IN SEARCH
OF STARIA

PEAGUM COLEMAN

ISBN – 978-1-78301-694-5

Except where actual historical events and characters are being described for the storyline of this novel, all situations in this publication are fictitious and any resemblance to living persons is purely coincidental.

Contact Details:
peagum.coleman@aol.com
or find me on facebook

To the memory of
Brenda Margaret Ashton
1921 – 1996

ACKNOWLEDGEMENTS

Given the solitary nature of the writing activity, it was so helpful to have friends around who were able to provide guidance and support as and when opportunities arose. Their comments kept me on track and, in no small measure, helped me maintain my confidence and momentum. For that I would like to thank Tina Daniels, Keith Robinson, Sonia Smith and Paul Ward for their invaluable contributions.

However, most of my gratitude must go to my wife, Geraldine, without whose enthusiasm and encouragement this book would never have been completed.

PROLOGUE

Coppergate,
York
20th December 1069

The Apothecary's wife hadn't been concerned until she heard the screaming. Up until then the only thing that she had noticed of the approaching Norman army was the smell of burning, not an unfamiliar odour in the city street. Now they seemed to be drawing far closer to her shop.

She had convinced herself that the invading troops would not ransack the city. After all, when they had first arrived two years earlier it had been a very bloodless affair. The gates had been opened by the city fathers and the Conqueror had just taken control. Many of the Saxon gentry had lost their lands, especially in the areas around the two new castle sites either side of the River Ouse, but most of York had been allowed to carry on as before, the only change being a new monarch on the throne. All was calm, almost peaceful.

But then Asbjorn had sailed up the river with his fleet of Viking ships and everything changed. Backed by King Swyen of Denmark they had retaken the city, brutally killing the entire Norman garrison. The citizens of York were given all the speeches of the North's Viking heritage and how they would be part of an empire stretching from Dublin to Denmark. She had never believed it, but others did. They were the ones that helped the Viking killers sweep through the ancient streets, butchering anyone who had even smiled at the Normans over the previous two years. They had truly thought that they could retake York, and from its ramparts establish a northern kingdom that would firstly rival and eventually topple the invaders from Normandy.

That was two months ago. Duke William, or rather King William as she was now getting used to calling him, was not going to allow any seeds of rebellion, however small, in his new domain. And York was not small. This had been the largest challenge to his power from anywhere in his new English territory. His response had been swift, massive and far more brutal than anything that she had seen in her lifetime. The Northern / Viking army had been massacred by the battle-hardened Norman troops who now had entered the city unopposed. Predictably, Asbjorn had vanished, his surviving troops melting as silently as they had arrived, leaving the ancient city to its gruesome fate.

She desperately wished that her husband was back. He had gone out earlier to collect herbs. She had warned him of the danger but, as usual, he was strangely calm, almost unworldly, about the situation. Normally that gave her a strange sense of security, but not today. Today she had been left to look after the shop alone until his return, and she was scared.

Suddenly she was brought back from her recollections by the sound of the shop door being kicked in. Three Norman soldiers entered, fully armed and dressed in helmets and chain mail. On seeing her, and that she was alone, they halted and smiled. Immediately, she knew what they had in mind for this unprotected woman.

One moved quickly across the floor of the small shop and pushed her back against the rough wood counter. He said something in a strange language and, when she did not respond, he struck out with his mailed fist. Thrown back onto the counter, she sent several earthenware pots and bowls spinning as she fell. In a single movement the soldier pinned her to the counter by her throat and pulled up the front of his tunic.

Once the three men had taken their turn at her, she was left lying on the counter as they moved towards the door. One paused and spoke to another, the one nearest to her, in their strange language. He shrugged, as if giving grudging consent, and moved once again to his victim. This time he withdrew his dagger from his belt and placed it at the nape of her neck. Leaning over, he stared into her eyes and, with a terrible grin, he pushed down quickly, causing the dagger to plunge through her throat, pinning her to the wooden counter beneath.

She gasped for breath but the air just wouldn't come. All she could taste was blood. Terrified, she tried to move but was fixed to the counter by the awful blade. Finally her head fell to one side. Her last memory was the sound of a low, guttural roar and the sight of her horrified husband standing in the doorway.

The Apothecary forced his way past the soldiers to get at his wife but quickly realised that he was too late. He was an elderly man, albeit of heavy build, and the soldiers quickly saw that he offered no threat and started to push him from one to another, as if in some awful playground game. At first he was stunned, overwhelmed by the dreadful sight before him, but he quickly recovered his wits as the soldiers began to strike him about the head. He twisted away from their grim circle of sport and fell against some shelves at the side of the shop. In a single, almost graceful, movement he scooped some orange grease from one of the broken bowls and mixed it with some green seeds taken from another. When the next blow came the Apothecary swayed beyond the reach of the assailant and, seizing his arm, slid back the chain mail covering and smeared the mixture upon the bare skin underneath. With surprising force the Apothecary pushed the soldier away, causing him to land in a heap at the feet of the other two.

Seeing their friend fallen, the foremost of the remaining two stepped forward and again tried to strike the Apothecary. As before, he skilfully swerved to avoid the blow and this time picked up a wide bowl from a higher shelf, containing a fine blue powder, ground down from a number of dried roots. He drew a deep breath and blew the contents into the soldier's face. Instantly the attack halted and the Norman staggered to the side of the shop, coughing violently as he sank to the ground.

The third Norman, the murderer of the Apothecary's wife, now stepped forward to finish their task, but hesitated on hearing a gasp from the first soldier to fall. Looking down he saw that his colleague had taken off his gauntlets and was fervently clawing at the paste on his arm. His evident pain seemed to worsen as the action spread the mixture across ever wider areas. With alarming speed, the skin on his arm and hands started to discolour and form into large red weals that instantly filled with a thick liquid. The smell of burning flesh began to fill the room as the terrified soldier wiped away the sweat, now pouring from his brow, but only succeeded in applying the deadly paste to an even wider area. Screaming, as pain swept through his body, the soldier tried to remove the heavy chain mail shirt, revealing a torso as yet untouched by the paste but already blistering heavily. Panic now overtook the soldier as he frantically tried to find some way of dealing with the intense pain now racking ever wider parts of his body. Horrified, he watched the blisters burst, causing a thick, black liquid to ooze over the surrounding areas, causing them to redden, blister and burst at an ever-widening circle of agony. His arms and hands were now sizzling like a spit roasted pig. Pulling himself to his feet, he tried to run from the shop but tripped and fell across the doorway. The pain was now overwhelming, worsened by his utter bewilderment as to what was happening to him. And it was in that moment of unknown terror that death brought him final relief.

The second soldier had remained seated on the floor throughout the death throes of his colleague. He had managed to move his back against the wall but somehow even that small effort seemed to have exhausted him. Pausing for a moment to gather his strength, he tried to rise but realised that he couldn't move his legs. All the energy in his body seemed to be just ebbing away. Suddenly he found that his arms were immobile, too heavy for his useless muscles to move. Looking up to his remaining colleague he tried to speak but found that he could make no sound, lacking the power even to move his mouth. Initially the Apothecary's second victim was surprised at the rapid turn of events but not yet concerned. Concern only started when he realised that this exhaustion was spreading to the muscles of his chest. Each breath was proving harder than the one before. This quickly changed to panic when his chest stopped moving. He tried to pull in at least some air, attempting a final, shallow, breath but even that failed him. With a unique combination of terror and silence, he slumped onto his side. It took him several moments to die.

Stunned by the mysterious deaths of his companions, the remaining soldier paused to look at their corpses. He was not sure which shocked him most, the stench of the first or the silence of the second. The pause was all the time the Apothecary needed. With surprising speed, he sprang forward and, with one cupped hand, caught and held the Norman beneath the chin. Moving to the side he spun round, placed his leg behind his opponent and, using his fearsome chin hold, he pulled the soldier backwards until his shoulders rested on the flat of the Apothecary's thigh. With a practised deliberation, he moved his other palm to the top of the Norman's helmet.

The Norman, stunned by the speed of the assault, struggled violently, but quickly found that he couldn't break free of the Apothecary's terrible grip. Slowly, the Apothecary started to bring his hands together, slowly crushing the murderer's skull.

As the Norman's teeth were ground together the pain began to build, rising quickly as the metal helmet began to deform under the Apothecary's powerful hands. It grew stronger still as the teeth began to crumble, grinding nerves into fragmenting stumps. The Norman began to groan, screaming being impossible with his jaws forced together under the Apothecary's almost inhuman strength. Yet more pressure caused the bones of the skull to grate together, bringing the Norman to the point of unconsciousness. Sensing this, the Apothecary paused and stared into the murderer's eyes, as this Norman had done to his wife moments before. Slowly he moved his thumb so that it was pressing upon the flat nose guard of the Norman's helmet. The soldier knew what was going to happen next. For the fourth time that day a look of abject terror appeared in the eyes of someone about to die. With a single powerful thrust, the Apothecary pushed the nose plate downwards into the Norman's skull. The metal plate and the crushed bones of his nose entered the brain cavity with a dreadful 'clunk'. It was the last sound that the Norman ever heard.

The Apothecary stood up, allowing the corpse to roll off his knee onto the stone-flagged floor. Moving across to his wife he pulled the dagger from her throat, releasing her body from its terrible fixture. Tenderly he leaned down, kissed her on the forehead, and whispered a final farewell. After a moment's thought, he stood up, conscious of what needed to be done and the brief time he had to do it. All too soon there would be other Norman soldiers coming into the shop, seeking out their missing companions.

He reached underneath the shop counter to find a small brown pouch made from animal skin. Opening the tie-cord, he moved around the shop collecting small quantities of various seeds and powders which he carefully poured into the pouch. In the case of some tiny black seeds, he found that the fighting had broken the bowl containing them, causing some to spill onto the floor and become mixed with a thick, brown oil from another broken bowl. Carefully he picked up these seeds, selecting only the clean ones, uncontaminated by the oil, which he added to the contents of the pouch. Finally, he pulled the drawstring tight and tied the pouch to a belt around his waist. He looked around his shop for what he knew would be the final time. Walking over to his wife's lifeless body, he bent down and kissed her one last time. Reluctantly, he walked through the doorway and out into Coppergate.

The street was a mass of running people, both city residents and Norman soldiers. The Apothecary knew that he must get away before the carnage in his shop was discovered and so turned to join the throng. He passed the shop of his friend and neighbour, Erik the Coppersmith. Inside he saw his friend handing over some of his best wares to rampaging Normans in a vain hope of bribing them, anything to persuade them to leave his shop. Erik glanced out through the doorway and saw the Apothecary looking in. The Apothecary waved his hand in farewell, a gesture immediately understood by the Coppersmith who nodded in response. The Apothecary turned and disappeared into the crowd.

Back in the Apothecary's shop all was silent for several minutes. Then, slowly at first but with an increasing urgency, the sound of stone sliding on stone was heard. Behind the counter one of the heavy floor slabs was gently pushed up and slid sideways, revealing an entrance to one of the few cellars in York. Out of this hole a small boy reached up and pulled himself clear. He was short for his age, which was about eight, but had a stocky build which gave him, accurately, the appearance of rude health. Once standing, he turned and reached down to help another child, this time a young girl, to climb into the shop. The girl was about six and dressed in a floor-length tunic of rough cloth. With her tiny hand she brushed off the dust from the front of her tunic and then reached into a side pocket from which she took a small doll made of dried grasses, cleverly tied together. Gently she kissed the doll's forehead and, tucking it under one arm, turned to face the boy.

Silently the two children stood for a moment looking at the body of the woman lying on the counter. Watched by the boy, the little girl stroked the hand of the woman. A small tear broke free of her eye and ran down her cheek. She turned to face the boy and saw that his eyes were also welling up. But he was determined not to cry. Crying would be weak and he knew that, from today, he must be strong, strong enough for both of them until the day when they would both be safe again. He vowed that only then would he allow himself to cry for his mother, now lying dead before them.

As the Apothecary had done moments before, the boy reached under the counter for another small pouch. This time the boy did not collect various seeds from the broken shelves but concentrated upon the small black seeds, all of which were now soaked in the thick, brown oil. Scooping up a handful, he placed them in his pouch.

Clutching the girl's wrist in one hand and the pouch in the other, he led her from the shop and out, into the street.

CHAPTER ONE

Woodburn Estate,
Bristol
Tuesday 21st August, in the present day.
9.30 p.m.

Looking back, Nathan Aluko could never recall the exact instant when he first saw the Old Man. This always struck him as a disappointment. Probably the most important moment of his life and he couldn't remember it.

Nathan had been in the police force for nearly seven months. As the only black man in his passing-out class he knew things would be tough but he seemed to be settling into his new role. His new colleagues, initially distant, had become closer over the weeks and now he was beginning to convince himself that he had made the right choice of career. In his close-knit group of family and friends, that put him in a minority of one.

That day he had turned up for the evening shift as usual, not expecting anything out of the ordinary. He had been allocated to the squad car, intended to tour a local housing estate looking for small-scale drug dealers. His companion, Bob Turnbull, was an experienced sergeant with many years of operating in this sort of role. Nathan had learned to trust Turnbull's judgement and was pleased to be working with him that evening.

They had spent an hour driving around the estate, watching groups of youths, all of whom dissolved into the seedy alleyways on catching sight of the police car. They were keeping the gangs moving, but achieving little else. Nathan could never see the point but kept his own counsel in the company of his more senior colleague.

'So why on earth does a graduate in medieval history choose to spend his days in this shit-tip?' Sergeant Turnbull posed a variation of the same question that people kept asking Nathan since he announced his decision to join the police force. He had never been able to come up with a convincing answer, either to himself or anyone else. Ever willing, he tried again.

'I wanted to make some sort of difference. Some contribution. I realise just how naive that sounds but it seemed a good idea at the time. Besides, you would be surprised how little demand there is for a guy with knowledge of medieval languages but not much else. I just thought that it might be interesting.'

'Well, believe me, if I had anything like your education you wouldn't find me spending my summer evenings chasing toe-rags like those.' As he spoke Turnbull nodded to his left. Looking in the direction of Turnbull's gesture Nathan saw yet another group of hooded youths slowly move into an alleyway. These estates were a warren of them. Over the last few weeks Nathan had often thought how perfectly designed they were for low level criminality. It was as if the planners had wanted these estates to turn out this way.

As the two policemen watched, the group started to speed up, looking back at the police in the car as they ran.

'They're up to something,' said Turnbull, his antennae sensing trouble. 'I know where that passage comes out. Quickly, drive around to the other end.'

Nathan's foot pressed down onto the pedal and the powerful car smoothly accelerated along the grim road.

A few moments later they pulled up at the end of a cul-de-sac, with the dark, narrow alleyway being the only way forward. There was no sign of the youths. A burnt-out car and a smashed street lamp were the only features on an otherwise blank canvas, bounded on all sides by the same run-down, low grade houses that seemed to comprise the entire estate.

'Something's going on,' said Turnbull, 'let's take a look.' He opened the car door and stepped out, reaching into the back seat for his hat.

'Shall I call it in?' said Nathan, feeling exposed in this dark, menacing place.

'Call in what? That we are about to be assaulted by an empty alleyway?' Turnbull's tone was meant to be mildly sarcastic but Nathan felt wounded by the remark, needing no reminder that he was new at this. He hoped that one day he would learn to overcome this feeling that he always got when in these situations, as if he was in some sort of danger. He also knew that it always sounded like fear. Perhaps one day, with more experience, he would cope better.

Turnbull walked a few paces towards the silent, dark alleyway. The few undamaged street lights illuminated the surrounding area but the entrance itself was a black void, providing an obvious focus for the two policemen.

Nathan moved alongside his colleague. 'Do we go in?' he asked, hoping that his fear didn't show.

All he got in reply was a pain-ridden gasp. Just as Turnbull turned towards his colleague to answer, a half brick had shot out of the darkness and struck him on the cheek, knocking him to the ground. Instantly Nathan crouched to avoid being hit by the wave of other bricks and bottles that followed, raining down upon them. Although stunned, he tried to rally his thoughts as his brain went into overdrive. He looked at Turnbull's fallen body, noticing the blood that was now spurting from the large, facial wound. He was surprised at how quickly the deep purple bruising spread around Turnbull's cheek. This examination came to an abrupt halt when he heard the crashing of broken glass, immediately followed by a loud roaring sound and a huge sheet of flame which knocked him down, sprawling over Turnbull's torso. The police car, their only means of escape, was now blazing furiously.

Another groan from Turnbull told Nathan that his colleague was still alive, but he realised that they needed better cover. They were totally exposed, both from any more missiles from the alleyway and the fall-out from the burning car. The alleyway was the source of both the bricks and the petrol bomb and so offered no exit that he wanted to risk. His thoughts were reinforced by a further hail of stones from the darkness. A gust of wind blew the black smoke, now massing above the car, aside for a brief moment, allowing Nathan to see a second, smaller passage off to one side, between the houses. He had no idea where it would lead but it was infinitely better than any other option that he could see. He gripped his colleague under the shoulders and heaved. Again, Turnbull groaned as Nathan dragged him the short distance into this second alleyway.

Looking back, Nathan could see a group of youths emerge from the darkness of the initial alley. They were all laughing and shouting, clearly high on something - possibly drugs, possibly adrenaline, probably both. With whoops of delight they swarmed towards the burning police car, seeking the occupants. It took Nathan a second to realise that the smoke was obscuring them from the gang and so they were safe, but only for a short time. Another gust of wind and the smoke could blow away at any time, leaving them at the mercy of the gang.

Leaning Turnbull's torso against the alley wall, he grasped his radio. 'PC 23748 calling,' Nathan tried to sound calm.

'Go ahead, 23748,' came the crackly reply

'Urgent call for assistance! Man down and severely injured. Group of youths attacking police car.'

'Stand by,' said the radio voice.

A second later, a more familiar voice came onto the radio. 'This is Inspector Greaves, 23748. Please report.'

'Sergeant Turnbull and I are in Graton Place, off Andrews Road on the Woodburn estate. We have been attacked by a group of youths, number unknown. He has been hit by a brick and has severe head trauma. We have left the patrol car, which has been fire bombed, and have taken refuge in an alleyway to the side of Graton Place. The youths have not seen us yet, but that could change at any time.'

'Understood. Help on the way. Please keep me informed. Greaves out.'

Nathan replaced the radio in the case and looked at Turnbull. His head wound was starting to clot, reducing the blood flow but Nathan could see that the damage was serious. Turnbull would need medical help and fast. Taking out his handkerchief he held it against the wound but it quickly became sodden.

With the noise of the youths getting louder and closer, the alleyway was rapidly losing its dubious appeal. Nathan saw the shapes of bodies jumping around the car, casting shadows on the walls of the surrounding houses. It would only take one of the gang to glance in his direction for them to be seen. Nathan knew that he had to find a safer place to hide, no matter what the risks were to his injured colleague. Grabbing Turnbull by the shoulders he pulled, pushed and dragged his colleague along this second alley, away from the firelight, smoke and noise. It opened unexpectedly onto a small courtyard, about 30 metres square, illuminated by a couple of lampposts around a dreary perimeter. On three sides of the courtyard were the drab council houses that comprised the Woodburn estate, all with tiny back 'gardens' of patchy, untended grass, surrounded by broken, rotting fences. However, the fourth side, directly in front of them, offered more hope. This edge was bounded by a low, churchyard wall, with an old wooden gate straight in front of them. Beyond the gate a flight of three stone steps rose up to a short path that led through a small graveyard to a church, some 40 metres beyond. The headstones offered much better cover so Nathan hoisted Turnbull onto his shoulders and scurried the short distance across the courtyard to the gate.

When he reached the entrance to the graveyard he heard a sound which made him turn, distracting his attention from the rotting gate. As Nathan pushed, the wood disintegrated, causing him to fall through the entrance, landing heavily on the stone steps beyond. Turnbull, crushed between the steps and the younger man's chest, screamed.

Nathan froze. The fall had winded him but otherwise he was still uninjured. Again, he looked towards the alleyway. Someone must have heard that scream, snatching away this fresh chance of survival. Seconds later he heard the sound he dreaded. Footfalls in the alleyway. The gang was coming.

The first arrivals were two small children, a boy and a girl. Despite being dressed in the anonymous, standard uniform of jeans and hoodies, Nathan guessed their ages at around eight or nine. His heart leapt. Perhaps they were not part of the gang. Perhaps they were refugees running from the mob. Kindred spirits in the unfolding nightmare.

The boy saw the two policemen first, his eyes coming to meet Nathan's. For a brief moment they held each other's stare. Nathan felt his life hanging in the balance, everything resting on what this small child chose to do next.

The boy saw the two policemen and smiled. 'They're over here!' he shouted at the top of his voice, 'On the church steps.' The girl laughed, her eyes glistening with excitement, at the knowledge of what was going to happen next, and their key part in causing it.

Beyond the courtyard, the noise seemed to pause for a second before returning, far louder than before, amplified by the narrow alleyway. All at once the gang poured into the square, filling it within seconds. Nathan tried to count them but the numbers were too high and rising rapidly. He stopped at fifteen, a mixture of ages and sizes. The average age would have been in the late teens but many were far younger. The only features that they shared were that they were all wild and all armed. Nathan saw no guns but could see knives, sticks and clubs but, again, too many to count. He could see that fighting the gang was out of the question, doubly so with Turnbull lying at his feet. However, to Nathan's surprise, the gang did not immediately engulf the pair. Seeing the helplessness of their quarry, they all paused, forming into a semi-circle around the two policemen.

Nathan realised that no one wanted to be the first to attack. He used their momentary hesitation to hoist Turnbull up the final step and lean him against a headstone. With both arms now free he took out his steel truncheon, extended it with a sweep of his arm, and turned back towards the gang. The click of the weapon as it reached its full length sounded foolishly reassuring. Knowing that there could now only be one outcome, he turned to face his attackers but the gang continued to hesitate. Each one urged others forward, wanting someone else to make the first step, someone else to take the inevitable blame whilst they could take the residual glory.

Initially unseen by all present, another person entered the courtyard. Although dressed in the same fashion as the others, anyone could see that this man was very different. Unlike all the other gang members, this one had a calmness about him. Slightly older than the others, perhaps around 21, he didn't shout or scream but moved confidently, covering the length of the courtyard in a few, almost jaunty, strides. As he moved into the crowd he touched people on the shoulder, only for them to move quickly aside when they recognised him. Nathan did not see him until he reached the front rank of the crowd, directly in front of the two policemen.

'Well, well. A black pig!' The newcomer spoke in a voice that was loud but without shouting. He didn't need to. All the gang had fallen silent when they saw their leader. 'You must be a fuckin' rarity. Ah well, so much the better. A great way of getting our message across, eh lads?'

The gang all shouted their collective approval and encouragement.

'Go on, Shaun.'

'Finish the bastard.'

'Stick him!'

Nathan's desperate thoughts raced. If there was to be a message then there must be a messenger. Perhaps they would get out of this alive after all.

The leader stepped out beyond the front rank of the crowd. Taking a baseball bat from the youth to his left, he moved towards Nathan. 'We're sick of your lot getting in the way of our business. You need to understand that we rule this estate. We don't need you and we don't want you. Perhaps a couple of dead coppers will make your boss understand.'

With that he lunged at Nathan, swinging the bat at his head. Swaying to one side, Nathan managed to avoid the blow but felt the wind of the weapon on the side of his cheek. Now the young policeman's training kicked in. Catching the gang leader off balance, Nathan brought up his truncheon hard into his opponent's side, striking into his ribcage, just below the armpit. The force of the blow lifted the gang leader off his feet, launching him onto the low wall to the side of the church gateway. His momentum caused him to roll further, falling off the top of the wall and dropping the short distance to the courtyard floor below. He grunted as he hit the tarmac surface.

The initial shock of their leader being repulsed did not last long. Two other youths dived in, grabbing Nathan by the arms. Another swung a bat at his head, catching him on the temple, knocking him senseless for a second.

In this dazed state, Nathan looked back towards the gang leader to see not one but two shapes rising from the ground. In addition to the sturdy frame of the youthful thug there was also the emaciated outline of an old man. Their arms and legs were interwoven, hindering the younger man's attempt to get to his feet. In his dazed state Nathan realised that the old man must have been hiding in the hedge on top of the wall and had been disturbed by the falling weight of the younger man. Such thoughts ended with another blow to his head, forcing him backwards onto the prostrate form of his sergeant. He knew that the end was near.

Sensing victory, the mob swarmed forward, grabbing and striking at the young policeman's limbs, making any defence impossible. The impact of one, final, blow twisted Nathan's head towards the two ill-matched shapes still grappling on the courtyard floor.

Having pushed the old man's body away, the gang leader was now back on his feet. He kicked out angrily at the elderly form, catching him in the stomach and making the old man cry out in pain. Yet amongst his anguished screams the old man somehow found the breath to cry out. 'Nei Meida, Onytr Sveinn!'

This strange outburst caused the thug to pause, but only for a second before he continued with his savage assault. Another vicious kick propelled the old man back to the low churchyard wall, leaving him sitting upright against the ancient stones.

Realizing the danger that he was in, the old man struggled painfully to his feet. In one, surprisingly swift, motion he brushed his hand along the seam of an old leather pouch tied to his belt and, reaching up, slapped the gang leader across the throat. The weakness of the 'blow' made the thug laugh. It was pathetic, almost as if he had been stroked by a child. Grinning, he grabbed the old man by the front of his rough tunic, hoisted him off the ground and, with a single, powerful movement, threw him into the centre of the mob, who continued the dreadful pummelling.

Finally, clear of restriction, the gang leader turned back towards Nathan, now lying across Turnbull's body and suffering a continuous beating from the other youths. Smiling at the prospect of finishing off the two policemen, now totally at his mercy, the gang leader paused to clear his throat to speak, to declare impending victory and urge his troops on to the finish. He coughed again to move some phlegm and, again, tried to shout but found that he still couldn't speak, such was the volume of fluid in his throat. Again, he hawked up a mouthful of saliva and spat it out, but it was quickly replaced by yet more of the sticky fluid. Now realising that something was very wrong, he spat once more but his throat seemed permanently filled with thick, red mucus. Struggling for breath he bent over and vomited copiously onto the courtyard floor but he still couldn't clear his throat. Sensing his discomfort, the mob paused in their assault on Nathan and the old man to watch as their leader fell to his knees, hacking vigorously and clutching at his throat. Horrified, he felt his fingers move through the barrier of his skin and into the widening void of his dissolving windpipe. His chest muscles heaved in a futile attempt to force air into his lungs, only to draw yet more of the thick liquid deep into his chest. Unable to breathe, he fell forwards onto the ground. Losing consciousness, his body continued to spasm for a few moments before death ended his confused suffering.

The gruesome death of their leader stunned the mob into a momentary silence which was broken suddenly by the sound of police sirens. Nathan, still dazed by the many blows to his head, tried but failed to make sense of the events quickly unravelling around him. He was only vaguely aware of the arrival of his police colleagues, smashing their way into the courtyard and through the rapidly dispersing mob. With friends in danger, the riot squad did not stand on ceremony. Cutting a swathe through the crowd, they thrashed to the left and right with batons and shields, clearing a path directly to the church steps.

Realising that he and Turnbull were safe, Nathan was overwhelmed by a sense of utter weariness. Still dazed, he looked around the courtyard to survey the maelstrom before him. The few gang members that chose to stand and fight were being treated as severely as they had treated him a few moments before. He also noticed the old man, surprisingly still alive, slowly crawling towards the body of the gang leader, now lying in a pool of his own body fluids. A strange thought drifted into the young policeman's barely conscious mind. Why, he wondered, in the midst of such a severe beating, did the old man cry out in the long-dead language of Old Norse?

As Nathan watched, the old man finally reached the body of the gang leader. Struggling to his feet, he carefully wiped his hands on the rough fabric of his tunic. Again, he touched the leather pouch at his waist, before dipping his hand into the pool of thickening, red liquid that stained the ground beneath the corpse. Lifting his hand, now coated with the sticky mucus, to his face, the old man paused and, very deliberately, licked his fingers.

The whole scene froze at the inhuman cacophony that followed. Rioters and police alike froze, all attention seized by the sight and sound of the old man. His elbows were drawn tightly into his sides, his hands outstretched and ending in rigid fingers pointing skyward, his head drawn back at an eerie angle. Yet it was the sound that caused all present that summer's evening to fall to their knees. He screamed a scream so high that everyone in the courtyard clamped their hands tightly over their ears, before it fell lower and lower as the old man's breath gradually left his body, finishing with a groan deeper than human memory, vibrating the very ground upon which they all stood. As the unearthly sound ended, the old man collapsed onto the body of the dead gang leader, both figures forming a heap on the stained courtyard floor.

As the welcome energy flowed, once again, through his broken body, just before he was overwhelmed by the familiar darkness, the old man's mind mused on how much the Others had learned since his last Return.

But how much more, so very much more, they had forgotten.

CHAPTER 2

Alton Grove Police Station,
Woodburn Estate
Wednesday 22nd August
6.30 a.m.

Even his eyelids ached. As Nathan gingerly raised his head the first thing he saw was surprisingly comforting. His eyes focused on a stainless-steel toilet and immediately he knew that he was safe. He was in one of the holding cells at Alton Grove Police Station, probably lying on one of the two bunks that each cell contained.

He turned his head and instantly regretted it. His head, his neck, his spine - indeed every part of his anatomy screamed at him, demanding that he stop all attempts at movement. He knew that, at the very least, he was badly bruised. However, so far as he could tell in this first moment of consciousness, no particular part of his body seemed to be especially painful. Taking comfort from this, he tried to move again. Slowly his other senses began to function. He became aware of his breathing, shallow and laboured, first through his mouth and then through his nose. Then the smell hit him. An awful, overpowering stench that almost made him retch, stopped only by the pain that came from his stomach muscles when he tried.

A moment later he discovered the source of the smell. Across the cell, lying very still on the other bunk was the Old Man. Slowly the memory of the attack came back and Nathan remembered the beating that the Old Man had taken. All those blows to the head, to the body … it was a surprise that he was still alive. Then the questions started to cascade into his mind. Why were either of them here? Surely they should be in hospital. And what of Turnbull? Where was he? And why were they in a cell? Nathan braced himself for the pain and sat up. The cell door was open and his consequent groans quickly alerted others to his condition.

'I think Aluko's awake, sir.'

Nathan recognized the voice of Tony Johnson, one of the sergeants from his station. The sound of footsteps quickly followed before Johnson and Inspector Greaves entered the cell.

The Inspector was the first to speak. 'Good to see you back with us, Nathan. You had us worried for a while.'

'What's happened, sir? Where's Sergeant Turnbull?'

'There will be time for the details later. You must rest for now. Turnbull was taken straight to hospital and we are waiting for news. The last we heard he was critical but stable, whatever that means. We are trying to get you into hospital but the riots are blocking all exits from the estate. Turnbull was taken by air ambulance just before the main rioting began. I made the judgment that you two,' Greaves nodded his head towards the Old Man, 'could be treated temporarily in the station, before taking you through the crowds under a police escort. In your case I was right. In his case,' again the nod, 'I was wrong. `

Nathan looked across at the elderly figure lying on the other bunk. It was the first time he had had a chance to really look at him. Lying down it was difficult to be accurate but Nathan judged him to be slightly below average height but with a broad, powerful chest. In his prime the Old Man must have cut an athletic figure, perhaps like a rugby forward, but that must have been a very long time ago. The figure before him was now frail, almost emaciated. The skin, so pale in colour, was stretched tightly across the face, making Nathan think of some sort of gruesome death mask. Yet even allowing for this, his facial features had a strange appearance. His nose was broad with wide nostrils, as if flattened by some old injury. His jawline jutted forward, giving the face a solidity that belied his overall condition. But the strangest thing was the eyes. Set deep into his face, shaded by eyebrows that emerged abruptly from a low forehead, they gave an expression that must have once been very intimidating. Now, framed by long, lank grey hair, the Old Man looked calm and restful. The image of a dead king or chieftain came into Nathan's mind. Clearly, he thought, this man must have demanded respect from those around him before age, infirmity and, finally, death had struck him down.

The body was dressed in a rough shirt or tunic and trousers made from a fabric unfamiliar to Nathan. Like the body, the clothes had seen far better days and there were no shoes on his grubby feet. The trousers were held up by some rudimentary rope belt, tied at the front. Attached to the belt was an old pouch, lying flat against his thigh, just big enough to take a man's hand. It seemed to be made of old leather, like the type used to clean windows yet darker in colour. It seemed to be moist, almost damp, with several coloured stains covering the surface. Apparently empty, whatever had caused the stains had long ago leached away leaving only the residual stench that had brought Nathan back to consciousness.

Greaves continued his story. 'The medics said that they weren't even sure that he was alive when they got to him. As they could only fit one casualty into the helicopter, and with Turnbull's head wound being so serious, well, they had to choose which one to take first.' It was clear that the Inspector felt the right decision had been made.

'He took a terrible beating.' Nathan recalled the force of the blows. 'He tried to defend himself but his assailant was too strong. The only defence that he could muster was a blow to the throat but it was barely more than a slap.'

The Inspector continued. 'We got you both back here to the station, but this cell was the only place to put you. The canteen is being used as a field hospital for all the walking wounded from the rioting and there was nowhere else with a bed.'

'What did you mean about riots?' Thinking about the Old Man reminded Nathan of his own struggles. 'Surely there were not enough in the courtyard to give our lads any real problems?'

'The guy who was killed was Shaun Callaghan, a major player in the drug trade around here. People were not too pleased when it got out that he was dead, especially in an incident that involved the police. News spread quickly and the next thing we knew the whole estate went up. We've got the lot. Burning cars barricading the main entry routes, petrol bombs, flag stones – anything that can fit into a hand is being used to throw at us. I've had to call in reinforcements from surrounding forces. We've currently got over 100 officers on that estate. I'm seriously thinking of calling in the army, it's got so bad. Things have improved over the last hour and I'm hoping that now we have got some daylight things will start to calm down.'

A voice outside the cell shouted something that Nathan couldn't hear clearly. The Inspector turned towards the voice. 'I'm coming out now. I'll meet you in the Ops. Room.' Then, this time to Nathan, 'Just try to rest for now. I'll bring you more news once I have it.'

Left alone, apart from the Old Man's body, Nathan started to gather his thoughts about the last few hours. He could remember the estate, the alleyway and the fight. He remembered the Old Man but not where he had appeared from. He must have fallen out of the hedge that topped the old wall. Mulling over this point, he fell back into a deep sleep.

A few minutes later the door opened again. A man in a white lab coat entered the cell and surveyed the two figures lying before him. He was carrying a small plastic tray on which lay a few glass tubes. He placed the tray across the top of the toilet and pulled a pair of latex gloves from his pocket. Taking a moment to put on the gloves, the technician looked at the Old Man. He picked up one of the glass tubes, unscrewed the sealed top and withdrew a long plastic stick which ended in a small cotton tip. With one hand he parted the Old Man's lips and inserted the tip of the stick gently into his mouth. He carefully wiped the cotton tip around the inside of the Old Man's cheek, removed the stick and replaced it in the glass tube. He removed the gloves, took a pen out of the coat pocket and wrote on the tube's paper label - *Elderly white male – deceased*. With all his kit now on the tray he picked it up and left the cell. He moved through the police station, reaching the storage room within a few strides. Inside, he opened the door of the refrigerated cabinet and placed the now-sealed tube in a rack on the top shelf which already contained other DNA samples that had been collected within the station over the previous 24 hours.

Dr Victoria Snow was annoyed. The call came when she was in the middle of her night shift and, although she had got here as quickly as she could, she knew that it wouldn't be soon enough. She glanced at the morning sun, rising across the city of Bristol laid out before her. Normally the spectacular view would have made her pause and gaze, but not today. With all the problems that she faced at present she really didn't need the hassle of getting her boyfriend out of trouble – again. As she parked the car, his car, outside the small police station she wondered, not for the first time, if this relationship was going to work. As she went through the front entrance, too deep in thought to notice the police rushing about, she resolved to bring things to a head. If he was going to carry on behaving like this then they could have no future together.

As she walked into the reception area the police officer behind the desk looked up and gave her an appreciative glance. She knew that she was no classic beauty but regarded herself as pretty enough to turn a man's head when required. Being slim, blue-eyed and having shoulder-length blonde hair didn't hurt either.

'My name is Dr Victoria Snow. I'm here to collect Julian St Clere.'

'How on earth did you get through the riots?' asked Sergeant Johnson. He was irritated that he should be doing the menial task of manning the front desk, but with all the chaos going on he had little option when his junior colleague requested a toilet break.

'I didn't see any rioting. Just a few youths on corners shouting abuse at your colleagues.'

'Thank heaven. It sounds like things are beginning to settle down. As you may have heard, we've had quite a night here. So we could do without folk like your Mr St Clere getting legless and trying to steal the warning signs around road works.' Johnson didn't try to hide his annoyance.

Vicky felt the usual embarrassment at dealing with these incidents. 'I'm so sorry. He does go a bit too far sometimes, but he means no harm. Will you be charging him?'

'We have more important things to concern us at present, so now that he has sobered up please take him home. I shall arrange for him to be brought through in a moment.' A thought occurred to the sergeant. 'Are you a doctor? A medical doctor, I mean.'

Vicky nodded. 'I'm a Registrar, working in A&E at St Luke`s'.

'Well, you could help us out while you're waiting. One of our lads was given a bad kicking earlier on and we have not been able to get him to hospital yet. I know that he's in a lot of pain. Would you take a look?'

Again, Vicky nodded. A chance to retrieve some credibility, perhaps.

Sergeant Johnson opened a side door and led Vicky through to the cell where Nathan was sleeping. He woke as she entered.

'I'm Dr Snow. I've been asked to check you over. Where does it hurt?' With professional thoroughness Vicky quickly examined the young man's body. She arrived at the same conclusion as Nathan. No major injuries but enough minor ones to cause him some discomfort over the next few days. 'You seem to have escaped the worst of things but your bruises will give you problems for a while. I'd say that you've been quite lucky.'

'It didn't seem that way last night. Obviously, you have a different definition of luck to the one I'm used to.' Nathan smiled at the attractive doctor in front of him.

Thinking of the A & E patients she had been treating all night, most of them with far more trivial injuries but with constant complaints, Vicky smiled back at Nathan. 'Good to see that your sense of humour appears undamaged. When I get back to the car I'll get something from my bag to help you with the pain.'

'It is a pity that you can't do the same for him.' Sergeant Johnson gestured towards the figure in the other bunk. Vicky moved over to the Old Man. She felt for a pulse but without success. The body was warmer than she would have expected but then it was quite hot in the cell. Turning her back on the body she spoke to the other two.

'No, I'm afraid you're right. He's dead.'

The voice from the bed behind her made her jump. 'You'll forgive me if I ask for another Physic, but you seem none too bright to me.' The Old Man sat up and rose to his feet, surprisingly sprightly given his recent diagnosis.

Vicky was stunned. She had been sure that this man was dead, as sure as she had ever been about anything. Yet here he was standing in front of her. She looked at the two policemen for some sort of explanation, but they were clearly as shocked as the young doctor.

Calmly the Old Man continued. 'Where is this place? What am I doing here? Are you King's men? I want to leave, now.' He moved towards the open cell door.

Sergeant Johnson was the first to overcome the surprise of the Old Man's recovery. He stepped into the doorway to block the exit. 'You're not going anywhere, old lad. I don't know what just happened here, but you are, at the very least, a witness to a violent death and you're staying put until we have some answers.'

'How are you called?' The Old Man faced up to Johnson. Realizing the sergeant didn't understand, the Old Man thought for a moment and asked again. 'What is your name?' This time the question was phrased slowly, in a deep west-country accent, revealing a Bristol upbringing.

'My name is Sergeant Johnson. I'm the custody officer at this station and I'm telling you that you're going nowhere.'

'Well met, Sergeant.' The Old Man held out his hand for the sergeant to shake. Only Nathan noticed the hand brush against the side of the Old Man's pouch as part of the upwards motion. Caught by surprise, Johnson automatically shook the proffered hand. 'Now, show me the way out.'

As the two hands met, the sergeant's demeanour changed completely. The stern face was replaced by an almost childlike smile. To the surprise of Vicky and Nathan the sergeant moved out of the doorway and, with a wave of his arm, indicated the exit. 'This way, sir. I shall get you outside in a jiffy.' The sergeant backed out into the corridor and pointed towards to door that led outside.

Nathan was the first to react to the rapidly unfolding events. 'What did you do then? What is in that pouch?'

The Old Man paused and turned to Nathan. 'You see much, young Kingsman. Perhaps more than is good for you.' He looked deep into Nathan's eyes. 'Your pain is great.' Again, the Old Man's hand brushed against the old pouch, this time along the lower seam. He reached out and touched Nathan's cheek. Instantly Nathan felt his pain vanish. Suddenly he felt wonderful, almost euphoric. All the aches and weariness of the last few hours just seemed to drain from him. He straightened up, rolling his shoulders to shake off the last of his fast disappearing stiffness. He looked across at Vicky. This time it was her turn to ask questions.

'What's going on here? One minute you're dead, the next you are very much alive and ordering policemen about. Who are you?'

'Ah yes, the Physic. You cannot understand what your eyes behold. You want explanations. Yet I cannot give them for I have to leave.' As before, he looked deep into her eyes. 'I see in you much promise. If you wish to learn great things you may join me, but it must be now, for I will stay no longer in a King's palace. Come with me and learn or remain and stay in ignorance. You must choose now. All is one to me.`

Vicky was confused. She was clearly intrigued by this Old Man, but her head demanded further details. 'I can't just wander off with a stranger, no matter how good his tricks are. As I said before, who are you?'

The Old Man took a step back and looked Vicky up and down. His next question rocked her. 'Your mother. Is she dead yet?'

Vicky looked at Nathan and Sergeant Johnson, once again seeking some form of explanation. Quickly realizing that these strangers couldn't possibly know about her mother's condition, she turned to face the Old Man. 'How do you know about my mother?'

'So, she lives. But she is near to death? Soon?'

'How can you possibly know that?'

'Tis simple. I see the seed of the gnawing plague within you. You carry your shoulder too stiff. Your arm does not hang straight. The pain is there but your mind forbids the knowing of it. It will be many years before you sense the killer within you. But your mother has spent her years. In her the seed will be full grown. It will be her death, but not yet from what you say?`

Vicky turned to the bewildered Nathan. 'My mother is in St Luke's with breast cancer. They have done all they can for her. She doesn't have long left.' Then, back to the Old Man, 'I don't understand how you could know about her, but if you do then you must also realise that all my time is devoted to her at present.' A shrill, ringing tone interrupted her explanation. She reached into the pocket of her coat and took out a mobile phone. A glance at the small screen told her that it must be answered immediately. 'Yes, this is Dr Snow. I see. Thanks for letting me know. I'll be there in twenty minutes.' She rang off and turned to the policemen. 'That was the hospital. My mother has gone into a coma. I must go.' With that she pushed past the Old Man and moved into the corridor. She glanced up at the tall figure of the sergeant, still smiling benignly, his arm motioning them all towards the exit.

'Then I will go with you.' The Old Man walked with her into the corridor, followed by Nathan who looked up uneasily at his sergeant. No word of complaint came from the sergeant's grinning face.

Chapter 3

Alton Grove Police Station,
Woodburn Estate,
Bristol.
Wednesday 22nd August
8.30 a.m.

It was a strange group that filed out of the cell into the corridor beyond. Sergeant Johnson took the lead, his eyes scanning ahead seeking someone, anyone, to order out of the way. Next came Vicky, looking down to fit her mobile phone back into her bag. For her, speed was now of the essence. She just wanted to get to the hospital in time. Behind her came the Old Man, moving more warily, looking all around him. Nathan brought up the rear, trying to make some sense of all he had just witnessed, so far without success.

As they entered the corridor the Old Man turned to Nathan. 'Why are you in a place that you clearly don't belong?'

'What?' replied Nathan, surprised by the unexpected question. For a moment he suspected some form of racist jibe but quickly realised that it had been posed in genuine curiosity, lacking the silent sneer that usually accompanied such remarks.

'Is the King now compelling men to do his bidding? It would not be the first time.'

'Look. After the day I've had I'm not in the mood for riddles.'

The Old Man hesitated for a moment, considering carefully Nathan's response before continuing. 'I am thinking why you are here, in a King's Palace, when your place is so obviously elsewhere. Yet I see you have been asking yourself that question for many weeks.'

Again, the remark surprised Nathan. How could the Old Man know of his reservations about his career choice? Before he could respond the Old Man continued. 'Perhaps some wanderings with a stranger would help you find a better path. Why not walk with me for some little time? Clear your mind of such concerns and maybe your face will not betray your fears.'

Before Nathan could reply the Old Man stopped dead in his tracks. Sniffing the muggy air in the corridor, he recognised a familiar odour. He pointed to the closed door of the cell next to the one they had just vacated.

'What is in there?' He posed the question to no one in particular but it was answered by a young constable, walking in the opposite direction.

'In there? Oh, that's our pet squaddie. Well worth leaving alone.' The Old Man looked at Nathan for further explanation.

'He was a paratrooper in Afghanistan until he was captured by the Taliban. They held him for a few hours before the Army got him back. Physically he is OK but his captors got him hooked on some sort of drug which he just can't get clear of. He was invalided out about three months ago and held in a secure detox centre a few miles from here. They try to treat him but his addiction is too strong so he keeps breaking out and causing havoc until he gets enough heroin to placate himself. He seems to need more each time and when he can't find enough he gets violent and so ends up in here until the detox boys come to collect him. We've learned the hard way that it's best to get him into the cell and then leave him alone.'

The Old Man nodded at Nathan by way of thanks, although he understood little of the explanation. He turned back to the constable. 'Open the door.'

'I don't think you understood, sir,' he replied. 'This man is a trained killer and extremely violent. Not what you'd call a good combination. We're far better off out here.`

Being called 'sir' by a Kingsman, however junior, made the Old Man pause for a moment but he quickly returned to his earlier request. He turned to the sergeant, who had returned to the group from the outer reception area, unaware that his charges had stopped. One glance was all that was needed. The sergeant entered the debate.

'Listen to me, Bradley. If this old gentleman wants to go into that cell then it's not for the likes of you to question him. Get that door open now or you'll be pulling night duty for the rest of the year.'

PC Bradley turned to Nathan for support but only got a shrug of the shoulders in reply. The sergeant was in charge and somehow the Old Man had him eating out of his hand. Reluctantly Bradley fished the key from his pocket, turned it in the heavy metal lock and pushed the door open. He stepped back quickly to allow the Old Man to enter first. He had a fair idea of how the inmate was going to respond and was not keen on taking the lead.

Inside the cell a tormented soul began to feel the return of the cravings. They seemed to be coming back more quickly with each passing day, his precious respite cut shorter and shorter. He had been thinking of the times before his capture, of his mates in the regiment, of the camaraderie, of the friendship. For a brief second he allowed himself a moment's hope that he would get back to those times one day. Then, as with every other day, his hopes were dashed with the return of his overwhelming yearning for the white dust that had blighted his life.

Sometimes, in clearer moments, he would recall the day of his capture. His squad had been involved in a skirmish with the rag-heads, one of which, a chief's son as it turned out, had been killed. Somehow, in all the turmoil, he became separated from his mates and was jumped by four of the bastards. Last thing he remembered was a crack on the back of his head. Next thing he knew he was in their camp, with the chief shouting at him in a language he couldn't understand. Even so he still got the message. They were going to kill him in revenge, but very slowly. With hundreds of years of experience they knew just how to achieve their objective with as much pain involved as possible, with heroin as their weapon of choice. It was to be a morale booster for their fighters and a message to the infidel invaders. What they didn't expect was the rescue mission. It was what Paras do, what mates do. No one gets left behind. Ever. No matter what.

He learned later that he was only in enemy hands for a day and a night but it had been enough. He knew that he was now beyond hope, addicted to the filth that they had dosed him with and there was nothing the medicos could do. In his heart he knew that his life was over. Deep down he hoped that one day, in an attempt to overcome his increasingly violent rages, someone would have the courage to shoot him dead. In his more lucid moments he often cursed that he didn't have the bollocks to do it himself. But he didn't. Not yet.

The Old Man entered the cell. Although identical to the one he had just left, this one seemed much smaller, dominated by the figure sitting on one of the beds, his head in his hands. The prisoner was one of the largest men the Old Man had ever seen. His head, his shoulders, his back were all massive, made more so by a thick covering of muscle and sinew. Even seated, the man seemed to fill the confined space. His arms were the thickness of most men's legs, the biceps bulging out of the short sleeves of a grubby tee shirt. Each forearm was covered in a series of tattoos, intricate Celtic patterns of interlacing, parallel forms, making the overall image even more menacing. As the Old Man entered, the prisoner lifted his huge head from his hands and a pair of wild, angry eyes focused on the new arrivals.

It was the Old Man who spoke first. 'Cyric?'

'What?' the prisoner snapped back.

Realising his mistake, the Old Man changed tack. 'How are you called?'

'What?' came the same reply, as if through some mental haze.

Before the Old Man could continue, the prisoner leapt to his feet and sent a massive fist flailing through the air towards his inquisitor.

From the corridor the watching group winced at the inevitable damage the blow would inflict when it reached the Old Man's head.

But the blow did not connect. Instead the Old Man simply swayed backward, moving from the waist just enough for the massive fist to miss by a hair's breadth. He felt only the breeze caused by the knuckles as they flashed past his cheek. The momentum caused the prisoner to continue his swing, spinning around and turning his back. In an instant the Old Man pounced onto the huge figure. His right hand pressed down on the prisoner's back, forcing him onto the surface of the bed. His left hand, again touching his pouch as part of yet another fluid movement, reached down and seized the prisoner by the ear lobe, squeezing hard between the thumb and index finger. The grip caused the prisoner to let out a loud scream. A second later the Old Man released his strange hold and stepped back.

The group waited for the prisoner to recover from this trivial attack and continue the assault. For a moment the large figure continued to lie, face down, on the bed. Slowly he eased himself back to his feet. With his back to the group he stretched his arms out to either side, as if waking from a long sleep. He turned to face the group and … nothing. Where there had been anger there was now calm. Tension had been replaced by peace. His eyes, now devoid of the wild glare from a moment before, came to rest upon the Old Man. 'What did you do to me?'

'There will be other days for such questions. For now, again, how are you called?'

'My name is Carl Curtis.'

'Carl Curtis, your odour proclaims you a warrior?' Carl nodded. 'I have need of a warrior. Will you journey with me? I do not yet know my destination, but every Return means a journey and warriors make sound companions. I see you are a slave to the poppy. Finding peace will be your life's quest. I can offer you the peace that you seek, the peace that you feel now.'

'If you can keep me feeling like this then I will follow you forever.'

'So then, until the end of days. It is settled. Now, we must leave.'

The Old Man turned and walked out of the cell followed by the confused prisoner.

PC Bradley, mindful of the mass of protocols and procedures that were about to be broken, tried to step forward and block the strange pair but a glare from his sergeant stopped him in mid stride.

In her hurry to leave, Vicky had pushed past the group around the cell door and had moved towards the outer reception area. As she opened the security door, unlocked from the inside, she heard a familiar voice. '... and if you should wish to progress further in what you, jokingly, call a career then I suggest that you should concentrate upon solving real crimes rather than stopping law-abiding citizens from having a moment's relaxation when they've had a drink or two.'

The voice belonged to her boyfriend, Julian St Clere. Although she had grown close to him during their twelve-month relationship there were times, such as today, when he was a total idiot. She winced as her partner continued to lambast the constable who had the bad luck to be on the front desk. The voice continued, 'Do you know that my father plays golf with both your present Chief Constable and the one before him? A word from me and you are history, my lad.'

Vicky looked at the tall, elegant figure looming over the counter at the policeman. She recalled how attractive she had found this aristocratic manner when they first met. How his over-riding confidence seemed to sweep him past all obstacles. Indeed, his very appearance and his overall bearing was often all that was needed to get out of the frequent scrapes that he found himself in. Now, with more experience, she saw this confidence as little more than a facade which, when challenged, fell quickly away to reveal a shallow, almost vacuous, interior. Seeing that such a challenge was imminent, she moved towards the counter, trying to intervene in time. She failed.

The policeman on the desk, having run out of patience, retaliated. 'I don't care who your father has in his social circle. And yes, I would much rather spend my time chasing real criminals. However, if you and your drunken friends are going to make pyramids from road works signs, leaving great holes in the road dangerously unmarked, then we're going to come down on you very hard. This isn't the first time you've given us problems and if it wasn't for last night's riots I would have left you in the cells much longer. If this happens again, Mr. St Clere, then your next social engagement will be in court, perhaps followed by a few weeks as a guest of Her Majesty. Is that clear? `

Seeing victory as unlikely Julian gave an exaggerated pout and turned away from the policeman's glare. As his gaze swept around the reception area he saw Vicky, standing in the doorway to the cells. After all the trouble she had been through to collect him it would have been nice to receive a friendly smile and a moment's appreciation. Experience had warned her to expect nothing of the kind. Experience won.

'At last! Where the hell have you been? I've been stuck here for hours. I told you on the phone that it was urgent.'

'Sorry, but I've been in A&E all night and the patients just wouldn't stop bleeding.' She tried and failed to keep her frustration out of her voice. 'Now just sign the paperwork and let's get out of here. I've heard from the hospital. Mum is getting worse.' Then, to the policeman, 'Can he go now?'

'All he has to do is sign for his personal effects.' The policeman nodded towards the clear plastic bag on the counter between them containing various keys, coins and a bulging wallet. 'However, as is usual with Mr St Clere, there's a problem.'

'How do I know that you haven't stolen something?' Julian glared across the counter at the policeman. 'I can't be expected to remember everything that I came in with. I don't know how much cash I was carrying and I certainly don't recall signing that.' Julian indicated a list of items stapled to the bag.

'Julian, I'm leaving for the hospital. You can either sign the form now and come with me, or sign the form later and walk. Your choice.' This time Vicky decided to let her anger show.

'Oh, go on then.' Julian snatched the form from the policeman's hand, scribbled a cursory signature and tossed it back. He opened the bag and allowed the contents to spill out onto the counter. He was still filling his pockets when the door from the cells swung open and the rest of the group swept in.

Led by the sergeant, they moved past Vicky and Julian, heading towards the exit. As they passed her she saw the large figure of Carl walking with the group. She gave Nathan a puzzled glance but he just shook his head in a way that suggested questions should be deferred for now.

'They are coming with us,' she told her bemused boyfriend and both joined the group as they all filed out of the station though the main door, held open by the sergeant, still frantic in his desire to help the Old Man leave the building.

Alton Grove Police Station was located on high ground on the edge of the housing estate that it was built to monitor. From this elevated position a casual observer could see a wide panorama, not just of the Woodburn estate but of the whole Bristol area. The view covered the tall buildings of the city centre in the middle distance and further, to the M5 motorway and the River Severn beyond, with its two bridges spanning the water like monstrous lizards. Several square miles of busy, modern life with all the associated activity were laid out before them. People, cars, buses and trains were all on view to the group as they walked quickly into the car park. All this was lost to Julian, Carl and Nathan as they followed Vicky towards her boyfriend's black Range Rover. She pressed the remote unlock button on the key fob and they all climbed in, Julian taking the front passenger seat.

All, that is, except the Old Man. Vicky quickly realised that they had lost him and so scanned the car park. She saw his stocky figure gazing out at the view over the city. He seemed stunned by what he saw. Anxious to get started, she beeped the car's horn at him but to no avail. Annoyed, she jumped out of the car and ran over to him.

'We need to go. I must get to the hospital.'

But the Old Man was not for moving. 'What have you done?' he gasped, seemingly unable to take in the view in front of him. 'So many structures! So many people! How can they all fit in? Nature cannot possibly accommodate so much. The spoil must be immense, the damage huge.' He drew in a large lungful of air through his nostrils and immediately began to cough and retch. 'This stench is dreadful. How can anything exist here?'

Vicky waved towards the car for Nathan and Carl, who got out and ran over to help. Predictably, Julian remained seated.

'We really should get him to A&E,' said Vicky as the two men arrived. 'I'll drop you all off as we go past. You two can take him in while I go to see my mother.'

With great difficulty the two men guided the Old Man, now clearly distressed, into the back seat of the Range Rover. Once seated between them he began to calm down, his coughing subsided and he seemed more settled. Vicky started the car and reversed out of the parking place. Changing gear, she drove out of the car park and onto the main road. Accelerating quickly, she began the short journey to the hospital. Her mind was on her mother. Would she get there in time? What was she going to find when she got there? What if she was too late? What if she wasn't?

As the car gained pace she became aware of something happening in the back seat. The Old Man, having been initially quiet, was now struggling violently with Carl and Nathan. 'What is happening?' he shouted out. 'What is this place? What are you doing to me?' His movements were so violent that Carl had to throw an arm across him to pin him to the seat. Nathan also held onto the Old Man's arm to stop him struggling. The writhing and twisting were causing the car to shake from side to side and, for a moment, Vicky was worried that she would lose control. Nathan was surprised at how strong the Old Man had suddenly become. Only Carl's great strength was keeping his elderly body pinned down in the seat. Nathan noticed the Old Man's hand stretching towards the pouch at his belt but Carl's grip prevented him reaching it.

'Calm down,' said Nathan in a voice that he hoped sounded soothing. 'You're safe. We are trying to help you. Stop struggling or you'll kill us all.'

31

Once he realised that he couldn't move, the Old Man ceased his struggle as swiftly as he began.

Nathan, keen to prevent another outburst, spoke to Carl. 'Keep hold of him until we get to the hospital. It's not far.'

Carl nodded and locked his arms into a wrestling grip. Now confident that he had the Old Man immobile, he was surprised at how much force had been needed to subdue him. The Old Man had been very close to breaking the hold of the muscular ex-paratrooper. Despite his size he was keen for the journey to end in case he should lose the next struggle. Fortunately the Old Man showed no sign of repeating his odd behaviour and so the group arrived at the hospital without further difficulty.

—∞—

Back at the police station Sergeant Johnson had followed the group out into the car park and watched in silence as they drove away. He was still absolutely convinced that helping the Old Man get out of the building had been the correct thing to do - indeed he regarded it as probably the most important task of his life to date. But as he saw the Range Rover drive down the hill a sense of dread began to grow within him. He became aware that he had done something terribly wrong. The feeling started small but grew quickly as he turned to walk back into the police station. Lost in thought, he held the door open for another man to enter the building in front of him. Once back in the station the sergeant decided to go for a coffee. He needed to think.

The man in front of the sergeant walked up to the counter and nodded to the constable on duty, who was chatting to another policeman. Without a word spoken the constable reached beneath the counter and pressed a release button for the security door.

The newcomer, obviously familiar with the layout, walked through to the back of the station and entered a small store room containing, amongst other things, a large refrigerator. Opening the door, he reached in. Ignoring the lunch boxes and bottles of milk, he reached to the back and took out the rack containing the several DNA samples taken over the previous 24 hours.

He moved the rack to a side table upon which sat a computer terminal. Logging on, the man entered the details from each of the glass tubes. A burring noise came from a printer at the side of the computer as it produced a series of bar-coded labels. Peeling each in turn from its backing paper, the man carefully applied a label to each tube, making sure that the correct label was applied to the correct sample. The printer burred again, this time producing two copies of a single sheet, which listed all the sample details together with the bar codes allocated to them. He took a pen from his jacket pocket and signed both documents. He picked up the sample tubes and placed them into a bag which he slung over his shoulder. Retracing his steps, the man returned to the reception area. He waved the two forms at the constable on duty before placing them flat on the counter. The constable gave them a moment's glance before adding his scribbled signature to each. The man picked up one of the forms, placed it into the shoulder bag and, with little more than a nodded farewell, walked out of the building. Once back in the car park the man unlocked his van, climbed in and drove away.

The door of the van was painted with a logo of a shield surrounded by some form of floral decoration, beneath which was written *'Forensic Science Service'*.

CHAPTER 4

St Luke's District Hospital,
Bristol
Wednesday 22nd August
8.45 a.m.

As the Range Rover pulled into the hospital car park Carl still held the Old Man firmly against the rear seat. In the front seat Julian watched his passengers with increasing unease. Seeing Vicky's evident concern about her mother had persuaded him to remain silent thus far but now he could hold back his questions no longer and so leaned across to whisper to his girlfriend. 'What is this menagerie? Why are they messing up my car?'

'Not now, Julian,' she replied. 'All I want to do at the moment is to get to Mum before it's too late. I promise I'll tell you what little I know later. Until then, please just work with me on this.'

Julian seemed momentarily appeased. He glanced once more at the strange trio on the back seat. He saw Nathan, still wearing his uniform, badly torn and dirty from the fighting of the previous evening. He saw Carl, his arms locking the Old Man into the seat, but also bearing the many puncture marks scarring the huge muscles. Finally, he looked at the Old Man who had now ceased any struggle but sat breathing deeply, his eyes tight shut. Increasingly concerned, Julian decided to ignore Vicky's request. 'Well that's all very well, old girl, but this is a £80,000 car and I don't want it damaged so soon after Dad gave it to me.' Vicky glared at him and would have started to shout, but they had reached the hospital car park. Swiftly she parked in one of the several vacant spaces, opened the door and jumped out.

Carl also flipped the catch to open his door. The moment the door was opened a fraction, the Old Man twisted his body so that his feet were flat against Nathan. Then, with a single movement, he straightened his legs, creating such a powerful force that both the Old Man and Carl were propelled rapidly out of the car, landing in a heap on the tarmac. The fall broke Carl's grip and instantly the Old Man rolled away and jumped to his feet, leaving Carl lying on the ground.

'What manner of creation is that?' he shouted, clearly upset by his recent experience. 'Why is it sealed like some metal coffin and how does it go so swiftly?'

By now Julian had climbed out and was inspecting the car to see if the violent struggle had caused any damage. 'This is a top-of-the-range Range Rover SE with all available options. It cost more money than you will see in your entire lifetime and I don't appreciate it being damaged by a travelling compost heap and his weird circus.'

The Old Man stared at Julian as he spoke. He understood nothing of the answer but he could recognise aggression when he saw it. Slowly he looked Julian up and down before reaching an unflattering conclusion. Quickly deciding that this man was irrelevant to any possible future plan, the Old Man chose to ignore him. He took a quick pace towards Julian, causing the younger man to take a step back, worried that he was about to be assaulted. In fact, the Old Man simply walked past him and into a flower bed along the edge of the car park where he began to rummage around in the sparse, assorted, vegetation.

'I must get to Mum,' shouted Vicky. 'You all go to A&E and get him sorted out,' she gestured towards the Old Man. 'We can meet back at the car later.' Turning her back on the group she walked quickly towards the block where she knew her mother lay dying.

The Old Man, having completed a swift survey of the flower bed, moved towards one particular plant. Pushing his fingers carefully into the hard, compacted earth, he was able to loosen the plant and pull it out, root and all. He tore off the upper foliage, leaving the small root in the palm of his hand. Brushing away the loose soil he tossed this root into his mouth and began to chew. Looking up, he saw the three men moving away. He could hear them arguing amongst themselves.

'Who are you calling weird, you posh tosser?' Carl was clearly over his fall.

'A super-sized druggie and a refugee from his own police station. That passes for normal in your world, does it?' Julian was not making any new friends today.

Ignoring them, and still chewing, the Old Man followed Vicky into the hospital.

It only took a few moments for Vicky to move through the familiar labyrinth of corridors that led to her mother's ward. As she entered she looked to the left, to the place that her mother had been on her last visit. The bay was empty. Thinking the worst, she then spun around, seeking an explanation. Fortunately the ward sister, June Sampson, spotted her and called out. 'Vicky! Over here.' As the young doctor approached her she continued, 'We've moved your mother to a side room. I thought it might be better for you both.' Vicky nodded her gratitude and walked in the direction indicated by the sister.

Her mother was in the only bed, looking as pale as the sheets that she lay upon. Casting her professional eye along the array of machines that her mother was connected to, Vicky saw that the readings were not good. Alongside the bed stood James Courtney, the consultant who had called her when she was in the police station. He looked grave.

'I'm glad you've got here in time. I'm sorry but she's fading fast. She drifts in and out of consciousness but I think she is aware of her surroundings. I think it might be time to say your farewells.'

Tears started to well up in Vicky's eyes. She knew that this day would come but hoped, against all the odds, that it wouldn't. However, even she had been surprised at the speed with which the cancer had overtaken the woman in the bed before her. Her mother just looked so ill. All the colour had drained from her cheeks and her breathing was laboured. Vicky knew that the end was near.

Her mind flew to other, happier times. Holidays, shopping trips, days out – so many to reflect upon but that would have to be for another day. Today she must say goodbye to her first and, as she now realised, her best friend. Stepping forward to the edge of the bed she reached out and held her mother's hand. It felt so light, so fragile. She wanted to grasp it tightly but worried that it might break. Moving aside the bedside table, bearing one of the many bouquets that decorated the room, Vicky stepped up to the side of the bed to half sit, half stand alongside her mother's head.

The consultant's angry voice brought her out of reverie. 'Who the hell is that?'

The Old Man had entered the room. His rough clothes and his dreadful smell, in stark contrast to the antiseptic surroundings of the hospital ward, demanded the attention of all present.

Vicky spoke first. 'He's with me. Please let him stay for a moment. He won't do any harm.'

The Old Man glanced at the woman in the bed and then at the consultant. He saw in the latter the stance of outraged authority. He had met many such people before but few with the insight to match their lordly manner. He faced up to the consultant and spoke to him in a clear, marginally hostile, voice.

'How are you called? What is your role here?'

The consultant was annoyed by the tone adopted by this scruffy visitor. He was used to a certain deference from visitors to his department and so chose an aggrieved, arrogant tone when he answered. 'I am James Courtney, Head of Oncology at this hospital.'

'So you are this woman's Physic. What cure are you using? When will she recover?'

The consultant smiled patronisingly at the naive questions. 'I'm afraid that it is too late to talk of cures. I've done all I can for her.'

'So you are only here to watch her die? Does such a task need much skill? I would have thought that any passing moron could do that!'

Anger blazed up in the consultant's mind but he checked himself. He was, after all, at someone's death bed. He turned to Vicky. Drawing her gently away from the bed he spoke to her in what he hoped was a soft, gentle voice.

'Vicky, I don't know who your friend is but I am concerned that the state he's in makes him a walking health hazard. Remember, we do have certain hygiene standards for visitors. I think that you should ask him to leave.'

During their conversation the two doctors had turned their backs on both the bed and the Old Man. Only Sister Sampson, on one side of the room, saw him approach the bed from the other. He glanced at the sister and smiled. She looked on in total horror as the Old Man leant over the patient's head and licked the pallid cheek. Speechless, she saw him pull a long-stemmed flower from one of the bouquets near the bed. With a well-practised movement, he ran his thumbnail down the full length of the stem, drawing out the plant's juice onto the palm of his hand. Oblivious to the sister's speechless stare, he spat out the pulped remains of the root he had been chewing since leaving the car park into the juice. Mixing the two ingredients together he raised his hand to his mouth and tasted the resulting gel. Clearly satisfied with the outcome, he leaned over the patient one last time and smeared the gel over her lips. He straightened up just as the two doctors turned to face him.

'I will leave now. All things will be well.` He looked at Vicky. 'I shall meet with you back at the Rover cart.' With a final, contemptuous, glance at the consultant he walked out of the room.

As he left, Vicky felt a moment's relief. She had not been looking forward to asking him to leave. She had enough on her plate at the moment. With this problem averted she returned to her final goodbye. As she moved back to the head of the bed she noticed June Sampson standing alongside her with an expression of open-mouthed horror. The Sister was just about to speak when another voice was heard in the room.

From the bed her mother spoke. 'Can I have a drink please, dear?'

Vicky, pleased that her mother had momentarily rallied, leaned over to pour her some water from the jug on the bedside table. As she did so she noticed the various machines giving details of her mother's condition had started to show quite different readings - those of a far healthier woman. Vicky knew that this equipment could often go wrong, especially if the sensors became dislodged from the skin surface. She turned to ensure that they were secure.

Then she noticed her mother's face. Her colour was rapidly improving. Vicky touched her cheek. It was warm and rapidly filling out, replacing the haggard look of the last few weeks. But it was not until her mother opened her eyes that Vicky realised that something truly remarkable was happening. Her eyes were a bright blue, with a sparkle that Vicky hadn't seen for years. All her vigour, her passion for life, her joie-de-vivre, all shone through. In a joyous instant Vicky knew that her mother had returned form the brink.

Without warning the patient sat up, pulling off several of the leads as she did so.

'I think that I would like to go home now, dear. I'm really feeling much better.' Then, to the consultant, 'Thank you so much, Mr Courtney. I'm not sure what you did but you really are a life saver.'

Stunned, Courtney nodded but couldn't speak. He had no idea what had just happened and so, possibly for the first time in his life, he had absolutely nothing to say.

The Forensic Science Service van drove along the Bristol side streets. Having picked up the samples from his morning round, the driver was returning to his base office. He approached the security gates of an unmarked, grey office block. Slowing down he produced an identity card from the glove box and waved it at the guard on the locked gates. The guard nodded at a colleague in a small building behind the fence and the gates swung slowly open. The driver drove through and covered the short distance to a car park. Reaching over to the passenger seat he picked up the satchel containing his morning's work and jumped out of the car. Half a dozen steps took him into the building.

The South West regional office of the Forensic Science Service, which the driver had now entered, provided all the laboratory facilities required by the Avon and Somerset Constabulary. Here all samples were analysed using some of the best facilities and equipment available. Staffed by some of the most able scientists in the UK, they provided the swift answers required by the police in pursuing their many enquiries. The driver walked up a flight of stairs, along a short corridor and entered one of these laboratories. On the door it read *Section 47E – DNA Analysis.*

Turning to the desk on the left he placed his satchel on the surface and took out the sample tubes. These he placed into a series of racks held within a refrigerated cabinet, fitted to the wall behind the desk. He placed the paperwork in a tray, turned and left the lab. His lunch and afternoon route beckoned.

A moment after he had departed a white coated technician approached the desk. His badge identified him as '*Ian Watkins – Lab Technician, Grade III*'. Picking up the racks he carefully carried them to his own work bench and, sitting down, began the process of sorting them into the different levels of importance. Those for serious crimes such as rape and murder were always processed first. The laboratory tried to get these results back to the police force within an hour of receiving the sample. Any samples taken from crime scenes of lesser note, such as assaults and robberies, were processed next. These had a promised turn-around time of up to one day. Any samples remaining, known within the department as the 'also-rans', were tested once all the others had been completed. They had no promised response time and so could often take days to process.

The technician picked up the sample taken from the Old Man. Noting that it had come from the corpse of a tramp and so was only needed for identification purposes, he placed it in the third category.

Glancing at the large number of samples that had just been delivered he thought it unlikely that the sample would be processed until the next day at the earliest, possibly even later if tomorrow's batches were as large as today's. He picked up the urgent samples and moved further into the laboratory to begin his analysis.

CHAPTER 5

St Luke's District Hospital,
Bristol
Wednesday 22nd August
9.30 a.m.

Nathan, Carl and Julian had returned to the car. Having arrived at the casualty department in the midst of a rancorous argument, they realised that their principal charge was not with them. The Old Man had just disappeared. They retraced their steps but could find no sign of him and so decided to remain by the car and await events.

'He can't have gone far,' said Nathan, 'and he seems to be able to look after himself.'

'Too right,' replied Carl, rubbing the bruise on his side where he had landed after being so forcefully propelled from the Range Rover.

'I'm not sure why Vicky is so keen on having him around.' Julian felt the need to explain her actions. 'She is usually a sucker for a sob story but this one seems to have taken the biscuit. A great collector of waifs and strays is my pet doctor. I remember one time when ...' His recollections were halted by the ringing of his mobile phone. He dug it out of his pocket and looked at the screen. 'Vicky,' he told the rest of the group before answering. 'Yes, dear?'

'Julian? Is the Old Man with you?' Vicky sounded somewhere between elated and desperate.

'No sign at present. He vanished as we were going to casualty. Small loss if you ask me. When can you get down here? I'm due back at the office as soon as ...'

'Something incredible has just happened and he is somehow involved. He said he was going back to the car. When he gets there you must not let him out of your sight. Take him back to the flat and stay with him until I get there. This is really important. Please say that you will do this for me.'

'Well, I can hang on for a few minutes but after that I must get going. If he turns up I'll get these two to look after him. I'm sure they must be marginally competent despite their appearance.'

'Don't prat about, Julian. I need you. For once, just help me.'

The tall man let out a deep sigh and replied reluctantly. 'Oh, all right.' Then, as an afterthought, 'How's your mother?' but Vicky had rung off.

Julian turned to the others. 'She says we are to wait here for that fossil to turn up and then take him to our flat. Something seems to have happened and she is convinced that he's in some way connected. Probably stole something. You can never trust such people. If you were any sort of policeman you would have spotted that.'

Nathan was about to defend himself when he saw the Old Man emerge from the hospital building and walk up behind Julian. He was surprised at how the Old Man seemed to be able to move so quietly, even across the gravel surface of the car park. Carl also saw the newcomer and was about to give Julian a warning but, after a shake of the head from Nathan, chose to say nothing.

Warming to his task, Julian continued his diatribe. 'I don't think we'll see him again. Probably grabbed a handful of drugs and was away on his toes.` Then, to Carl, 'Pity you didn't go with him. You'll have to buy them from him now.'

Silently the Old Man stepped up immediately behind Julian but didn't interrupt his flow.

'No, the thing that I've learned in life is how to judge character. You two just saw a broken down-and-out, whereas I could see a public liability. A good job that he's gone. Saves me the trouble of running him in.'

From a point just behind Julian's ear, the Old Man spoke. 'We are indeed fortunate to have such a wealth of wisdom within our company.'

Julian jumped. 'In God's name! Where did you come from? You could kill people by creeping about like that.' Taking a moment to compose himself he continued. 'Anyway, thank heaven you're here. Vicky says that I am to take you back to the flat.' Then, to the others, 'OK then you two. You can go now. I'm sure that you have other things to do.'

'These men are now part of my company. They go where I go. Lead us to this place that is flat.' The Old Man had acquired a commanding air which seemed to offer defiance to any who would disagree. Picking up on this, Julian chose not to argue and stepped towards the car.

'Oh no!' said the Old Man. 'The Rover cart has no use for me. It smells, moves too quickly and entombs those who ride within. I will not travel in its bowels again. We will walk.'

'Walk! But it's over a mile up that steep hill.' Julian, appalled at the idea of such exertion, indicated the vague direction. 'I haven't got time for that. And where am I going to leave the car? If it stays here for more than an hour I'll come back to find it on bricks. Do you know how appalling the police are around here?'

Once again, Nathan chose not to rise to the provocations that Julian seemed to continually offer. Was he doing this on purpose or was he genuinely unaware of the offence that he gave? Or perhaps he knew but just didn't care? In any case Nathan had already spotted that the best response was to ignore these pointed remarks. This seemed to irritate Julian more than any riposte. 'If it's only a mile then walking won't be too bad. I, for one, could do with some fresh air.' Nathan looked at Carl for agreement and got a nod in return.

''Tis settled then,' replied the Old Man. 'Let us all follow Vicky's servant.'

'I'm not her servant!' Julian was highly indignant at the suggestion.

'Then we shall have to wait until your true function becomes apparent.'

Without waiting for a response the Old Man began to walk in the direction of the hill. Nathan and Carl followed, smiling at Julian's discomfort.

Julian followed in a bemused silence.

—∞—

Back at Alton Grove police station, Sergeant Johnson closed the door behind him as he left the Inspector's office. It had not been a comfortable meeting. Not unreasonably, the Inspector had demanded to know why he, a senior member of the station's management team, had overridden all police procedures and regulations to allow (the phrase used was 'actively conspire') a suspect in a suspicious death to leave the station. Not only had he ordered all his subordinates to grant the suspect full assistance but he had even held the door open for him as he left the building. To make matters worse, the suspect was involved in not just any suspicious death but the one that had caused the whole of the Woodburn estate to erupt in rioting for the previous 12 hours. Finally, to make his predicament even worse, the suspect had been allowed to team up with a known violent offender, thus making his future capture even more difficult.

Johnson knew that he had done all those things but couldn't for the life of him recall why. At the time it had seemed the most reasonable, most obvious thing to do. In all his life he had never been more certain of the correctness of his actions. However, in the few hours since waving them goodbye from the car park – he was very pleased that no one had seen that particular action – all certainty had fallen away and he was now utterly perplexed by what he had done.

He had been able to convince the Inspector, temporarily at least, that he had been the victim of some form of drug that removed his judgement. The Inspector had ordered him to prove this vague hypothesis by recapturing the suspect very quickly and 'rescue' the three hostages that the suspect had 'kidnapped' during the escape. This last part was the result of Johnson's quick thinking during the meeting. It was the only reason he could think of as to why anyone would go off with such an odd character.

At least he was in no doubt about his next course of action. The Inspector had made it very plain. Either he re-captured the suspect and so proved the 'drugged compliance' theory or he would be charged with aiding and abetting a fugitive from justice. He had been given 12 hours to complete his task, less if the press got hold of the story.

Johnson walked into the canteen where he knew all his team would be waiting. The general chatter fell away as he walked to the front and addressed the group. They all knew that he would be angry, but when he began to speak they realised just how angry he was.

'As you all know, earlier today a suspect was brought into the station. He was found in the centre of the rioting and was initially thought to be dead and so laid out in the cells to await collection. The initial view as to his condition now seems to have been premature as he regained consciousness some hours later.'

So far Johnson's tone had been worryingly polite and professional. His audience knew that it was the calm before the storm and so sat in a hesitant silence. The sergeant continued. 'At some stage soon after, this suspect was able to walk out of this station, in total contravention of every rule in the book, having somehow persuaded me to help him!' Suddenly, Johnson slammed his hand down onto the table in front of him, the noise startling his audience. Now Johnson began to shout. 'I've been a copper for almost 25 years and in all that time no one has made me look as stupid as this bastard did. I'm now told that if we don't find him, and soon, bad things will fall down upon me. And in this totally unfair world, if bad things fall upon me, even worse things will fall upon you.' The group began to shift in their collective seats.

'So I want you to stop all other activities, no matter what they are, and find me this bastard. No other actions, no excuses, just get him back into this station and soon. You lot ...' he indicated a group of six sitting in the corner, 'break into pairs and start combing the area. You two …' now pointing at other staff, 'find all you can on that doctor and her boyfriend that left with him. You …' directed at another policeman, 'try and track down Nathan through his radio or his mobile.` Finally, to no one in particular, 'Does anyone know if we took any samples before he pulled his Lazarus trick?' One person at the back nodded. 'Right, get onto the forensic team and get his samples processed. I want those results back within the hour. Now, is anyone in any doubt about how badly I want this bloke?' No one spoke. 'Right then, get out there and get him back here.'

With this final, screamed, remark Johnson reached down to the edge of the table in front of him and flipped it into the air. The crash with which it, and the attendant plates, cups and cutlery, landed, made all present jump once again.

Suitably motivated, they all rushed out of the room.

—∞—

Ian Watkins had been working on the current crop of DNA samples for most of the morning. He had completed all of the urgent samples and now was working his way through the second level. Glancing up at the racks he could see that he might get those finished but the third group, those marked as non-urgent, would have to wait until tomorrow. Except that tomorrow would bring in a new crop, with its own set of priorities and demands. Even the arrival of the new testing kit could not keep pace with the constant arrival of samples for analysis. Still, he had to admit that this new kit was the real deal. This was a Paternoster 4400E, the Rolls Royce of DNA testing equipment. All he had to do was load the glass phial containing the sample and that was it. The machine took in the phial, broke the seal, took a small amount of the sample taken at the scene, carried out the test and displayed the results on the computer screen alongside the testing kit. It even read the bar-coded label on the side of the phial before re-sealing and returning the sample to the technician via a sliding tray. Once the test was complete the results were sent down the attached computer line to the Home Office DNA database where a match was sought. If found, the results screen was updated with the identified person's details and, when prompted by the technician, the final result was sent electronically to the police station that had provided the sample. The whole thing took less than a minute. Ian Watkins was impressed. The machine was a step change improvement on the previous version, a Paternoster 250GH.

The technician would have been even more impressed if he knew what else happened to the information collected by the machine. Unknown to him, indeed unknown to anyone outside Paternoster Industries, the electronic details were also sent to a large, nondescript office block in a science park on the outskirts of Cambridge, along a digital pathway that was, allegedly, for automatic software upgrades.

As with the equivalent Home Office set-up, a comparison was made with a large database, built up over many years of operations. However, unlike the official records, these details were not subject to any form of government scrutiny. No awkward questions were ever raised about who should go on this database and, more pertinently, who should be taken off. In fact, no one was ever removed. Once a person's details were added this information would be available to the database owner for ever. In direct contravention of every law ever passed on the topic, Paternoster Industries had built up information on over 45 million citizens of the United Kingdom. Had they known about the database, Parliament and all the civil liberties groups would have been incandescent. But they didn't know. Only the owners of the database knew and Paternoster Industries were keen not to tell anyone.

By careful pricing they had been able to place Paternoster testers in over 85 per cent of the testing locations across the UK. Of the remainder, 10 per cent of the test houses were using equipment supplied by a 'competitor' of Paternoster who was, in reality, a secret subsidiary. The other 5 per cent were mostly University departments who used DNA for research purposes and so only made a small number of tests per year, far fewer than the tens of thousands carried out by the police and medical facilities, already covered by the Paternoster empire. However, even these university departments were subjected to a constant stream of marketing literature that offered Paternoster machines at below market prices. Paternoster Industries were anxious to ensure that no one could slip their expensive net.

In the background Ian Watkins heard a phone ring. One of his colleagues answered the call and Ian could hear him take down some details. Once the call was completed the colleague shouted across to him. 'Are you doing the work from the northern stations at the moment?'

'Yes. I've nearly finished the second group. Why?'

'Well, in the also-rans there is a sample that they want doing right away.' He gave the details to Watkins who checked them against his list.

'According to the notes that sample came from a corpse. They weren't too bothered before. Why is it suddenly so important now?' asked Watkins.

His colleague shrugged his shoulders. 'Ours is not to reason why, Ian, old friend. Perhaps he got better.'

Ian smiled at his friend's flippant remark. He located the glass phial from the rack and fed it into the machine. Waiting for the process time to elapse he leaned back into his seat and watched the screen. As the results came up he frowned. The pattern displayed was unlike any that he had ever seen before. In fact they were so wrong that it must be a malfunction of the equipment. No one could ever have provided a sample that looked like that. The machine must be acting up. As if to prove this developing theory, the testing machine suddenly seemed to shut down, with the screen blanking out, but not before destroying the sample, thus preventing any further tests being carried out.

However, despite appearances, the testing machine, following core programming written into every Paternoster machine since the very beginning of the company's activities, continued to send the results down the computer line. A split second later the information was received by the Paternoster server and compared to the millions held on file. Like Ian Watkins a moment earlier, the system confirmed that the sample was quite unlike anything previously collected and stored on the massive database.

However, unlike Ian Watkins, the system did not diagnose a malfunction but took a very different course of action. In the Paternoster central control room a loud klaxon began to sound and several computer screens began to flash, all displaying the same simple message.

'Critical Match Confirmed.'

CHAPTER 6

Paternoster Industries International Headquarters,
Cambridge
Wednesday 22nd August
11.45 a.m.

Years earlier the Paternoster control system had been designed to operate completely automatically. The input data from thousands of testing machines, all over the country, fed into anonymous banks of computers. These hummed quietly, processing this data, with the results destined for the large bank of servers that contained the DNA results of almost the whole of the adult UK population. For years this area had been a calm oasis, a place of peace and almost total tranquillity, just waiting to find one person, the single needle in the most immense of haystacks.

However, once that needle was found, the system was designed to move to a different mode, very definitely a manual one. Human intervention was required and now the system called for it, indeed loudly demanded it. The klaxons, the flashing screens, all the elements now merged together to call for an instantaneous response from the creators of the system. They must be made aware that the whole mechanism that was Paternoster Industries had just borne fruit. The single individual, the focus of countless hours of processing, had been found. The system had done its work. The next step required human hands.

Six people burst through the double doors and raced into the control room. In the lead was a white coated individual, his name badge proclaiming him to be Mike Aspinall – Operations Director. He ran to the largest, most central, of the computer screens. The other five staff, also white coated, dispersed themselves around the room to the remaining terminals. All of their movements had an air of a well-drilled operation, practised many times. Aspinall was the first to speak. 'Right. Calm down, everyone. Let's take this step by step. Do we all agree that this is not a drill?' He looked around at his colleagues all now tapping on keyboards and staring at screens. Each, in turn, shouted a similar response. 'Confirmed!'

'OK. Now can we establish that the signal is not any form of malfunction. Ged?'

The tall man at the next screen typed in some code. A tense moment passed as all present watched his screen from their respective stations. A graphic pattern appeared which the System Maintenance engineer, Ged, scanned with both eye and finger.

'I confirm that there has been no malfunction. The signal is genuine.'

'Thank you. Can anyone else see anything unplanned? Do you all agree that we have a positive here?' Aspinall looked around the room at each colleague in turn, getting a nod from each as he did so. 'Right, we all agree that a positive response has been found. Start the tracing process. I want to know all about that sample.' Three of the operatives started to tap questions into keyboards. Aspinall turned to his deputy, seated on his left-hand side. 'We had better tell the Boss.'

'Don't bother. He already knows.' A tall, elegant man walked into the control room through the double doors. Late fifties, his grey hair slightly receding, his accent, his manner, his Savile Row suit, all contributed to the impression of command. This was John Eriksson, Chief Executive Officer of Paternoster Industries, or, to give him his preferred title, the Boss. Moving across the control room in his usual fashion, one that gave the impression of speed yet not haste, he took up position alongside the seated Aspinall. 'We're absolutely sure that it is not a false reading?'

Aspinall nodded and replied, 'All indications are that we've found him.' Eriksson moved to the next screen and continued his questions.

'What do we know about the sample, Julie?'

At another screen Julie Griffiths, the object of the question, replied without raising her head. 'It came from an old man found at the scene of a riot on a Bristol estate. It was put through as an identification trace because … Oh!'

'Go on!' demanded Eriksson.

'I'm so sorry but it appears that the person who gave the sample was deceased.'

With one exception, everyone in the control room gave out a collective gasp. Had all this been for nothing? Were they too late?

All eyes were on Eriksson to see his reaction. 'I suspect that you might find him to be a little more durable than you think.' Eriksson spun round to face yet another colleague. 'Alan, I want you to get into the computer system at the police station and get all the reports relating to this riot.'

Alan, IT specialist, replied, 'No problem but it might take a minute or so.'

Eriksson nodded for Alan to proceed before returning to Aspinall. 'I think that we should inform the owners. Get them on the speakerphone.' A few taps on the phone pad later and Eriksson spoke again, this time into the open air. 'This is John. I think that we might have some good news at last.'

The voice that replied was very high pitched, obviously heavily disguised by the electronics. 'Are you sure, John? We both know that we have had disappointments before.'

'Well, we're as certain as we can be so far. I'm getting more details now. I shall let you know the moment I hear any more news.'

Another disguised voice joined the conversation. 'It has been such a long time, John. I'm sure we can wait a little longer. Just follow the agreed plan. Speak to you soon.' The high-pitched voice rang off.

Alan was the next to speak. 'Right sir, I've got into their system. It seems the sample provider came into the station during the night, accompanied by an injured policeman. Local rioting meant that they couldn't get him to a hospital and so both were treated in the station. He was sampled whilst asleep but was later pronounced dead.'

Aspinall interrupted, 'That would explain how they got the sample. He would never have given one voluntarily.' Eriksson nodded.

Alan continued, 'There is another report about a sergeant in the station who appears to have helped the old man to leave, together with the injured policeman, a hospital doctor who was there to get her drunken boyfriend out of the cells, and a drug addicted ex-paratrooper. It appears that the sergeant is in quite a bit of trouble. No one's sure why he did it, including the sergeant, it appears.'

'Not bad going for a corpse,' quipped Eriksson. 'Does it say what language the old man was speaking?'

'No mention at all. But there was no request for a translator so I would think that he must have been speaking in English.'

Eriksson turned to Aspinall. 'So he has assimilated.'

Aspinall nodded. 'Do you want me to send a team out?'

'Yes. I think we have enough now to be fairly sure that it's him. Who do we have down there?'

'Our main guy is Colin Warren. Do you remember him?' Eriksson shook his head so Aspinall continued. 'Ex major, paratroopers and Special Forces. A very good man and with a good team around him.'

'Get him on the speakerphone.' A moment later the connection was made.

'Major Warren? This is John Eriksson, CEO of Paternoster. I'm sending you down some details of a man that we want you to find. Do you think you can do that for me?'

The voice that replied spoke with a North Country accent, possibly Yorkshire, thought Eriksson. 'Don't see a problem, sir. Can you give me any initial details?'

'He is an old man who has recently been injured in a riot. He is probably travelling on foot, possibly accompanied by a small group of individuals. He was in Bristol a few hours ago but we don't know anything since. Obviously we shall keep you updated as more information becomes available.'

'I'm sure that me and my team can get to him in no time.'

'Whilst I admire your confidence, Major, I feel that I must urge you to use a high level of caution. Believe me, you have never met anyone like this man before. He has skills and knowledge that are way outside your experience. In fact, I would suggest that he could do more damage armed only with a florist's shop than you and your team could do with a Chieftain tank. For your own sake do not, under any circumstances, confront him directly. I want no one hurt in this endeavour. Do I make myself clear?'

'Completely clear, sir.'

'OK then, Major, we will speak again soon.' Eriksson ended the transmission with a touch on the phone pad and turned towards the door. 'I'm going to be with the owners. Keep me informed of developments, Mike.'

As he reached the door he paused and turned back. 'We must have sent a false sample back to the testing machine?'

Aspinall nodded.

'Who did we send?' asked Eriksson.

'The computer selected someone with about the same details. You know - male, about the right height, same sort of age.'

'Same sort of age? Oh I don't think so, Mike. I really don't think so.' With an amused chuckle, Eriksson turned and walked out of the control room.

—∞—

Back at the Forensic Laboratory Ian Watkins was trying to restart the testing machine. Having tried and failed with all the obvious steps, he had now resorted, in desperation, to reading the instruction manual. As he thumbed through to the section on 'Common Errors' the lights on the machine began to flicker. A moment later Ian saw the tester automatically start the familiar warm–up routine which, he knew, was a prelude to the system becoming functional again. A few seconds later the tester and associated computer returned to full operational mode.

Ian was also pleased to see that the results of the previous test, the one which had caused the machine to fail, were still displayed on the screen. This time the results were far more normal, similar to a thousand other samples that Ian had processed over the years. He had been sure that the previous one, displayed just before the tester shut down, could not have been correct. It was just too odd. Fortunately the system had found a match with a record on the Home Office database. A face appeared on the computer screen together with brief details of its owner.

'Edward James Rylands,' Ian mused aloud. 'Where have I heard that name before?'

He was still trying to recognise the name as he pressed the 'Send' button, dispatching the results to the waiting police station.

The name gradually faded from his thoughts as he pressed on with the next sample.

CHAPTER 7

Canford Park,
Bristol
Wednesday 22nd August
1.45 p.m.

The tramp waddled across the open parkland towards the waste bin. Rummaging through the day's detritus he found a pizza box which yielded a hardened crust, rejected as inedible by the previous owner. Happy with this unforeseen bounty, the tramp sat down on the grass to enjoy his lunch.

As he nibbled along one edge he saw that the nearby bench was unoccupied, but before he could move towards it he noticed another man walking from the car park. This man, middle aged and dressed in a cheap suit, was clearly intent on sitting on this bench. As the man's eyes saw the tramp his pace quickened almost, but not quite, to a run. On reaching the bench he sat down and looked at the tramp in a glance that hovered between disdain and hostile. The tramp got the message and, keen to finish his meal in peace, moved and sat down on the grass a few yards further away.

Minutes later, the calm of the summer afternoon was disturbed by another arrival. A new Jaguar saloon swept gracefully into the car park and moved into a space not far from the bench. The driver, another middle-aged man, got out and sauntered over to the bench. The tramp could see that the new arrival was an altogether different type of individual. From his clothes to his shoes, to the confident way he walked, this was a man who knew what he wanted and was generally successful in getting it.

The new arrival nodded to the man seated on the bench. 'Good afternoon, Councillor.'

The seated man nodded in response and gestured for the newcomer to sit.

At first, the newcomer hesitated, unhappy with the state of the bench but, after a moment's thought, decided that the meeting would go better if he was seated and so he decided to risk the damage to his expensive suit and sat next to his companion.

'How goes things at our wonderful Council?'

'Oh, you know, all very busy, full of debate and discussion. Same as ever really. At the moment I think the best way of summing things up would be ...' the Councillor hesitated for a moment as if struggling for the right word, ` ... balanced. Perhaps even finely balanced.'

'Ah, balanced. I do often feel that balance is not always the best situation for local democracy. It tends to lead to impasse, delay, a lack of progress towards the better things in life for your constituents. Don't you agree?'

The Councillor shrugged with an air of neither agreement nor disagreement. It was a gesture that he had honed to perfection over 20 years in local government.

The newcomer continued, 'No. I sometimes feel that what's needed is for someone of stature to take the lead, to push through these impediments, to take a stand for the best interests of local people and make sure that they get the facilities and services that they deserve.'

This time the Councillor made a slight nodding movement but, again, said nothing.

'I have been watching your endeavours over the past few weeks and I have to say that I see, in you, just such a person. So I decided to arrange this little chat to see how I might help you in areas where we might be able to work together. Areas where we could help both the local economy and, who knows, assist you in your important work.'

At last the Councillor spoke. 'Well, Mr Grayson, I am always interested in areas where business and local politics can work in a more cohesive fashion. Perhaps you could give me an example of where such an approach could prove useful?'

'Strangely enough I had just such a circumstance on my desk this morning. As you may be aware, my company is trying to build some new housing on the old industrial zone. Sadly, not everyone on the Council sees this as a useful contribution. There are some who feel this area should be retained for industrial use, some vain hope that new factories might be built there in the future. I ask you, factories indeed! We don't make things in this country any more so why do we need factories? Mark my words, if we wait for new factories then that land will remain unused and derelict for decades. What sort of contribution to society is that?'

'Funny you should mention that project. You may not be aware of this, but I have some small involvement in these matters and I know how split we are. It may well be that I have to cast the deciding vote. If I am to use it in favour of your development how will that contribute to the local society?'

'Well, clearly the houses that we will build will create work for local trades in the area during construction and then local people will have the chance to ...'

'Perhaps I did not pose the question correctly,' the Councillor interrupted before the conversation moved too far from his desired agenda. 'How would you be able to contribute to the development of local democracy in this area?'

'I quite understand. As I see it, the main problem is that good people such as yourself are hindered by the appalling lack of 'gratitude' that you obtain for your excellent services. My company would be only too happy to provide you with such further support if only it could be done... sensitively. Sadly there are those who might not share my enthusiasm for such direct support. Some might see this in a more negative light.'

Both men turned as the tramp, sitting on the grass several metres away, chose this moment to screw up the now empty pizza box and try to throw it into the waste bin. It hit the edge and bounced onto the ground.

After a few seconds of reflective silence the newcomer continued but with a new tack. 'How's the family doing? Both of your children must be at university by now. Getting on well, are they?'

'Yes, thank you. Ian is at Birmingham doing Civil Engineering. Grace is at St Andrew's studying Politics and Media.'

'Such an expensive time these days, what with student loans and so on,' said Grayson.

The Councillor nodded and, for the first time since he sat down, smiled.

Sensing the first signs of enthusiasm, Grayson pressed on. 'Perhaps we could arrange some form of sponsorship for them with my company. We're always looking for good people. We could pay off their student loans and provide them with a few thousand pounds in bursary. Even guarantee them employment once they have qualified if that would help. Maybe they could work on that new development we were discussing, assuming that it gets past planning of course.'

'That would be very kind. I'm sure they would be most grateful.'

'I'm also concerned about you. I hope you don't mind me saying this, but you do look very tired. The demands of the job are obviously taking their toll. We need to look after ourselves at our age. A few years ago I bought a small villa in the Caribbean. Why don't you pop over for a couple of weeks? I'm sure you would enjoy it. All expenses covered of course. You and your wife – ' the Councillor frowned so the businessman quickly changed tack, ' - or indeed anyone that you might wish to take, would have a great time. In fact, I can suggest a number of lady friends that would be only too delighted to accompany you. All of them would be very flexible to your needs. Actually, one of them is so flexible that she can …'

'ARMED POLICE. STAND UP WITH YOUR ARMS OUTSTRETCHED!'

A loudhailer boomed the message across the park as several police, clad in full body armour, helmets and rifles, burst out of the bushes and knelt around the bench. All weapons were pointed directly at the small group.

The two men jumped to their feet and quickly extended their arms, as instructed. The speed of the interruption had stunned them both.

A second later two more policemen ran into this, now secure, ring. However, they ran straight past the Councillor and the businessman and, to their joint astonishment, jumped on the tramp.

'Edward James Rylands. I am arresting you in connection with the suspicious death of Shaun Callaghan. You have the right to remain silent but ... `

'Shit! Could you not have waited for just two more minutes?' the tramp shouted angrily. He reached up to his head, pulled off a wig and peeled off his beard to reveal a clean shaven, close cropped appearance. He looked towards the car park and made a slicing motion across his throat before shouting, 'Cut.' As he did so, the back doors of a Ford transit van burst open and several people jumped out. One was holding a large, expensive looking TV camera. Another was carrying a dish microphone, clearly used to record conversations at a distance. A third, obviously in charge, ran over to the policeman in the process of cautioning the 'tramp' and shouted, 'What the fuck are you doing?'

The 'tramp' threw down his wig and continued his tirade against the policeman. 'Six months` work ruined. We've been chasing these bent bastards ...' he indicated the two men by the bench ... 'for weeks. We were within an ace of catching them red- handed. Another two minutes and it would have been on the evening news. But now...'

'Sorry sir, but this is part of a major police investigation in which, we believe, you are implicated.' The senior policeman was bemused but still intent on finishing his task. 'I must ask you to accompany me to our station where my sergeant is very keen to speak to you.'

As he was talking, a large police van drove into the car park. The 'tramp', or Eddie Rylands, Investigative Journalist, as he was known by millions of TV viewers, was roughly bundled into the back of the van which then drove away, spinning its tyres on the car park gravel. The rest of the TV team all jumped back into their van and sped after the police vehicle. The remaining armed police melted back into the bushes on their way back to their own transport.

This left just the Councillor and the businessman standing, arms still outstretched, besides the bench. A silent moment passed during which the full implications of their predicament began to dawn on them. At the same instant both men dropped their arms and began to walk hurriedly back to their respective cars.

—∞—

The four men arrived at Vicky's flat. The walk should only have taken a few minutes but hours had passed since they had left the car park. It had proved impossible to persuade the Old Man to walk in a direct route. He had constantly strayed away from the other three, wandering off to look at things that had caught his attention. Shop windows, flower beds, trees – all manner of everyday things that made the Old Man stop and examine them as if for the first time. Nathan had lost count of the number of times that the Old Man had picked leaves from a flower or a tree. Each time he studied them minutely, closely observing them and, in some cases, placing them into his mouth and chewing them. Some leaves were spat out almost immediately, often into the Old Man's palm, followed by another close inspection. Other times the Old Man swallowed the leaf before moving onto the next. Carl and Nathan were fascinated by the Old Man's actions. Julian was just irritated. But no amount of hint, insult or threat would make the Old Man move any more swiftly towards their destination. Ignoring Julian's urging and, without anything approaching an explanation, he just carried on with his investigations.

Reaching into his pocket for a key, Julian opened the door of the flat and went in, followed by the other three. He guided them into the main lounge area. Leaving aside the normal pleasantries, he was about to launch into a string of dire threats about what would happen if his audience did not respect Vicky's property when the Old Man swept past him and sat in a large armchair.

'I shall rest here until the return of the Physic.' Without any further comment the Old Man closed his eyes and was immediately asleep.

Julian was pleased to have finally coaxed his charges to the requested destination. He felt he had discharged his promise to Vicky and so had no further responsibility. He moved back towards the front door. 'I really must get back to work. I'm going to collect the car and then I'm off to the office. You two can just look after yourselves until Vicky gets back. Tell her to call me.'

Before Nathan or Carl could reply he was gone.

Nathan had known of Carl's problems because of his reputation within the police station but he had never met him directly, let alone speak to him. This was the first opportunity to begin to get to know him. Nathan sensed that, as possible companions in the Old Man's unspecified venture, they would be together for some time. He decided to start some form of conversation. 'How are you feeling?'

Carl seemed to be in some sort of haze. His reply was slow in coming, wary and surprised. 'I feel great. The best I've felt for months. What was it that the old guy did to me?'

'I didn't really see. It all happened so quickly. He seemed to just pinch your ear but it must have been more than that.' Nathan reflected again on the incident in the police cell. He recalled the movement of the Old Man's hand and realised that, once again, the pouch at his belt was involved. 'He touched that pouch just before he pushed you.'

'All I can remember is taking a swing at him, somehow missing. Next thing he is pressing me down and I get a massive pain inside my head. I must have blacked out for a second but when I came to, all my cravings had gone. It was as if all the Afghan stuff – you know about that?... Nathan nodded '... just never happened. Do you think this will be permanent? I just couldn't cope if I had to go back to that state again.' As he spoke he sat down on the large sofa. Looking down on the immense figure before him, Nathan recalled just how violent Carl could be and hoped that whatever the Old Man had done, it didn't wear off any time soon.

It was Carl's turn to ask some questions. 'How did you meet him?'

Nathan told him of the riot in the estate and how he woke up in the cell with the Old Man's 'corpse'. He spoke of Vicky's involvement, bringing Carl up to the point when the Old Man entered the paratrooper's cell.

'How does he do all these things?' Carl posed the question that Nathan had been asking himself all morning. Nathan's reply reflected his lack of success so far.

'I really don't know. Perhaps we'll have a chance to ask him when he wakes up.'

Carl stood up and walked towards the kitchen.

'Do you think the doctor would mind if we got some lunch?'

'I'm sure we could get something and sort it out later.'

'I'll see what I can find. You interested?' Nathan nodded.

Now in the kitchen Carl called to his new companion. 'Right then, Squaddie's rules apply. Always eat when you get the chance. You may not get another. She's sure to have some eggs. You want some?'

Again Nathan nodded.

While the paratrooper prepared some food Nathan thought about his own situation. He had just walked out of the station and, so far, had not been in contact. He was rather surprised that they had not tried to call him. Reaching into his pocket he took out his mobile phone. Seeing that it was switched off, he recalled that it had been low on power the previous evening. Clearly it had run down and switched itself off - something that had gone unnoticed during the morning's events.

Looking around the room he saw that Vicky had a compatible phone charger on a small table near the window. He picked up the charger and plugged it into his phone. The small screen lit up and indicated several missed calls. Pressing another key told him that they had all come from his station. A further key put him in contact.

'Alton Grove Police Station. PC Bradley speaking.'

'Alan. It's Nathan.'

'Nathan! Where the hell have you been? We've been chasing you all morning. Sergeant Johnson is on the warpath.' Bradley described the events following Nathan's departure. 'So the current view is that you have been kidnapped and we are trying to get you back here, pronto. Sounds like rubbish to me but arguing with Johnson in his current state would be a bit career-limiting.'

'You're right, Alan, I was certainly not kidnapped. In fact ...' Nathan paused for a moment in his explanation. Was this a good time to bring his contact with the Old Man to an end? He glanced at the figure sleeping in the chair in front of him. There was something about him that made Nathan want to stay around. Not just these tricks with the pouch but something more basic, more fundamental. The Old Man seemed to generate an aura of quiet confidence and wisdom, something that offered Nathan a resolution to the dilemmas that beset him. He decided to take a course of action that could also turn into a career-limiting move. 'In fact, Alan, they just gave me a lift to the hospital where I spent the morning in the casualty department. They make you switch your phone off, so this is the first chance I've had to call. I'm going back home now to get some rest. I might be going away for a while to recuperate. I'll call back in a few days when I'm feeling better. Bye then.'

'Hang on,' the anxiety sounded in Bradley's voice. 'Johnson is going to want to speak to you. I'll put him on. Just wait a moment.'

Nathan ended the call and switched off the phone, a step that gave him a surprising amount of pleasure. Almost cathartic. Perhaps this was a new beginning? Maybe a few days away from the daily grind might give him a chance to take a wider view? Was that what the Old Man had been suggesting? He was still reflecting on this when Carl came in carrying two plates of scrambled eggs.

'What now?' asked Carl, after they had both devoured the simple meal.

Nathan noted the weariness in Carl's voice. He nodded at the figure of the Old Man sleeping in the chair. 'I think he has the right idea. Perhaps we should do the same. You look the way I feel. You take the sofa, I'll take the chair.' He made himself comfortable and almost immediately fell asleep.

Carl moved one of the cushions under his head and listened to Nathan's gentle snoring until he also dropped off.

CHAPTER 8

Victoria Snow's Flat,
Bristol
Wednesday 22nd August
5.00 p.m.

The Old Man awoke, instantly aware that something was about to happen. He sniffed the air and recognised a familiar scent. He stood up and walked across the room into the hallway, taking up a position facing the front door. Once there he paused, waiting.

A moment later there was the sound of a key in the lock, the door opened and Vicky walked into her home. Seeing the Old Man she felt a rush of elation. This was the one who had, somehow, saved her mother's life. In the hours since their last meeting her life had been a whirlwind. She rushed forward, threw her arms around the waiting figure and hugged him. 'I have no idea what you did but thank you from the bottom of my heart.'

The Old Man was clearly taken aback by Vicky's display of gratitude and gently unpeeled her arms from around his neck.

'I am pleased that your mother has recovered,' the Old Man said with an almost embarrassed air.

'Recovered doesn't even begin to describe things. Yesterday she was struggling for breath and now I've just left her planning her next holiday!' In truth, the hardest part of the morning had been persuading her mother to remain in the hospital ward. The old woman felt so full of energy that she didn't want to waste a single moment of this new lease of life that she had been so unexpectedly granted.

However, the hospital staff, led by a stunned Head of Oncology, were equally adamant that she should stay. They pointed out that the improvement might be temporary, that further tests would be needed, that the hospital was the best place for her over the next few days. None of them had seen anything quite so dramatic before and they were all desperate to find out what had caused this miraculous recovery.

Once her mother had agreed to stay, James Courtney took Vicky to one side. He had realised that Vicky's visitor had played some important part in the morning's drama and so he wanted to know more about him. Vicky had told him all that she knew but was conscious of how little that was.

Courtney was clear what the next step should be. If at all possible, she was to get him back to the hospital. If that proved impossible then she was to stay with him for as long as she needed to discover what he had done to cause such a change in her mother's condition. Now, with the Old Man in front of her, she began her questioning. 'So ... God, I don't even know your name.'

The Old Man shrugged. 'I have been called by many names, each one less important than the one before. Call me what you wish. Or, indeed, nothing at all.'

'Well, whatever your name is, what did you do to my mother?'

The Old Man let out a deep sigh, turned and walked back into the lounge. 'This is the hardest part of every Return. Questions. Always so many questions. And every answer just begets more questions, in a never-ending stream. Why can you never accept that things just happen? This curiosity, this constant search for explanations, it will be the death of you.'

The noise had woken Nathan and Carl who now sat up as Vicky and the Old Man entered the room. They saw a determined Vicky, who was not going to be halted in her quest.

'No. Not again. I remember that you were able to deflect any explanations in the police station with this 'Man of Mystery' routine.'

She gently placed her hands on his shoulders and guided him towards an armchair. He reluctantly allowed himself to be pushed down into the seat.

'What's happened? How is your Mum?' Nathan's voice sounded almost incidental in the background.

'Better than she has been for years. I have just spent the last four hours with her and she is rushing around like a thing possessed. Something happened at her bedside in the hospital ward, something that this man did, and I want to know what it was and I want to know it now.'

The Old Man placed his head in his hands and let out a large sigh. 'What do you want to know?'

'Simple. What did you do to her?'

'Yes, it is simple. But it is also difficult. And I know that you will ignore the simple and choose the difficult. Well, to answer your question, I have some small knowledge of plants, built up over many Returns. I know what many of them do, and how that can be used in combination. So I know that knapwort, mixed with the flux of the aldbune leaf, makes a juice that destroys the gnawing plague. I also know that the knapwort root is too tough to use without chewing it to a pulp before you make the mixture, and that smearing the lips is the swiftest way for the treatment to work. Will you accept my answer or must you continue?'

'What are knapwort and aldbune? What is it about them that causes the cure? Why the lips?' Vicky's torrent of questions stopped only for her to draw breath but before she could continue the Old Man spoke again.

'You see! For each answer, another question. It has no end. It just goes on forever. Why can you not just accept the 'what'? Why do you have to know the 'how' and the 'why'? It is always the same. Can you all never learn that there is a time to stop asking questions and start seeking other routes to knowledge?' The Old Man shook his head sadly.

Seeing that he was becoming irritated, Vicky decided to change tack. 'How can I learn these things without asking questions?' She smiled at her question and its inherent contradiction.

The Old Man smiled back. He walked across the room to the window and looked down to the street below. The evening traffic was starting to build up, with its attendant noise and smells. Taking all this in with a single glance, he turned back to face the group. 'It might have been good to pass on some of this wisdom to you. As a Physic I'm sure that you would make much use of it, although little of it for Nature's benefit. But this Return is not to be a long one. The world is fouled beyond measure and I have no desire to await the cleansing.' He turned back towards the window and fell into silent reflection.

Nathan was the next to speak. 'You keep talking about 'Returns'. What do you mean?'

'Ah, my errant Kingsman. I will be sad not to journey with you. I see in you a trustworthy companion. So, in recompense for taking you away from your old path, I shall answer your question.' He paused for a second before pressing on. 'You must understand that my life has been one long series of Rests and Returns. At each Return I can, as I choose, remain for some small while or, if the world has turned against Nature, take my Rest once more.' He gestured out of the window again. 'In all my time I have never seen the world so set against Nature's path and so, this time, my Return will be short and so my next Rest awaits.'

'I'm sorry but I still don't understand. How will you take this 'Rest'?'

'Through my knowledge of plants. Tell me, do you know how a bear can sleep through the winter's cold?'

Nathan had no idea. 'I think it just falls asleep.'

'Yet it falls asleep each night. Why does it not also sleep through the summer?' Again, Nathan shrugged. He looked for support from Carl or Vicky but none was forthcoming.

The Old Man continued, 'Many years since, I watched bears in their preparation for winter. They ate many things, some flesh, some plants. I tried each of these in turn. The trials took many years but in the end, I found the right one. It was a small plant, almost too tiny to see. It had yellow flowers and a tiny black seed, little more than a speck of dust. It grows just as the first snow of the winter falls. I found that it was this plant that makes the bears sleep through the winter. I began to mix the different parts with other plants. I found that the flowers, dusted with frommel petals, can delay sleep for many days. Yet if you mix the seeds with the juice of the kabline leaf and the stem of the younson then its potency increases manyfold. This potion can make a person sleep for years and years. I use the seeds of this plant to give me my Rest.`

'What is the plant called?' asked Vicky, hoping that the Old Man would not clam up again.

'Staria. The plant is named staria.'

'I remember seeing bears in Canada on one of my overseas postings.' It was Carl's turn to enter the conversation. 'Amazing things they were. Massive. Powerful. Where did you see them?'

'I saw them in the land of the Picts. I walked in those realms in the days of my youth.'

Carl looked puzzled. 'Where's that? I've never heard of it.'

The Old Man looked confused as if surprised that anyone should ask such a simple question.

Nathan stepped in. 'It's an old name for Scotland. But that can't be right. There haven't been bears in Scotland for centuries. They were all wiped out long ago.'

The Old Man looked around the small group, now all looking at him waiting for his answer.

He hesitated, unwilling to say the words. He always tried to keep this explanation back because he knew what would follow. The waiting only seemed to increase the tension. 'I make no error. The bears were in the land you now call Scotland and it was a very long time ago.'

He looked at each of the faces. Each had the look he had come to expect. Not being able to accept the truth of his explanation yet unable to express their doubts, their politeness stopping them from directly questioning the sanity of their new acquaintance. He took a deep breath and pressed on. 'What King reigns?'

Vicky was the first to speak. 'Oh no, you're not changing the subject now. How can you have seen bears in Scotland centuries ago?'

The Old Man felt the familiar feeling of disbelief, of not comprehending. He had been through this routine so many times before. As they all stared at him he pondered how his explanation would be taken this time. Acceptance? Probably not. Rejection? Hopefully not. Understanding? Definitely not.

He continued, 'Staria causes a sleep of not hours or days but of years, of lifetimes. The sum of all my Rests is beyond your measure. I have known a lifetime of lifetimes. I have walked this land from the very beginning and I have learned many things. I have told very few of my history and have met fewer still that believed it.' He surveyed the three faces before him, all open- mouthed with amazement.

Nathan was the first to respond. 'So you are some form of time-traveller, sleeping through great swathes of years before waking, spending some time on what you call a `Return' before using the staria to go back to sleep again? Is that your claim? You expect us to believe that?'

'I claim nothing. I have simply spoken the truth. I am a traveller but time is nothing more than the road upon which I wander. Time holds all of us in its grip. For me, the grip is merely a little looser.'

It was Vicky's turn to speak. 'How long have you been having these feelings?'
Her words, spoken with a manner of professional sympathy, betrayed a direction that the Old Man sensed instantly. Angrily, he replied. 'So you think me mad? Well, this is not the first time I have been so accused. So riddle me this, Physic. How can a wandering madman strike the gnawing plague from your dying mother when the best your own shaman can do is to watch her perish?' He turned to Nathan, 'How can I walk out of a King's palace with one of his own captains holding open the door?' Finally, to Carl, 'How can I take away the madness of the poppy with a single squeeze of your ear?' He could see his audience start to reconsider and the first beginnings of doubt take hold. He knew that, as so many had before, they would start with disbelief, before moving to confusion, as the evidence of their eyes began to contradict the logic of their minds. In time, he knew that they would have believed him as this evidence became overwhelming.

'So why have you returned now? What causes you to wake up?' asked Vicky.

'Usually, I sleep until the potency of the staria falls to naught. Unless, that is, something happens to disturb my slumber. I try to find peaceful places that are unlikely to be disrupted, such as amongst the roots of the ancient yew tree in the churchyard at the village of Woodburn. Long had I rested there, until I was woken by that angry young lord who fell upon me.'

Nathan recalled how he had thrown the gang leader against the old wall of the church yard. The stones must have become loosened by his impact, causing the Old Man to fall out.

'So how long are you going to stay this time?' said Vicky. She was anxious for him to be around long enough for her to learn about his medical skills. A second later she realised that she was being drawn into his delusions.

'As I said, this Return will not be a long one. I can sense terrible things are about to happen. I must find a sanctuary and then take my Rest before Nature strikes.'

He began to prepare the staria mixture. Reaching to his waist, the Old Man opened the neck of the hide pouch tied to his belt. Pushing his hand inside he withdrew a tightly clenched fist which he opened carefully to reveal a mixture of dried seeds, roots and petals. He moved a finger of his other hand around the palm, seeking one particular type. Clearly unsuccessful, he placed the contents on the coffee table before plunging into the pouch a second time. Again he opened his palm and moved the variety of seeds and roots around but still failed to find the ones that he sought. Adding this second handful to the first, he turned his attention to his pouch. He carefully examined the animal skin, especially the closely stitched edges and seams. After a moment he gave out an irritated sigh. He held out the bag towards the others and they saw, in a corner where two seams met, a small hole.

'This gap is too small to allow larger seeds to fall out but not the smallest. Staria has the smallest seeds of all and so all my stock has been lost. Yet this is but a small problem. I must collect more and it will take a little time. It is an unfortunate distraction but I shall find some before long.'

As he spoke, in such a matter-of- fact way, the implications of his claims began to spread into the minds of his audience.

Nathan was struck silent by the Old Man's story. It was simply incredible - beyond all possibility of belief. All his considerable intelligence demanded that he should challenge the strange figure in front of him, analysing the absurdity of his fairy tale before intellectually tearing it to shreds. Yet looking at the Old Man he was taken by the manner in which he had told his strange story, almost reluctantly, and with an air that almost invited rejection. Even this early in his police career Nathan had met liars, many of them great liars. This Old Man was either the best liar he had ever seen, or - but no. The alternative just was not credible, so obviously beyond all chance of acceptance. Yet at the back of his mind, in the small part most sheltered from logic, questions still raged. It wasn't just this talk of plants but his strange clothes, his constant state of surprise at common, everyday things, his manner of speech.

Then Nathan remembered something else. From the moment that the Old Man had woken up in the cell Nathan had a strange feeling of familiarity. He was sure that he had heard the Old Man's voice before. The Bristol accent, the tone, the inflexion, Nathan could not pin it down. But something in that voice was calling to him, giving a feeling of apprehension that he just could not explain. Perhaps discovering the answer to that riddle alone was enough reason to play along with the Old Man's delusions, even if it was just for the time being.

Carl was also struggling with the Old Man's story. To him it all just sounded like total crap. All this talk of plants and sleeping for years was so bogus that he was tempted to just walk away and leave the Old Man to his fantasy. Then he remembered his own recent hallucinations, how vivid they had been, and how terrifying. Yet he had been clear of them for several hours, the longest period since his return from Afghanistan. There had been none of the desperate cravings that had wrecked his recent months. Was this really all down to the Old Man's actions in the cell? As the thought crossed his mind he began to sense the feelings that he knew, in time, would grow into an insatiable demand for the accursed powder. Perhaps the Old Man had not cured him but only found another way to fulfil the demand, albeit temporarily. For Carl, going back was not an option. He decided that he must stay with the Old Man in the hope that the respite given him was not an isolated event but the first stage towards something more permanent.

And yet there was more than that. Carl also sensed a strong affinity with the Old Man. Perhaps it was just another of his plant tricks but deep-down Carl doubted it. He actually felt a strong kinship between them, built in some unfathomable way over a long period of time. He knew that this kinship meant that his role was to protect the Old Man from harm even at the cost of his own life. He didn't know why, but he also knew that this was not the first time he had been given this task.

Vicky was also stunned by the revelations made by the Old Man. She was struggling to balance the total absurdity of his time-travelling claims with the spectacular improvement in her mother's condition. All her scientific instincts wanted her to settle the matter immediately but she could see that this was not the time for confrontation. She would try to help him with his delusions later. Right now the best approach was to establish some form of rapport, perhaps offer him some support for his actions. Maybe then she would stand a chance of learning from him. 'So you need to find this plant? I think I can help you there.' She walked into one of the bedrooms that she used as a study and returned carrying a laptop computer.

The Old Man was perplexed when he saw it, even more so when she opened the lid and the screen lit up. As she began to type onto the keyboard, the Old Man moved around the back of the machine, trying to see where the pictures were coming from.

After a moment Vicky continued, 'Right, this is a gardening website that my mother is always using. It has a plant-finder section.' She typed in the plant name and waited while the internet found the distant database. 'No. It doesn't recognise that name. Perhaps we can find it by its description. So, you said that it is small with a yellow flower and that it flowers in late autumn.' She entered the details. A moment later several pictures of different flowers that might match the description were displayed. 'Which one is it?'

The Old Man was fascinated by the laptop and the pictures now displayed on the screen. He carefully examined each of the pictures in turn before pointing to one of them. 'That has the likeness of staria.'

Vicky moved the cursor to the picture and clicked the button on her wireless mouse. Within a second a larger image of the plant appeared together with some text. She quickly read through the text, seeking locations where the plant could be found. However, what she discovered made her look up at Nathan and Carl, who had also seen the section of the text that had made her pause. She looked directly at the Old Man, not sure how he would receive this news. 'I'm sorry, but according to this, staria is now extinct.'

—∞—

The screen on Colin Warren's mobile flashed 'Eriksson' as it rang.

'Major Warren? I have some more information on the whereabouts of your target. It seems that he left the police station with a small group and drove to St Luke's hospital. I'm confident that he can't drive so he must have been taken by one of his new companions. We still have no details of the other group members but we do know something of the car. It is a black Range Rover, quite new. I suggest that you get over to the hospital and see what you can find. Keep me informed.' Eriksson rang off without waiting for a reply.

Warren was momentarily irritated by the abruptness of Eriksson's telephone manner but his years of army life had taught him how to cope with senior officers barking orders and this was little different. His mind moved to the task in hand. Since Eriksson's first contact he had used his time well. A few calls had brought together most of his team. Like him they were all ex-forces, specialists in their chosen fields. Surveillance, weapons, transport, communications – all the skills that would be needed for the task in hand. Paternoster were paying top rate for the best that he could find and he was pleased with the faces ranged in front of him, waiting for him to pass on the orders that would flow from his call.

'Right. We've got our starting line. Time to go.'

The team filed out of the garage that had been their assembly point. Dressed in a range of clothing around a common theme of dark tops and jeans, they moved across to two unmarked, dark blue Ford Transit vans parked on the tarmac. Silently the team climbed into the vans. The engines fired up and the vans swung onto the road, blending into the anonymity of the evening traffic.

The man-hunt had begun.

CHAPTER 9

Victoria Snow's Flat,
Bristol
Wednesday 22nd August
5.30 p.m.

'What means this word 'extinct'?' The puzzlement in the Old Man's voice was evident.

The Old Man scanned the three faces, urgently seeking an answer.

Nathan thought, if this guy is really play-acting then he deserves an Oscar. 'It means that it has died out. It is not alive anywhere anymore.' He tried to soften the bad news but could only do so much.

'No longer alive! How can that be? I could find it everywhere on my last Return.' Then, to Vicky, nodding towards the laptop, 'Your wisdom box plays you false. Staria cannot have died out. I am familiar with the notion. Indeed, I have seen many beasts and plants fall from Nature's plan but this takes many lifetimes. This cannot have happened during a single Rest.'

Nathan continued with his explanation. 'We are seeing many changes at the moment, often much faster than the world has seen before. If your staria was sensitive to increases in acidity then the rainfall might have killed it off, let alone the effects of carbon dioxide and climate change.' As he spoke Nathan realised that he was also being drawn into accepting his foolishness as reality.

'So it is just as I feared. You have poisoned your nest so badly that Nature is replying in kind. Well, I have seen her awesome wrath. She cares not what she destroys in regaining her balance. This makes it ever more vital that I start my Rest. I just cannot believe your wisdom box. I must find some staria somewhere and I must start now.' He moved towards the door, clearly intent upon leaving.

'Wait!' Vicky had continued to work on her laptop. 'I think I can find a place where we might find some. Do you need the whole plant or just the seeds?'

'Only the seeds are needed for the Resting potion,' replied the Old Man. 'Does your box speak of such a place?'

Vicky swung the laptop around to show the others the website that she had been looking at.

'According to their site, this place might have some.'

The three men closely examined the picture that Vicky had found.

Nathan scanned the screen, quickly realising the idea that Vicky was suggesting. 'What a great idea. Well done. If anywhere has seeds then it's that place. Can you be sure? It's a long way to go for nothing.'

'I'm sure. I've just looked through their catalogue and the modern name of the plant is listed so they definitely have some. Whether they would give it to us is a different question.'

The Old Man continued to stare at the screen. The curves of the modern, sleek buildings displayed on the screen were utterly new to him, quite unlike any structure that he had seen before. 'Where is this strange palace?'

A further click of the mouse and a map of the location was displayed.

'I know that place. It is near to an Army barracks where I was billeted once. We could get there in a few hours if we used your boyfriend's car.' Carl seemed to have the habit of speaking so infrequently that he was often forgotten.

'Not I. I will never travel again in that Rover cart. It is beyond nature and, I'm sure, not safe.'

'It's up to you but without using the car we can't get there.' Vicky tried to placate the Old Man. This was not a good time to start confronting the delusions, but his hatred of all things modern was an interesting symptom.

The Old Man was staring closely at the map on the screen. Most of the symbols were beyond his knowledge but he could recognise the layout of the roads, rivers and surrounding hills. He reached back into his memory and tried to recall this part of the country. Initially he was unsuccessful until he saw a particular symbol.

'What does that mark denote?'

Nathan bent over to look as closely as the Old Man had done.

'It means an ancient barrow. A sort of tomb.'

'And that one?'

'A stately home called Wakehurst Place.'

The Old Man pondered for a second before walking over to the window and looking up at the sky. He seemed to be looking at the position of the sun. After a moment's thought he turned back to the group.

'I know this dwelling. It is many days' walk from here but the way is not harsh. So we shall have our journey together after all. We must start at the sun's first light. For now, we must rest.' He moved across to the settee and lay down, full length.

'Hang on,' said Vicky. 'Do you expect us to drop everything and walk with you for days on end, and all on the off chance that this place will just give up some endangered seeds if you ask them nicely?'

But there was no reply. The Old Man was asleep.

—∞—

'Eriksson speaking'

'This is Warren. We are at the hospital.'

'Have you been able to track down the car?'

'It's no longer here but we spoke with the car park attendant. He remembers it very clearly. It appears that it outstayed the free period and so he put a wheel clamp and a fine notice onto it. When the owner came back he was none too pleased and called the attendant some names that would have made my troopers blush. Not surprisingly the attendant remembers him quite clearly.'

'Details, please.'

'The name is Julian St Clere. He is middle-to-late 20s, tall with dark brown hair. The attendant described him as well dressed and well spoken, at least when he is not cursing. I've seen the clamp release documentation which gives the car registration number as ...' Warren read off the details from his notes.

'Stand by, Major.' Eriksson turned to his IT specialist sitting in the corner of the control room. 'Got that?' The IT guy nodded as he fed the information into his system. A moment later he replied.

'The DVLA system gives the owner of that car as Julian St Clere, address Apartment 4a, Sophia View, Reaning, Bristol. The Local Authority database confirms that information. Social Security systems give his age as 27 and that he is unmarried. Companies House list him as a director in several small businesses, most of which have failed in the first few months of trading. He has ...' the IT guy paused as he counted the lines on the screen, 'eight credit cards which he uses regularly, building up some very large debts which he normally manages to pay off quite quickly. His most recent bank statement gives his only significant source of income as ... Mr Alain St Clere of Hanover Square, London, relationship – Father. He doesn't have a criminal record but the 'under-the-counter' police database notes several warnings for minor misdemeanours, mostly vandalism whilst drunk.' The IT guy smiled as he read ahead. 'This unofficial system is not restricted by the conventions of political correctness and so they can often give quite revealing summaries of the people in question.'

'And what description have they given to Mr St Clere?'

'Tosser!'

Eriksson returned to Colin Warren.

'Did you catch all that, Major? I think that a little social call on friend Julian might prove educational.'

'Would you rather we staked out his flat until morning? We could then go in as part of the everyday bustle of city life. Going in now might not be as unobtrusive as you would wish.'

'I understand your point, Major, but time is of the essence. I want our target under your control as soon as humanly possible. Please therefore proceed with all possible speed. Eriksson out.'

—∞—

Sensing Vicky's frustration, Nathan reached over and tapped the Old Man's shoulder but without success. He tried again, this time a little more vigorously, but still without waking him. Finally he stood over the Old Man's sleeping form and, lifting him by both shoulders, he shook the Old Man again but more forcefully, but still to no avail.

'I'm sorry, but he's dead to the world. I don't think anything is going to wake him until morning.'

'Well, it looks like all other questions will have to wait.' Vicky was clearly disappointed. She was anxious to get more details of the medications that the Old Man had used on her mother. Her boss, James Courtney, had told her to get this information, come what may. He hadn't specifically included going off on some form of ramble across southern England but if that was what it was going to take then so be it.

Her mind moved to more practical issues. 'It looks like you two are going to be my guests for tonight. The spare room has two single beds. Please make yourselves at home. I'm just going to get changed and then I'll make us something to eat.' She stood up and walked across the room to her bedroom, closing the door behind her. The two men looked at each other in silence, each waiting for the other to speak, to start some form of normal conversation despite the story they had just heard. Nathan tried first.

'It looks like we are going to be travelling companions for a while. How are you feeling?'

'Fine.' Carl was reluctant to discuss his addiction with so slight an acquaintance but saw that they had very little else in common. 'I don't remember the last time I went so long without feeling the craving. How are you after your pummelling?'

'A bit stiff, especially where the bruises are starting to appear. Still, I seem to have got off pretty lightly.' Again, the stunted silence. It was becoming clear that avoiding the obvious topic was not going to be an option. Someone was going to have to grasp this verbal nettle. Nathan decided that it should be him. 'So what did you think of his story?'

'He tells a good tale right enough, but it's got to be a load of bollocks.'

'That's exactly how I feel. It cannot be true. It's just too unbelievable. But ...'

'Yes?' Carl leaned forward. He had been expecting the 'but'.

'There is something about him. If any normal person had spouted this tosh I would be calling the men in white coats. But, well, look at him. He hasn't done anything even half normal since he woke up in the cell. Everything he does seems to be at best eccentric and at worst downright weird.'

'He is certainly the strangest bloke I've ever met and no mistake. Don't make his story any more truthful though.'

'So what do you plan to do? Are you going to go with him tomorrow?'

Carl frowned. 'Don't see as I've much choice. Whatever he did to me seems to have done the trick but how do I know it'll be permanent? If I don't go with him I might be screaming the place down by this time tomorrow. No, I think that staying with him seems like my best plan at present. How about you?'

'If I have any sense at all I should go back to the station tomorrow, probably taking him ...' Nathan nodded to the sleeping form on the sofa, '... with me.'

Carl nodded. Now it was his turn to press for a finish to the sentence. 'But ...'

Nathan smiled, 'I just don't know why but all my instincts tell me that would be a bad move. This guy keeps saying things to me that cut right to the heart of my worries. Questions that I've been struggling with for weeks. He seems to offer answers and I just feel that I need to be around to hear them.'

'So you're up for this walk then?'

'Seems like it.'

'Tell you what,' Carl continued, 'I'll stick with him as long as you stick with him. Deal?' Carl extended his huge hand towards Nathan.

Nathan sensed a possible ally reaching out, someone seeking support for the strange times to come. He grasped the hand in front of him and shook it. 'Deal!'

They had been so deep in their conversation that they did not hear the front door open. Nor did they notice a large figure standing in the doorway. In fact they had been completely unaware of this person until they heard a familiar voice.

'Oh God. Don't tell me you lot are still here.'

Julian had returned.

The motorbike flashed around the street corner into the small cul-de-sac. The rider slowed down momentarily to look around. A quiet suburban street, all peace and tranquillity. Middle England in microcosm. In fact, he saw only two things that were even slightly out of keeping. Away from the comforting security of the street lamps sat two Ford Transit vans, their darkened windows offering the only hint of a threat to the sleepy urban scene.

The rider moved his bike alongside the leading van. Once in position he knocked quietly on the driver's door. In reply, the window moved down slowly.

'Major Warren?'

The driver nodded. The rider turned to open the container fixed behind his seat. He removed a large brown envelope and handed it to the driver.

'A present from a friend at Paternoster.'

Warren took the package and nodded his thanks. The window slowly returned to its closed position.

His task completed, the rider drove slowly back to the entrance to the cul-de-sac before revving his engine and disappearing into the night.

Back in the van, Warren was unimpressed at the rider's triumphal exit. A racket like that he could do without. He threw the package to one of his team in the back of the van and moved to sit next to him on the van's floor.

Opening the package, the trooper withdrew a large piece of paper. Unfolding it several times he spread it onto the van floor alongside Warren.

'What's this?' said the trooper.

'The building plans of those flats over there.' Warren nodded to an impressive building at the end of the cul-de-sac. 'We are interested in this one.' He pointed at the drawing. 'Apartment 4a, Sophia View.'

'Shit. How did he get these so quickly? We've only been here five minutes.'

Warren smiled. 'Friends in low places.' Although he chose not to show it, he was actually very impressed. This Paternoster outfit seemed to be the real deal when it came to this type of work.

He called his team to order. 'Right. So how do we get into this place, remove one old man and get away again before his mates even know we've been to visit? Ideas please.'

The group began to plan their night's work.

—∞—

Vicky heard Julian's voice from her bedroom and moved swiftly into the lounge. She had hoped that she could intercept him before he saw the others but his silent arrival ended any chance of that.

'Julian. I need a word.'

The couple moved into the kitchen and so out of sight of Nathan and Carl. Only the sounds told them of how the couple's conversation progressed. Starting out as a series of whispers their voices quickly rose through normal to loud to shouting and finally to screaming.

Vicky was the first to emerge. 'Well, I have tried to tell Julian about today's events and it won't surprise you to learn that he is not keen on joining our little expedition.'

'That's putting it mildly.' Julian had joined them from the kitchen area. 'I'm not surprised that Laurel and Hardy here have fallen for this rubbish - but you! You're supposed to be a doctor, a scientist, someone with at least something in the way of critical reasoning. Yet you let some wandering tramp walk into your life, spin a tale of time-sleeping and suddenly you're off on some mystery tour to help him find some magic beans!'

'Not beans, seeds.' Carl was trying to be helpful but somehow his intervention did little to stop Julian's invective flow.

'Thanks for the botany lesson, Darwin, but I think my point still holds, don't you? Perhaps you could return to your specialist subject, which would be ...?' Julian struck an exaggerated, thoughtful pose. 'The life and works of the Brothers Grimm?'

Carl quickly stood and went nose-to-nose with Julian.

Nathan intervened before the threatened violence ensued. 'Listen, Julian.'

Julian turned away from Carl towards the policeman. 'I think that Mr St Clere would be more appropriate, Constable. I find a degree of formality so important when dealing with the mentally challenged.'

'Oh, stop being such a prat, Julian.' Vicky's voice seemed to make her boyfriend at least pause in his dangerous upward spiral. 'Whether you like it or not, strange things have happened today and, yes, I'm a scientist and I want answers. Of course I have severe doubts about the answers I've had so far but that doesn't mean I should stop looking. So yes, I'm going with this strange man to find his staria seeds. And if, along the way, I find out more of how he cured my mother then I cannot tell you how important that would be. Now if you wish to join us then I, at least, would welcome you. However, if you don't want to go then that's also fine by me. I think I'll have all the company I need?'

This last remark was directed at Nathan and Carl. Both nodded.

Julian saw that he was not going to win Vicky over and so decided to launch into a big finish. 'Fine. If that's what you want, then go. Just don't come crying back to me when your professional reputation is in tatters!' With a dramatic flourish he flounced into the kitchen.

Vicky felt the need to say something to her new companions about her boyfriend's behaviour. 'I know how he seems to come across, but he can be good fun once you get to know him. I really would like him to join us if at all possible. I'll have another go at persuading him later, this time on our own. You never know, he might change his mind.'

'Yes. That would be great,' Nathan lied.

'Don't try too hard,' said Carl, with brutal truthfulness.

'Please help yourselves to some food. The kitchen is well stocked. I'm going to call Mum from my bedroom and then I'll probably turn in. See you all in the morning. Perhaps things will make more sense then.'

—⊗—

Warren glanced at his watch. It was now 2.00 a.m. He turned to the sleeping group lying in the back of the van.

'Time to go, boys.'

Each of them woke quickly and shrugged off the stiffness brought on by sleeping in such a confined space. Quietly they climbed out of the Transit and grouped together on the pavement. One of the team walked over to the other Transit and tapped quietly on the side. Moments later the scene was repeated as the second group took their places.

'OK, any final questions?' All eyes were on Warren. There were none. 'Right then, let's do it.'

Most of the group started to move towards the apartments, leaving only two who climbed back into the Transits. They were to move the vans, ready for a quick departure when the team came back with their quarry.

Once they reached the front door, one of the team reached into the black bag and removed a small electronic device, about the size of a mobile phone. He attached this to the keypad at the side of the entrance. Switching it on brought a buzzing sound as the device wirelessly interrogated the door's keypad. A second later a series of digits were displayed. Warren tapped the figures in and the door opened with a comforting click.

The team were now in the main hallway of the apartment block. Fully illuminated throughout the night, the lights made them feel very exposed. For choice Warren would have preferred to go in during the day, when so many more people were about, but he had been overruled. A second later the lights went out, again down to the relevant specialist in Warren's team.

They knew that the flat was on the second floor and so they quietly moved up the stairs. A few more seconds brought them to their target, clearly marked 'Apartment 4a'. A nod from Warren and another of the team withdrew some putty-like material which he shaped with his gloved hands and applied to three sections of the door, in the areas of the hinges and of the lock. A further team member had withdrawn some sacks, made from thick plastic. These he distributed to others, together with small metal cylinders. These cylinders were screwed onto specially designed connectors and almost immediately the sacks began to inflate.

Once the putty had been applied to the door the sacks were placed on top, fixed in place by several pieces of strong black tape. Peeling the tape from the roll had been the loudest part of the whole process. Finally a large suction cup was applied to the centre of the door. A rope was tied through a loop in the cup's handle, run across the hallway and tied to the banister on the stairs several metres away.

The group now split into two sections. One moved further up the staircase, taking refuge on the third floor. The other, including Warren, ducked under the rope now tied across their path and stepped quickly down to the entrance hall.

Once all his men were in position Warren removed a small handset, keyed in a code number and pressed a large green button along the top edge.

Both groups felt a sudden rush of air as the pressure wave from the explosion flashed past them. At the same instant a bright, but mercifully short, light illuminated the staircase. The only sound was a muffled 'thump'.

Warren smiled. The explosive had worked well. Designed to have a maximum impact yet minimum sound, it was perfect for this type of job. At first, he had been surprised that Paternoster could get hold of any, as it was still in the top secret, development stage. However, he was getting to know his employers a little better now, so such surprises were getting fewer.

Both teams moved back in front of the apartment door. The silent explosion had badly damaged the edges of the door, especially where the putty had been directly applied. Yet the door was still standing. This was the function of the suction cup, still fixed to the centre of the door. There was no point in having a silent explosion if the noise of the door falling in woke the sleeping residents. The rope was untied from the banister and held, awaiting Warren's order.

Meanwhile all the members of the team took gas masks from their bags and fitted them carefully over their faces. These masks were also fitted with night-vision goggles, giving them all complete visibility for the task to come.

Slowly the rope was slackened, allowing the door, now completely detached from the frame, to be lowered to the ground, touching the carpet inside the apartment with barely a sound. The burglar alarm started to beep, softly at this stage. Warren knew that they had 15 seconds before, without the right code, the main alarm would sound and a message would be sent through the telephone line to the private security firm contracted to guard the premises. The team's electronics specialist stepped forward. Again the detector was attached to the alarm keypad and, again, the required digits were identified and keyed in. The beeping stopped and the tense silence returned.

Once again Warren checked that all his men were ready. After receiving a nod from each he, in turn, nodded back to one of them. This man took a different cylinder from the bag that he carried. Dislodging a ring-pull at one end caused a fine mist to emerge. Quickly the man tossed the cylinder into the darkened hallway and withdrew.

Warren now waited. This was always the hard part. The team were so keyed up they always wanted to burst in at this point. But Warren knew that the gas would need a few moments to take full effect. It was designed to incapacitate rather than kill, but the victims must have a few lungfuls before it took full effect. If he went in too soon and someone was still awake, well, that's how accidents happen. Warren didn't like accidents. Accidents often led to shooting and then to deaths. It had been made very clear to him that the death of this target was not an option.

After what seemed like an age Warren gave the final nod and the group rushed into the apartment. Following the agreed plan they split up into the various rooms that the building plans had told them to expect. Each room had two of the team allocated to it. Instructions were clear. Find the old man, lift him out, carry him down. All others were to be left where they slept.

With professional, silent haste the team fanned out, entering all of the rooms at the same moment. Their heat-sensitive goggles enabled them to see through both the darkness and the mist generated by the gas cylinder, now lying empty on the hall floor.

As each room was searched it became apparent that there was a problem. The two bedrooms, the lounge, even the bathroom, were searched for the sleeping occupants. In each case the searchers called out the same response.

'All clear!'

Warren quickly realised that, although his plan had worked perfectly, he had failed in his night's mission.

The apartment was completely unoccupied.

CHAPTER 10

The sun rose gloriously over Alphington Terrace, in the Handrel area of the city. Vicky had chosen this particular flat because of the view from the lounge, especially in the morning. For those awake to see it, the sunrise was as impressive as ever.

This particular morning only the Old Man sat and watched the spectacle. For him it was the one unchanging aspect of the world around him. In all his Returns, through all of the changes that Nature had wrought, this one sight remained inviolate. For more times than he could count, he had watched the sun emerge above the horizon, yet it always made his spirits rise and his skin tingle. Nature was indeed magnificent. It had always been so and would forever be so, no matter what the Others did to despoil it.

His mind again considered this latest Return. How could there be such devastation? It cannot have been so long since his last Return and yet every aspect of the world seemed to be ruined. He looked down from the window to the buildings that surrounded him and saw how packed together they were. If all these dwellings were filled with people then there must be far more than the earth could sustain. So how could they survive? He had seen cities before but never on such a scale. He was sure that Nature might be tricked into such widespread provision for a short time but she would have her retribution in the end. And, based upon what he had seen so far, this latest trick had been massive and so, in reply, he knew that this retribution would be of a comparable order, and so truly grotesque. He had seen Nature re-establish her balance many times. Her weapons were truly awesome - plague, famine, flood and fire. He had seen them all. He wondered which would be used this time. Perhaps it would be a combination of all four. Or perhaps something different: a new response for a new corruption. Whatever was to happen, and all his senses told him it would be soon, he did not want to be around to see it. Some staria must be found, and quickly.

Reluctantly he moved away from the window and moved through the flat. 'Awake! We must prepare for our journey!' His loud voice rang out, certain to bring everyone out of their slumbers.

Nathan was the first to stir. He walked into the lounge in time to see the Old Man moving towards the front door. 'Hang on. We'll all need to get ready first.'

'What do you mean, 'get ready'?' replied the Old Man, annoyed at the delay.

'You know, get washed, have breakfast. If you want to make some decent progress today then you really need to give us a few minutes to prepare.'

'Ah yes. The breaking of the night's fast. I had forgotten the habit of eating at set times. It always seemed strange to me when food is always at hand throughout the day. Yet you are right. You must all take nourishment before we depart. But make haste as I want to make the most of the daylight hours.'

Nathan walked to the TV set in the corner of the lounge and switched it on.

'Right. Let's see what the weather's going to do.'

'The weather? Surely we already know. Any fool can see that from the clouds. Our need now is to …' The Old Man stopped in mid-sentence. The TV set was showing the local news and, specifically, a very accurate drawing of his face. Both men listened to the voice overlaying the image.

'Police are anxious to speak with this man in connection with the suspicious death of a local businessman during the recent rioting on the Woodburn estate. He is described as being around 60 years of age, of medium height with a stocky build, grey hair and beard. He was last seen dressed as a vagrant. It is believed that he escaped early yesterday morning from a local police station, kidnapping a policeman and several members of the public. Members of the public are warned not to approach him but to call 999 or contact their nearest police station.'

Nathan ran to the lounge door and called to the others. The Old Man remained in front of the TV.

'In other news it has been confirmed that the two swans found dead in a Bristol park did carry the H5N1 strain of the bird flu virus, known to be the most dangerous to humans. The local Health Authority has said that local residents should not be alarmed but report any flu-like symptoms to their doctor.

Finally, in the city, the FT index rose by 3.5% on news of an increase in …..'

'What are you shouting about?' Vicky had rushed into the lounge, responding to Nathan's call. Carl was only a stride behind her.

'His face was on the local news,' said Nathan. 'They said that he escaped from the police station and he kidnapped all of us.'

'That's ridiculous. We all walked out together. There was no question of being forced.' Vicky spoke the words that they were all thinking.

'It's stranger than that,' Nathan replied. 'I phoned the station yesterday to let them know I was OK and told them we weren't kidnapped. Yet they put out this story to the press. Why should they do that?'

'The King's captain is trying to explain why he permitted me to leave. Doubtless his superiors were angry at the manner of our departure and this answer was the best that he could devise. I'm surprised. I did not think him so bright. But it should not deflect us from our task. So they speak untruths. Kingsmen have done so since the days of the Romans. It is to be expected.'

Nathan chose not to argue. The evidence against him seemed rather strong and besides, they now had other problems.

'You don't understand,' he said. 'This changes everything. Now they will be looking for us. All ways out of the city will be watched. Roads, railway stations, the airport, everything. Believe me, they are very good at this. And when they look they find, almost all of the time.'

'What's more, I don't think we will make a particularly difficult quarry.' It was Carl's turn to speak.

'What do you mean?' said Vicky.

'Well, frankly, there'll be four of us. But consider the size of me, the uniform of him,' he pointed at Nathan, 'and the state of him.' The last comment was directed at the Old Man, for whom the TV's description of vagrant was depressingly appropriate. 'We're hardly incognito, are we?' Carl looked around the group awaiting disagreement. As a former paratrooper, moving undetected through enemy terrain was his speciality and he was glad for the chance to contribute.

The Old Man dismissed their concerns with a sweep of his hand. 'The paths that we shall follow have not been walked for many years. The Kingsmen will not be watching them and so I have no fear of discovery. But you speak the truth regarding our appearance. We may well be spotted by local peasants and reported. We must change to blend in more with the countryside and other travellers moving through it. Warrior, can you do this? Can you prepare us for such a journey?'

Carl grinned. 'No problem. I know just the place for what we need.'

'Good. Then let us break our fast and prepare.'

The group moved into the kitchen and the next few minutes were spent eating cereals and drinking coffee. The Old Man watched the others carefully but took nothing to eat or drink. They had almost finished when their thoughtful silence was broken.

'Any coffee going?' Julian had now woken and joined them. Vicky explained the plan as she poured him a cup.

'So you're serious, then? You really are going to wander off with this ...' he struggled for a polite description, but not for long, '... nutter, leaving all your lives on hold for as long as it takes? You really are going to buy into his fairy stories?' He looked from face to face getting no verbal reply but he could see his answer from their expressions. 'Oh God. Surely someone can show this tale up for the rubbish it truly is?' Again silence. 'Right then. Looks like it's down to me.' He turned to the Old Man. 'So let's get this straight, Worzel. You claim to have been asleep for a few hundred years and only woke up when PC Plod here dropped a thug on your head? Have I got that right so far?'

The Old Man could see that Julian was an unlikely follower and so was tempted to ignore him but he also knew that the others were not yet fully convinced. He decided that he would have to deal with Julian's questions or risk losing them all. He could cope without them but the journey would be much more pleasant with them along.

'Your brevity misses much but is, in essence, correct.'

'Right then,' Julian exclaimed, with the air of a barrister about to destroy a hostile witness. 'So how is it that you can speak such modern English? Surely when you fell asleep it was all thee's and thou's? Get out of that one then!'

'I assimilated.'

'You what?'

'I assimilated with the first suitable subject that I saw.'

'Very good, but once again please, only without the psychobabble.'

The Old Man turned to Nathan. 'Do you recall what happened at the end of that first night? Just before you passed out?'

'Not really. It's all still a bit hazy.'

The Old Man squeezed the seam of his pouch and rubbed his finger and thumb under Nathan's nose. 'Try once more.'

Nathan thought for a moment. A strange scent drifted into his nose which seemed to somehow clear his head. Details that he had forgotten slowly came back to him. 'Yes, I remember now. Just as I was passing out I saw you crawl across to the body of the thug and dip your hand into the pool of liquid. You licked your fingers. I remember being utterly disgusted. Then you gave out a sound, the like of which I have never heard before. A high pitched scream which became gradually deeper until you fell into your coma. It is the last thing that I can remember.'

'Your memory plays you truly. That was my assimilation. As Vicky's servant says ...' the Old Man nodded towards Julian, who thought about challenging him but thought better of it, ' ... I come into each new Return with no knowledge of recent events. If I am to survive I must gain this knowledge as soon as I can. To achieve this I must select a target and assimilate with them.'

'What do you mean by assimilate?' Vicky joined in the questioning. She was keen to learn all that this man had to teach and was not going to let another opportunity slip.

'We all carry our wisdom deep within us. A mixture of oil of halswort and the dust from the malue flower draws out this wisdom and passes it to another. All that is required is that you blend the mixture with some waters from your target, drink of the resulting brew and their knowledge becomes your knowledge. The passing of the wisdom causes the mind to withdraw for a few hours but the wisdom is worth the distress.'

'So that is why you seemed to be dead when I examined you. Your system had shut down while this halswort stuff did its work,' said Vicky, struggling with the answer to an issue that had been bothering her since their time in the police cell.

'To the most raw of apprentices my state may, indeed, be mistaken for death, but anyone with even a small knowledge should have spotted the signs of life.'

Suitably chastised, Vicky fell silent so it was left to Nathan to continue the questioning. 'But why choose him? He was a low-life thug. Of all the people to pick, why him?'

'I fear that you may be right in your judgement. Yet, at the time, I thought him some minor lordling, and so a good source of current wisdom. I now realise that his knowledge was low and base. I gained the basics of modern speech but very little else.'

Nathan suddenly realised what had been bothering him about the Old Man. Even though he had been sure they had never met, there had been something familiar about him, something that had made his stomach lurch every time the Old Man spoke.

'You speak with his accent! Your voice sounds just like his! That's what made me so apprehensive towards you.'

'He almost killed you. No need to be ashamed of your reaction to his voice. As I now know better than anyone, he was a cruel and evil creature. The world is better off without him walking upon it.'

'Is that why you killed him?'

The Old Man hesitated before answering. 'To kill is a most grievous step. I did not take his life willingly. I was still waking when he attacked me. I was a stranger to him yet he tried to destroy me. I had to defend myself. Perhaps, with a little more time, my mind might have been clearer and my defence a little less severe. But he chose the fight and so had to suffer the consequence.'

'Yet both your defence and your assimilation were instantaneous. There was no time to mix any pastes or potions. How did you have these things to hand so readily?'

'I have all that I need here.' The Old Man lifted the pouch at his belt. It was made of some old leather-type material, stained with different shades of brown across its surface. An equally ancient cord provided both the means of drawing the pouch closed and of attaching it to his belt. 'This is made from the skin of the otter, tanned in greden juice. There is nothing better for keeping moist the oils and pastes that I need. Here, let me show you.' The Old Man pointed to a particularly dark stain near the top edge of the pouch. 'This is the juice of the pulsper mixed with dynige. The scent can bring back the memories of distant events. I used it a moment ago to make you recall the fighting. Here again,' the Old Man moved to a lighter stain near the lower seam, 'This is ramese oil mixed with the juice of the ceaf bush. I used this to persuade your Kingsman to allow us out of his palace. And here ...'

the Old Man indicated yet another stain '… is the mixture that causes flesh to melt like butter in the sun.'

Nathan recalled the appalling death of the gang leader and shuddered.

Fascinated, but conscious that the Old Man might clam up at any moment, Vicky decided to push the questioning just a little further. 'Yet your flesh didn't melt. How did you avoid being injured by your own defence?'

The Old Man's finger tapped onto another stained area of the pouch.

'Here is a grease made from feldmore and lafer. It acts as a barrier to all the other lotions. I rub my fingers across this part first and then move to whichever grease that I need.'

'And which is the stain that helped you steal the doubtless extensive brainpower of the gang leader?' Julian's tone was still disbelieving yet the Old Man could see the stirrings of change in his demeanour.

'It is this part of the pouch, in the lower corner near the seam.'

'So why not repeat the exercise? I suspect that any of us could provide a better set of brains than your average low-life.'

'The shock of assimilation is too great a shock to the mind and body. It can only be done once in each Return. A second attempt risks death. But enough of these endless questions. We must depart. Come, let us make ready.'

As the group moved around the flat, pulling together the various items that they would need, the Old Man watched Julian. He remained seated in the kitchen, deep in thought. Eventually he stood up and walked into the bedroom. Emerging a few moments later, now dressed for a journey, he made an almost regal announcement to the group. 'It is obvious to me that this whole thing is nothing more than a fool's errand. But as your partner, Vicky, I feel a responsibility for your welfare and I'm not at all happy about you disappearing into the wilds of the English countryside with only these three to protect you. I shall therefore tag along until I'm satisfied as to your safety.' With that he opened the front door and led the group out.

102

None of the others believed a word of Julian's speech but Vicky seemed happy that he was joining them. Only the Old Man wondered what had made Julian change his mind so suddenly. He reflected on the events of the morning so far and quickly realised Julian's true motive. Strange how little things have changed in the minds of men, he thought, as he walked out of the flat.

His thoughts were broken by Nathan.

'What else did you learn from the thug?'

'As I said before, nothing of any great note. His mind had very few significant insights. In fact, I can only think of one major truth that seemed to drive him on, far beyond all other thoughts. Yet this truth is very strange. It means nothing to me but, to him, it was absolutely vital. A passion that governed his very being.'

'So what was this great truth?'

'Bristol Rovers are utter crap!'

Nathan smiled at the Old Man's puzzled expression as they both walked out of the flat.

—∞—

The Old Man was not the only one to see the sun rise that morning. Eddie Rylands walked out of the police station just in time to watch the spectacle but, as with the others the previous day, its grandeur was lost on him. His mind was taken up with other things. In the dozen or so hours since being arrested in the park, he had been stripped, probed, sampled and questioned. The latter activity had been done by several officers, all of whom were highly intimidating in their style and violent in their conduct. No one had actually hit him but there had been much banging of tables and kicking of chairs. He had been involved with the police several times before - it rather went with the job of investigative journalist - but he had never seen them behave like this before. It was as if they were driven by the fear of failure.

All the time they kept asking him about the death of some gang leader on a local estate. He had tried telling them that he knew nothing about it, that he didn't know the man, and that he was nowhere near the estate in question. Sadly, they simply were not listening. They were far too concerned to prove his guilt to bother about his explanations, especially if they didn't conform to the required script. Things took a downward turn when the results of his DNA test came in, only an hour after he gave the sample, which 'proved' that he had been in this station only a few hours before. For Eddie that was the blackest moment of the whole evening. For a few moments, even he began to think that he had been responsible for the man's death. Fortunately, just after that, word came in confirming his alibi. He had been appearing on a live, late-night chat show for a local TV station, discussing the pros and cons of a Privacy Bill with the show's host and a local MP. Even allowing for the low audience figures of non-terrestrial channels, this still gave him several thousand witnesses.

This should have been enough of an alibi for most situations but the police were still hesitant about releasing him. Until, that is, the arrival of a particular police sergeant. This guy was clearly in charge of this whole venture and he wasn't taking any crap from anyone. Eddie heard him shouting in the corridor outside the cell before he even entered.

'I don't give a toss what his alibi is, I want this bastard nailed!' The voice sounded extremely angry. Someone else replied to him, but in muffled tones that Eddie could not hear. 'Well, if you lot can't get the truth out of him then I will.'

The door of the interview room burst open to reveal a large man in a police sergeant's uniform, looking even more furious than his voice had suggested. He looked down at Eddie seated at the small table. Clearly, he was not impressed by what he saw. The sight of Eddie made him even more angry.

'Who the fuck is this?'

The constable sitting with Eddie rose and answered, 'This is Edward Rylands. His DNA puts him in here last night.'

'What are you talking about? This is not the man we're after. He doesn't even look the same.'

Later Eddie recalled this to be the moment when most of the chair kicking took place.

The sergeant turned to leave.

'What do you want us to do with him?' Eddie noted the pleading tone in the constable's question.

'I don't give a toss. Get him out of my sight and get on with catching the right one. '

By the time he had finished the sentence the sergeant had reached the corridor and was out of Eddie's sight. The hurricane seemed to have passed.

It took about five minutes for Eddie to be shown the door and another few seconds for him to be roughly pushed through it. Now, standing in the station car park, Eddie at last had a moment to reflect upon the strange events that he had just endured. His initial rage had gradually subsided to anger and then, as the absurdity of his situation had become apparent, to bewilderment. Now, standing in the car park, still dressed in his tramp's outfit, he began to think. What had happened to him over the last few hours? Why were the police so convinced that he was their man? What had made them change their minds so completely, and so abruptly?

His musings were interrupted by his mobile, recently returned by his captors yet lying forgotten in his pocket. He glanced at the screen and, seeing that it was his commissioning editor, decided to answer. 'Greetings, Alan. Bet this is the first time you've seen five in the morning?'

'I see the attentions of the constabulary haven't improved your humour. But I didn't call to bandy words. The crew told me about what happened at the park. No chance of getting that project back on the rails, I suppose?'

'I'm fine after my night in the cells. Thanks for asking. I was hoping that my colleagues with the cameras might have waited for me but they are nowhere to be seen.'

'Sorry, Eddie. My fault. Afraid they lost interest once I told them that there was no cash for overtime. Don't take it personally. Just business. Anyway, what about our corrupt councillor and his pal? As I said before, any prospect of me getting that programme?'

'More chance of knitting fog, I'm afraid. Judging from the look on their faces as I was being carted off, I think that they will border on the angelic from now on. A small victory, perhaps, but I'm sure you agree it was worth all the effort.' Eddie squeezed as much cynicism into his voice as he could.

'Very commendable, but we are still left with a large hole in the budget and without a programme for the good viewers. The accountants will be cross.'

'Sad but true, Alan, sad but true.' As he spoke, his thoughts, grinding away in the back of his mind, began to solidify into the germ of an idea. 'Still, perhaps this debacle might give a profit after all.'

'I've heard that tone before. Normally means that you have a new lead, usually an expensive one. What do you have in mind?'

'It seems that I'm here because someone cocked up a DNA sample.'

'I thought DNA was the New Jerusalem for our boys in blue. Still, to err is human and besides, as we both know, technical is boring. Forget it.'

'No, this is not that simple. This was no human error. The feds checked several times and always came back with the same answer. For some reason they were convinced that I was arrested at a local riot last night. It was only when a nice police sergeant told them it wasn't me that they let me go. He was so pleased.'

'I'm still not convinced.'

'Don't give up on me yet. There seems to be something quite fundamentally wrong here. Give me a day or so to clear my head and we will talk again.'

'Not yet found a way of stopping you, once you get one of your ideas. So go for it. Just don't spend any money. Or time.'

'Knew I could rely on your support. Speak soon.' Eddie closed the phone and waved down a passing taxi. The driver paused before stopping, balancing the twin problems of a lack of early morning fares with the risk of picking up a tramp. It took Eddie a few choice phrases to convince the driver to take him home. As he sat down in the back seat and watched the police station disappear into the distance he recalled that he was carrying no money.

He sighed. Life was treating him as well as ever.

CHAPTER 11

A Paternoster Safe House,
Bristol
Thursday 23rd August
8.30 a.m.

The ring tone brought Warren back from his brief slumber. He had allocated the theme tune from 'Mission Impossible' to Eriksson. It seemed strangely appropriate. He flipped open the phone. 'Yes, Boss?'

'All recovered from your evening out?'

'Hardly recovered. We got back to the base house about three hours ago. The troops are sleeping now. Any new information?'

'It seems that he is now a TV star. The local station is broadcasting a story about how our target has broken out of a police station, taking some hostages with him. All nonsense, of course. He has a history of pulling a group around him but the thought of him dragging folk along, kicking and screaming, is just preposterous. All our information suggests that people seem to flock to him.'

'How do you know all this? What are your sources? How reliable are they?'

'Well, to be honest, you can only put so much credence into something written on parchment but we have no reason to doubt.'

'Parchment?'

'Need to know basis, Major. Sure you understand.'

Warren did. He had spent his whole career chasing the shadows cast by 'need to know' ghosts. This was always the way that senior officers ended debate. He took the hint. 'So what's next?'

'Just stand by for now. I'll be in touch as soon as we have any more data. Be ready to move quickly when I call you again.' Eriksson rang off.

Warren rolled over and went back to sleep. Soon he was dreaming. About parchment.

—∞—

For the tenth time that morning Rhona reached into her bag and took out the small mirror. The rash was definitely getting worse. A few weeks ago it was only on her shoulder and neck but fortunately below her collar. Now it had reached up to her jawline. There was just no way of disguising it. It seemed to be spreading further each day. Nothing she did seemed to halt its progress. Not creams, not lotions, nothing. The doctor said that was it was down to her nerves and so she should relax about it. Very helpful! How could any teenage girl do anything but worry about her appearance?

She had always wanted to work in the make-up department of a local store, but the rash had put that ambition beyond hope for the time being. The people at the store were nice about it but made it clear that if she couldn't promote the products herself then she should look elsewhere. She decided to try to get some experience of shop work in the hope that she could return to her dream job one day. To her disappointment all that she could get was in this huge warehouse, selling military surplus to passing weirdos. Knives, boots and jackets, in any colour you like so long as it's camouflaged. She hated the job but it paid the bills.

She moved across to take up her position behind the till counter and nodded to the manager, who reached up and unlocked the front doors. Experience told them that this wasn't the sort of shop that got a sudden opening rush so, pulling rank, he went for a tea break, leaving her alone on the large sales floor.

Once he was out of sight she took out her mirror again and checked her neck for the eleventh time. Looking up, she saw the first customers of the morning come in. A group of five entered, led by a huge man with tattooed arms who eagerly rushed towards the racks bearing the clothing. In contrast to his enthusiasm a guy dressed as a tramp brought up the rear. He looked totally uninterested, almost reluctant to enter. More weirdos, she thought, and returned to her mirror.

Since leaving the flat, over an hour before, Carl had led the group across Bristol to this military surplus warehouse. True to form, the Old Man had adamantly refused to use the Range Rover, preferring to wander at his sedate pace through the side roads and back streets. Nathan had been trying to hurry the group along, fearing identification by his colleagues at any moment, but the more he encouraged haste, the slower the Old Man walked. He seemed far more interested in the vegetation along the way. Several times he knelt down to smell the flowers and plants, sometimes pulling off leaves to chew and either swallow or spit out. Several times Vicky asked him about these strange habits, continuing her mission to get information from him, but each request brought silence and a dismissive wave of the hand.

On entering the shop Carl began by rummaging amongst the many racks of military clothing. He lifted off jackets several times, examining each in turn before returning them to the hanger. Nathan moved alongside him, wanting to help. He picked up a jacket, almost at random, and started to try it on.

'Don't bother, that stuff's all crap,' said Carl, now moving further down the racks.

'Why? It seems OK to me.'

'Standard British Army kit, all useless. Believe me, I know.'

'So what are we looking for?'

'Special Forces gear would be best but they probably won't have that here. Try and find some German army stuff - or better still, Canadian, if you can see any.'

Vicky had joined the two men and overheard their conversation. 'I'm not interested in who made it. I'm more worried about the thought of wearing it. Do we really have to dress in this?' She held up a camouflage jacket bearing a particularly bold print. 'It looks awful and I'm not at all convinced that it's necessary.'

'According to the Old Man we will be passing through country terrain for most of the journey. These clothes are our best chance of not being noticed.' Carl was not used to his opinions being questioned, especially in matters such as these, but Vicky was still not persuaded.

'Yes, but surely we won't be in woods and fields for the whole journey. Some of the time we shall have to go into towns and villages, to buy supplies if nothing else. Wearing this stuff will make us very obvious. It will look as if we are trying to invade. Hardly circumspect.'

Carl hid his irritation but had to concede the point. 'So what do you suggest?'

'Perhaps a combination of this stuff and something a little more civilian. I saw another store just along the road. If we could pop into there once we've finished here, then ...'

'No!' shouted the Old Man. He had walked up behind the bickering group. 'This whole venture is causing us much delay. We need to depart soon. Get what you need from this place and then we must leave.'

Carl, Vicky and Nathan all felt suitably chastised. The two men chose to accept the Old Man's warning. Vicky did not. She decided to return to the fray.

'Yes, but what if ...'

'Perhaps I can help, Madam.' Rhona had heard the rising voices and had moved away from her sales counter to join the group. She heard the exchange and had a solution. 'We do have a range of clothes that are not quite so - well, belligerent. I wouldn't call them high fashion but you might like to take a look. They are over there at the back of the sales floor.' She indicated a corner area that was almost hidden behind a display of tents. Vicky smiled in thanks and wandered over to it.

Julian, strangely silent during the exchange, followed her. Nathan and Carl continued to rummage.

Over the next twenty minutes Carl amassed a huge pile of clothes and equipment for the journey. Starting with clothing (jackets, trousers, vests, socks) he then moved onto boots (he proved surprisingly accurate in selecting sizes) and then to tents, cooking equipment, portable stoves and ration packs. Twice he had sent Nathan back to the store entrance for more wheeled baskets. He then selected four rucksacks large enough to carry all the equipment out of the shop.

Finally, his eyes noticed a glass case containing some large hunting knives. He was drawn to one in particular. It was magnificent. High grade stainless steel blade fitted to a carved bone-effect handle. He opened the case and took out the weapon. The balance was perfect, telling the ex-para that it would make an excellent throwing weapon. Slots running the length of each side of the blade might look purely decorative to the casual observer but told the trained killer that blood would have an escape route when this blade was used, making it easier to withdraw. This knife was made by a real craftsman. The end of the handle unscrewed to reveal a compass and a length of fishing twine, including a hook. Finally the sheath had a section for a second steel piece which, when fitted to a lug on the main blade, enabled the knife to be used for cutting through wire. Then Carl noticed the price: £258.50. Ridiculous, even for so fine a piece. He replaced the knife and took out another. Although inferior in every respect, he had to admit that it would fulfil all the likely needs on the journey. This knife cost £15.35. For the first time the issue of payment entered his head. He looked around the store and spoke, quite loudly, to any or all of the group.

'Who's paying for all this?'

Without even looking at her boyfriend Vicky replied. 'Julian.'

Julian looked a little surprised but shrugged his shoulders and continued to examine the racks without comment.

Carl smiled wryly as he retrieved the expensive knife from the glass case and placed it in his basket.

A few minutes later the group, with the exception of the Old Man, congregated around the sales counter. He chose to remain near the door, dividing the time between studiously ignoring all of the shop's contents and glancing up at the sky to note the position of the sun.

Carl had amassed the largest pile but the others had also decided to get a few items, mostly from the non-belligerent section.

At the sales counter Rhona patiently moved all the bar-coded items through the laser scanner, noting with pleasure the rising total. This was going to be a good day for her sales bonus. Once completed, she informed the large man of the total. He smiled and turned to Julian.

'Come on then, Goldenballs, time to show us your worth.'

Julian moved to the counter and, ignoring the jibes from Carl, proffered his gold credit card. Rhona inserted the card into the relevant slot, entered the sales total and presented the unit back to Julian. Very deliberately he turned his back on Carl and Nathan, typed in his PIN and passed the small machine back to the sales assistant. The group then waited for the unit to authorise the transaction and print off a receipt.

It was only a short wait but still too long for the Old Man. He had reached the end of his patience. Using a quicker pace than any of them had seen in their short acquaintance, he strode over to the sales desk.

'What is this delay? We must make haste if we are to progress this day. How much longer do you ... ' He paused in mid-sentence, staring at something by the side of the till. 'What manner of pouch is that?'

This question was directed at Rhona. At first she hesitated, not realising what had caught the Old Man's attention. After a second she saw that he was looking at a small polythene bag. About 4 inches square, she used them at the end of each day to collect up all the coins from the till before moving them upstairs to the safe. She picked up the bag and handed it to him. He examined it carefully, all time pressure now seemingly vanished. He looked through the transparent film, he sniffed at it, he pushed his fingers inside and squeezed the material between his finger and thumb. He pressed together the rolled seam at the top, realising how this sealed the bag. He was clearly fascinated.

'At last I have found something of purpose in these dreadful days. This is truly wondrous. Anything placed within would not lose moisture. Such a pouch will have a value beyond coin, yet I would know the price as I must possess it.'

Rhona barely understood the Old Man's words but got the main message from his gestures. 'Sorry, but we don't sell those.'

A look of disappointment passed across the Old Man's face. He began to reach towards his own pouch.

Rhona continued, 'No, you don't understand. We just use them to cash up the till at the end of the day. Look, I have dozens of them.' She reached under the counter, grabbed a handful of the cash bags and laid them out onto the flat surface. 'Please, if you want some, just take them.'

Now it was the Old Man's turn to struggle with words. 'You give these to me, freely and without payment or coercion?'

Rhona smiled and nodded.

The Old Man, clearly stunned by such a step, picked up the bags. 'Such kindness should be rewarded with the riches of kings but I have none to give save the thanks of an old traveller.' He reached across to Rhona and, in a manner that reminded her of her long dead grandfather, patted her on the cheek. Most times she would draw back from such a familiar gesture, especially from an old, scruffy stranger, but this seemed so natural that no one could have taken offence, so she simply smiled back at him.

With a further nod of thanks, the Old Man turned and walked out of the shop. His companions hoisted their new possessions and followed him.

—∞—

Eriksson sat in his office, staring at the files piled on the desk in front of him. He hadn't slept since the news came through of the latest Return. Tired, he picked up the top file once again, hoping that this would give him some clue about what the Old Man was planning. The file was labelled 'Aluko, Nathan'. His team had generated similar files about all the members of the target group. Why them? Of all the possible companions available, why had these been selected?

He forced himself to concentrate on the papers before him. 'Born September 13th 1987 in Lambeth, London. Attended the local comprehensive where he obtained sufficiently good grades in his GCSEs and A levels before moving on to Winchester University to study Medieval History.` Wonder if that is relevant, thought Eriksson, before returning to the report. 'Obtained a 2:1 Honours. Declined offers of research positions and chose to join the Avon and Somerset police on their graduate accelerated promotion scheme. Reports from his basic training course indicate a bright mind, quick to develop new ideas and excellent at establishing good working relationships with those around him. On the negative side his tutors noted that he still seemed less than fully committed to his new career, with one even suggesting that he would not see out the year. Sent for his first probationary period to the Woodburn station, Bristol.' Eriksson put down the report and rubbed his eyes. Perhaps it was weariness but he just couldn't see any reason behind Aluko's selection. Maybe it was just a random act, him being in the right (or wrong) place and at the right (or wrong) time.

He picked up the next file, this one headed 'Curtis, Carl`. The file contained a photo of the ex-paratrooper, and Eriksson paused for a moment to stare at the face. He had always prided himself on his innate ability to judge a person upon first sight. This picture spoke to him of a tough fighter, with a vicious streak that valued results above regulations. Yet there was something else about the eyes. They spoke of a lack of direction, of a confusion that needed a guiding influence, telling him which battles to fight and which to flee. Certainly a useful man to have on any team, but this was not just any team. The Old Man would have no need of protection – he was more than capable of looking after himself – so why bring this damaged soldier along? Perhaps another random choice, but that made two. Randomness was stacking up here in a fashion that was beginning to concern him.

He replaced the picture in the file and picked up the next. 'Snow, Victoria'. He began to read once again but stopped after the first few lines. There was nothing new here. All this had been reported to him before and re-reading them was just giving him a headache. Whatever the Old Man's plans were, Eriksson would just have to await events. Not a position that he liked but his choices were slim at present. Fortunately, the next event was not long in coming.

Mike Aspinall rushed into the office. The lack of the customary deferential knock told Eriksson that his Operations Director had something important to say.

'St Clere has just used his credit card.' Eriksson sat bolt upright in his seat, his former tiredness now forgotten.

'Where?'

'At a Military Surplus warehouse on the outskirts of Bristol. He seems to have bought a mountain of kit, far more than he could possibly need for himself alone.'

'Have you informed Major Warren?'

'As soon as I got the details. He is setting off now but says that the traffic will delay most of his team. He is going to take one team member and go ahead by motorcycles. The others are going to follow him in the Transits.'

'Excellent. Thanks, Mike. Keep me informed.'

Aspinall nodded and left the office.

Eriksson leaned back in his seat and began to ponder. So, he thought, they are either going to invade somewhere or they are going for a clandestine walk. Or, possibly, both.

—∞—

Rhona had been busy all morning. First that large group with the strange old man, then a school party preparing for a camping trip. She couldn't remember such a hectic first hour. She looked at her watch. It was almost time for her break.

'Pardon me, Miss.' The voice came from one of two young-ish men in motorcycle leathers. The politeness was in sharp contrast to their rugged appearance. She gave them her best sales-assistant smile by way of response. 'I'm looking for my uncle. We were supposed to meet him here but we were delayed. Has he been here yet?'

'We've been quite busy here this morning. What does your uncle look like?'

'You wouldn't forget him. He's a bit of an eccentric. Dresses very scruffily. He was here with my sister and a few friends.'

'Oh yes, I remember him. He was here when we opened. They bought a load of stuff.' As she spoke she was aware of the second man smiling at her over the shoulder of the first. It was a smile that she had not seen for ages but recognised it immediately.

The first man spoke again, forcing her to return her attention to him. 'Look, this is a bit of a cheek, but I was going to buy him a present and, as I wasn't here, I don't know what they got for him. Is there any way that you could tell us what they bought? You know, to make sure that I don't duplicate anything.'

Rhona knew that this was perfectly possible but would be frowned upon by her boss. She was about to explain about Customer Data Protection but saw the second man smiling at her again. No doubt about it, she thought, he's definitely interested. That settled the matter. She went over to the sales computer next to the cash till and printed off a copy of the receipt that gave a complete list of all the items purchased. Handing it over, she smiled at both of them, but mostly the second guy.

The first man took a moment to study the list while the other man continued the conversation.

'How long ago did they leave?' He had a deep, rich voice. Rhona was becoming more attracted by the minute.

'It would be about an hour ago.'

'Did you see which direction they went?'

'Sorry, but the shop was busy. I didn't notice.'

Now it was the first man's turn to speak. 'Thanks for this. I'm afraid that he's already bought all that I was going to get him so I'll have to think again. Thanks anyway.' He turned to leave, followed, to Rhona's disappointment, by his companion. However, after a few steps the second man stopped and returned to the counter.

'I know that this is a real cheek but I may not have another chance. My name is Mark Preston. I'm a bit bogged down with a bit of a project at the moment but when it's finished do you think we could go out for a drink or something? I know you don't know me but I promise you that I'm almost totally harmless.'

Rhona was both pleased and surprised. She found a scrap of paper and wrote down her number. 'Call me when you're less bogged down,' she said, handing him the note, trying to sound casual. He smiled, turned and jogged to catch up with his colleague.

Once he had left the shop Rhona paused to think about what had just happened. She had never just given her number away like that before. She must be mad. Still, he seemed interested, which was especially surprising given the state of her skin. Reminded, she reached into her bag for her mirror. She hadn't had time to check all morning. Reluctantly she peered at her reflection, hoping that the rash hadn't spread even further. What she saw stunned her. She looked a second time, this time far more carefully.

There could be no doubt. The rash had completely vanished.

Chapter 12

Eddie Rylands had also been busy that morning. Phone calls, a few threats and cashing in a few favours had brought him to this large Mexican themed restaurant in Bristol's main shopping mall. He had chosen it carefully. It was anonymously large yet still had several dark alcoves, perfect for clandestine meetings. He had timed the meeting to be during the lunchtime rush and so sufficiently full of customers to provide a basic cover.

As he arrived the waiter, complete with synthetic welcome, tried to guide him to a more open table in the central area but Eddie selected a corner booth, far more suited to the task in hand.

'I'm expecting someone to join me,' he said, partly in an inadequate explanation but mostly as information. 'He will be asking for Mr Smith.' The waiter nodded and left Rylands to peruse the folded, laminated menu.

He only had to wait a few minutes before his guest joined him. Even out of uniform his appearance still screamed 'copper' to all who saw him.

'Mr Smith. Good to see you again.'

'Well, PC Bradley. What a pleasant surprise.'

Bradley swiftly glanced around him, concerned that his name should have been heard by any nearby diners. Fortunately, it hadn't been as they were some distance from the nearest occupied table. Rylands had chosen his meeting point well.

'It was quite a surprise to get your phone call.' Even though he was confident that he was not being overheard, Bradley could not help lowering his voice. Rylands realised that the young constable must be new to this. The journalist wanted to press on to the main purpose of the meeting before the policeman had a chance to change his mind but they were interrupted by the arrival of the waiter. Without asking his guest, Rylands ordered two coffees and waited until the waiter was out of earshot.

'So, what was that pantomime all about this morning?'

'It really was quite traumatic, wasn't it? I felt so stressed afterwards. I think I may need some time off. A holiday perhaps,' replied Bradley.

'Ah,' said Rylands. Perhaps the constable was not quite as new to this as he pretended.

'You did say something about a contribution to my holiday fund.'

'Would you like something to eat?' Rylands slid the menu across the table. A casual glance would have seen nothing unusual in the action. A keener observer may have noticed that the menu was not quite flat, as if something was contained within its folded pages. Fortunately for both men there were no observers, keen or otherwise. Bradley lifted the document as if to choose and allowed the envelope contained within to drop onto his lap. Once it was out of sight, Bradley examined the collection of ten pound notes that the envelope contained. Satisfied, he continued with the conversation.

'So what do you want to know?'

'In the words of the old song, 'Let's start at the very beginning, for that's a very good place to start.' Rylands smiled at the waiter as he brought the coffee. 'Thanks very much. I'll call you if we need anything else.'

Over the next ten minutes Bradley described carefully the events of the previous evening. From when the Old Man was brought in, through the strange behaviour of the sergeant, right up to when the group walked out of the station. Throughout the constable's monologue Rylands listened carefully but took no notes. He had no need to. Unknown to Bradley he was taping the conversation using his mobile phone.

Once the young policeman had finished Rylands summarised. 'So an old tramp recovers from a beating and walks out of the station, taking a few new chums with him. Unusual but hardly newsworthy.'

'Perhaps so. But if you had seen this old guy. There was something about him. Something strange. The way he looked. The way he dressed. The way he could make people, very difficult people, do whatever he wanted. He's your story.'

'Perhaps if I was writing an article for Saga magazine, but I've heard nothing yet to interest the TV channels. I've also yet to hear why I was dragged into this sorry tale. Why me?'

'While the old guy was asleep – actually we all thought that he was dead – the station techie took a DNA sample. Once the sergeant put his weight behind it the result came in quite quickly, but after the Old Man had gone. The DNA result placed you dead centre of the frame. We found out where you were working from your production company. A snatch squad was dispatched and the rest you know. Finding you dressed as a tramp was the final piece in the jigsaw.'

'Apart from the inconvenient fact that I was not the guy involved.'

'You are lucky that your alibi was watertight. Anything less and you would still be a guest of my sergeant.'

'So what caused it? Some sort of technical cock-up?'

'No. The forensic nerds have been over the whole system a dozen times and found everything working fine. They are still adamant that you were the guy in the cells and nothing as trivial as an alibi is going to persuade them otherwise. Your sample has really upset them.'

'I shouldn't expect a Christmas card, then?' Rylands paused to think for a moment and decided to change tack. 'Do you know where the group is now?'

'Last seen heading for the hospital to see the girl's mother. After that we have no idea. We've got the whole force chasing them but they've just disappeared. Sergeant Johnson is frothing at the mouth.

He stands to lose out big time if we don't find them soon. The kidnap story is just his way of explaining his bizarre actions to the Inspector.'

'He did strike me as the caring sort. You also know this guy, Nathan Aluko. What do you reckon is his take on this?'

'He called me. Said he was taking some time off, which was fair enough, as he was given a real battering.'

'But?'

'Well, he's also vanished. That's not like him at all. He is a very regular guy, always predictable. Not been with the police long but seemed to be settling in. Always seemed a bit distant, though. As if he hadn't fully signed up yet.'

'Anything you can tell me about the others in the group?'

'Not really. The ex-para is simply a nutter to be avoided at all costs. The doctor was only in to collect her flash boyfriend, who we only know from his drunken rants.'

'Is that it?' Rylands was conscious that the conversation was drawing to a close.

'Thought you might like this.' The policeman slid a piece of card, face down, across the table. 'See it as an early postcard from my holiday.'

Bradley stood and walked out of the restaurant, failing to look even remotely casual.

Rylands watched his departing shape until it was out of sight. He reached down and flipped over the card. It was a photograph taken from a CCTV camera. Rylands recognised the scene as the police station reception area. It showed the sergeant leading the group across the public area. Most of the group were looking towards the door but one was looking directly at the camera.

For the first time Rylands looked upon the face of the Old Man.

—∞—

The group had been walking for nearly two hours. In that time they had paused to change into their new clothes and so now looked more like ramblers. Carl had made the suggestion as they passed some public toilets, intending them to be used as changing rooms but, before they could stop him, the Old Man had stripped off his old clothes and discarded them at the side of the road. This very public act had shocked the others, who had managed to push him into the toilets before too many passers-by noticed.

Not for the first time that day Nathan had worried about being seen by his colleagues. He felt that it was only a matter of time before they were caught and arrested.

Vicky was also perplexed. This public striptease had revealed the Old Man to have a broad chest, densely matted with hair, powerful arms and well-muscled legs. She also noticed that he had very little fat on him, the skin stretched tautly across his frame. He might claim to be very old but he had the physique of a much younger man.

Broadly, the Old Man was leading them south, but modern civilisation was getting in his way. Time and again a particular building would block their path, causing the Old Man to backtrack and try to find an alternative route. So far they had always been able to find one, albeit at some cost in terms of time. Finally, his alternatives seemed to run out and exasperation began to creep in.

They had entered a large, modern housing estate comprising several dozen executive houses, each of impressive proportions. The layout of the estate took the roads through several twists and back loops. This, plus the similarity in the design of the houses, made it difficult for the Old Man to hold to his southward course. Eventually he seemed to give up trying to find a way through. He paused in front of an especially large mock Tudor residence and looked up at the sky.

'Our path is this way but this Lord has built his hall across the route. I cannot see why they must build their manors so close together. There is no way between. It is not my wish to intrude upon them but they leave me no choice.' Without further explanation he stepped forward onto the manicured lawn and began to walk towards the side of the house.

'Wait!' shouted Nathan. 'You just can't wander around like that. This is someone's house.' As he spoke he looked around to see if they were being observed. There was no challenge from the house and, unlike the houses on either side, there were no cars in the driveway.

'Perhaps the owners are out.' Vicky was clearly as concerned as Nathan.

'Tis of no import. We shall be on this manor for but a moment before entering the woodland beyond.' The Old Man had reached the wooden side gate which he found unlocked. Opening the gate he walked down the passage at the side of the house towards the large garden at the rear. The others followed reluctantly, apart from Carl who pushed himself to the front. All day he had felt strangely driven to protect the Old Man from harm. Entering this unknown garden was his first chance to play an active part and he took it gladly, leading the group to the end of the passage. As the narrow pathway widened out to the full width of the garden Carl paused and peered around the corner. His training told him not to walk into unknown territory without checking. That training saved his life.

As his head moved beyond the shelter of the corner he caught the blur of a moving creature. He threw himself backwards just in time to avoid the savage attack of a huge dog. A mixture of training and instinct brought him back to his feet, ready to grapple with the impact of the animal's next charge.

The guard dog, a large Rottweiler, leapt again at the ex-paratrooper who readied himself for the impact, but the dog was halted in mid-flight, inches short of Carl's throat. A chain from the dog's collar to a large staple fixed to the house wall prevented the dog from reaching its target. Expertly, Carl rolled sideways to take him further beyond the dog's attack range.

Realising that its prey was beyond reach, the animal went berserk. Trained to be silent until the attack began, it now barked and snarled. Throwing itself towards Carl the dog was again and again held back by the chain. Frustration only drove it into a further frenzy, causing it to pull even harder on the restraining link.

Still in the safety of the side passage, Nathan noticed that whoever had fixed the chain had miscalculated. Fortunately for Carl, the length restricted the dog's movements but it also provided a narrow corridor of safety down the side of the garden.

Seizing Vicky's hand, he placed his back flat against the wooden fence panels and moved sideways, just beyond the range of the guard dog, onto the manicured lawn beyond. Vicky allowed herself to be guided by Nathan and, once clear, gestured to Julian to follow suit. At first Julian hesitated, reluctant to go anywhere near the slavering jaws of the Rottweiler, but a none-too-gentle push from the Old Man forced him against the fence so that the only way out was to follow Vicky. A moment later all five had moved beyond the dog's attack radius and were running towards the rear of the garden, the direction indicated by the Old Man.

When they reached the fence at the back of the garden, the Old Man spoke to Carl.

'You go over first and check that all is clear.'

Carl nodded. Quickly peeling the rucksack from his back he threw it over the fence and into the woodland beyond. Hoisting up his large frame, he swung his legs athletically over the top of the fence and disappeared from view. A second later his voice called back.

'All clear.'

The Old Man gestured to Vicky that she should go next. She placed her hands on top of the fence but struggled to haul her body to the top. Nathan and the Old Man stepped in to help her.

Julian glanced back to the house where the dog continued to throw itself against the taut chain. What he saw worried him.

'Hate to tell you this, chaps, but that staple is about to break.'

Nathan, Vicky and the Old Man all looked back towards the house. It was just as Julian had said. The power of the dog's exertions was causing the staple that fixed the chain to the wall to slowly bend. Each new jerk of the dog's huge frame pulled the metal apart a little further.

With renewed urgency Nathan and the Old Man pushed Vicky up to the top of the fence. Once over, she fell into the waiting arms of Carl.

Nathan and Julian also removed their rucksacks, throwing them over the fence in a similar fashion to Carl. Now clear of their impediments they launched themselves at the fence panel. Nathan, the fitter of the two, managed to climb over without difficulty. Julian's scramble, driven more by fear than any athletic ability, meant that he dropped rather than jumped down onto the figures below. All attempts by Carl and Vicky to catch him proved futile and all three ended up in a heap at the foot of the fence.

This left only the Old Man still on the garden side. As he reached up to the fence he glanced back at the house just in time to see the dog give one final jerk which caused the staple to give way. Relieved of all constraint, the dog began to race towards the Old Man. A dozen strides were all that was needed for it to reach its victim.

Calmly, the Old Man abandoned any attempt to scale the fence. He turned towards the advancing dog, pulled himself up to his full height and filled his chest with air. He furrowed his brows, drawing his eyes even deeper into his face. The action also drew his scalp taut, causing his hair to flare out into a magnificent mane.

On the other side of the fence the group were still struggling to their feet. They heard the staple break and the sound of the chain being dragged. They could hear the snarls of the dog as it rushed towards the Old Man. Nathan and Carl threw themselves at the fence and began to climb but stopped when they heard a sudden, awesome sound. It halted them in their tracks, rooting them to the ground.

As children they had heard lions and tigers roar, either at the zoo or in television programmes. They had been impressed by the majestic power that could be produced by such wild creatures, intent on intimidating all before them. Yet the roar from the garden surpassed anything they had ever heard before. Deeper, louder, stronger than any modern predator, the sound seemed to shake the ground on which they stood, proclaiming enormous power in the creature that produced it, and causing utter terror in anything that opposed it.

The ensuing silence was broken by Vicky, posing the question to herself as much as anyone else. 'What on earth was that?'

Once the sound subsided the two men managed to re-gather their wits and again flung themselves at the fence but they were only half way up when the face of the Old Man appeared. Pulling himself up by his arms he sprang across the top edge, over both climbing bodies and, in a surprisingly sprightly fashion, landed gently on the ground beyond. Calmly, he addressed the group.

'Our path leads hence.' He indicated a path through the rough woodland beyond and stepped towards it.

'What was that sound?' Vicky spoke for the stunned group.

'What sound?' The Old Man replied and, in a manner that precluded further debate, walked towards the trees.

Exchanging glances, Nathan and Carl pulled themselves to the top of the fence and looked around the garden. All signs of the dog had gone yet there were no marks of any struggle, no clue as to what had happened a moment before. Nathan saw Carl nod towards a large kennel at the far end of the garden, next to the house. In front, trailing through the kennel's entrance, lay the length of chain. Following the chain, his eyes were drawn into the darkened interior. As he watched he saw two bright eyes peering out at him from the gloom within. In those eyes Nathan saw but a single emotion. This creature, so ferocious but a short time before, was now utterly terrified. As they watched, a thin stream of clear liquid trickled from the kennel and dripped onto the flagstones beneath.

Confused, Nathan and Carl allowed themselves to drop back onto the ground and followed the others into the woodland beyond.

The group walked a short distance through the trees before they emerged into a more agricultural landscape of fields and hedges stretching for miles in all directions. The Old Man raised his arm and pointed towards the highest point on the skyline, towards the south-east.

'That is our first waymark. We go to Maes Knoll. Warrior, you take the lead.' Carl saw a rough path through the grass-covered fields before him and started to stride out towards it. Vicky and Nathan fell in behind, followed by Julian.

The Old Man held back from the group. Once he was confident that they were following the right path he reached down and picked some small purple flowers, growing in a clump around the base of a horse chestnut tree. Stepping back into the trees he began to look around for something else. After a few seconds he shook his head in desperation before he saw what he needed. Kneeling beside a bank of nettles, he carefully moved away the surrounding grass to reveal a patch of a small plant, dark green in colour with an almost black vein running through each leaf. He pulled away a handful of the leaves, carefully ensuring that sufficient remained to allow the plant to continue growing. Combining the leaves with the purple flowers, he placed the ensuing assortment on the ground in front of him. Without even a cautionary glance he loosened his new trousers and urinated onto the mixture. Once finished he rearranged his clothing before picking up the now-sodden vegetation and squeezed it into a pulp. Returning to the horse chestnut tree, he smeared the pulp around the trunk, up to the height of the surrounding grass stalks.

His labours completed, he followed the path his companions had taken into the fields.

CHAPTER 13

Military Surplus Store,
Bristol
Thursday 23rd August
2.00 p.m.

Warren and his second-in-command were just leaving the Military Surplus warehouse as the two Transits arrived carrying the rest of the troop. Although they had left at the same time as the two motorbikes, the traffic had delayed them significantly. The vans parked next to the motorbikes and the troopers piled out. Now dressed in civilian clothes, they blended in more with the public but anyone could see that this was no ordinary group as they still seemed to give off an aura of organised menace.

Conscious of this, Warren called them together. He wanted to brief them and get them onto their next task as quickly as possible. 'Right. The targets left here about an hour ago. They bought a large amount of hiking and camping stuff so it looks like they're going to be travelling over open country.'

'Sounds to me like they know they're being chased.' One of the team expressed a thought that had occurred to Warren.

'So it would seem, but Paternoster assures me that there is no way they can know about us. I reckon they are trying to avoid the police.' Warren was having to think on his feet, a talent that he had been selected for. 'Either way, if they are in hiding it only makes our task harder. Who's got the map?'

A large-scale map of the area was produced and laid out on the ground.

'Now, we are here,' Warren indicated their location to the group. The warehouse had been built on the site of an old factory, located in the middle of a large industrial and residential area. The patchwork of small streets spread out in all directions. 'We've no way of knowing which way they went. It is possible that they are heading for open country but that is miles to the south. Equally, they might be heading for somewhere else first, so we will have to cover all options.'

'What transport will they be using?' another of the troopers asked.

'That's one piece of luck we do have. It seems that our main target has a hatred of all things mechanical. Paternoster thinks it highly unlikely that they will be using anything motorised.'

'So they will be walking?'

'Seems so.'

'So we should split into small teams and reconnoitre the area in all directions. We can report back if we find anything.' The trooper seemed pleased with his suggestion.

Warren chose not to tell him that the idea had been in his own mind for several minutes. Good team management, according to the books. 'Sounds good to me. Teams of two, all taking different directions.' Warren indicated the possible routes on the map. 'Talk to people, look for signs, anything to find our target. Don't forget that they are quite a noticeable group, especially the big bloke. If you find anything, call it in. We'll give it two hours before re-grouping.' He looked around the troopers. 'Questions?' No answer. 'OK then, move out.'

The group split up and each pair half walked, half jogged, firstly to the entrance to the retail estate and then into the maze of streets beyond.

It was over half an hour before one of the pairs called in. Warren answered the phone with the air of a desperate man, keen to grab at whatever straw fate sent his way.

'Warren here.'

'This is Collier, sir. Forster and I think we may have something.'

'Not a good time for mysteries, Collier. Get on with it. What have you found?'

'Seems that about an hour ago the target team stopped at some public bogs to change clothes. Problem was the old guy didn't see the need for cover and so stripped off in the street. Caused quite a stir. I spoke to the owner of the shop opposite who was on the verge of calling the police.'

'I hope you have dissuaded him from doing so?'

'It's a her, sir, and yes, she has been too busy with customers and can't see the point now.'

'Good. Now give me your location and I shall get the others over to you.' Warren paused as a thought struck him. 'Collier, do you know what happened to the old bloke's clothes?'

'They're still lying in the street, sir. I can see them from here.'

'Right, the pair of you get over there and stand guard over them. Don't either of you touch them and don't let anyone else near them either. I'll be with you in the next five minutes.' Warren ended the call and typed in the Paternoster number. Eriksson answered.

'Major, I hope you bring good news.'

Warren quickly covered the recent developments and explained what he wanted for the next stage in the pursuit. Eriksson listened carefully before replying.

'That's not something we keep on tap but I shall ensure that your requirements will be fulfilled within the hour.' Hanging up, Eriksson turned to his Operations Manager.

'What do they need?' Mike Aspinall asked.

'Mike, I think it's time to get out the cheque book.'

—∞—

The Old Man had taken up his now traditional position, some twenty metres behind the group. He walked slowly, continually checking the plant life around him, sniffing, tasting, swallowing or spitting as the fancy took him. Sometimes he retraced his steps to find a plant that he had passed by, often to mix it with another that he held in his large hands. This process of careful examination was repeated over and over again. However, if he reached any conclusions he kept them to himself.

The other four had to constantly check that they were not getting too far ahead as they wandered through the fields. Following the Old Man's initial guidance, they were heading in the general direction towards the hilltop about a mile and a half away. Initially the land was quite flat but, as they approached the hill, the route became steeper and steeper. Despite his drug problems Carl was the fittest of the four by some measure and his long strides ate up the ground ahead. Nathan came next, bent under the weight of the rucksack, but determined not to embarrass himself by what should have been a brisk, but not too demanding, walk. He needn't have worried. Vicky and Julian, bringing up the rear of their foursome, were clearly struggling with the increasing slope. Vicky was trying to cope as silently as she could but Julian had no such qualms. Every step was accompanied by a regular stream of grunts and sighs, wordlessly communicating to all around that he was an unhappy traveller in this strange quest. However, Vicky was surprised that he chose not to put his discomfort into words. She would have expected him to be producing a stream of complaints, insults and other expressions of dissatisfaction. She knew that his lack of comments could only mean one thing. He was plotting something.

After walking for about forty-five minutes the group reached the top of the hill and were faced with a large, flat, broadly circular field, about the size of two football pitches. The summit upon which they stood formed a raised hump at the north-west end of this plateau, some ten metres above the level of the remaining area. From this vantage point they could see for miles in all directions. In the afternoon sunlight all four paused to take in the magnificent view around them.

Nathan also noticed something odd about the field that lay just below them. The boundaries of the field seemed to fall away sharply, at a very steep angle, giving the area within the appearance of a huge table top, with a cloth draped across it, a shape that was very familiar to him.

'This is a hill fort.'

'A what?' said Julian.

'A hill fort, built long ago to protect the tribe around here in times of danger. Look, you can see the outer edge falls away steeply, too steeply for it to be natural. This plateau was made by humans.'

'It's a good defensive position and no mistake. Nobody's going to creep up on you here. You would be able to see an enemy from miles away.' Carl, seeing it from a military viewpoint, was most impressed. 'Whoever chose this place certainly knew what he was doing.'

'She.' The Old Man had now caught up with the group and seemed to enjoy correcting the soldier.

'What's that you say?' said Carl.

'It was not a 'he' but a 'she'. Her name was Igerna. She was a chieftain of the Dobunni tribe. A brilliant leader but an awful cook.' Without further explanation he descended the slope to arrive on the wide plateau. The others followed, stumbling as they went. Once all were at the base, Nathan started the questioning.

'What did you say just then?'

'The Kingsman is right. This was a hill fort, known to later people as Maes Knoll. It was built by Igerna, the second wife of Oghar, a chieftain of the tribe that dominated this area in the days before the Romans. She came from another tribe, many days' walk to the north, as a peace gift. Oghar's first wife had died so he took Igerna as his second. He was in his final days so all thought that she would just warm his bed until his end came but he seeded her and, to the surprise of all, she gave him a son.'

As the Old Man was speaking, Julian collapsed in an exhausted heap. 'If it's going to be story time again, then let's take a rest.'

The Old Man nodded in agreement and the others sat down alongside Julian. Carl removed his rucksack and took out some ration packs that he had bought at the warehouse. Each comprised a block of some form of mint cake which he distributed among the others, together with some bottles of water. When the rations reached the Old Man he declined them with a shake of his head.

'You were telling us about Igerna,' said Vicky before beginning to chew on the sticky white bar. She was keen partly to hear more of this story but also wanted to get the Old Man used to talking about himself. She knew that he could teach her so much but only if she could get him chatting.

'The son was born fit and strong. She called him Baclan, after her own father. He was important to the tribe, as Oghar's first wife was barren. Baclan was now the heir and was treasured by the tribe, especially as Oghar died in the second summer after the birth. Igerna, as the mother of the chief-child, had to lead the tribe until her son's manhood. Many of the tribal elders were against her and, given time, they would have driven her out and chosen a new chief from their own families. It was Igerna's good fortune that they were attacked by another tribe before that could happen.'

As the Old Man spoke, Nathan looked around the faces of the group. All of them were engrossed in the Old Man's story. Even Julian had stopped his griping, although Nathan accepted that this might be as much about getting a rest as hearing about these long-dead characters. Once again Nathan realised that all of them were being drawn, little by little, into the Old Man's fantasy. He certainly told a good tale, weaving together the characters into a wholly believable plot. The fact that they were sitting in this ancient place gave even more depth to the narrative.

The Old Man continued. 'The attackers were seen some way off and so the elders planned to rush out and confront them on the flat ground that led to the village. They knew that the tactic was risky and would cost many lives, but such was their way in the making of war. Igerna, still having the authority of the heir's mother, overruled the plan. She demanded that the tribe's warriors split into two groups and hide in the trees that lay either side of the pathway into the village.

She then told all the women and children to sit in front of the round houses, in plain view of the attackers.'

'Bait for a trap, you mean?' said Carl.

'Just so,' replied the Old Man. 'Once the leader of the raiding party saw that the village was undefended he couldn't restrain himself. He led all his warriors in a massed charge towards the women and children, promising them all the slaves that they could catch. The blood lust was upon them all and so they failed to see the Dobunni menfolk in the trees on either side of them. At a signal from Igerna all her warriors emerged from their hiding places and swarmed over the enemy. Breathless from the charge and confused by the surprise attack, they offered little opposition. The Dobunni assault was short and brutal. So great were the numbers of attackers killed in that first charge that the rest threw down their spears and pleaded for mercy.

Yet that was not the Dobunni way and the elders wanted to slaughter them all but Igerna intervened. She claimed that hers was the victory and so hers were the captives, to treat as she saw fit. She selected five of the biggest warriors to be her personal slaves. The rest were sent back to their tribal home, stripped naked and each with a deep gash upon their cheek. All were told that, in the future days, anyone bearing such a mark found on the Dobunni lands would be killed instantly. The five slaves became her bodyguard, devoted to her well-being as they knew that if she was killed then the elders would go back to their original plan and they would not long survive. Yet, in time, I suspect that all of them would have preferred to be scarred and sent back, naked, to their homeland.

'Why was that?' said Vicky.

'For the rest of their lives they had to deal with a dreadful penance that Igerna subjected them to.'

Nathan tried to imagine what this awful vengeance might be. 'What was it that she did?'

The Old Man looked around the group and saw that he had them all riveted by his tale. He shook his head sadly and said, 'She used to cook for them.'

Warren looked down on the collection of rags that the Old Man had discarded. Since his call to Eriksson he had moved the vans and motorbikes to this new location. Now parked down a side street, the vans were filling up with members of his team as they gradually arrived back from their search areas.

Not wanting to make their presence too obvious, only he and the two finders were waiting on the pavement. He looked again at his watch. Perhaps this latest request had stalled even the mighty Paternoster. He was taking a moment of grim pleasure in this small but significant achievement when a small van pulled up alongside him. The driver rolled down the window and spoke to the threesome.

'Is one of you Warren?'

'That's me.'

'Well, perhaps you can tell me what the bloody hell is going on?'

'What?' Warren replied, trying to hold back his irritation at the man's outburst.

'Thing is,' continued the driver, 'I've just had a call from my boss who tells me that he has just sold the business and that I'm now working for you. Then he tells me that I was to load up these buggers ...' he indicated towards the back of the van, 'and get round here pronto.'

Warren, now confused, said, 'What buggers?'

The driver got out of the car and walked to the back of the van. He opened the door and quickly stepped out of the way. 'These buggers!'

Out of the van jumped two Springer spaniels. One rushed up playfully to Warren. The other ran over to the other two troopers on the pavement who began to fuss over it, to the obvious delight of both dog and troopers.

'What is it that your company does?' said Warren, now beginning to see the hand of Paternoster in this confusion.

'We train up sniffer dogs for use in airports. You know, to find drugs and stuff like that. These two have just finished their training and were about to be sent to Heathrow. Until I got the call to bring them over to you, that is.'

As he spoke the two dogs transferred their attentions to the pile of rags on the ground. 'So these dogs are trained to follow a scent?' asked Warren.

'Once they're latched on, you'll struggle to stop them.'

'Right. I want them to follow the trail of the guy who left those clothes. Can they do that?'

'No problem.' With that the driver snapped his fingers, causing both dogs to run towards him and sit by his ankles. He then stepped towards the clothes, pointing to them as he moved. 'These rags stink so much I reckon I could follow the bloke's trail myself.' The two dogs spent a few more moments fervently sniffing at the ancient fabric, during which the driver returned to the van. Reaching in, he took out two long leads which he fitted to the dogs' collars. Finally he raised both hands and shouted 'Find!' at which the dogs sped off down the street.

Warren left word for the troopers to get another three of their colleagues from the vans and set off after the dogs, who were now dragging the unfortunate driver behind them.

The dogs sped through the streets, covering over a mile in what seemed to Warren to be no time at all. He knew that, at this rate, they would overtake the target in the very near future. His five troopers had caught up and rushed after the dogs. Only the driver was struggling with the hectic pace. As he kept on pointing out, airport security areas were nowhere near this big and so he was ill-prepared for such a chase. Warren suggested that one of his troopers could take over the leads but the driver pointed out that only he could call the dogs off when they reached the target.

Their chase took the group down several blind trails, where – according to the driver – the target had gone and then returned, until they found themselves in front of a large, modern house on the far edge of an estate of similar properties. Both dogs were straining at their lead to go towards the house but Warren wanted them held back. If the target group were inside then he wanted his full team with him when they entered the place. He was on the phone to call up the vans when the driver, now seriously out of breath, accidentally let slip one of the leads. Now free, the dog concerned rushed towards the house, not to the front door but down the side of the house, through an already opened side gate and into the garden at the back. From their vantage point on the pavement they could see the dog rush down to the very end of the garden, where it paused in front of a large wooden fence.

'There's no way that your man's in that house,' the driver said. 'He must have gone down that path, into the garden and over the fence at the back.'

'Then so will we,' said Warren, leading the group, the driver and the remaining dog along the trail blazed by the first dog a moment before.

As they entered the rear garden Warren saw the large kennel with the chain leading into it. Ignoring the frantic barking of the spaniel at the rear fence, he jogged over to the kennel and looked inside. At the very back lay a large dog which, on seeing Warren, began to whimper plaintively. The driver now arrived at the kennel and also looked in.

'That dog's terrified,' he said. 'Must have been abused for years to turn out like that. Terrible thing, animal cruelty. Strange choice for a guard dog, though.'

'So no danger to us, then,' said Warren as he stood up and jogged down to the rear fence where his troopers had managed to prise up one of the main panels, allowing the dogs, now both firmly held by the driver, and the troopers to leave the garden and enter the woodlands beyond. A few strides further on and they emerged into a rural landscape, with open fields stretching in all directions as far as the eye could see.

'Finding the target in all this would be a nightmare,' he said, to himself as much as anyone. 'Thank God we have the dogs.' But as he said it he realised that there was a problem. The barking of the dogs, which had been a constant source of loud noise for the whole of the chase, had now reached a crescendo. Both animals were going wild, barking more loudly than at any point since they jumped out of the van.

'Something's not right,' said the driver, his concern evident in the tone of his voice.

The focus of the dogs' attention was one tree in particular where they were sniffing dementedly around the base of the trunk. The driver tried to pull them away, but to no avail. Each time they were withdrawn they just returned to the horse chestnut tree that seemed to fascinate them beyond measure. Even when the troopers picked the dogs up and carried them to a point over 100 metres away, they still rushed back to the same tree.

After an hour of trying to persuade the dogs to continue with the trail, the driver was forced to give up. 'I've never seen anything like this. It's as if that tree is the most important thing that these dogs have ever found. I'm sorry but I can't do any more with them. We'll have to carry them back to the van.'

Reluctantly, Warren agreed. He called his troops back together and ordered them back to base. As he turned his back on the rolling fields that his target had undoubtedly taken, he paused to look at the tree. He was sure that this was no coincidence. This was the Old Man's doing. There was clearly more to him than Warren had anticipated. With a grudging admiration, and now devoid of leads to follow, he followed his troops back towards the housing estate.

CHAPTER 14.

Maes Knoll Hill Fort
South of Bristol
Thursday 23rd August
3.00 p.m.

The Old Man had fallen silent. In his mind's eye he wandered back over the centuries to the last time he had sat on this spot. So much was different - the crops in the fields, the sheep grazing within the fort area, the total lack of any roundhouses or barns. Yet there was still sufficient to stir his memories. Despite the overwhelming stench of this modern world, here he could still catch the scent of the cammoc from some distant hedgerow. This, plus the calling of the ever present birds above him, drew him to those dangerous, but still somehow happier, times.

'So what part did you play in Igerna's story?' Vicky's voice pulled him back to his current Return. Her questions seemed less intrusive now. He realised that she wanted his knowledge and he appreciated her attempts to make her learning more conversational.

'I came this way many years later. By then she had taken firm control of the tribe, partly through her keen wisdom in so many matters but also, it must be said, through the presence of her personal guards. Through her stewardship the tribe prospered. Their lands were extended in all directions, either through war or marriage, until they had all the food and slaves that they could ever need. Yet this wealth came to the notice of other, more distant, tribes who wanted to take for themselves that which the Dobunni owned. Such is the way of the Others.'

'Who were these Others? Some other local tribe?' At first Nathan's question annoyed Vicky, as she was keen to hold the attention of the Old Man, but then she saw that spreading the questions around the group might make her task easier.

'The Others? They are a foul pestilence that blight this world. You will know much when you know them. Yet the Physic wants to know of Igerna so let us not stray from her questions.'

'I wish you would call me Vicky.'

'So it shall be. Well, Vicky, Igerna reasoned that her tribe needed a place of safety, of security. A stronghold into which they could retreat when the dangers came. This place was part of her tribal lands and so she chose here.'

'It was a good choice.' Carl spoke for the first time since they had sat down. What sort of fortifications did they have?'

'Firstly she set slaves to shape the summit of the hill. The top was flattened and the spoil pushed down the sides to make these steep slopes around the rim. Only this large mound, known in later days as the Tump, against which we sit, was left higher than the summit surface. Indeed it was made higher by adding some of the spoil, supported by large rocks at the base. This served as both a watch tower and a place where a bonfire was lit to warn of attack.

'And was there some form of wall around the edge?'

'Quite so, Warrior.'

'If you can call her Vicky then I think you can call me Carl.'

'As with her so it shall be with you. So then, Carl, your instincts guide you well. Igerna set a wooden palisade, the height of a man with another sitting on his shoulders, all around the summit, broken only by two gates aligned with the rising and the setting sun at the summer solstice.'

Vicky looked across the wide expanse of grassland that now covered the summit. Even now, divided in two by modern fields, she could see that it was a vast area. The work that the Old Man had described must have been a truly monumental task. 'She must have been quite a woman. But you still haven't told us how you were involved. Did you have something to do with the building work?'

'Over my Returns I have played many roles, but I have never been a slave nor shall I ever be.' The Old Man sounded quite indignant and, for a moment, Vicky worried that she might have pushed him into yet another silence. Fortunately his face softened and he continued with his story. 'I came this way as they were almost completing the palisade. I had not planned to stay as they were wary of my companionship. My plans changed when Baclan was severely wounded.'

'Baclan, Igerna's son?' Vicky asked.

'Just so, yet he was now grown in years. A few more summers and he would have become Chieftain, after his mother's plan. He had become a fine warrior and often led war bands against any local tribes that rebelled against Dobunni rule. This day he had taken a spear thrust to his side and was near to death. Fever was overwhelming him. Igerna directed the tribe's Druid to save him but he was of no use. Seeing Baclan's condition he abandoned all hope and told Igerna to prepare for his passing. He had ceased to acquire wisdom, you see. He felt that he was too important to learn. Rather like your master, Vicky.'

'He means my senior consultant, Mr Courtney. They had something of a clash at the hospital,' she explained to the others. Then, to the Old Man, 'You shouldn't be too hard on him. He is a very good doctor.'

'Once arrogance starts, the search for wisdom ends. It is always so. In all my Returns it is the one thing that I have found most often.' He was about to continue on this topic until he saw the concern in Vicky's face. Reluctantly, he returned to his story. 'I told Igerna that I could keep her son in this world and she, for want of other choices, believed me. It was a simple matter, merely a poultice of magepe and cassia, together with some persogg to strengthen his blood. His fever broke within the day but it took several more weeks before he could walk again.' Then, again to Vicky and almost by way of an apology, 'My wisdom was not so wide in those times. Today, I could have had him walking within the hour but I had not learned of galban then.'

Vicky found herself nodding sympathetically but in truth she had no idea what he was talking about.

The Old Man continued. 'Igerna was so grateful that she made me Healer for the tribe. I stayed with them for many summers.'

'I'm sure that your presence was a joy to them all,' said Julian, his heavy sarcasm noted but ignored by the Old Man.

Throughout the Old Man's tale Nathan had been looking around nervously. He was worried about his colleagues searching for them. Even out here in the countryside they were still likely to be spotted, if only by a passing farmer concerned by trespassing townies. He felt that it was time to move. 'I'm not sure that the locals would appreciate our presence here,' he said. 'I think it is time to get going.'

'Igerna gave me leave to return here without limit of time. No future lord can overturn her decree.'

Julian had heard enough. His plan to keep calm and silent evaporated in the warm afternoon sunshine. He just couldn't help himself from intervening. 'Oh, please! Enough of this drivel. Ancient Celtic harpies giving everlasting consent. I can't see a modern Farmer Giles buying that without something more than just your word for it.'

'She said the same on the day of my leaving. So she had me leave my mark.'

'Please, no more of this fantasy. This lot might be falling for it but I'm not that stupid.'

The Old Man looked across to Carl who was sitting on the grass, leaning back against the steep slope of the mound. 'Carl, take that wondrous knife and dig into the turf, an arm's length from your right side.'

Carl started to dig in the spot that the Old Man had indicated. After a few cuts he hit rock. Removing the knife he continued with his bare hands until he had cleared away the covering soil to reveal a large, flat stone standing on its edge. It was clearly part of a larger structure, possibly the base of the ancient wall that had once supported the mound. As he swept away the last of the soil he saw that the surface was not simply hewn to give the flat appearance - something else had been carefully carved into the face. A few more sweeps of his hand revealed a set of indentations, initially indistinct but clearly visible. He picked up his knife again and used the tip to clear away the soil that was embedded into the deeper sections of the fast emerging shape. A few moments later he had finished his work.

The pattern, carefully carved into the stone, was now clearly identifiable. It was that of a large hand print, so clear as to be almost as if the hand's owner had pressed it into wet mud. Yet this was not soft mud but hard granite. A craftsman had obviously laboured for some time to carve this. Reaching for his bottle, Carl splashed the shape with water, removing the last of the soil in the finer crevices to reveal an astonishing level of detail. The muscles of the palm, the length of the fingers, widening to encompass the broad knuckles, by any standard this was a remarkable piece of carving.

Nathan, Vicky and Julian had all grouped around Carl to watch as the shape emerged from the stone face. Once finished, he leaned back to allow the others a closer look. All then turned to face the Old Man, seeking some form of explanation. None came. Instead the Old Man stood up, walked across to the newly cleared stone and placed his hand into the carving. It was a perfect fit.

'This is my mark, made by her master mason at Igerna's decree. It tells all who see it that the owner of the hand can pass this way without limit of time.' The group looked from one to another, the evidence before them clashing with the lingering disbelief in their minds.

Predictably it was Julian who spoke first. 'This proves nothing. For all we know you could have carved that last month. It was you that chose to come this way and to sit down here.'

The Old Man looked around the other three. Julian had simply spoken the words that were in their minds. 'I do not offer this mark as proof. It is for each of you to accept my story or not, according to your own wisdom. Yet in one respect Vicky's servant speaks the truth.

No ancient mark will convince the farmer who tills these fields today. We must move on.'

'How many times must I tell you that I'm not Vicky's servant!'

'Then soon you must educate me on your true role, but not now.' The Old Man rose to his feet, pulling up a handful of turf as he did so. Carefully spreading the stalks across his palm he selected one small plant. Shorter than the others, it had a thin, broader leaf and, upon closer inspection, was a slightly different shade of green. Discarding the other stalks he motioned for the others to gather around him. 'This is wastem. I have need of many handfuls. I wish that each of you should collect some from the ground around us. Do this swiftly that we might leave the sooner.'

'So the fairy stories have stopped and now we're into another botany lesson.' Julian seemed less than thrilled at the prospect of crawling around on his knees.

'I reckon you need all the exercise you can get. Think of it as being good for your health ...' Carl loomed over Julian as he spoke, 'because the alternative won't be!'

'How much do you want us to collect?' Nathan asked, trying to defuse the situation.

'Each of you must have cupped hands filled to overflowing.'

'Why do we need so much?' asked Vicky

'All will become clear,' the Old Man replied.

The group spread out to carry out their task. Initially each had problems as the plant that they sought was so similar to other grasses surrounding it but, as their familiarity grew, they quickly began to collect the required amount. Nathan was the first to finish. Standing up, he looked around for the Old Man, eventually seeing him in a hedgerow some distance from the base of the hill fort ramparts. He, too, was collecting something, this time some green berries from deep within the overgrown hedge. Once he had found the required quantity, about a single handful, he turned and climbed the steep slope to re-join the others.

'Enough,' he called. 'Come now to me and place the wastem into a single mound.' They did as he requested, although it was phrased more in terms of a demand. 'Now, all gather behind me and stay close.' With that he squeezed the juice of the berries onto the newly created mound. Once all the juice had been extracted he tossed the grass and juice mixture, rather as a cook would toss a salad. All four of his companions were focusing on the now sticky concoction that the Old Man had created, and so missed the first stirrings of the surrounding fauna.

As soon as the juice touched the wastem the several dozen sheep scattered around the field raised their heads. Each one sniffed the air, turned towards the group and trotted towards them. Within a minute the five figures were surrounded by a large flock, all pushing towards the sticky mixture, braying loudly in apparent frustration. At the Old Man's direction, each member of the group grabbed two handfuls of the mixture and held them above the reach of the advancing sheep.

'What now?' said Nathan, more than a little uncomfortable in the midst of such an animated flock.

'We must move slowly towards the distant trees, scattering small pieces of the dampened wastem as we go,' replied the Old Man. As he spoke he dropped a small lump onto the ground. Several sheep rushed to the area where it fell and started to push each other violently in a desperate attempt to eat it. Vicky had been brought up on a farm and so was more used to sheep than the others but she had never seen these docile creatures act so aggressively.

Slowly the group moved towards the trees indicated by the Old Man, located in the western edge of the hill fort, some 100 metres from their starting point. It took them several minutes to cover the distance. All the way they were surrounded by the sheep, still vigorously contesting the small supply of the damp mixture that the Old Man kept dropping onto the grass. As his supply ran out he directed the others to drop their portion in a similar fashion. Eventually they reached the line of trees. Still dropping the mixture they followed the trees until they reached a hedge, running across their path and so providing a boundary to the field upon which the hill fort stood. With some difficulty they clambered through this hedge and into the field beyond. The sheep, now separated from their treat, continued the loud braying noise for several minutes until they realised that no more was to be had and so dispersed back around the hill fort fields.

Once in the adjacent field the group paused to catch their breath after their exertions in climbing through the hedge.

Julian looked down at the remains of the sticky mess that now adhered to his hands. 'What was all that about?'

'You truly saw no purpose in that venture? Nothing at all?' said the Old Man.

'Well, we wound up some sheep and I tore my shirt climbing through the hedge, but apart from that, no,' replied Julian.

Shaking his head, either in sadness or disbelief - the group was not sure - the Old Man turned and continued to follow the line of trees down the slope. Carl, Nathan and Vicky, all as ignorant as Julian concerning their recent performance, chose to remain silent as they followed the Old Man.

—∞—

'Mr Courtney, wait a moment.'

James Courtney paused for a moment. He was not used to being shouted at, especially on a hospital ward. He turned to see a scruffy man hurrying after him, gently pushing through the crowd of nurses, cleaners and visitors. In the moment it took to decide whether to pause his rounds or ignore him and continue to the next patient, the man caught up.

'Thanks for waiting. My name is Eddie Rylands. I'm a journalist doing a piece for one of the Sunday colour supplements on the role of women in the upper echelons of the Health Service.'

'I'm sorry, Mr Rylands. I'm doing my rounds at present. If you call my secretary I'm sure that we can set up a more suitable time.' Courtney turned away in a fashion that, he hoped, had an aura of irritated impatience.

Rylands had already tried the secretary and got nowhere. He realised that this direct approach was unlikely to succeed but his experience had told him that it was always worth a try, especially when there was no alternative. 'I'm trying to contact Vicky Snow.'

At the mention of Vicky's name Courtney stopped and turned to face Rylands. 'What do you want with Dr Snow?'

'I'm told that she would be a good example of a high-flyer on the way up in the medical profession. Problem is that no one seems to know where she is. I wondered if you could help me find her?'

'Dr Snow is on a short sabbatical, doing some important research for me. It is vital that she is not disturbed. I suggest that you find someone else as an example for your piece.'

'Yes, but ...'

'So if you have no further business here, I suggest that you stop pestering me and let me get on with my important work. If you continue to follow me I shall have the security staff eject you.' With that he turned into a side ward, brusquely closing the door behind him.

Rylands could see that this time his 'no alternative' approach would not be paying off. He was about to leave when he saw one of the nursing staff, a Sister no less, waving at him. Having caught his attention she silently indicated that he should follow her through a side door off the main ward which, on entering, turned out to be a linen store.

'What do you want with Vicky?' said the Sister, coming straight to the point.

'I'm interested in doing a piece on her for a Sunday supplement and I was ...'

'Don't ever play poker, Mr Rylands. Courtney didn't believe your story and neither do I. So if you wish this conversation to continue, tell me the truth. Once again, what do you want with Vicky?'

Rylands rather liked playing poker but usually lost, sometimes heavily. He began to see why. 'May I know who it is that's shredding my cover story?'

'My name is June Sampson. I'm the Sister in charge of this ward but, more to the point, I'm a close friend of Vicky Snow.'

Rylands nodded. He could see that directness and honesty would be the best policy here so decided to stray into this unfamiliar territory. 'My name really is Rylands and I am a journalist. I'm trying to find Vicky because she was last seen in the company of someone that I'm interested in.'

'You can only mean the Old Man.'

'You've met him?' Rylands tried to hide his surprise. He failed, but now he was conscious of his failure. Time perhaps to forget the poker.

'Once seen never forgotten. He makes quite an impression.'

Rylands took out his wallet and withdrew the photograph given to him by Bradley. 'Just to be sure. This is the man I'm trying to find.'

June looked down at the picture. 'Yes, that's him.'

'How do you know him?'

June quickly related the events of the Old Man's visit. Rylands listened with increasing astonishment at the enfolding story. When June finished Rylands paused, trying to make some sense of it all.

'So he took a woman, at death's door with breast cancer, and cured her with a daffodil!'

'It wasn't a daffodil. Plus, he added something that he had been chewing when he arrived.'

'Even so, I've got to assume that this treatment is not normal medical practice.'

'Certainly not. We have no idea what he did.'

'And Vicky and Courtney saw all this?'

'Not exactly. They both had their backs turned. The treatment was over in a flash. The Old Man said that all things would be well – he has a strange way of speaking - and he walked off. Vicky's mother started to recover almost immediately which, as you can imagine, caused quite a stir. She wanted to get up and go home but we persuaded her to stay. We told her that the improvement might only be temporary and that we should do more tests.'

'True enough, surely?'

'Perhaps half true. In reality all the tests confirmed that she has made a full recovery. She is now as healthy as you or I, probably healthier.'

'So can I see her?'

'That's why I'm desperate to contact Vicky. Courtney has moved her into a private room on an equally private ward. He has got his own staff looking after her 24 hours per day. None of us can get near her.'

'Sounds like an excellent care package. He did strike me as a caring individual.'

'But what if she's now fully recovered? When does 'excellent care' stop and 'imprisonment' begin?'

'Point taken.'

'All I know is that Courtney is desperate to find out what the Old Man did. I'd like to say that his motive is for the betterment of humanity but I suspect that enormous wealth and the Nobel Prize for Medicine are more likely targets.'

'You think it could be that big?'

'And then some. This would be the biggest step forward in medicine since antibiotics, probably bigger.'

'So where is Vicky?'

'Courtney has given her extended leave to track down the Old Man and get the details of the treatment. Nobody has seen her since she left the ward yesterday.'

'Does she know about Courtney's care package for her mother?'

'I doubt it and I'm sure that she would not be impressed if she did.'

'Would she not see her Nobel Prize as being an adequate reward for locking up her old Mum for a few days?'

'Absolutely not. Everything I know about Vicky tells me that she is the polar opposite of Courtney. For her, the betterment of humanity would come first, second and third. She would probably use a Nobel Prize to prop open her kitchen door. Yet all that is totally academic. Once she has passed the information to Courtney, I'm sure that her role in this would be dramatically downplayed. Our Mr Courtney is not the sharing kind.'

'You astound me,' replied Rylands. 'So have you tried to contact Vicky and tell her all this?'

'I've called her mobile phone and her home number every hour since 9.00 this morning. She has switched off her mobile and her home line is just taking messages. I'm really worried about her. It is not like her to go 'incommunicado' like this.'

'So what do you plan to do?'

'I've no idea. I can't contact the police after such a short time, they would just laugh at me. Then a few minutes ago I had this great idea. I would contact a top-notch investigative journalist, tell him my story and get him to track her down. So I was wondering if you might know any?'

Rylands wasn't sure if the remark was meant as a barb or an attempt at humour. He chose the latter. 'Strangely enough, I can think of someone. He's not very bright but he's very reliable.'

'And he's bad at poker?' June smiled. 'So now you tell me your side of this tale. How do you know this Old Man?'

'We have a great deal in common. Specifically, we seem to have the same DNA.'

'Sorry?'

Rylands related his story. At the end of it, June shook her head.

'No, that simply cannot be right. I sometimes work in A&E and the police often come in to take DNA samples of patients whom they suspect for whatever reason. They are always very careful. If your sample is the same as his, which it can't be, then it is either a cock-up ...'

'They assure me that it wasn't,' said Rylands.

' ... or someone is messing around with the testing process. Perhaps that is your next step.'

'Thanks for the tip. Look, if anything comes up, I wonder if you could call me.' He gave her a card. 'This is my number. Obviously I'll call you here at the hospital if I contact Vicky. Deal?'

'Deal. Now you just wait here for a few minutes after I leave. I don't think it will do either of us any good if Courtney saw us together.'

'Keep in touch, Sister.'

June nodded and left.

Chapter 15

Open countryside, south-east of Bristol
Thursday 23rd August
6.00 p.m.

In the few hours since leaving Maes Knoll, the Old Man had led the group in a roughly easterly direction. Sometimes they followed country lanes, sometimes ill-defined paths across open fields. Unusually the Old Man had taken the lead, partly as he was the only one who knew where they were going, but also because the other four had started to fall back, mostly due to the tiredness of Vicky and Julian.

Seeing that the Old Man was out of earshot, Nathan took the opportunity to discuss their route with Carl.

'How do you think he knows the way?'

'Obvious to me that he's been this way before. Either that or he's making it up as he goes, and he seems too confident for that.'

'We seem to be headed in more or less a straight line.'

'Yes, I know, slightly south of east.'

'But how is he keeping to that heading? I've not seen him use any compass.'

'The only compass on this expedition is in my pocket,' replied the big soldier. 'That's how I know the direction and how closely he is following it. But how he is doing it, God only knows.'

The two men walked in silence for a few minutes before Carl continued.

'Have you noticed the trackway across this field?'

'What trackway?'

'You have to look very carefully but if you do you can see a slight rise on one side of our route and a slight dip on the other.'

Once it was pointed out Nathan could see it quite clearly. Looking back he saw that it was running the full length of the field. More importantly, this trackway precisely followed the route that the group were taking.

'Must be worn down by cattle,' Nathan replied.

'Don't think so. Firstly, that would explain the dip but not the rise. Secondly, the track doesn't align with the field gates. Look, it's going to take us right through that hedge.'

'So we'll be clambering through more hawthorn. I can hear Julian's whingeing already,' said Nathan, grinning.

'You've missed my point. If the trackway doesn't align with the gates then it must have been in use before the field was created. You're the history nerd. When were these field boundaries set up?'

'Not sure that I like being called a nerd, especially by some wandering squaddie.' Nathan felt that his relationship with Carl could now move into the 'banter' phase.

Fortunately, Carl thought so too. He smiled before replying. 'Like I give a toss what you think. So come on then, college boy. When were these fields created?'

'Well, it's hard to say. I'd need to check on old maps, perhaps dig up some hedges and look for finds to date. Not easy to be precise.'

'Typical academic. Too cautious, never prepared to commit, never make a decision that might fall back on you. You'd make a good officer.'

'Thanks for the character analysis, flawed though it is. If you had let me finish I was going to say they would probably have been made in medieval times, possibly a hundred years either side of 1300 AD.'

'So this trackway would be older than that?'

'Possibly, but why is that important? It's only in this field.'

'Sorry, Professor, but you're wrong. I first noticed this trackway three fields ago and I can see traces of it in the next two, as they rise up that hill.'

Nathan saw that Carl was right. The Old Man was following the track, at least for the last few fields, but possibly since they had left the hill fort. Before they could continue their debate the main group had reached the hedge. The Old Man had already climbed through and waited for them on the other side. Nathan and Carl helped Vicky clamber through, a task which they had yet to master as each of them, unlike the Old Man, collected several cuts and scratches. Once on the other side the threesome joined the Old Man to await Julian. Strangely, in Julian's case no offer of help was forthcoming.

As they waited the Old Man walked up to Nathan and Carl.

'Tell me, please, what is a nerd? It is a term I've not met before and I should like to know its meaning.'

Instantly both men realised that the Old Man had heard everything that they had said. They searched their memories to recall if they had said anything derogatory.

The look of concern on both their faces amused the Old Man, who smiled before continuing. 'Your observation does you credit, Carl. We are indeed following an ancient pathway. We walk the Wansdyke.'

'I've heard of that but I never knew where it was.' Vicky had overheard the conversation. 'What is it?'

'What 'was' it would be more accurate,' Nathan explained. 'It was an ancient protective barrier, probably built by the Celts at a time when the Anglo-Saxons were sweeping across the south of England, perhaps around 700 to 800 AD. Some think that it was in two sections. The one we are on now stretches around the south of Bath, the other is further west, near Marlborough. Others think that it was a single, long earthwork, with the two sections connected by a length of Roman road. I really should have remembered it, but I forgot that it was around here.'

Carl looked down at the small ridge and ditch stretching out before them. 'Doesn't look like much of a defence now. It must have been much bigger then.'

'Very much so' replied Nathan, now in his element. 'The ditch would have been dug to the depth of a man, with the spoil then piled up to make the ridge. On top of that it would have had a wooden fence running the full length. It must have been quite an enterprise to build it.'

His lecture was stopped by the crashing sound of Julian falling through the hedge.

'Why do we have to keep climbing through bushes?' Julian shouted as he pulled yet more thorns out of his hands.

The others looked at each other, picked up their rucksacks and continued along the path.

After a few strides the Old Man turned to Carl.

'That was most helpful,' he said, 'I now know what a nerd is.'

Colin Warren looked across at his second-in-command and posed the question both of them had been struggling with.

'Well, what do we do now?'

Mark Preston had been with Warren, in and out of the army, for over 15 years, but he had never seen him like this before. He had seen him frustrated many times but somehow this time it went deeper. Warren was taking this situation almost as a personal affront to his abilities and Preston could tell that this was getting to his old friend. Fortunately he had a short-term answer that had always worked before.

'I think a drink is called for.' Preston was pleased that a smile appeared on Warren's face, the first for several hours.

'Good plan. I'll have the usual.'

Preston walked across to the small bar, went behind the counter and helped himself to two large measures of Glenmorangie. Returning to the table, he handed over the glass and the two of them continued their thoughtful silence as they sipped their single malts.

As Warren stared out of the window, Preston looked around the bar area of the small hotel that was now their base. After spending several fruitless hours combing the fields around where they had lost contact with the quarry, they had reluctantly called in details of their failure to Paternoster. From what Warren had said Eriksson had taken the news surprisingly well, almost as though he was expecting it. The troop had been told to move to this hotel, called The Hallows, book in and await instructions.

They arrived to see the previous guests being driven away in a fleet of taxis. The team were soon to discover that the hotel owner was a former Paternoster man. At the request of his former employers, he had booked all his guests into other, higher grade accommodation in the local area and sent them on their way, each with an envelope containing £500 in cash, 'for their inconvenience'. Each trooper was allocated a room and told to meet in the 'free' bar at 7.00 in time for a meal to be served at 7.30. Clearly, Paternoster had block booked the hotel for the foreseeable future. Judging by the smile on the owner's face, Preston was sure that he was going to do very well out of the deal. His thoughts returned to Warren who was still staring out of the window.

'Any ideas?'

'None, said his leader, gloomily. 'Looks like we are back to waiting for them to make another mistake. Not a happy place to be.'

Both men lapsed into thoughtful silence, broken a few moments later by Preston as he saw a car, a brand new Bentley no less, pull into the drive in front of the hotel. 'Looks like one of the guests didn't get the message.'

'Mine Host will get rid of him quick enough,' replied Warren, distractedly.

A chauffeur got out of the car and opened one of the rear doors to allow his passenger to get out. Preston saw that he was a tall man dressed in a suit that, he reckoned, cost enough for a winter cruise. From his thinning hair, cut short in a business-like style, to his shoes, polished to a high lustre, this man looked every inch the leader of industry. His confident style, plus the chauffeur-driven Bentley, should have given Preston a warning but his mind was on other things. Warren continued to stare sightlessly across the car park.

'We're closed, mate,' Preston mouthed through the window, backing up his message with suitable gestures. The visitor saw the performance going on behind the window but chose to ignore them and walked briskly towards the front door.

'Piss off, you stupid prat.' Preston's gestured message became more forceful, but was again ignored by the visitor who reached the front door just as it was opened by the hotel owner. Preston saw the two men initially shake hands, followed by a more heartfelt embrace, as if they were old friends who had not seen each other for some time. The visitor took a step back to admire the front of the hotel, making some complimentary remark before the smiling owner ushered him into the lobby. A few seconds later both men entered the bar.

The hotel owner spoke first. 'Gentlemen, may I have your attention, please.' The troopers all stopped whatever they were doing and turned towards the newcomer. 'I would like to present to you all Mr John Eriksson, Chief Executive Officer of Paternoster Industries.'

'Oh shit,' said Preston, mostly to himself but loudly enough to shake Warren out of his thoughtful silence. Eriksson crossed the bar area and extended a hand to Warren who was, by now, rising from his seat.

'I'm pleased to meet you in person, at last, Major.'

'Hello.' It was all Warren could think to say. Fortunately he shook off his surprised state swiftly enough to introduce his friend. 'This is Captain Mark Preston, my second-in-command.'

'Ah yes. Judging from your gestures a moment ago, I have to conclude that you are in Communications!'

'I'm so sorry, sir. I had no idea that ...'

'No offence taken, Captain. Think nothing of it. Now, Major, I would be grateful if you could introduce me to the rest of the team.'

Nice touch, thought Warren, who went around the group as requested. In every case, Eriksson made some form of remark that showed he had read up on each trooper in turn. Perhaps where they had come from, where they had served, what their specialism was or something about their family circumstances. The whole process only took a few minutes but by the end each trooper seemed lifted by the experience. Warren was impressed. This guy knew how to get the best out of people.

Once Eriksson had completed the introductions he addressed the whole group. 'Well, I mustn't keep you from your dinner a moment longer. If you could all move through to the restaurant I'm confident that the hotel has prepared a meal worthy of you all.' The group started to move into the next room.

Eriksson turned to Warren and Preston. 'Except for you two gentlemen. I wonder if we might delay our food a little further to discuss our future tactics.' The three men sat down again around the window table. 'More drinks might help I think. Glenmorangie for you both, isn't it?' Again Warren was impressed. Eriksson clearly knew the importance of the little details.

Once the drinks were brought the three men turned to the matter in hand. Eriksson began. 'So, as I understand it, we lost the Old Man's trail when he pulled that trick with the dogs?'

'That's right,' replied Warren. 'No one has any idea how he did it but he completely screwed up the scent trail. We moved the vans to a more central position in the countryside and I sent teams off in all directions but it was needle-in-haystack stuff. After a few hours I had to call them off and come back here.'

Eriksson nodded sympathetically. 'Once we got your message we tried to send up some helicopters but it appears that area is on the flight path for Bristol Airport so we couldn't get any off the ground. Pity. This would have been our best bet.'

'Any further news from the police?' asked Warren, keen to move the conversation away from his own failures.

'Nothing as yet. They have been covering Bristol city centre and the suburbs. Obviously they don't know that the group have left the area and I'm not about to tell them. I suspect that their efforts will diminish as other priorities come along. I'm keeping a team monitoring their communications but I'm not hopeful.'

'So what now?' Preston felt that someone had to ask the question and was keen to take some of the pressure off Warren.

'Succinctly put, Captain,' replied Eriksson, 'and the main reason for my visit. Obviously I have all the resources of Paternoster looking for our targets but I'm worried that they may not make too many more mistakes. I was hoping that you chaps may have some ideas that are a little more pro-active. So, any suggestions?'

A tangible silence followed. With nothing to say, Warren and Preston could only stare out of the window, seeking some form of inspiration that just wouldn't come. Eriksson let the silence run for a few moments but then stood up to leave.

'Well, gentlemen, perhaps we should leave it at that for the time being.'

As he spoke Preston watched as a blackbird hopped over the hedge surrounding the hotel. It settled onto a pile of logs and began to search for food. Preston smiled as the solution hit him.

'Chogan!' he shouted.

'Yes,' said Warren, jumping to his feet, 'that's it!'

'What, pray, is Chogan?' asked Eriksson.

'Not what - who!' said Preston. 'Private Pierre Chogan of the Canadian Special Forces.'

'Go on,' said Eriksson.

'When we served in Bosnia we teamed up with some Canadian Specials, trying to track down various undesirables. Chogan was part of their team. He was supposed to be there for his explosives knowledge but we used him more for a skill that he picked up as a child.' Preston stopped for breath but Warren jumped in before he could continue.

'Pierre is a Red Indian, of the Algonquin tribe.'

Eriksson winced. 'I think that you might find that 'Native American' is a little more acceptable these days.'

'Call him whatever you like, but, as the saying goes, just call him. We need him here as soon as possible,' Preston continued.

'I'm happy to bring Mr Chogan into our little community but what particular skill would he bring that you do not already have?'

'He is a tracker,' replied Preston.

'Oh no, no, no,' interrupted Warren. 'He is THE tracker! The best. He found bad guys hidden all over Bosnia, following trails often days or even weeks old.'

'How can I find him?' replied Eriksson, now seeing where this thread was taking them.

'He came from Quebec. I'm certain that he will have gone back there if he has left the military. With all your resources I'm sure you can catch up with him.' Warren smiled as he passed over the information.

'Consider it done. I shall get your former colleague here as quickly as possible.' Eriksson turned to leave but paused. 'What made you think of him?'

Warren smiled and nodded out into the garden. 'As he never tired of telling us, in the Algonquin language Chogan means Blackbird.'

CHAPTER 16

The Wansdyke
Thursday 23rd August
9.00 p.m.

T he group had continued along the often indistinct line of the
Wansdyke all afternoon. Most of the journey had been across
open fields, much to the discomfort of Nathan and Carl, who kept on
requesting a route that gave a bit more cover. The Old Man had just
ignored them and pressed on. He kept plucking leaves, berries and
flowers as he walked, tasting them in various combinations either to
be swallowed or spat out according to some unwritten plan known to
him alone.

At one point the route had taken them close to the village of
Compton Dando. At Vicky's suggestion, the group had left the path
to visit the village shop to stock up on supplies of food and drinks.
Nathan had not been keen but eventually bowed to Vicky's argument
that they would soon tire of Carl's army rations. The implied criticism
had mildly irritated the ex-paratrooper but he agreed to the diversion
when Vicky pointed out that buying fresh food whenever possible
would make the ration packs last longer.

Once in the village Nathan was pleasantly surprised at how little
reaction they seemed to cause. Clearly hikers were not an uncommon
sight in these parts, something that he hoped would continue to prove
useful in the days ahead. Unfortunately it soon became apparent that

the village did not have a shop so, in one way, it was a wasted trip. However, they were able to use the village bridge to cross a small river, thus preventing them from getting wet so late in the day.

Once over the bridge Julian was keen to visit the local pub, an idea that Carl and Nathan supported but Vicky, mindful of Julian's recent record with alcohol, was dead against it. The matter was eventually settled when they noticed that the Old Man had not stopped to engage in the argument but had pressed ahead. Now he was almost out of sight on the road out of the village, and had they not followed they would have lost contact. Since this was out of the question, the four travellers hurried after him. Within a few minutes they were back on the Wansdyke which they continued to follow, across a main road and up a wooded hill. Climbing through the steep wooded slope the group emerged into a clearing at the summit.

'This is Stantonbury,' explained the Old Man. 'It is another hill fort built by the Dobunni in the time of Igerna. We sleep here this night.'

Without waiting to be asked, Carl quickly took over and distributed the four tents around the group. After some initial difficulty they were erected around a central area where Carl had set up the small stove on which he had planned to boil water for the evening meal.

On seeing the stove the Old Man laughed. 'What use is this against the cold breezes of the night? No. We must make a fire here. You three ...' he pointed at the men, 'go and collect firewood.'

'And what do you propose to do while we are working?' Julian was feeling weary and didn't worry about showing it.

'I shall sit here and decide the best punishment for a lazy servant!'

'Now listen to me, you old relic ...' Julian's words were cut short by Carl's strong hand grasping him by the collar and dragging him into the surrounding woodland.

Vicky looked across the clearing at the Old Man, now squatting by the embryonic camp fire. She was getting nowhere in her objective of getting him to share his medicinal secrets. All afternoon she had walked beside him, trying to engage him in conversation. Each time he had shaken his head and gone off into one of his silences or given her just enough information to show her how much she still needed to know. Now, after a full day in his company, she was ready to give up.

The Old Man looked across at her. Somehow he seemed to sense her frustration. 'Do not be downhearted, Vicky. I understand your purpose here, but you must see that wisdom that took a lifetime of lifetimes to acquire cannot be passed on in a few short hours. The way of my people is not to question but to test. Many times, most times, I fail but sometimes I succeed and so my wisdom grows.'

'But I do not have your lifetime of lifetimes. How can I get this wisdom in the short time that we have together?'

The Old Man stared thoughtfully at the ground where the fire would be lit. After a few moments he seemed to reach a decision. 'So be it. I shall try to help you as best I can in the time that we are spared. We shall use both your way and mine. It may be enlightening as to which proves the better. Yet be warned. I am told that I do not handle questions well. There are those who have said I can be a little ...' he seemed to struggle for the right word, 'prickly.'

'They're right,' replied Vicky, deciding that a direct approach might be better than false diplomacy. 'You can be really cantankerous.'

The Old Man smiled, a rare thing in itself. 'I have learned that showing false feelings only serves ill. Yet do not be diverted from your purpose, even if I am, as you say, can-tank-er-ous. Press on until I make it clear that I wish for your questions to cease.'

'It's a deal.' Vicky proffered her hand for the Old Man to shake. Once he took it, Vicky shook his hand, smiling at the major step that she was sure they had just made.

'So let us start by me asking you one of your beloved questions,' said the Old Man.

Vicky was bemused for a second. She had expected this to be the other way around but still nodded in agreement.

'Earlier today Nathan was talking about the Wansdyke. He did well. Almost half of what he said was correct.' Vicky smiled, but let the Old Man continue. 'He told us that he had all this knowledge yet he had forgotten where the Wansdyke lay.'

'Yes. I remember him saying that. What's your question?'

'Tell me, please, what is this word 'forgotten'?'

'Forgotten?'

'Yes. I have heard it spoken before and I think I know something of its meaning but I struggle to understand. I would find it helpful for you to tell me about this word.'

'Well, it means that you cannot remember something,' replied Vicky, slightly surprised.

'That has always been my understanding. Yet that must mean that something that is known would somehow become not known. How can that be? Once wisdom has been captured how can it be lost?'

'But everyone forgets things. No one retains all the information that they capture, as you put it.'

'Not I.'

'What?'

'All that I have ever known, I still know. All the wisdom gathered over my time is still in my mind. Is this not so with all creatures?'

Vicky paused for a moment to consider what the Old Man had just said. 'So you have never forgotten anything? Everything that you have seen and done over all the lifetimes you say you have lived, all of that you can still recall?'

'Not just what I have seen and done but also everything that I have smelt, tasted, heard and touched. Again I ask, is this not so for all creatures?'

'I can't speak for all creatures but it is certainly not the case for me, nor anyone that I've ever met. Everyone forgets things. Sometimes small things, like where you have put the car keys, sometimes big, important things, such as which doses are needed for particular medicines. That's why we write things down, so that we don't need to remember them.'

'Hence the need for the huge number of books that I have seen on my travels. Yes, I can see now. So your need for writing springs from your poor recollection, and your need of reading becomes vital to gather this lost wisdom. Thank you, Vicky. Your words clear the confusion of many Returns.'

'Are you saying that you cannot read and write?'

'I have mastered these skills several times but they change greatly for each Return. Also they are all so tedious to acquire and, until now, I never understood their true purpose.'

'So let me get this straight. You can read and write but see no use for doing so   because you can retain all the information that is presented to you?'

The Old Man nodded.

'OK then, what was hanging over the bed in my mother's ward room?'

'Ha, so it is a test, then? Well, so be it. For that is my method, testing things above questions. So, let this test begin.' The Old Man paused, as if to think, but he saw the three men returning, all carrying various lengths of tree branches. 'Oh no! What have they brought?'

Carl led the group into the circle of tents and dropped his load of wood onto the ground, to be followed in quick succession by Nathan and Julian. Between them they had collected an impressive pile and so looked towards Vicky and the Old Man for some form of congratulation. Instead, all they got was a look of disbelief from the Old Man.

'What use is this?' he said, looking from one puzzled face to another. No answer came. 'I told you to get some firewood.'

'And that is what we collected,' replied Carl, confused by the Old Man's angry response.

The Old Man stood and started to rummage through the wood pile. 'You have brought chestnut, oak and alder. What use are they?'

'It's all wood, isn't it?' Julian was tired and so in no mood for a lecture.

'All wood? But surely you must know which types of wood to collect?'

The three men just looked at him, an embarrassed silence holding sway.

'The first thing a child learns once they are able to walk is from which trees to collect firewood. It is their only task for the early years of life.' He turned to Vicky for support but saw a similar confusion on her face. 'So none of you has learned even this basic wisdom?'

Again the silence told the answer.

'Your choices could not have been worse. This,' he picked up a large log from the top of the pile, 'is chestnut. Its flame is weak and so is its warmth. All it will make is sparks that will burn holes in your cloaks.' He threw the log back into the trees and picked up another. 'This is alder. What little warmth it gives is so short lived that you would have to spend all the dark hours feeding the flames. It is only good for making charcoal. Do any of you know how to make charcoal?' All four shook their heads. The alder log joined the chestnut back in the woods. 'But this one is the worst of all.' He held up the largest of the logs from the pile. 'This is oak. Old and dry, this is the best of all firewood. Yet fresh and damp, this gives little heat but great plumes of acrid smoke that will leave you coughing for days.'

'So which trees should we have chosen?' asked Nathan, seeing where the Old Man's problem lay.

'Blackthorn would be best. Ash or beech would also make a good blaze. Cedar is also good but often hard to find. Even elm would suffice, yet I have seen few of them on this Return.'

'So what does blackthorn look like?' Nathan was trying to find a way out of this lambasting but unwittingly only made matters worse.

On hearing the question the Old Man's shoulders sagged. He turned to Vicky and held out his hands. 'You see, a lifetime of lifetimes gathering wisdom and only a single Return to pass it on.'

'You have to start somewhere and this would seem a good place.' Vicky tried to sound conciliatory but knew her argument lacked conviction. She was beginning to see why he found her questions so frustrating.

'Perhaps you are right, Physic. Let it be so,' said the Old Man, hurling the large oak log a surprising distance into the woods.

He looked down on the remaining logs in the pile. Mentally rejecting them all, he turned back to the foursome, intending to lead the group back into the woods, but as he did so he stopped. Something in the pile had caught his eye. Bending down he picked up one of the logs, one that had some leaves of another plant caught between two small branches. He carefully pulled out these leaves, allowing the log to fall back onto the pile. They were as long as a man's hand but narrower across the width. They were a dark green colour, made deeper by the glossy coating that covered one side. The Old Man examined them carefully before turning back to the group. 'Which of you collected this log?'

'I did,' said Julian.

'Can you recall where it was found?'

'I think so. It was over on the far side, almost on the edge of the wood.'

'Take me there.' His tone had changed completely. Now the Old Man had lost his exasperated look, replacing it with one of earnest curiosity. As instructed, Julian led the group back into the woods. It only took a couple of minutes to lead them to the glade where the plant grew. He indicated the spot where he found the branch. It was alongside a huge bush which completely dominated the surrounding area. Higher than a man and broadly circular with a diameter of around 15 metres, it had densely packed foliage that covered the ground so completely that it cut off the light to any aspiring growth underneath its canopy.

The Old Man was fascinated by what he saw. He pulled off a leaf and nibbled at its edge before spitting out the remnants into the palm of his hand for closer study. He repeated with some bark scraped from one of the larger branches.

'Your knife, Warrior!' The Old Man gestured impatiently at Carl who quickly placed the weapon into the Old Man's outstretched hand. He checked the sharpness of the edge before he fell to his knees and crawled under the canopy and out of sight of the others.

'What is he doing?' whispered Julian to his equally confused companions.

'Blowed if I know,' replied Carl, looking at Nathan for some suggestion but getting none.

'He's examining this bush. It is obviously something new to him and this is how he acquires knowledge,' said Vicky, thinking back to the conversation that she had with the Old Man before the others returned. She wanted to explain more but was stopped by the reappearance of the Old Man, now clutching a length of root. Once clear of the bush, he squatted down on his haunches and carefully whittled away some of the root covering before tossing the knife back to Carl. As with the leaves, he popped the root cuttings into his mouth and chewed them for a moment. This time he spat them onto the ground and stood up to stare at the huge bush.

'This plant has no place here. It has immense power, too much for the other plants around it. See how it chokes all those that try to grow in its shadow. In all my Returns I have not seen the like of it before.'

'But it's only a rhododendron.' Julian's casual manner was in stark contrast to the earnest concern of the Old Man.

'You have some knowledge of this?' he replied. 'Then share your wisdom with me.'

'My mother has them on our estate. She cultivates them. She's quite proud of her collection. I think she has over 150 varieties now. Many of them are new but some are from the very first cuttings brought into this country.'

'What is meant by 'first brought into the country'?'

'Well, history is not my strong suit but I seem to recall her going on about how the original plants were brought into this country by plant collectors back in the Victorian era, probably about a hundred and fifty years ago.'

'And from where did these fools bring this plant?'

'Sorry, but I can't remember any more. Surprised that I can recall even that.' Julian smiled, missing the deep frown that was forming on the Old Man's face. Nathan was more aware of the Old Man's changing mood and so picked up the story.

'They brought it from the slopes of the Himalayas.'

'And this is far away?'

'It is on the other side of the world.'

For a moment the Old Man was speechless, whether from rage or exasperation the others could not tell. He turned his back on them and took a few paces into the glade before rounding on them. 'Have you lost all reason? Have you any concept of the consequences of your actions?' He looked from face to face but only saw confusion. 'This plant, this rho-do-den-dron, is a plague. Nature had no purpose for it in this land yet you have decided to ignore her wisdom and grow it anyway. So, what enemies have you brought in to halt its spread? Nature always acts in balance, spawning plants and animals that both spread and curtail in equal measure, taking eternities to achieve such a state. Yet you have chosen to destroy that balance. In a few short lifetimes this pestilence ...' he flailed an arm helplessly at the huge bush, 'has escaped the clutches of the morons that brought it and poisoned the very earth upon which you live. See how, even in this small space, how many of these plague plants now grow.'

The Old Man pointed into the woods that surrounded them. It was as if their eyes had just been opened. Now, all of them saw that several rhododendron bushes were growing around the clearing. Although all smaller than the one they were examining, each was dominating its growing space. Only large trees, probably pre-dating the bushes, managed to survive by pushing through the dense foliage. Once they died, as one day they must, only the rhododendrons would remain.

'So, they can be cut down, pulled up, rooted out. It would be something of a chore but where's the problem?' said Nathan.

'You are wrong, Kingsman,' replied the Old Man sadly. 'I have never known such a taste or smell before, but I can sense great power here. This plant will be very hard to destroy. Even a small trace left in the ground will be enough for the growth to resume. I foresee that, on my next Return, these woods and all that Nature planned for them, will be gone. All I will see is huge vistas of this plague plant rolling across the hillsides.'

He turned and started walking back towards the camp. After a few steps he stopped and turned to the following group. 'How many more plagues have you visited upon yourselves? How much more destruction must Nature have to overcome? My search for staria becomes ever more urgent. I must return to my Rest before Nature begins her restoration.'

In silence, the group returned to the camp.

—∞—

Ian Watkins returned to his flat both late and tired. His day at the laboratory had been a real hassle. The number of tests allocated to him had been far too high and so he had fallen behind his schedule. His schedule! That was a joke. He had very little to do with it. His boss simply gave him the list and told him to get on with it. As ever, the number of tests required was greater than his ability to get through in the time available. So he just worked longer. Again. Once or twice was not a problem but this was now a regular feature of his working day. He had hoped that the arrival of the new Paternoster machine would help solve this problem, as it was far quicker to do the DNA testing, but all that happened was that the number of tests was extended to reflect the greater speed. 'Oh, the more it changes, the more it stays the same.' He had heard that somewhere. Very apt, he thought, as he switched on his home computer.

He planned to sort out any e-mails before he went down to the pub for a drink with his mates. He typed in his password with his mind on the first pint. He swiftly scanned the titles of the nine that he found, noting the usual mix of online pharmacy offers and dubious bank alerts. However, one caught his eye. It was headed 'Job Opportunity – Urgent'. He clicked on the heading and read:

Dear Mr Watson,

I represent a client who is considering opening a new, state-of-the-art Biological Testing Laboratory in the South West of England, probably in the Bristol area. I am currently seeking the right person to take on the role of Technical Director for this exciting venture.

This will provide an excellent opportunity for the successful candidate to be involved in all aspects of the development of the facility 'from the ground up', covering both technical and people issues.

The position will command an excellent salary, substantially in excess of current rates of remuneration in the public sector. The package will also include a company car (probably a BMW), a non-contributory pension scheme and generous holidays. A share-option scheme is also being considered and may form part of the final package upon appointment.

Your name has been put to me, by a mutual contact, as the sort of talented person who might find this project to be of interest. It would be useful if we meet to discuss this directly in the near future, as my client is keen to move quickly on this appointment.

I am staying at the Marriott in Bristol all this week. Would it be convenient to meet in the bar tomorrow evening? May I suggest 7.30?

Perhaps you could e-mail a reply as soon as possible. If you could attach a copy of your current CV that would also be helpful.

Regards

Michael Prentice
Director
BioTech Appointments

The pint forgotten, Ian sat down to prepare his reply.

CHAPTER 17

Quebec, Canada
Thursday 23rd August
8.00 p.m. Canadian Time

As his wife handed him a beer, Pierre Chogan reflected on how wonderful things had been since leaving the army. His family, his house, his car – everything had worked out exactly as planned. The income from his military career plus a small inheritance had funded all that he and his wife had dreamed of. All he had to do was to get a little job to top up his income and they would be made for life. He should be as carefree as the blackbird that he was named after. Sadly, he wasn't.

Problem was that the 'little job' had proved to be more elusive than anticipated. After he left the forces he had expected to be able to pick up work with no problems. With the skills that he had acquired in the army, especially in the Special Forces, he thought he would walk into employment, a view reinforced by the careers team allocated to him once his leaving date was agreed. 'No problem,' they said. 'Sure thing,' they said. 'Call these numbers,' they said. So he did and quickly found that, out of uniform, there were many problems and no sure things. An expert knowledge of how to blow things up somehow didn't seem too important to companies involved in more commercial pursuits. So, after a few months of getting nowhere, he had lowered his sights. He took a string of low paid jobs around the city, each one more downbeat than the last. He had ended up doing a labouring job in the paper industry but even that had ended a week ago. Due to the recession, he was told, as if that helped.

He glanced across at his wife, sitting next to him. She was now heavily pregnant with their fourth child, and he had decided not to burden her with his problems. She had enough on her plate at present. As he looked at her she smiled across at him. He tried to smile back but the memory of today's mail prevented all but a very meagre attempt. This morning he had received their bank statement which told him that the inevitable, dreadful day had arrived. Their little inheritance was now used up and they had no more money to live on. Tomorrow he would have to put the house on the market. Tomorrow he would have to tell his wife and kids that he had failed them, and that their little piece of heaven would soon be gone. He was determined to leave the news until tomorrow. Tonight was going to be their last night of ignorance. He would wait until tomorrow before giving them the dreadful news.

He shuffled himself into a still more comfortable position in his hammock and allowed the warmth of the early evening to draw him into one last dreamy sleep. It was in that space, between dreams and wakefulness, that he heard the distant ring of his doorbell.

—∞—

As she unzipped the flap of the small tent, Vicky thought she was the first one awake. All the other tents around the now-extinguished fire were still sealed up against the strong morning breeze. Crawling out, she felt the knot in her back that had ensured a poor night's sleep. Standing upright she stretched out her arms to relieve the pains of sleeping on the ground, separated only by a thin mattress, and reminded herself to thank Carl personally for his lack of foresight in not purchasing air beds.

She was about to start shaking the other tents to rouse her companions when she saw the Old Man emerging from the woods. Grasped in one of his large fists were parts of the rhododendron plant from the night before, including leaves and roots. However, it was his other fist that he waved at Vicky.

'Good morrow, Physic. I have brought you something to break your fast.' He waved two rabbits in her direction before laying them at her feet. 'I recall that your tribe place great importance on the first meal, and I wish to cover a large distance today.' Without further comment he turned and went back into the woods.

It took a moment or so before Vicky realised that the Old Man expected her to prepare and cook the rabbits. Her medical training meant that she had no fear of the innards but she had absolutely no idea how to remove them, let alone cook the cleaned creatures. Fortunately, her plight was ended by Carl who had climbed out of his tent when he heard the others talking.

'Just you leave them to me, Doc. I'll rustle us up some grub in no time. Why don't you wake the other two?'

'Oh, thanks,' she replied gratefully, all thoughts of air beds swept away.

About forty-five minutes later the Old Man had still not returned. The others were sitting around the reignited fire over which Carl had made an impromptu spit upon which the rabbits had been roasted and distributed around the group. The ex-para had made an excellent job of field-chef and everyone, after a little hesitation, had thoroughly enjoyed their breakfast. Only a small portion remained, awaiting the return of the Old Man. Vicky had taken the opportunity to tell the others of her conversation the previous evening. Predictably it was Julian who was proving the most dubious.

'So, he's saying that he never forgets anything?'

'That's what he claims,' Vicky replied.

'And not just sights and sounds but tastes and smells?'

'That's right.'

'And you continue to believe him?' Julian looked around the group for at least some support. The nearest he got was from Nathan.

'I know it sounds unlikely but it is only the latest in a string of unbelievable claims. Yesterday it seemed so easy to reject all of them, but today? Well, I'm not so sure.'

'Oh, come on! Please don't tell me you are starting to fall for this fiction as heavily as my pretty doctor?'

'As a whole, of course, his story is nonsense. Yet consider any of the elements and tell me how it was done? I saw him kill a fully grown thug with a mere slap. Vicky tells us that her mother is now alive when she shouldn't be. What did he do to that massive dog in the garden back there? Until I hear some answers to those questions I'm reluctant to write off the whole story. I'm keeping an open mind for the moment and I suggest that you should as well. Who knows, there may be something immense happening here. Do you want to miss it for the sake of a few days in the countryside?'

'Well said, Kingsman.' The Old Man had returned to the group. He had moved so silently that no one had heard his approach. 'An open mind. I can ask for no more.'

'We've saved you some rabbit,' said Vicky, trying to move on from what she felt was an awkward moment.

The Old Man shook his head. 'That was a kindness but I rarely feed upon flesh.'

'So, you are some form of part-time vegetarian?' said Julian, sarcastically. 'If you care so much for the bunnies why did you kill them?'

'Of all the things that I have found on this Return, your words always seem the most confusing to me.'

'He means that a concern for the welfare of animals does not sit well with your obvious role as a hunter,' said Nathan.

'Concern for the welfare of … what foolishness is this? You are either prey or preyed upon. 'Tis nature's way. I began my life as an eater of flesh but now choose plants whenever possible. I have learned the dangers of eating too much meat.'

'What dangers?' Out of habit Vicky tried not to sound too keen but then remembered her agreement with the Old Man.

'I found that eating flesh gave, in some small measure, a degree of assimilation with the animal that provided it.'

'Go on.' It was Julian's turn to encourage the Old Man.

Mentally the Old Man noted his interest. 'In Vicky's flat I related that halswort and malue, mixed in the right quantities, caused the wisdom of one to flow into another.' The Old Man paused while Vicky, Nathan and Julian nodded.

'Yes. I remember that you used that stain in the corner of your pouch,' said Vicky.

'Yet that is not the only way of extracting inner wisdom. Long ago I discovered that eating the flesh of another animal gives you, in small measure, the knowledge of that animal. Yet if that animal is utterly stupid, such as a cow or a sheep, then your mind becomes clogged with this useless wisdom, reducing your power of thought. Repeated over a lifetime, the mind becomes so clogged as to be almost useless. So I choose not to eat flesh if I can find alternatives.'

'Nice of you to get us the rabbits, then,' said Julian.

'I fear that it is too late for many of your kind - a fear that is strengthened with your every word,' replied the Old Man.

Vicky intervened before Julian could reply. 'So what do you eat? In fact, when do you eat? I've not seen you take any food in all the time we've been on this trip.'

'I have not stopped feeding throughout the entire journey. You just don't see it.' Seeing that Vicky was puzzled with his answer he continued, 'Have you not noticed that I am constantly picking leaves, flowers and roots?'

'Yes, but you explained that yesterday. You are doing some form of ongoing trials to discover more about them.'

'In some cases, yes, but in others I am simply using wisdom already learned, taking plants that provide me with the nourishment that I require. Each plant may contain only a small quantity but over the hours of daylight I can usually obtain sufficient for my needs.'

'Could you show me some examples?'

The Old Man reached down to the ground next to where he was standing and pulled up a handful of the turf, pretty much at random. He moved across and squatted alongside her. With the turf in one hand he picked through it with his other, pulling out different leaves and grasses as he went. 'Consider this.' He plucked out a small leaf, circular and about the size of a fingernail. 'This is good for energy. It can sustain you through a long, active day. Yet it can bloat the insides with unfortunate consequences so I eat an equal measure of this one.' He picked another, this time a type of grass with a long thin green stalk. 'This causes the bloating to cease. Yet be warned. You must not take any of this plant.' He picked a third one, this time another grass. 'This, even in small measures, causes the insides to become loose and flow down the back of the legs. It has great use as a medicine but none as a food. Fortunately, as you can see, they are quite different, so only a fool would take one in error.' He nodded at Vicky as he spoke, keen for her to understand the knowledge that he was imparting.

Vicky looked closely at the two grasses. After a moment's study she looked up at the others, only to see the same blank expression that she knew must be on her face. Once again she looked at the two stalks, this time even more closely than before, only to reach the same conclusion. As far as she could see they were identical. If there were any differences then she couldn't see them. She hesitated, unsure how to tell the Old Man of her plight. Unfortunately she waited too long and he jumped to his feet.

'Good,' he said, 'See how your wisdom grows. Perhaps I have misjudged you. It may be possible for you to learn what you seek during our journey after all.' Without further debate, he strode across the clearing and back into the woods. 'Come now, we must continue along the Wansdyke. I wish to be across the Fosse Way before the sun is at its zenith.'

Behind him the rest of the group struggled to collect together the tents and packs before hurrying after him.

As he got into the front passenger seat of the Jaguar saloon, Pierre Chogan felt the overwhelming need to pinch himself. So much had happened in the last few hours that he was expecting to wake up and find himself back on his porch, finishing his beer. He glanced at his watch which told him that it was 7.14 a.m. Quebec time. He glanced at the clock on the gleaming dashboard which told him that it was 12.14 p.m. local time, British time.

The driver smiled at him before starting the car which smoothly accelerated across the airport tarmac and through an open gate in the perimeter fence. Pierre had just enough time to read a sign saying 'Thank you for using Bristol Airport' before he was swept away into a series of narrow roads.

Somewhere a telephone rang. He looked at the driver who nodded towards the glove box. Pierre pressed the catch and a large section of the dashboard gently lowered itself to reveal a mobile phone, ringing and vibrating. He took out the phone and pressed what he hoped would be the correct key.

'Welcome to the United Kingdom, Mr Chogan. My name is John Eriksson, Chief Executive of Paternoster Industries. There are some things that I need to acquaint you with, but before that I have someone who wants to talk to you. Please hold for a moment.'

Pierre heard a few clicks before a familiar voice spoke.

'Pierre, is that you?'

'Pattie?'

'Oh, it's great to hear your voice. How is England?'

'Hard to say. I only just got here. It all seems very green. Oh, and they drive on the wrong side of the road.' He grinned at the driver who smiled back.

'How are you? How was the flight? Did you get any sleep? Have you …'

'Slow down, will you. I can't keep up. Yes, I'm fine. The flight was great.' He thought back to the flight. As the only passenger on an executive Learjet, the term 'great' didn't even come close. All the food and drink that he wanted, although he had declined most of the proffered alcohol, and a full-length bed to sleep in. This outfit certainly knew how to look after their workers. 'I grabbed a few hours' sleep but to be honest, my mind is still spinning with the pace of everything. Enough about me. How are you and the kids?'

'We're fine. Everything has happened just as the Paternoster guy said. A few minutes after you left this other guy turns up, telling me that he is there to help me. I keep calling him a butler but he prefers domestic assistant. He's doing everything. Cooking, cleaning, everything. Then a midwife appeared. She is going to stay with me until the baby is born. She brought with her so much kit that it's like a hospital here now.'

'What about the car?'

'Yes, I checked a moment ago. There is a Mercedes station wagon on the drive with yet another guy sitting in it. The butler – sorry, domestic assistant - tells me that the guy is our chauffeur but he looks like one tough hombre. I sure wouldn't wanna mess with him.'

Chogan smiled. The man was more than a chauffeur, he was a bodyguard. It was one of his conditions. The guy was ex-Special Forces, an old friend of Pierre who needed the work. Pierre would entrust the safety of his family to no-one else. He hadn't mentioned this part to Pattie. There was no need to worry her as, in reality, there was no threat, but Paternoster seemed keen on putting his mind at rest during his absence. 'Sounds like you're set up really well. Remember the deal. You are to relax until I get back. Are the kids OK?'

'They're all fine. They are just getting breakfast now.'

'I'll call when I can. Love to you all.'

'Love you too, honey.'

The line went dead for a second before Eriksson came back on.

'So, Mr Chogan, I hope you agree that we have kept to our side of the agreement. I should also tell you that the initial sum has now been deposited into your bank account. You may check if you wish as your bank's details have been programmed into the memory of the phone that you are holding. As agreed, the bonus sum will be paid upon the successful completion of the contract.'

'OK, Mr Eriksson, but soon you will need to tell me what it is that you want me to do. I explained to the guy in Quebec that I am happy to blow up whatever you want but I won't kill anybody. I hope that's clear.'

'So you think that we are employing you for your explosives skills? My word, how very North American.' Chogan heard a slight chuckle down the line before Eriksson continued. 'I think it best that explanations should wait until you meet up with the chase team. You will see some familiar faces and the mission details will come better from them. Please retain this mobile - sorry, cell phone - for use during the contract. I hope to meet up with you over the next few days but for now farewell and good hunting.'

Chogan was still trying to consider Eriksson's remarks as the Jaguar swept into the driveway of a small hotel. Pulling up outside the front door the driver asked Pierre to get out and go inside while he sorted out the luggage. As Pierre entered the hotel foyer, he heard a familiar voice.

'Choggy, what took you so long?'

Pierre turned to see Colin Warren and Mark Preston walking towards him.

'So you two are at the bottom of all this? I should have guessed once I heard that I was coming to England.' The three men embraced in the manner of old friends everywhere. 'How long has it been? 10 years?'

'You haven't changed a bit. Well, apart from the hair.' Preston ruffled the thick black locks of his old friend. 'What do you think, Col? An improvement upon the Canadian forces crew-cut?'

'Can't blame the hair, Mark. He always was an ugly bastard!'

Pierre was taken aback for a moment at Warren's comment before remembering about English banter. He realised how much he had missed it as he recalled the rules. It was always meant in jest, only done to good friends and, to survive, you must give back as good as you got, the quicker the better.

'Never mind about me. What's happened to you two guys? Have you both put on weight or are you now into balloon smuggling?' Laughing, the three friends linked arms and walked into the bar, where 'Choggy' met up with more old friends and was introduced to several new ones.

Once the welcomes were complete, Warren and Preston seated Chogan at the window table that had become Warren's base-of-operations. All jocularity was now set aside as their professionalism came to the fore.

'OK then, so why have I been flown in at such short notice?'

'What have they told you so far?' said Warren.

'If you assume nothing then you won't be far off. I had assumed it was some form of covert explosives job until a few minutes ago.'

'God, no! If things need blowing up then we will have gone seriously off script.' Warren then went on to explain about the Old Man, his companions, and the task that Paternoster wanted undertaken. He related their progress so far, up to the point where the dogs had lost the trail in the woods behind the housing estate.

'So why do they want this guy so badly?' Chogan was relieved about the skills he was to use but still worried about potential outcomes. 'How can you be sure that he is not for the chop once we catch him?'

'No guarantees, I'm afraid, but the one thing that they have continually emphasised to me is that the old guy must come to no harm. That is a mission imperative.'

'So why the delay? I can see the big ex-para might be a handful but the others must be soft targets.

'I was told from the outset not to underestimate this old bloke. Of course, at first I used the standard army method for dealing with intelligence given at start-up meetings.'

'Nod wisely then ignore.' Pierre was surprised at how quickly he was falling back into military mode.

'But I was wrong, very wrong, in this case. This guy has more twists than a bent corkscrew. He has pulled some strokes in the last 36 hours that I haven't seen in 20 years of soldiering. He seems to know what you are planning even before you do. We must all be very careful in the steps that we are going to take, especially you, as you are going to be our front man.'

'Message received, Major. So what now?'

'Depends on you. If you are up for it, we go back to where we lost the trail and see if you can pick it up again. Did you get any sleep on the plane?'

'More than enough. Let's get this show on the road.'

Within the hour the team were back at the site of their recent failure. Warren was concerned that he would not be able to identify the tree that had attracted the dogs on the previous visit but he needn't have worried. Even twenty-four hours on, the tree was still surrounded by dogs sniffing wildly around the trunk, frustrated owners pulling them away to resume what was supposed to be a peaceful walk. The rather intimidating appearance of the troopers only served to increase their enthusiasm to be elsewhere.

Once the dogs were driven away Chogan was able to examine the tree trunk. He had seen the effect that it had on dogs and had heard Warren's account of the previous day. Kneeling down, he smelt at the bark. He took out a knife and hacked off a small piece, placing it into his mouth to chew for a moment before spitting it out.

'No. I have no idea what he has done here. I can't recognise anything about the smell or the taste. We're not going to get anything from this.' He fell to his knees and began to carefully examine the ground around the base of the tree. After a moment he looked up again. 'Of course it might have been better if you guys had not used this place for your ballroom dancing competition. There are just so many tracks here. How can I know which is which?'

'If it was easy we wouldn't have needed the Learjet,' Preston smiled and received a grin in return.

Chogan continued to work around the tree. He moved in circles, each one slightly further out than before. After many shakes of his head, and much tutting, he suddenly halted. It was clear that he had found something.

'Are these the same troopers that were here yesterday?' he shouted to Warren.

'The very same,' the team leader replied.

'OK then,' said the Canadian, jumping to his feet. 'I want you all to line up in front of me. Come on, quickly. Everyone, including you two.' He indicated Warren and Preston. Once they were all in a straight line Chogan gave another order. 'Right. I want you all to kneel down.' The task was done with much muttering and not a little complaint. Chogan then went around the back of the line and looked at the boots of each trooper in turn. Once he had worked the length of the line he allowed them all to stand up and walked over to Warren and Preston, both engaged in brushing the soil from their trousers. 'Don't worry, ladies. It'll wash off.'

'What was that little pantomime all about?' said Warren.

'Just as I thought. All wearing military issue Doc Martens. You 're all so predictable in the British Army.'

'So how does that pearl of wisdom help us?'

'Well, fortunately, there's a guy out there ...' Chogan waved his hand at the inspected ground, 'wearing a pair of Canadian military boots which, doubly fortunately, have a distinctive tread pattern. Now it is possible that one of your local dog-walkers has a thing for Canadian footwear but I think it more likely that it is one of our targets.'

'Hang on a minute.' Preston reached into his pocket and withdrew the list of purchases made by the group at the military surplus warehouse. After a moment spent scanning the sheet, he gave the result they all wanted to hear. 'You're right. One of them bought a pair of Canadian military boots, size 9.'

To the cheers of the troopers Warren put his arm around the Canadian's shoulders. 'Nice one, Choggy.' He turned to Preston, 'Call Eriksson. Tell him the Learjet was worth it. We're back in business.'

CHAPTER 18

The Wansdyke
Friday 24th August
1.00 p.m.

They had been walking for several hours. Carl paused and waited for the rest of the group to catch up. He was conscious that his pace was far quicker than the others and so if he didn't make these regular stops he would pull too far ahead. The Old Man seemed happy to let him take the lead, only calling on him once or twice to change direction slightly. The Wansdyke, still visible for most of the morning, was taking them broadly eastward, making it very easy to follow.

He took the moment's rest to reflect upon his new companions. Before his capture he had always delighted in being described as 'the strong silent type'. He knew his enforced addiction had radically changed his personality but now, at least temporarily clear of the dreadful cravings, he was enjoying the return to his former self. So it was mostly in silence that he had been watching the others.

Right from the start he had concluded that Vicky was a driven woman. Her desire to obtain information from the Old Man seemed to affect everything that she did. In the beginning it had been incessant. With her constant pestering, Carl almost felt sorry for the Old Man. It seemed to irritate him at first but then the Old Man had decided just to ignore the young doctor. It had taken a while for Vicky to catch on but once she did, the journey became far more peaceful. Carl had watched as Vicky had become so dispirited that he thought she was going to pull out of the trip. That was until last evening. The conversation between them while Carl and the others had been collecting wood seemed to have settled both of them. They had been chatting freely throughout the morning and Carl detected a more relaxed attitude between them.

Nathan, he just didn't understand. A nice bloke, very bright in his own way, good education, good career stretching out before him – yet he had decided to go AWOL and join up with a group of strangers who were assisting a wanted fugitive. A strange decision if ever there was one. Even so, Carl was glad that he had come along. Of all his new companions, he felt closest to Nathan. It was good to have someone to talk with along the way - something that Nathan also seemed to feel. The young policeman seemed to be grateful for conversation, perhaps as a respite from the inner questions that seemed to beset him.

Upon his first meeting with Julian in the police station, Carl knew that he was always going to detest him. Unearned wealth and a total lack of talent were never going to be an easy combination to cope with. When added to an overwhelming confidence that regularly strayed into outright arrogance, Carl knew that any form of friendship was out of the question. He just hoped that he could get as far as their destination without giving him a smack.

And the Old Man? Carl was as bewildered as ever. The more he listened to his stories the less he believed. Several times along the journey he had been able to convince himself that it was all 'just total bollocks!' Then he would remember the words of the others which made him pause for further thought. Then he would remember that he had not felt any cravings for almost three days now so he would decide that the Old Man had been telling the truth all along and so Carl should go with him, helping where he could. Finally he would get that strange feeling that he had been through this thought process many times before and had always reached the same conclusion.

As the group caught up with him, Carl saw that Nathan and Vicky were in deep conversation with the Old Man who, for the moment, seemed happy to talk.

'So if you can remember everything you have ever seen, how far back do your memories go? What can you recall of your childhood, for example?' asked Nathan.

'My earliest recollections are, I confess, rather hazy. I recall my tribe living on a vast plain, teeming with forests and animals. I can picture the menfolk regularly bringing back animals that they had hunted for the women to skin and prepare. My clearest memory is a particular summer when we settled at the foot of some enormous cliffs to the North and East of here. They stretched out for a day's walk either side of our camp. The leaders had chosen the place because it was so good for hunting yet still close to forests so that we could also pick fruits and berries.'

'What were your parents like?' It was Vicky's turn. She had noticed that the Old Man seemed less hostile if the questions were asked by more than one of them, so she and Nathan had fallen into the unspoken habit of alternating the questions.

'I never knew which of the menfolk was my father. I think that he was one of the hunters but I can't be sure. My tribe never placed the same importance upon the father and son link as your tribes do.'

'Your mother then?' asked Nathan, picking up his turn.

'I remember her very well. My earliest memory is moving around the camp, clutching onto her clothes as she walked ahead of me. She was the tribe's Healer, an important position. Her knowledge of plants was vital to the tribe's survival.'

'So it was from her that you got your knowledge?'

'I owe her that but so much more. It was she that saved me from the flood.' He paused in mid stride, for a moment lost in thought. This time neither Nathan nor Vicky felt the need for more questions. Something important in the Old Man's life was about to be related.

'I recall the day very clearly. The hunters had found the trail of a large herd of auroch.'

Vicky flashed a puzzled glance at Nathan.

'Wild cattle,' Nathan replied quietly. 'Much larger than modern ones.'

'They wanted to try and kill as many as possible in a single hunt. The whole tribe was to go with them, out onto the plain to help bring back the carcasses before the wolves got to them. It would give us meat for weeks and the skins would be vital in the cold times. Yet my mother was not for going. She had almost used up her stock of a herb that was needed to slow the rotting of the meat. Without it there was no point in killing such a large herd in a single hunt. She knew of a place where the herb grew but it was on a plateau at the top of the cliffs. So, when the tribe set off on the hunt, she led me up a path that she had found that led to the place of the herb. I recall being sad that I was not going on the hunt with my friends, even more so as the path was so steep and hard to climb.'

'When we reached the top, the sun was almost at its peak. My mother began to collect the herbs that we needed as she was keen to get back to the camp before the hunters returned. I wandered to the edge and looked down onto the plains, trying to see my tribe in the distance but they were too small and too far away. All I could see were the forests and grasslands leading down to, in the far distance, a mighty river. The hunters had told us children about this river, about how wide and fast it was but none of the children had ever seen it because it was over a day's walk away. I realised that I was now the only child in the tribe to have seen it and remember looking forward to boasting about it to my friends around the camp fire that evening.'

'I turned to call my mother over to look at the wonderful view but she just glanced up and smiled at me. She was too busy collecting the herbs and putting them into a sack. I turned back to see the river but something had changed. It somehow seemed closer than before. I remember rubbing my eyes, thinking it some trick of the light but when I looked again I knew that it was so. The river seemed to be moving closer. Then I realised what was happening. It was not moving closer but getting wider, covering more and more of the plains as it grew. I did not know the word then but I now know that the river was flooding. In the space of a few heartbeats the water covered half of the ground before me. Such a quantity of water as I have never seen since burst over the dry lands, driving all before it.'

'Again I called to my mother to come. This time she stopped and walked over to me. Her horrified look told me that we were watching something truly terrible. Before she could speak she saw something in the distance and pointed. I followed the line of her arm and saw the tiny figures of our tribe trying to outrun the rising water, but they stood no chance. Almost as soon as I saw them they were overwhelmed. The water rose over their heads and they were gone.'

'My mother started to cry and pulled me towards her, pressing my face into her fur cloak. We seemed to hold each other for an age, not wanting to look again at the disaster below. When she finally released me I looked down again. The water was crashing against the foot of the cliffs below. The plains and forests were gone. The flooding was complete and all I could see, stretching far into the distance, was the grey water.`

All four of the group had clustered around the Old Man to hear his story, horrified at what they had heard.

'So what did you do?' said Vicky.

'What could we do? Our tribe was gone and all the lands we knew with them. We could only walk away from the water, towards territory unknown to us. Somehow we survived, mostly due to my mother's wisdom with plants. You must understand that I was little more than a babe in arms. I was no use to her in those first years. I learned how harsh was the world when you have no tribe to support you. Yet our wandering took its toll on my mother. She lived to see my early manhood but died soon after, exhausted by her endeavours. In our wanderings we had reached the lands that would one day be the home of the Picts. It was after I had buried her that I started to watch the bears, worried that they might dig up her bones, and so it was that I found the secret of staria. It was her final gift to me.'

'So what about ...' said Vicky, but The Old Man, clearly upset, waved his hand at her.

'Enough. We chatter too much and walk too little.' He strode away, an air of finality in his every step.

'So, what do you make of that?' said Vicky to no one in particular.

'Just another fairy story,' said Julian.

'Well, that's one possibility,' Nathan spoke thoughtfully, as if still reaching a conclusion.

'Oh, come on. What else could it be?'

'Look, you heard just as much as me, so think. Cliffs, aurochs, large plains suddenly flooded....' Nathan paused.

'Go on,' said Vicky.

Nathan seemed almost unwilling to say the words. 'Sounded to me like an eye-witness statement of the flooding of the English Channel.'

'And when was that?'

'About 8,000 years ago.'

—∞—

The group had been following the trail of the Canadian boots all afternoon. The tracks had led them across some fields before rising sharply up a steep hill. It had been slow progress. Fortunately Warren had seen his friend in action before and so knew better than to expect the Hollywood style, where the tracker can run along the invisible pathway, sometimes even on horseback, stopping only for breath every few miles. Chogan worked differently. He moved slowly, studying the ground in front of him. Quite often he dropped to his knees and examined the grass in minute detail. Once or twice he seemed to have lost the trail but he simply doubled back to the previous trace, re-found the trail and continued on his deliberate path.

Warren had sent most of the troop back to the Transits with orders to go back to the hotel and collect their belongings. They were to drive to a convenient location, some miles ahead, and wait for a shout. He had kept Preston and four of the others with him. He hoped that the six of them, plus Chogan, would be enough manpower to subdue the Old Man's team when they caught up with them.

The ground became steeper as they walked. Looking ahead, Warren could see the rough direction that they travelled. It led up to a ridge that spread out on either side, dominating the landscape. Automatically, his military mind recognised it as a good defensive position but the thought was dismissed as soon as it occurred. Without realising it, he wandered ahead of his tracker, now lying flat trying to see some indications in the flattened grass.

'Have you ever considered becoming a tracker yourself?' asked the prostrate Canadian.

'No, not really,' replied Warren, confused by the sudden question.

'Good, because you're crap at it. Get back behind me and stop screwing up my trail!'

Suitably chastened, the team leader returned to his position at the rear.

The group continued in silence until they reached the top of the slope. Cresting the hill they found themselves on the top of a small hillock, some 10 metres above a wide circular plain bounded on all sides by a steep bank that fell away at an unnatural angle in all directions. Some of them paused to admire the fantastic view, but not Chogan. His focus on the task in hand took him down the other side of the steep slope. He stopped where the hillock ended and the plain began. He raised his hand to the following group, halting them in their downward momentum.

'You guys stay there,' called the tracker, 'something's happened down here.'

He took a few moments to carefully walk around the area at the foot of the slope. Once satisfied he called up to Warren, 'Looks like they stopped here to chow down. I think they've stopped worrying about being followed. Look, they've made a heck of a mess.' He made a sweeping gesture with his hand around the area as if to emphasise his point.

'Yes,' said Warren, not seeing anything at all, 'obviously.' Looking for support he turned to Preston, standing next to him, but only received a disbelieving smirk.

'One sat over there, another here and two more against the slope,' continued Chogan to no one in particular. 'What's this?' He folded back a large square of turf that had been roughly laid down against the base of the steep slope, revealing a large, almost vertical, flat stone, in the centre which was a large beautifully carved hand print. 'I think you should get down here and see this.'

Warren jumped the small distance down to the base of the slope, quickly followed by Preston, sliding down on the seat of his trousers. The three men gathered around the carving, impressed by what they saw.

'What is it?' Preston was the first to speak.

'God knows,' replied Warren, 'but we should get a picture back to Eriksson. It's clearly very old and he's been giving me constant remarks about history ever since we started this job.' He took out his mobile phone and a second later the image was dispatched to their employer, accompanied a second later by an explanatory text message.

'It's just exquisite. Look at the detail. I've never seen stone carving like it,' said Preston

'It's remarkable, no question,' said Chogan, who was now studying the carving in great detail, 'but something's not right.'

'What do you mean?' Warren had learned to listen to the Canadian when he used that tone of voice.

'I'm not sure. If you look at the detail you just have to assume that whoever carved this knew their trade.'

'Seems reasonable. So what's your point?' Warren replied, but the answer was interrupted by the strains of Mission Impossible. He turned his back as he took the phone out of his pocket. 'Yes, sir. I thought you'd be interested.' A pause followed whilst Eriksson spoke. 'That's all very interesting, sir, but not much use to us. Look, I'll send you our co-ordinates so you can send in a tame archaeologist if you like but I need to press on. OK? Good. Warren out.'

'What's the boss man say?' asked Preston.

'It seems that the carving is a site marker. Used in the Iron Age to confirm some sort of title for a local chief. Eriksson is getting very high on the news but it's sod-all use to us.' Then, to Chogan, 'Time to press on.'

The tracker turned away from the carving with evident reluctance. Warren was now looking across at the wide plain before them so it was Preston who picked up on Chogan's concern.

'What were you saying?'

'Something's just not right. The carver got so much detail into the stone and yet got one thing completely wrong.'

'Looks OK to me.'

'That's because you are too close. Take a step back and look at the whole imprint.'

Preston did as requested but still saw nothing out of place.

'How can you miss it? It's so obvious. Look at the size of the hand.' Chogan was getting frustrated.

'He was a big bugger, that I can see.'

'Yes, but there's more. Look at the proportions. Look at the length. Look at the width. Compare them to your own hand.'

Preston did as he was told but still without any idea of the point the tracker was making.

'Oh, surely you can see the problem. This hand is far too wide in comparison to its length. The whole thing is totally the wrong shape. No one that I've ever met has hands like that. It's almost like the guy isn't human.'

'So perhaps the carver wasn't so good after all?'

'That must be it. Still, it seems strange that he got so much else right,' replied the tracker in a tone that suggested he was still unconvinced.

His musings were broken by a shout from in front of them.

'Come on, you two. I want to get as far as I can before we lose the light.' Warren was calling the team back together at the foot of the hillock. 'Choggy, nose back to the grindstone, old son.'

Half an hour later the group were still gathered in the same place. Chogan had spent the time crawling around the grassy areas that formed the closest part of the wide plain. Every few minutes he returned to the group and set off in a different direction, only to return moments later. Eventually he was forced to admit defeat.

'Sorry, but I can't see where they went from here.'

'What's the problem?' said Warren, evidently concerned.

'It's those furry bastards,' said the tracker, indicating the sheep spread across the whole plain. 'They've screwed up all traces of the group.'

'The sheep? But surely they can't have walked around that much in such a short time? When do you reckon the targets were here?'

'I think around early afternoon yesterday and, yes, you're right. I wouldn't have expected the sheep to have been so active but they have been. There are just no signs of our targets. It's as if the sheep had been persuaded to trample over the tracks, but that's just ridiculous.'

Warren remembered the trick with the dogs and the tree. 'Ridiculous comes as standard with this guy. So what do we do now? Please don't tell me we're snookered?'

From his high vantage point Chogan could see all the surrounding fields. The flat top of the hill, and the steep bank surrounding it, was further ringed by a grassy band some twenty metres wide. Beyond that a thick hawthorn hedge marked the boundary of the field, running around the full perimeter. The fields beyond were rich in grass and waving corn and pleasingly devoid of any sheep. 'They must have left this field at some point. I can see a gateway down there ...' he pointed down to his right, 'but somehow I can't see them using the obvious exit.'

Warren nodded. 'Go on. So what's the plan?'

'I need to go right around the edge of the field. Somewhere they had to crash through that hedge and that would be impossible to conceal. Once we can locate the exit point I should be able to pick up their trail in the fields beyond. '

'So you need to go right around the boundary of this huge field checking the hedges for damage. How long is that going to take?'

'If I'm lucky I might find it in minutes. If not, it could take hours. Problem is that we'll lose the light well within that time.'

'But you're sure you can find the trail eventually?'

Chogan nodded. 'I just need time and light.'

'Right, you carry on as long as you can. I'll call in the Transits and we will camp here for the night.'

Chogan started to jog across the wide, circular plain and down the banking to the hedge. This would be a good time to be lucky, he thought, but somehow he knew that luck would not be with him this evening.

CHAPTER 19

Marriott Hotel, Bristol
Friday 24th August
7.30 p.m.

Ian Watkins walked hesitantly into the reception area of the Marriott Hotel. A glance at his watch told him that he was bang on time, surely a good sign to any potential employer. He caught sight of himself in the large glass doors and once again questioned his choice of clothes. Initially he had decided to go for a business suit, to give the young, professional image he was sure was required. Then he thought that, being outside office hours, it might be better to go for the 'smart yet casual' look, perhaps not looking too eager. The matter was finally decided when he remembered that his only business suit lay at the bottom of his wardrobe, a casualty of his sister's wedding the previous year. Getting it cleaned at such short notice was out of the question so 'smart yet casual' was the look for the evening. But then, how smart and how casual? Perhaps …

'Mr Watkins?' The question came from a rather scruffy looking, middle aged man walking towards him from the reception desk. His suit looked as crumpled as the lines on his face. Odd, thought Ian, but then how should an international head hunter dress? Never having met one, Ian had no idea.

'Mr Prentice?'

The man smiled and gestured towards some leather sofas further inside the hotel. 'Let's sit down. Can I get you a drink?'

'Thanks. I'll have a whisky, on the rocks,' replied Ian, remembering to choose something more sophisticated than his usual tipple, which came in pints.

The man waved across to a waiter and ordered the whisky and a pint of lager. Damn, thought Ian.

'Find the place all right?'

'Yes, no problem, thanks.'

'Of course. I forgot. You're a local, aren't you?'

Ian smiled in reply and tried to look relaxed in the deep leather. A moment of silence followed as the waiter brought the drinks.

'Right,' said the man. 'To business. I'd like to start off by giving you this.' He reached into an inside pocket and withdrew a brown paper envelope. Opening it, Ian saw that it contained a number of £50 notes. Surprised, he looked back across the glass table between them.

'What's this for?'

'To help you get over your disappointment.'

'Disappointment?'

'I'm afraid you didn't get the job.'

'Why not?'

'Because there wasn't one. Sorry about that.'

Initially Ian was hit by a wave of bewilderment, quickly followed by irritation and then anger. 'Then what am I doing here? What the hell are you playing at?'

'You feel pissed off. I can understand that. I've felt that way myself quite a bit of late. That's what the £500 is for. But if I were you I'd try to get over it as soon as you can. That way you can best deal with the next question.' He took out a second envelope, similarly filled, and laid it on the table between them.

'What's that for?' said Ian, now utterly confused.

'Excellent question. I knew you'd get the hang of it.'

'Now listen to me, Mr Prentice.'

'My name's not Prentice.'

'So who are you and what do you want?'

'More excellent questions. You're really quite good at this. Now I'm not normally one for giving out my real name but today is different. We won't make much progress without it. My name is Rylands, Eddie Rylands.' He paused for a moment. He was used to people recalling his limited TV stardom and so prepared to put on his well-practised 'embarrassed celebrity' pose.

'Never heard of you.'

Overcoming his injured ego, Rylands pressed on. 'Oh but you have, Ian. I have it on good authority that my name flashed through your life in the very recent past, and that ...' he indicated the second envelope '... is to help you remember.'

Ian was still angry at the trick played upon him but Rylands was right. The second envelope lying on the table was certainly helping him overcome his disappointment.

'Why should I have seen your name? In what context? Perhaps if you give me the circumstances then I might remember?'

'It was a few days ago. You were doing some tests on DNA from a police station in Bristol.'

'I spend my life doing DNA tests from police stations in Bristol. You'll have to be a bit more specific, I'm afraid.'

'You did a test on a sample from an old man who had been involved in a riot.'

Ian shrugged. 'Means nothing to me. I never know the circumstances. All I ever see are the test tubes.'

'This test didn't go smoothly. Something about it was out of the ordinary. Your lab had to repeat the test several times over in the days that followed.'

Ian began to shake his head again but then suddenly remembered. 'Edward James Rylands. Of course. You were the corpse that came back to life. Caused quite a stir in the lab. We don't get many of those.'

'Spare me the comedy! I want to know what happened to that test sample. I want the details and I want them now.'

'Sorry, but that information is classif ...' then Ian saw the second envelope and realised the true purpose of the meeting.

'Think of it as a contribution to your holiday fund,' said Rylands, following Ian's gaze. Ian's last holiday had been two years before. It had involved a cheap hotel on the Costa del Sol. In the week that followed he had only been able to get off the toilet for long enough to rub cream into his insect bites. The decision was not a difficult one and so Ian spent the next 15 minutes telling his new sponsor all he could recall of the testing activities on that day. He described the normal testing routine and how that now-famous sample had followed the process in the same way as any other.

'So there was nothing unusual about it at all?' Rylands was clearly disappointed but tried not to let it show in his voice.

'Absolutely not. We've already had an internal inquiry on this very subject and I'm telling you the same as I've told them. That sample followed the same routine as any other, from the moment it was taken to the moment the results were sent.'

'So everything went fine apart from the inconvenient fact that I was not the man at the scene of the riot.'

'Look, Mr Rylands. I cannot help what you told the police about your movements that night, but as far as the forensics are concerned, the sample taken matches the one that we have on file for you, taken several years ago I understand for an incident involving ...'

'An unfortunate misunderstanding that never went to court. That's not the issue here.' Rylands was keen not to pursue that line.

'So there are only two possibilities. Either there are two of you with the same DNA fingerprint – which is as near to statistically impossible as makes no difference – or you were at the scene of the riot that night.'

Rylands was beginning to see that his return on the £1000 invested in this meeting was going to be minimal. He tried to think of a new line of questioning.

'You're sure that the sample could not have been contaminated in some way?'

'It doesn't work like that. If the sample was corrupted it wouldn't change from one individual to another, it would just become meaningless. Besides, there were several samples taken, from the initial one taken in the cell right through to the three taken from you after your arrest.'

'So you can be sure that the initial sample was the same as the ones taken later from me?'

'Absolutely.' Watkins paused, suddenly recalling something that he had forgotten up until this point. 'Well, most likely, anyway.'

Rylands immediately picked up on the hesitation in the young technician. 'What do you mean 'most likely'?'

'Well, we couldn't do a direct comparison involving the original sample.' Watkins hesitated, embarrassed at what was about to come out.

'Go on'

'I've just remembered. Right after it took your first reading the measurement equipment threw a moody.'

'A what?'

'It sort-of crashed. It threw up a totally ridiculous result and then shut down. A moment later it re-started itself and identified you.'

'So what about the original sample?'

'I'm afraid that was destroyed when the machine crashed. But it's not a problem because we did get the result.'

'You said that at first it threw up a ridiculous result. What was that?'

'Well, I only saw it for a split second but it was just way out of court. I'd not seen anything like it before. It couldn't have come from anything human. Honestly, it was just a glitch in the machine.'

'And does this machine make a habit of such glitches?'

'Absolutely not.' Watkins sounded almost indignant at the suggestion. 'It is a Paternoster 4400E, the best that you can get. We've only had it a few weeks so it's nearly new, plus it is connected to the manufacturers over the internet for regular software updates.'

'So this paragon of technical virtue has only crashed once?'

'Yes.'

'And that was when it was testing 'my' sample?'

'That's right.'

'And you think that was a coincidence?'

'It must have been.'

Rylands picked up the second envelope and tossed it across the table where it was caught clumsily by the young technician. 'Enjoy your holiday. Don't send me a card. In fact, don't try to make contact with me in any way. Understand?' Watkins nodded. He paused long enough to finish his whisky before standing up and walking out of the hotel.

Once the glass door of the hotel had swung shut behind his guest, Rylands picked up his mobile phone from the table. He stopped the recording function and moved to the screen showing contact numbers. Selecting one, he leaned back on his sofa, listening to the ringing tone at the other end. A familiar voice answered.

'Hello Eddie. Long time no hear.'

'Hello Tom. Got a moment to chat?'

'Always time for you, Eddie. You always have such interesting stories to tell. How are things going? I heard about the tramp fiasco.'

'Not my greatest hour but never a door closes but another opens. Need a favour.'

'Ask away.'

'I want the full monty on a company that manufactures DNA testing machines. So I need a top-flight financial journalist to investigate them for me. Sadly he was out so I'm calling you.' Rylands smiled.

'Very funny, Eddie. Who wrote that one for you?'

'I got it from a Nursing Sister, actually. Glad you like it. So will you help me, then?'

'No problem. Who are they?'

'The name's Paternoster.'

'Not one that I've heard of. Give me a couple of days and I'll get back to you. Why are you interested in them?'

'Because I don't believe in coincidence. Speak with you soon. Take care, Tom.' Rylands rang off and stared thoughtfully into his lager.

—∞—

A few miles to the south-east Nathan also stared into his drink. It had been a struggle but Vicky and Julian had persuaded the group to end the day in The Wheelwright's Arms, a pub in the village of Monkton Combe, to the south of Bath, or 'Aqua Sulis' as the Old Man insisted on calling it. Nathan had not been keen, still concerned that his former colleagues might still be seeking them, but less so as each day passed. He stopped himself in mid-thought. Former colleagues? Had he started to make decisions unconsciously? Was this trip really answering his worries as the Old Man had proposed?

The day's journey had been difficult. The time spent walking had taken a toll on all four of them in one way or another. Vicky and Julian were struggling with the physical efforts. Nathan and Carl were struggling with Vicky and Julian. For the latter the day had been one long complaint. If it wasn't his boots, it was his pack. If not the route then the weather, which Nathan thought had been surprisingly good but far too hot for Julian. Heaven help us if it starts to rain, thought the young policeman. He and Carl had watched as Vicky's patient silence had progressively disintegrated. She had finished the day with the last of several angry jibes at her partner followed by a loud cry of 'I need a drink!' It was this remark that had resulted in them sitting around the table in this pleasant country pub, waiting for the food that they had ordered.

Since they left the camp that morning they had continued to follow the Wansdyke across open fields and through wooded valleys. The path had been following a south-easterly direction for most of the morning but had turned abruptly south just after they had gone through the village of Englishcombe. Nathan's protests about travelling through public places had been met with the familiar refusal to deviate from the ancient pathway in any way. Fortunately their rambler disguise, made ever more convincing by the dearth of washing facilities along the way, ensured that they progressed successfully.

The Old Man had been keen to cross 'The Fosse' before noon. Nathan knew this to be the Fosse Way, the main Roman road into Bath from the south-west. Foolishly he mentioned this in Julian's hearing, resulting in caustic remarks about the likelihood of being arrested by some 2000 -year-old legionaries. As usual, the Old Man had ignored the jibes, Vicky had grimaced in yet another embarrassed silence and Carl had loomed over Julian and growled one of the many threats that he had learned in the army. This had proved to be one of the few effective ways of shutting Julian up, at least for a few minutes.

'The Fosse' turned out to be nothing more than a modern A road which the group crossed without incident before plunging into the outskirts of Bath. After a few minutes Nathan gratefully found that they returned into the secure anonymity of the woods, following a valley until they arrived at their current location.

After his comments about his childhood, the Old Man had lapsed into his familiar silence. Nathan had watched him all day as he continued his perpetual experimentation with the local plant life, or perhaps he was just feeding. No one could tell which. It was probably a combination of both.

At one point, as they emerged from the Bath suburbs and entered a wooded valley, they had to climb across an old stile, cut into a large hawthorn hedge that ran for some distance on either side. As was becoming the custom Carl had gone first, followed by Vicky and Julian. Nathan had climbed over next and walked several paces down the path before turning to see if the Old Man had managed the slippery wooden structure successfully. Nimble as ever, he vaulted the stile but had paused to rummage under the hedge to the side of the stile. Unaware that Nathan was watching, he emerged with several small, pale yellow flowers laid carefully across his open palm. Using his other hand he withdrew his leather pouch, opened the drawstring and took out some grey seeds, placing them upon his palm alongside the flowers. Grinding his hands together he turned the flowers and seeds into a thick paste which he thinned down by the addition of some spit. Holding the resulting pool of liquid in the palm of one hand he approached the hawthorn where it overhung the stile. He carefully selected a thin branch, about the height of a man's shoulder. At the end of this branch, which was little more than a twig, there were three small red berries. Holding his cupped palm under the twig he carefully dipped the berries into the liquid. Once satisfied that they were all fully coated he wiped his hands on his coat before returning to the branch. With great care he snapped the twig but ensured that it did not break completely but was left hanging by a thin strip of undamaged bark. His work complete, the Old Man turned back to the path to re-join the group. He smiled at Nathan as he passed but offered no explanation for his actions. Nathan chose not to seek one. There seemed little point.

Nathan's thoughts were disturbed by the waitress serving the food that four of them had ordered. It was no surprise that the Old Man had chosen not to eat the food offered by the pub menu but that did not stop him from staring at each of the plates as they were set on the table. Reaching out, he took a chip from Vicky's plate and examined it closely before putting it carefully into his mouth. A second later he spat it out onto the floor, much to the annoyance of the landlord who had been watching this strange group from across the bar.

'Now then,' the landlord shouted, 'A bit of decorum if you please or I shall have to ask you to leave.' As he spoke he looked at Carl and prayed that things would not come to that.

'Please forgive my friend,' replied Vicky in her sweetest voice. 'He has not been well. We'll make sure that he behaves.'

The landlord nodded, temporarily appeased.

'What manner of food is this?' said the Old Man between sharp intakes of breath to cool his burnt mouth.

'It is a chip. Made from potato. Surely you have seen them before?' Julian's tone continued to betray his disbelief in the Old Man's stories.

'Potato? Why yes, in a previous Return, but never prepared in this fashion. Is this a common means of nourishment in these dreadful times?'

'We eat rather a lot. Perhaps too many. They are almost a staple food for most people,' replied Vicky.

'That explains much,' commented the Old Man, almost to himself. He scanned the other meals without further comment before moving around the dining area, looking closely at the pictures on the walls and the old farming implements fixed to the ceiling. Eventually his examinations took him into the next bar, out of sight of the others who continued with their meals.

Once the Old Man was gone Vicky turned to Carl and Nathan.

'I know I was pushing my luck to get you two in here for a meal but I want to go further still.'

'Go on,' said Nathan.

'I think we should stay here tonight. When I came in I saw that they had some rooms vacant so I want us to take them.'

'Risky,' said Carl. 'We would be sitting ducks if any of the local plod shows up.'

'I agree that it's a risk,' replied Vicky, 'but look at the advantages. Julian and I are just about all in. Another night sleeping on the ground will finish us off. If you think we slowed you down today how much slower will we be tomorrow?'

'Well, why don't you just drop out?' said Nathan, trying to be as gentle as possible. He was expecting a blitz of reasons from Vicky about how important this trip was to her but what he got surprised him.

'Don't you take that tone with her, Constable.' Julian had unexpectedly entered the discussion. 'Even I can see how important this little hike is to her. She is trying to learn something important from that old relic, something that could make the world a better place. She has already invested so much time and energy that there is no way that

210

I'm going to allow a failure like you to stop her from doing something important with her life.'

'I'm not trying to do anything of the sort,' snapped Nathan, annoyed at Julian's rather pompous speech, but also surprised at this unexpected defence of his girlfriend. 'I'm just trying to be practical. I can't see the trip getting any easier but, in the end, it has to be for each of us to decide how long we stay aboard.'

'That's right,' said Vicky, even more surprised by Julian's words. 'but there is no point in making it harder than it need be. A bath and a good night's sleep will help all of us in the days ahead. And, as for the local police, I'd be surprised if there are any for miles around.'

Nathan, with an insider's knowledge of the manning levels of rural police forces, reluctantly agreed.

'Excellent,' said Vicky. Finishing her meal, she rose and went to find the landlord to book the rooms.

The landlord had been reluctant to accept the room bookings but he had been persuaded by the twin forces of Vicky's smile and the slim likelihood of getting any alternative bookings so late in the day. Having gained his agreement, she went to tell the Old Man of the changes to the plan. She found him at the other end of the long bar. He was standing looking up at a wide-screen TV fixed high up on one of the walls, showing a game of football. As she approached him she was expecting an argument about her decision.

'I didn't know that you followed football?' she said, grateful for such a good opening to their conversation.

'What is football?' replied the Old Man.

'The game you are watching on the screen.'

The Old Man looked at Vicky. 'I'm trying to see how these wisdom boxes function. I can see them having great purpose. Can you teach me of such mysteries?'

Vicky was about to reply that she had no idea about technology when the screen suddenly changed. A serious looking TV presenter appeared.

'We interrupt this programme to make an emergency news announcement.'

Vicky and the Old Man exchanged glances before returning their attention to the screen. The presenter continued:

'The following statement was issued by the Department of Health at 17.00 this afternoon. Tests have now confirmed that the two council employees who died earlier today had contracted the H5N1 strain of Avian Influenza from swans found dead at a Bristol park a few days ago. All isolation measures have been taken and the NHS is extremely confident that these steps will ensure no further outbreaks. The public are therefore encouraged to continue their normal working patterns until further notice. However, anyone with concerns should call the NHS helpline where comprehensive advice is available. Persons feeling any flu-like symptoms should rest and take regular liquids. Only contact your GP if the symptoms worsen. Further announcements will be made as and when the Department of Health feel them to be appropriate.'

The screen returned to the football.

'Bird flu,' said Vicky. 'It was only a matter of time.'

'What is this 'bird flu'?' asked the Old Man.

Vicky saw that some chairs had become available next to the log fire, lit by the landlord against the chill of the late summer evening. Moving across, they sat down and, in a few moments, she told him all that she knew about the disease. Throughout the explanation the Old Man remained silent, only nodding as the young doctor spoke. When she had finished he continued his silence for a few moments more.

'So it is to be plague, then?' he said, darkly.

'What do you mean?'

'This news brings me no surprise. I knew that Nature would have her say before long, only her methods were in question. I have known plagues from past times. The culling will be harsh but her purpose will be achieved.'

'You've survived a plague? You were really lucky if all I have read about them is true.' As she spoke Vicky wasn't sure if she was saying this to placate him or if she was actually starting to believe his impossible tales. His next remark shook her out of her internal debate.

'Luck played no part in it.'

'Pardon?'

'It is not a question of luck. With every plague comes a means of escape for those with the skills to find it.'

'Go on,' said Vicky, praying that he would not choose that moment to go silent.

'Nature never obliterates with pestilence. For that she chooses the flood or earthquake. Plagues are for thinning out the herds, not destroying them. Every plague carries within it the seeds of survival.'

'I'm sorry but I don't understand.'

'Consider the plague known as the Black Death, in the days of the third King Edward. Know you of this?'

Vicky nodded. 'I know that it killed almost a third of the population.'

'And yet one creature flourished. I was in a village not far from here when the plague came. I saw many die, both people and animals. Yet very few horses were struck down.'

'I didn't know that.'

''Twas so. I mused about what kept the pestilence from the horses. I tried many things but found, at length, that a pottage of tyrwert and welnae mixed with the sweat of a young stallion saved the life of any that took it.'

As usual, Vicky had no idea what tyrwert or welnae were but chose to press on regardless. 'How did you apply it?'

'Drunk by those who had no plague symptoms, smeared on the boils of those who had.'

'So you think there would be a similar cure for bird flu?'

''Tis certain. Nature always matches death with salvation.'

'So you could teach me how to find a such a cure?'

The Old Man shrugged. 'It would take some time to discover it but it will be there for those with the skills and knowledge to find it.'

Vicky leaned towards her unlikely mentor. 'You must show me those skills, teach me that knowledge,' she said earnestly.

The Old Man let out a deep sigh. He stared at the floor for several moments before looking up to return Vicky's imploring stare. 'There will be a cure for this plague, Vicky, but I will play no part either in seeking it or helping you to do so.'

'Why not?' Vicky was horrified.

'Because there is a purpose in Nature's ways. Your world is foul and corrupted. This plague is her way of cleansing the filth that you have created.'

Vicky was silent for a moment, stunned by what she had heard. She struggled to find a counter argument, something with which to challenge the Old Man. Suddenly a possibility struck her.

'Then why did you find a cure for the Black Death? Surely you went against Nature then?'

'I did not save the world, only a village that had befriended me. My cure went no further than the village bounds.'

'Yes, but …'

'No, Vicky,' he shouted, causing everyone in the pub to look at the pair. 'I have learned that to oppose Nature is to fail. I will take no part in this. My only wish is to find some staria and take my rest.'

The tension was broken by Nathan's voice, anxious to end this very public disagreement. 'This sounds serious. May we join you?'

The others had finished eating and had walked through to find their companions. They took the remaining seats around the log fire. Vicky chose to let their discussion drop and so the group spent the rest of the evening in a strained silence, staring into the flames.

All, bar one, of the group just let the warmth of the fire and the food in their stomachs lull them into a comfortable doze. Only Vicky spent time in any form of cogent thought. After what she had just heard she was more determined than ever to learn the Old Man's secrets. This was now more than a search for his cure for her mother's cancer. Vicky realised that her task had widened massively, becoming a matter of life and death for potentially millions of people, on a scale that she was struggling to comprehend. From now on there could be no talk of dropping out, no matter how hard the journey became. Even the search for her mother's cure must now take second place. Nothing must be allowed to prevent her discovering the cure for what she knew would become humanity's next, and possibly final, catastrophe.

CHAPTER 20

Maes Knoll Hill Fort
Saturday 25th August
7.00 a.m.

Chogan was the first to wake. Slipping his outer clothes over his underwear, he unzipped the tent flap and stepped out into the bright sunshine of another glorious morning. As he pulled on his boots he nodded to the two troopers standing guard over the little collection of tents. Old habits die hard in the military, he thought. Even though there was little chance of the group being attacked, Warren had detailed pairs of troopers to stand watch, changing at two-hour intervals throughout the hours of darkness.

'Now that someone's up, I'll start the breakfast going. Bacon rolls OK ?' said one of the guards.

'That would be swell,' replied Chogan. 'I'll be down by the hedge. Call me when it's ready.'

Throughout the night, between periods of fitful sleep, Chogan had carefully considered how he was going to pick up the lost trail. He reckoned that the fields had a perimeter of about a mile. Somewhere around that circle his quarry must have broken through the hawthorn hedge that surrounded the field. He was sure that no one, not even the clever bastard that he was tracking, could get a group of people through a hedge without leaving some signs. If he had to examine the entire perimeter then it would take most of the morning. The Canadian realised that he would have to start somewhere and so chose to begin his painstaking search around the gate in the south-east corner of the field. In his heart he was sure that such an exit would be too obvious for his skilful prey, but perhaps it could be using a double-bluff – not expecting anyone to consider this route out.

After walking down to the metal gate he carefully examined all the ground in front of it. It took him only a few minutes to decide that nothing was to be found within the field so he carefully opened the gate and checked the grass and mud beyond. He had just concluded that the target group had not walked this way when he heard a familiar voice, calling to him.

'Choggy! Where are you?' Warren appeared on the other side of the gate carrying a bacon roll and a mug of steaming tea.

Chogan walked back to the gate and accepted the breakfast.

'What do you reckon?' Warren tried and failed to keep his concern out of his voice.

'They didn't come through here, so they must have got through the hedge. Problem is where?'

Warren looked along the line of the hedge stretching for hundreds of yards on either side of the gate. 'So what happens now?'

'We only have two choices. I can either follow the hedge clockwise or anti-clockwise. It's anyone's guess which way would be most successful.'

'Well, perhaps not quite so difficult. Remember that they came in from the west. Surely it follows that they are heading broadly eastwards and so the most likely crossing point is on that side of the field.' Warren emphasised his opinion with a wave of his arm.

'So your vote is that I work anti-clockwise, covering the east side first?'

'Sounds right to me.'

'Unless this clever bastard wants us to think that and so heads west.' Chogan spoke through a mouthful of bread and bacon.

Warren shrugged. 'That's the risk we have to take. Anything the rest of us can do to help?'

'Two things. Firstly, keep away from the hedge. My job is tough enough without you guys stomping all over the ground.'

'No problem. And the second?'

Chogan held up the almost consumed bacon roll. 'Keep me supplied with these babies.'

—∞—

Several miles to the east the bright morning sunlight also woke Vicky. She looked across at Julian, still sleeping alongside her, and her mind returned to her thoughts of the previous night.

When they first met Julian had seemed such a pleasant change from the men she had known before. His confidence, spirit and general joy of life entranced her. Life with him had been an endless series of parties and weekends away. She had known about his wealth and family connections from very early in their relationship but she always felt that they did not influence her view of him, good or bad. To her he was always a tonic, much needed in the rigorous life of a junior doctor battling her way up the foothills of the medical profession. She was even beginning to feel that there might be a long-term future for them together - a first for her.

But then things began to change. She wasn't sure if it was him or her, but gradually the wild drinking parties became a source of embarrassment rather than happiness. She began to see his overwhelming confidence move into outright arrogance. What had been appealing as a strident young man trying to make his mark in the world had now become a long series of rather boorish complaints.

Perhaps it wasn't him who had changed, but rather her. It was as if she had moved on, grown up in her outlook, leaving him behind. Whatever the reason, she felt that their time together was coming to an end. The last few days had given her an insight into Julian's character and she had not liked what she saw. Before long she knew that she must end their relationship. But when? And how? These were always difficult questions for her, ones that her previous experiences had never helped her to answer. There was never a 'good' time and never a 'good' way but her current situation made the timing even worse.

Her mind moved on to the remarks of the Old Man the previous evening. Could he really find a cure for the flu pandemic that was to come? During her studies she had researched previous pandemics for a final year essay on the Spanish flu of 1918. She recalled the appalling reality of the disease. How it had struck a weakened population in the aftermath of the First World War. How it claimed more victims than all the battles fought over that terrible period. How it had, preferentially, claimed the lives of the young and fit rather than the old and weak. Her research told her that the next time it would be even worse. The world population was more concentrated into huge cities, often with poor sanitation. International travel was now commonplace, even to the most distant parts of the globe. All the indications were that the next time influenza struck it would be catastrophic and the Old Man's knowledge could be the only way to stop it.

But was that right? Perhaps she was simply being drawn into the fantasy of a deluded fool? She had tried to keep an open mind on this since that evening in her flat when he had first told them of his history. She had tried so hard to be the detached, medical professional that she considered herself to be. Yet, as her time with this man increased, she was more and more taken in by his story, the way he related it and the fact that he was completely unconcerned whether the rest of the group believed him or not. And there was always her mother. She had been dying, of that there was no doubt. Something remarkable happened in that hospital room and Vicky could not believe that the presence of the Old Man was a coincidence, leading to the inevitable conclusion that he saved her. That fact alone, for it was a cold, hard fact, convinced her that the Old Man was something different, something special. So, once again, she decided to continue on this journey, even if that meant being drawn into his 'delusion' and all the problems that such a step gave to a detached, medical professional.

The thought of her mother made her realise that she had not kept in touch as she had promised. Nathan had been adamant that all mobiles must be switched off to prevent the police from tracking them so Vicky had no means of communication. She looked across at the hotel phone on the bedside table, considering the possibility of using that but quickly rejected the idea for another that occurred to her. Rolling out of the bed, she crossed the room and reached into her open backpack, sitting on a chair by the window. She withdrew a small, flat nylon case which she unzipped to reveal a small notebook computer. This had been included as an afterthought, just as she was leaving the flat. She had decided that its size wouldn't add too much weight and it could prove very useful on the trip.

After starting up the computer she opened a side pouch and withdrew a plastic tube with a metal connector at one end. The man in the shop had said that it was called a dongle but she was sure he was winding her up. This device gave her access to the internet anywhere across the UK and, crucially, as she had paid for it in cash, she was sure that it could not be traced.

A moment later she was looking at her e-mail account which showed that she had 23 messages. Running quickly through them she deleted the dubious ones (Nigerian bankers wanting to give you free cash – did anyone really fall for that?) before focusing on five. These she downloaded onto her notebook before logging off and breaking the connection. Four of the five were from her boss, James Courtney. The first was a polite enquiry about how she was getting on and what information she had been able to find out. Clearly her lack of replies had worried him as the next four, whilst seeking much the same information, were expressed in ever more desperate terms, with the final one bordering on threats if she didn't return his calls or messages. The other message was from June Sampson, her friend the ward sister who was looking after her mother. This message told Vicky that her Mum was making excellent progress and was now completely clear of the cancer that had almost killed her. She also told Vicky about how Courtney was holding her mother in a private ward, allegedly for more tests. In June's opinion this was more about a Nobel prize than any concern about her mother's welfare, and so urged Vicky to get back as soon as she could. She also warned about being too open with Courtney in any messages to him. Finally, she told Vicky about the visit of a journalist, concluding that he didn't seem too worrying but that she should know that he was trying to contact her.

In reply, Vicky typed two messages. In the first she gave Courtney a very brief update but without giving any location details. She promised to keep in touch as often as she could. In the second she told June a little more about her situation, but again without any details of the journey or location. She thanked her for looking after her mother and, once again, promised to keep in touch. She re-connected to the internet, sent the messages and quickly disconnected again.

The bedside phone rang loudly, perhaps too loudly. Certainly it was far louder than was needed to bring Eriksson out of his slumber. He took a moment to shrug off the tiredness he felt before realising the he was not at home but in the small, temporary bedroom that had been set up for him alongside his office at Paternoster headquarters. First thing for today, he thought to himself, new phone. Next thing, a new bed, as he stretched the stiffness out of his back and shoulders. Once done he rolled over and picked up the phone.

'Vicky Snow has answered her e-mails,' an excited Mike Aspinall shouted down the phone at him.

Instantly Eriksson was fully awake. 'Go on.'

'She downloaded five, mostly from her boss asking, then demanding, to know what she is up to. The remaining one was from a friend at her hospital giving her an update on her mother's condition.'

'Did she reply to any?'

'Yes, she sent two. One to her boss and one to her friend.'

'Did she give any indication of her location?'

'None. She was very cagey with the boss and a bit more open with the friend but still gave no details on location to either of them.'

'Good fortune, then, that our expensive IT set-up will be able to find her for us.'

'Ah.' Eriksson did not like the tone of his Operations Manager's voice. 'I'm afraid she is using a mobile broadband dongle. These things can be bought over the counter in any phone shop, often with cash.'

'So what are you saying?'

'There is no easy way of tracking down which dongle was used to collect the messages. Plus the fact that she was actually online for only two very brief periods.'

'Is there no useful information at all?'

'Well, we were able to get a very approximate idea as to her location. We know that she is somewhere south of Bath but more than that we are still working on.'

'So that would put them to the east of Major Warren's team.'

'That's right.'

'OK. Pass the information to them straight away. I'm not sure that it will be of much use to them but, who knows, it may assist them somehow.'

Eriksson replaced the telephone and lay on his back, considering his current status. They were so close to finding the Old Man. Could he really be the one to succeed where so many had failed? It would be such an achievement if Paternoster's Core Purpose could be achieved on his watch. If, after so many years, he was the one to catch up with the Old Man.

—∞—

Chogan had spent the last two hours on his knees, crawling alongside the tall hawthorn. He had been carefully examining both the ground in front of the hedge and the myriad thin branches that made hawthorn so dense, almost impenetrable to all but the most determined souls. His total lack of success was starting to depress him. Perhaps he had met his match. Perhaps here was the one individual who could not be followed, so perfectly did he cover his trail. Then he remembered the words of his father, his tutor in this specialist skill. 'There are no perfectly hidden trails – only lazy trackers who stop looking.'

He decided that he needed a moment's break so he stood up to stretch out his back and arms. As he stood he glanced up the hill towards the small encampment where his friends awaited the outcome of his labours. By standing up he had alerted them, and so made them all look towards him.

'Any joy?' Warren called down.

'Not yet,' Chogan shouted back, trying to keep the frustration out of his voice. The group returned to their card game.

From his standing position the Canadian looked around the hillside as it led down to the hedge. He had been trying to maintain this open view all morning but had to admit to himself that he had spent too much time focusing on his close examination of the hedge. Once again the words of his father came back to him.

'Study both the leaves and the forest, for the path lies in both.'

But there was no forest here. Just a sloping field covered in annoying sheep tracks. The damned creatures had been all over this field, hiding whatever had been beneath. Looking further along the hedge he could see still more of the stupid tracks. As he stared he realised that, in one area, they seemed much more densely packed than others, almost as if the sheep had congregated there. He jogged over to this spot and found that he was right. The tracks were far more concentrated here. Looking back up the hill he realised that this was not just where he stood but followed a very broad swath, cutting across the field towards the place where, he knew, his quarry had eaten their lunch. How had the Old Man done this, mused the tracker. It was as if he had persuaded the sheep to group around them as they moved across the field, masking their foot prints. He had never seen such a thing before but quickly realised that such methods were the stock-in-trade of the genius - there could be no other word - that he was tracking. Now that he knew what to look for he followed their trail down the hill to the point where it intersected the hedge. By pushing apart the outer foliage he saw exactly what he had hoped for. In the inner section of the hedge were several broken branches - unavoidable damage for anyone climbing through - and the final proof that he had picked up their trail again. He then saw a scrap of fabric, evidently recently torn from a shirt. He took a moment to silently thank his father before putting his head back and gave out a loud, high pitched, Algonquin war cry.

The strange sound made the group of troopers quickly get to their feet.

'Think he's found something!' said Preston, just in time to see his commander sprint down the hill. 'Right, you lot. Break camp. I think we'll be on the move again very soon.'

As Warren reached the hedge he called to Chogan.

'Have you found it? Are we back in business?'

'Damn right,' he replied. As Warren watched, Chogan reached into the centre of the bush to retrieve the strip of fabric torn off by the recent passage of their quarry. He held up his prize to Warren as proof of his success before carefully picking off a bright red berry from a branch that must have been snapped as one of the group had clambered through. Moving a step along the hedge he picked a second berry, this time from an unbroken branch. He tossed the first berry into his mouth and chewed it for a moment before spitting it out. He then repeated the process with the second berry.

'It that your way of asking for another bacon roll?' quipped Warren.

Chogan smiled at his commander's ignorance. 'An old tracker's trick. The sugar in the fruit falls away very quickly once it has been separated from the host plant. By comparing the taste of these two berries I can get an idea about how long ago the branch was broken.'

'And?'

'Just under 48 hours ago. Exactly when we would expect. There can be no doubt. We're back on their trail.'

Warren smiled and gave his friend a heavy pat on the shoulder. He turned and waved to the team, now moving down the hillside towards the hedge. He was about to call something but was interrupted by the Mission Impossible theme coming from his mobile phone.

'Yes, Boss? OK, thanks for that. That's very helpful.' Warren closed the phone, breaking the connection.

'What did they say?' asked Chogan

'They said that they have picked up some comms data from our target. It appears that they are to the east of here.' Warren grinned. 'So it's not just military top brass that do that.'

'Do what?'

'Give you highly useful intelligence, but always about two hours too late.'

—∞—

As Vicky led Julian into the dining area of the pub she could hear the voices of Carl and Nathan ahead of her. They were sitting around a large table bearing a collection of breakfast cereals, a large jug of milk and steaming pots of tea and coffee. Both their companions had progressed beyond the cereals and were tucking into large cooked breakfasts. There was no sign of the Old Man.

Nathan waved towards the remaining seats. 'Please, join us. The landlord told us to help ourselves. He'll be back in a minute to take your order if you want something cooked.'

The two newcomers took seats across the table and Vicky reached for a box of muesli.

'I don't reckon that rabbit food will get you very far, Doctor. I suggest you get a real breakfast inside you,' said Carl in a manner that was attempting to be helpful in his brusque, clumsy fashion. Vicky had still to decide about the big soldier. Initially she had disliked him and they had clashed several times early on in the journey. Now, as she got to know him better, she was beginning to see him as a useful person to have around in times of need. She had started to see his intimidating size as a source of comfort rather than apprehension. Even his direct manner of speech, with his thick Bristolean accent, she now saw as a source of good, sensible advice, albeit wrapped up in the blunt vocabulary of the armed forces. Her thoughts were broken by the arrival of the landlord.

'A full, cooked breakfast for you both?'

Vicky glanced across to Carl and smiled. 'Yes please. `

'Sounds good to me,' agreed Julian.

'And a generous second helping for me,' said Carl, handing his empty plate to the landlord, who considered mentioning additional costs but quickly decided against it.

'Sleep well?' asked Nathan.

'Wonderfully,' answered Julian for both of them. 'This was a really good idea of yours, Vicky. We must do this more often.'

Vicky nodded at the compliment before launching into a full description of her conversation of the previous evening. 'So, this trip has become more crucial than you can possibly know. I have got to get him to either stop this epidemic or teach me how to do it. You must all understand the criticality of this. It is imperative that we persuade him to help us, so we must stick together on this journey until we have achieved his agreement. Are we agreed on that?'

'No problem here,' said Carl. 'I'm in for the duration anyway.'

'Count me in as well,' said Nathan. 'If you're even half right about this then it's more important than anything else on my current agenda.'

Vicky smiled in gratitude at both of them before turning to Julian. 'And you? Will you stick with this journey?'

Julian let out a long sigh. 'To be honest, this was what I had feared. I only came on this little trek because I was worried that you would be swept up in this loon's fantasy. You are too gullible for your own good sometimes, my love, and so I'm here to protect you from yourself. So yes, I will keep jogging along behind but not for the reasons you describe. I just want to be there to pick you up when this whole venture goes belly up, something that I'm much more qualified for than Tweedledum and Tweedledee over there.'

Vicky's response was interrupted by the arrival of the breakfast plates. Once he had placed them in front of his guests the landlord asked, 'Is the old gentleman joining you for breakfast?'

'Good question. Where is His Lordship, anyway?' Julian looked around the group but got no answer. 'Well, someone better stir the lazy sod. I'm closest so it looks like I'm elected.' With that he squeezed himself from behind the table and climbed the stairs, leaving behind the puzzled glances of his fellow travellers, surprised at his helpful actions.

Once on the top corridor he identified the Old Man's room and knocked softly. Receiving no reply he turned the handle to find the door unlocked. A second later Julian had entered the room and found himself standing before the Old Man's bed. It was empty and clearly had not been slept in the previous night. For a second Julian panicked. Perhaps the Old Man had left without them, choosing to continue the journey alone. Despite his laid-back response to Vicky's bombshell, this possibility appalled him. He had his own reasons for being on this trip, reasons that required the Old Man's presence – at least for the time being. He swiftly moved across to the bedroom window in the vague hope that he might see the departing form of the Old Man. The window looked out onto the beer garden, used by the pub to give extra seating in the warm, summer evenings. The garden was bounded by thick privet hedging beneath which, to his immense relief, Julian saw the sleeping form of the Old Man.

Carefully, Julian came down the stairs and walked through the pub towards the beer garden, taking a route through the bar to avoid his colleagues, still eating their breakfast. A moment later he was crouching over the Old Man, now lying on his back, still fast asleep. He was still wearing the clothes from the previous evening, notably the walking jacket obtained from the warehouse. Julian knew that the Old Man had placed his otter-skin pouch in the left, side pocket of this jacket, a pocket that now gaped temptingly open. As silently as he could, Julian moved his hand towards the pocket. Just before he pushed his hand inside, he glanced back at the Old Man's face, to see that his eyes had opened and he was staring at Julian with a look that seemed to bore into his very soul.

Instantly Julian jumped to his feet, shocked both by the Old Man's sudden wakefulness but also by that awful stare. It was as if the Old Man could see all Julian's plans and schemes, laid out before him on some vast mental table. The image momentarily scared Julian but he quickly regained his composure sufficiently to speak.

'We'll be ready to leave soon. The others sent me to find you.'

The Old Man remained silent as he got to his feet and, ignoring Julian, walked across the garden and into the pub. Julian followed on behind, still shaken by the strange experience.

Carl, Nathan and Vicky were just finishing their breakfast when the other two entered the dining area. The Old Man looked perfectly calm but Vicky could see that something had shocked Julian. She had known him long enough to see the signs, probably invisible to the others. A slight reddening to the face, a little out of breath and, perhaps the most telling, a reluctance to engage in eye-to-eye contact.

'What's happened?' she asked but only received a cursory shake of the head in response. She wanted to press the matter further but was interrupted by the Old Man.

'It is good that you have broken your fast. We have far to go today and the wisdom box tells of ill tidings. We should start now.'

'It'll take me a few minutes to pack our things,' said Vicky to the group. Then, to Julian, 'You stay here and finish your breakfast. I'll be down as soon as I can.'

The Old Man seemed to want to challenge this but Vicky had left before he had the chance. Instead he sat at the table and began a silent contemplation of the day ahead.

The landlord entered the dining area and broke the silence by asking who was going to settle the bill, nodding towards the folded piece of paper on a plate that he was carrying. Nathan picked up the paper, unfolded it and grimaced at the amount. Carl looked over his shoulder at the amount.

'Too rich for my blood, boy. Another one for Goldenballs over there, I think.'

Julian took the note from Nathan, looked at the total and shrugged. 'No problem, except that I don't have that much cash on me. I'll have to use a card.'

The landlord nodded and walked back to the bar to get the payment machine. Once he was out of earshot, Nathan whispered to Julian.

'I'm not sure that's a great idea. The police might be checking on card payments.'

'Well, sorry, Constable, but I'm fresh out of alternatives. Unless you favour making a run for it, which seems to me even more likely to attract the local plod. Besides, I used the card in the warehouse for all the hiking stuff and they didn't seem to pick up on that.' Julian paused to eat a small piece of sausage before continuing. 'Perhaps they haven't made a link between us. Just because we left the police station at the same time doesn't mean that we are joined at the hip.'

Nathan was about to point out that his sergeant watching them all climb into Julian's car and waving them off probably constituted some form of clue but he was interrupted by the return of the landlord with the card reader. Taking Julian's card he inserted it into the machine, typed in the relevant numbers and presented it to Julian to type in his PIN code. Julian placed the reader on the table and began to feed in the number.

Carl lifted up his cup and passed it to the landlord. 'Any danger of a final cup of tea for the journey?' As his hand moved across the table his elbow caught the top edge of the large milk jug, causing it to topple and spill its contents across the table and, more importantly, all over the card reader. The machine let out a sizzling noise and a small amount of grey smoke before the display vanished.

Julian jumped up to avoid the milk rushing across the table towards him. 'You clumsy prat!'

'I'm so sorry,' exclaimed Carl, jumping up to start a vain attempt at mopping up the milk with his napkin.

'Not a problem, sir,' said the landlord, clearly not meaning a word. He removed Julian's card from the now defunct machine. 'We don't have another electronic reader. I shall have to get the old, hand-cranked one. He returned a moment later with a dusty, manual device that involved an imprint of Julian's card being made on a slip of paper which he then duly signed.

Further discussions were interrupted by Vicky's return carrying the two rucksacks. Nathan and Carl had already brought their rucksacks down and so hoisted them onto their shoulders, before the four of them walked through the pub and out into the bright morning sunshine.

Nathan looked suspiciously at Carl. 'You did that on purpose.'

'Did what?' said the big Para innocently.

'Knocked over the jug of milk.'

'No, not me, boy. Always was a clumsy bastard. Ask anyone. Comes with having such big arms.'

'And the fact that our payment details will now be slowed down by a couple of days is just a happy coincidence?'

'Is that a fact? Well, I wouldn't know about that. I don't do technical.' A wry grin spread across the big man's face as he strode across the car park.

Nathan realised that his respect for his new friend was slowly growing. He was about to walk after him when he realised that the Old Man was still in the pub. Looking back through the open doorway he saw him talking to the landlord.

'My gratitude to you, Innkeeper, for your kindness,' said the Old Man, extending his hand for a goodbye handshake.

The landlord took the proffered hand and shook it politely.

'You run a fine tavern here. May your efforts prosper and your kin survive the bad times to come.'

He tried to withdraw his hand but the Old Man held on for a second longer than seemed polite, then released it before turning and walking out to join the others in the car park.

The landlord watched the group walk away before returning to his work, preparing the pub for the day ahead. As he reached the bar he flicked on the radio, expecting some music to help him through his tasks. Instead it was a news report. He was barely listening to the newsreader's words, waiting for the music that would inevitably follow.

The NHS has now confirmed that several school children from the Bristol area have been diagnosed with flu-like symptoms and are being held in isolation facilities at an unnamed location. The spokesman for the South West Area Health Authority said that these measures were purely precautionary and urged the press not to link this news with any other recent incidents. When questioned about rumours that these children had been playing in a Bristol park where two park attendants were based before succumbing to the bird flu, the spokesman stated that, while the recent movements of the children were being investigated, it was too soon to make any firm conclusions and that more information would be released as soon as it became available.'

CHAPTER 21

The Wansdyke
Saturday 25th August
1.00 p.m.

Warren was pleased with the progress of the chase team. After so many problems and distractions they were back on the Old Man's trail. The breakthrough had been Chogan finding the point where their quarry had broken through the hedge. Once through, the Old Man had seemed to stop being so careful about covering his tracks. It was almost as if he was confident that no one would pick up the trail after his latest ruse.

Chogan had told Warren about the trick with the flock of sheep. The Canadian had spoken in almost reverential tones, so high was his regard for the skills of the man they were tracking. Once again, Warren offered up a silent prayer for the idea of getting Chogan onto the team. The cost must have been vast but it was certainly proving worthwhile. He had made the point to Eriksson during each of their hourly feedback calls, but his boss always seemed totally unconcerned about the money that was being expended, focussing only on the progress being made towards capturing the Old Man. Many times Warren had wondered why Paternoster was so desperate to catch this strange character but all attempts to glean any details from Eriksson were elegantly rebuffed. Even so, Warren knew that such an immense cost would only have been incurred for someone that they were desperate to catch.

His team had spent the day following the tracks left by the Old Man and his group. Now that the trail was far clearer than before, Chogan had been able to move more quickly and most of the day had been spent in a brisk jog. This pace was not a problem for trained professionals but Warren doubted that the five people ahead of him were fit enough to move so quickly, leading to the reasonable assumption that his team were gaining ground on their target. The tracker had confirmed this, using several methods that Warren could only guess at.

Their route had mostly taken them across open fields which gave very little by way of cover from any aerial reconnaissance. The Old Man had been fortunate that Paternoster could not send up any helicopters. He made a mental note to pass this on to Eriksson when, or perhaps if, they were able to move out of the restricted airspace. However, apart from crossing some country roads and going through a few small villages, the team had seen very few signs of human contact. They had asked amongst the locals in the hamlet of Compton Dando but, apart from vague references to various groups of hikers – a common sight in these parts in high summer – they gleaned no specific information about the Old Man and his companions.

Warren was surprised at the straightness of the route that they were following. In many cases the Old Man followed a line that defied common sense. Several times he had ignored what seemed to be a perfectly good pathway simply because it deviated slightly from their direction of travel. Many times they had climbed through hedges even though field gates were a few dozen yards to the left or right. Such directness suited Chogan as it gave regular confirmations of the trail, but Warren just could not see any sense in such foolish actions.

Yet Warren had learned the hard way that this individual was not at all foolish, so the route must have been chosen for a reason. Several times Warren had tried to see some pattern but had so far failed completely. At one point he thought he could make out the merest hint of a trackway in one of the fields that they had crossed, a slight linear depression running across the pasture, broadly in their direction of travel. Looking even harder he almost convinced himself that there was an even less discernible raised section running alongside the depression. However, after a while he was sure that he was just seeing things. He decided that they were probably caused by cattle, or perhaps a geological feature, certainly nothing worthy of mention.

By lunchtime the team had reached Stantonbury Hill where Chogan found evidence of the group having spent the night. Even the Old Man could not hide the presence of a fire around which the Canadian was able to point out the locations that various tents had been erected. Warren chose to give the team a 30 minute break for a rest and some food, during which he called over Chogan and Preston for a round-up session.

'So then. Any ideas so far on where they might be heading?'

Chogan was the first to speak. 'We have been moving in an almost straight line, broadly easterly.'

Preston spread a map across the grass beneath them, weighing down each corner with a stone. 'That direction takes us to the south of Bath. We should be hitting the suburbs before the end of the day.'

'More chance of being spotted by the locals, then,' said Warren.

'Yes, but more difficult to track them across concrete and asphalt,' replied Chogan.

'Is there any point in calling in the rest of the team to patrol the areas ahead of us? They are just sitting around in the Transits at present, bored to death I should think,' said Preston.

'No. It's too big an area at the moment. Plus we cannot be sure that the quarry won't change tack. I don't want the vans to be too far behind though. Move them to around here.' Warren indicated an area broadly to the south of Bath. 'Tell them to sit tight and keep out of trouble. Hopefully we should be able to regroup before too much longer.' Then, to Chogan, 'We've been going at quite a pace this morning. We must be catching them up. How far ahead do you think they are?'

'They are moving at a slow pace so far but I can't be sure that they won't speed up. Assuming they don't, we should catch them around mid-morning tomorrow.'

'Excellent. Right, you guys go and get some grub. I'll report in.'
The group split up as directed.

The afternoon passed in much the same pattern. After yet more open fields, the path took the chase team right through the centre of the village of Englishcombe, again much to the surprise of Warren who thought it would have been much safer to work their way around the small cluster of buildings. Questioning of the locals had a more positive outcome here, as two teenagers recalled seeing the big paratrooper and the black policeman, but couldn't recall the others. They had passed through around lunchtime the previous day.

Shortly after leaving the village the trail took its first deviation from a straight line, turning south following the brow of some high ground. As they walked along the ridge, Preston noticed the way the land fell away quite steeply on the eastern side. His military mind reflected upon how good a defensive position this pathway was. It would have been very difficult for infantry to assault this ridge from the east, especially if the defenders were behind some form of fortification. His musings were interrupted by one of the troopers stumbling ahead of him, rolling a few yards down the steep slope. To much banter and laughter, the embarrassed trooper picked himself up and re-joined the jogging line.

Following the trail, Chogan took the group down a steep slope into a small wooded area that emerged onto a main road. Once across, the Canadian entered a built-up area, causing him to pause. As expected, the trail was much more difficult to follow through an urban environment so he trusted to luck and pressed on in the broad south-eastern direction that he had been following all day. His luck paid off as, after only a few hundred yards the path emerged onto some more fields which the trail skirted before crossing a roundabout and plunging into a steep wooded valley, marked on the map as Horsecombe Vale.

The pathway into the woodland was blocked by a stile, almost overgrown by the hawthorn hedges that bushed out on either side.

As he approached the Canadian noticed that a single, thin branch of hawthorn had been snapped by someone recently crossing over the stile. The marks on the ground convinced him that only the Old Man's group had come this way in the recent past. Closer inspection of the snapped branch indicated that it carried two or three berries, hanging by the thinnest of threads from the surrounding plant. He picked one and tossed it into his mouth, briefly chewing before spitting it out. He reached out for another berry from an undamaged part of the hedge just as Warren walked up alongside him.

'So how far do you think they are ahead of us now?'

Chogan turned, but instead of answering he fell headlong into the arms of his friend. Warren caught him and rolled him over, laying him on his back in front of the stile.

'Medic!' he screamed.

One of the group rushed to his side and, sliding off a pack containing a military medical kit, quickly carried out an initial examination.

'Well?' said Warren, 'What's happened to him?'

The medic looked up with a puzzled frown. 'I'm not sure. All his vital signs are fine. He just seems to have fallen asleep.'

'So wake him up,' replied Warren, now increasingly concerned by the look on the medic's face.

'That's the problem. I can't. He seems to have gone into some form of coma.'

Nathan looked along the track to see the Old Man striding out ahead of him. The pace had really picked up since the group had left the pub a few hours earlier. The news of the bird flu outbreak had certainly changed things, especially for Vicky. With the Old Man now in front the group had covered several miles at a speed that even Carl, with his habitual understatement, described as 'steady'.

Nathan was struggling a little but he was mainly concerned with the young doctor. She walked in silence a few paces behind him but he could see that this increased pace was quickly using up her last reserves of energy. Yet at no time did she utter anything even approaching a complaint. A steely determination seemed to have overtaken her which was driving her on, at least for the present. Nathan knew how much the journey meant to her even before, but the news of the bird flu or, more specifically, the Old Man's response to it, had galvanised her even more.

Carl could see it too and was as worried as Nathan. 'She can't keep this pace up,' he had whispered to Nathan, 'no matter how much she wants this cure. Sooner or later her system will just give up and then she won't be going nowhere until she rests awhile.'

'Problem is that I can't see the old guy slowing up. He seems very keen today.'

'Why don't you go and have a word? You never know. He might want a break himself. Meantime I'll go and help Vicky.' Carl walked back the few paces to the young doctor, reached out his hand and nodded at the rucksack on her back. Vicky, realising the help being offered, slid the pack off and passed it across. Carl swung it over his shoulder, alongside his own, and fell into step with Vicky.

Nathan walked up alongside the Old Man. Although he was moving more quickly than previous days he still continued his habit of plucking various leaves and grasses from their path, chewing them and spitting them out. He glanced at Nathan as the two drew level.

'I'm thinking it might be a good time for a few minutes` rest. Any chance?' asked Nathan, trying not to show his breathlessness.

The Old Man glanced across at Nathan and turned to look at the others, stretched out over 50 metres behind him. He immediately noticed Vicky and the evident distress that she was in. He nodded at Nathan, who swung off his pack and sat down on the side of the path, to be joined by the other three a few moments later. The Old Man did not sit with them but wandered off into a field at the side of the track.

'How far do you think we have come?' asked Vicky, of no one in particular.

'Too far for my liking,' replied Julian. 'We must have walked about 20 miles at least.'

'You really are a wimp, aren't you, Goldenballs?' replied Carl. 'OK, we are a bit quicker than yesterday, I grant you. But twenty miles, no way. Ten possibly, twelve at most.'

'So how much further then, Godzilla?'

'Not sure of the route that his nibs wants to take. He seems to be heading in a straight line eastwards. I reckon, if we keep up this pace, we should reach our destination in about five days.'

Julian groaned and looked to Vicky for support. She glanced at him for a moment before looking away, trying to hide the look of concern on her face.

As he drank from his water bottle, Nathan reflected on the route that they had taken since leaving the pub. The small road had taken them towards the River Avon, which they had crossed using a footpath over the Dundas aqueduct, named after the chairman of the company that built it according to an information board alongside the pathway.

'No mention of the poor bastards that actually got their hands dirty,' declared Carl, on reading the sign.

Nathan was about to reply but then noticed the Old Man hesitate and look over the stone wall at the river flowing several hundred feet beneath. He seemed to need to convince himself that there was no danger before trotting across the aqueduct, slowing only when he was safe on the other side.

As ever, their path had continued eastwards, taking them into some steep woodland which they struggled through until they reached another footpath that ran across them, following the north - south line of a ridge which marked the top edge of the valley cut by the River Avon aeons before. The Old Man took the north-bound direction into more woodland. Occasionally they could see through the trees down to the river in the valley below, so Nathan could see that they were following its path, albeit several hundred feet higher than the sparkling waters. They followed this northerly path for about an hour before it turned east, leaving the path of the Avon and following the high ground above another, smaller waterway that could be seen down to their left.

A short while later the group left the cover of the woods and emerged into fields again, much to the disappointment of Carl and Nathan. Both had been far more comfortable walking under the tree canopy, and the return to open ground increased their chances of being seen from the air.

The Old Man had spotted a large mound in the corner of one of the fields - something that he was evidently expecting. He used this to take a bearing slightly more to the north-east, a direction that they had been following ever since. Sometimes there was a clear pathway, other times only the slightest hint of the direction to follow but mostly nothing at all to guide them on their way. Initially Nathan was lost but after a few miles there were enough indications to convince him that he knew at least something of the route they were taking. Straight as an arrow, not changing even to go around small hills, there was only one type of route that took such a direct line. Nathan realised that the group was now walking along a Roman road.

The Old Man's return broke into Nathan's thoughts. Climbing over a low stone wall, he stepped back onto the trackway. Crouching down on his haunches he spread out several strands of grass. They all looked the same to Nathan but he was learning fast that such observations meant nothing.

Picking up the longest strand the Old Man pulled it between his thumbnail and forefinger, stripping away some seeds from the top of the plant, which fell expertly into his palm. He repeated the process with another stalk, which Nathan now noticed was a slightly deeper shade of green. However, this time it was the sticky juice from within the stalk that ended up in his palm. Finally the petals of a tiny white flower were added. Using the thumb of his other hand, he mixed his ingredients into a paste which gradually solidified as the moisture from the pulp was absorbed by the other ingredients. The Old Man continued until he had worked the mixture into a ball about two centimetres across. He glanced up at Vicky, still seated on the path, leaning against a stone wall. Her eyes were closed, making the most of her brief rest. Nathan watched as the Old Man seemed to be weighing her up in his mind. Finally he reached a decision and split the ball into three equal parts, each of which was then rolled into smaller pellets.

Standing up from his crouched position the Old Man walked across to Vicky and gently touched her shoulder. She opened her eyes and smiled at him. He lifted one of her hands and placed a pellet in the palm.

'Take this. Chew it slowly until it has melted away.' Without further comment he turned and called brusquely to the others, 'Enough rest. We leave now,' before striding out on the ancient road.

Nathan looked across at Vicky. She hesitated for a moment before putting the pellet into her mouth. He moved his glance to Carl who had also been watching the Old Man and was now looking at Vicky, his face showing concern for the young doctor.

As she chewed, Vicky's face seemed to lose the pale quality that had marked her falling energy levels. At first Nathan thought she was blushing, but the redness in her face continued until she looked almost sunburnt. The glow seemed to ebb away as fast as it had arrived, leaving her with her normal complexion. She got to her feet and seemed to shake out her legs, as if to remove some stiffness, before striding over to where Carl was sitting. Reaching down, she picked up her pack lying beside him and swung it onto her back.

'Come then, campers,' she said with a smile they had not seen for hours. 'We're not going to save the world by sitting here all day.' She turned and jogged along the trail to catch up with the Old Man.

Nathan and Carl quickly pulled on their packs and followed them, pausing only to rouse the dozing Julian, who had missed the whole incident.

Warren and Preston stumbled into the car park of the Wheelwright's Arms, carrying the unconscious body of their friend. Gratefully they handed him over to other members of the troop who had driven down in the Transits to meet them.

Once the shock of Chogan's collapse had worn off, Warren had checked the map to find a suitable rendezvous. The group medic had recommended that their fallen colleague should be taken to a medical facility as soon as possible. He made it clear that camping down at their present location and waiting for him to wake up was not an option.

'That could take days, Boss. Plus, he seems to be OK apart from being asleep but I can't be sure that there aren't other things going on inside his head. The truth is that I don't know what's happening to him. It's way outside my experience for someone to just keel over like that.'

'I hate to get all professional about this,' interjected Preston, 'but the longer he sleeps, the further away the quarry gets. We really need to get him specialist help as soon as possible.'

Warren nodded but, in truth, his concern for the Canadian's welfare had already made the decision for him. It was time to call in the might of Paternoster.

The only sensible meeting point was about a mile away, following a steep valley until it came to a village called Monkton Combe. The map showed the location of a pub, so that was identified as their meeting point. Preston put in a call to the rest of the troop to drive down and meet up with them in the pub car park.

Warren called Eriksson to explain the situation and request medical support to meet up with them at the same location. Even taking turns to carry Chogan's body, it had taken them almost 45 minutes to cover the distance along the valley floor, but he was still surprised to see the two Transit vans waiting for them, especially when the troopers within all jumped out to relieve him of his burden.

He was met at the door of the pub by the landlord. 'Mr Smith?' the landlord asked.

Warren nodded, seeing Eriksson's hand in this.

'Excellent. Nice to meet you. I have set up everything just as your head office has requested. I have set aside the largest bedroom for your injured friend and allocated the other rooms for the rest of you. Please let me show you the way.'

Turning, he went up the staircase, followed by Warren, Preston and the trooper carrying Chogan over his shoulder.

Once in the bedroom, with Chogan gently laid onto the bed, the landlord turned again to Warren. 'OK, then, Mr Smith. Here are the keys to all the rooms. Please make yourselves at home.' He then leaned forward, bringing his head closer to Warren's and dropped his voice to a conspiratorial whisper. 'Please don't think me rude, but I'm not stupid. I can see that something odd is going on here but, in view of the very generous fee that your head office have paid, I'm happy to go along with whatever you want, as per their instructions. I've sent all the other guests to alternative accommodation so you have the place to yourselves. My staff will be around to provide your team with whatever you need. My only condition, and I have said this to your boss, is that I will not be party to anything illegal. Do I have your promise that nothing like that is going on?'

Warren nodded his head and was about to reply but was interrupted by the sound of sirens coming from the road outside. He looked out of the window to see a large Audi saloon screech to a halt in the car park. This was swiftly followed by a private ambulance and yet another Transit van. A small man, smartly dressed in a business suit, jumped out of the Audi and rushed into the pub, quickly followed by two nurses from the ambulance. Warren left the bedroom and met the new group halfway down the stairs. The man in the business suit spoke first.

'I am Professor Charles Willis, head of High Dependency Medicine at Swindon University Hospital. Where is the patient?'

After a hectic few hours Warren allowed himself a moment to relax in the bar. The medical team had taken over Chogan's treatment, which seemed to have involved turning the bedroom into a private ward, complete with a small-scale laboratory with which they were testing regular blood samples. Despite all the medical technology and expertise on parade, all he could get out of the professor was that the patient was 'comfortable'. When pressed for a more comprehensive diagnosis, he would only expand the remark as far as that 'he is as well as can be expected.' Warren took this to mean that the medical team was as flummoxed as his medic had been. Still, Choggy was now in good hands and Warren was grateful for that small mercy.

The landlord brought Warren another drink as he took the opportunity to get back to the main task.

'We're looking for a group of people who might have passed this way a few hours ahead of us. I wonder if they might have come through here?'

'It's possible. This is the only pub around here. What can you tell me about them?'

'There are five of them. They're led by an old man but they also include a girl in her mid-twenties and three blokes, one posh, one black and one huge. Ring any bells?'

'To be honest, Mr Smith, my memory is not what it was, especially over the last few days. But from your description I'm sure that I'd remember a group like that.'

'So have you seen them?'

'No. Sorry. No one like that has been through here recently.'

CHAPTER 22

The Wansdyke
Sunday 26th August
10.00 a.m.

Vicky looked along the line of figures ahead of her. Although they
had been walking for several hours, she felt none of the tiredness
that had beset her earlier in their journey. The Old Man had given her
another pellet before they had set off that morning which seemed to
provide her with sufficient energy for the whole day. She now walked
at the back of the group, not out of tiredness but in order to keep
behind Julian. He was now the weakest member of the team, and
therefore the slowest. By walking behind him she tried to ensure he
wasn't left behind. She had suggested to the Old Man that he might
give a pellet to her boyfriend but he warned against it, though without
giving any reason. She was left with the impression that it was more
down to his opinion of Julian than any medicinal reason.

Yesterday they had continued until darkness fell. They had camped
on some high ground which, when she had woken that morning, had
given them spectacular views in all directions. These, plus the warm
morning sunshine, seemed to lift the spirits of the whole team. Even
the Old Man seemed less grumpy. While the rest of the team made
breakfast he had spent the time wandering around the area on which
they had camped. Evidently pleased at what he had found, he had
taken her by the hand and pointed out the large variety of plants that

seemed to cover the hill top. He had spoken at length about their properties, about how one was good for stomach cramp and another cleared up leg ulcers overnight. He also said how rare they seemed to be in this modern time, although they had been commonplace in his previous Returns.

'This is clearly a special place,' he said. 'As yet it has not been despoiled by the Others.'

'You have mentioned them before,' she replied. 'Who are these Others?' But the Old Man had just smiled before wandering off in search of more plants.

A few minutes later the group had packed up and started out on the next leg of their trek. As they started to go downhill Vicky passed a sign. It read:

'*Morgan's Hill, Chalk Downland Landscape – Site of Special Scientific Interest.*'

The path continued to run relentlessly eastwards. After following the invisible Roman road section, the Wansdyke became far more distinctive here, with the raised bank in some places as much as two metres above the base of the ditch that ran alongside. In other sections the trackway had been completely ploughed out, but the Old Man was still able to confidently follow the ancient route.

For most of the morning the trackway had taken them through open fields but as they approached midday the path took them through some woodland before emerging at the top of a gentle slope. This gradually lead them down across a small road running along the base of a valley before rising to the top of a hill beyond.

As they emerged from the wood Carl looked at his watch. 'We've been going now for about three hours. Time for a break, I reckon.' He looked towards the Old Man but got only the merest hint of a nod. Taking this as agreement, he swung the large pack off his shoulders and began to take out some drinks and army rations. The others followed his lead and, within a few minutes, they were sitting in a group enjoying both the rest and the morning sunshine. The Old Man did not join them but turned and walked back into the woodland.

Looking towards the north Nathan could see the distant buildings of a large town.

'That must be Marlborough,' he said, before realising that no one was listening.

Vicky was thinking over the events of the morning, particularly her conversation with the Old Man about the flowers. Try as she might she could not recall any of the details of the flowers and their uses. The information was presented too quickly and she had no time to take any notes. Once again she questioned why she had chosen to make this journey if there was to be no practical outcome. She also wondered if the Old Man's talents were confined to a phenomenal knowledge of plants or if he had any practical skills that she might be able to learn. Fate was to answer her question sooner than she expected.

Three hundred metres down the hill in front of the group ran one of the two main roads that entered Marlborough from the south. On that road there was a bus stop at which a mother and her two small children were waiting to go on their weekly trip to the local swimming pool. The mother, standing at one end of the steel and glass structure, looked at her watch. The bus was slightly late and she was worried that they might miss the starting time for her son's swimming lesson. She glanced back into the bus shelter to see Adam, aged five, steal his sister's rolled-up towel. Emily, aged seven, immediately gave out a loud shriek.

'Mum, tell Adam to give me my towel back!'

'Adam! Behave,' replied the woman, in the tone used by mothers everywhere. With a giggling reluctance the boy returned the towel.

They were getting bored, she thought. As the wife of a local farmer she was familiar with the problems of rural transport. Normally she would have used her own car but it had broken down the previous day. Nor was her husband's Land Rover available, as he said he needed it for some unspecified purpose. As she watched her two children begin to bicker again she hoped that his unspecified purpose was worth it.

Looking up, she saw two horses, side by side, trotting along the road past the bus stop. She recognised the riders as friends, the wife and daughter of another farmer.

'Hi, Pam,' called out the older of the riders. 'Off swimming?'

'It's Adam's last lesson. He gets his certificate today.'

'Well done, Adam,' said the rider. Adam smiled back, his pride at his achievement evident.

'I got my certificate last year,' called out Emily, not wishing to be outdone by her younger brother.

'Then well done to you, too,' replied the rider. 'Must go. Got to sort out the lunch. Bye.'

The mother waved goodbye as the riders trotted past.

Half a mile to the north a girl in her late teens was driving her BMW Mini southwards, back to her home in Pewsey.

God, what a party that was, she thought, as she revved the engine on her new car, making it move even faster along the quiet country road. What a state they had all been in. Absolutely legless by the time they all fell asleep. She woke up feeling dreadful but it had been worth it. It had been the best party she had attended for ages, at least the parts that she could remember. All she wanted to do now was to get home as soon as possible. Her parents were away for an overnight stay in London and if she could get back before they did, things would be so much easier.

The car came out of a slow corner and moved onto a long straight, giving the girl the chance to accelerate further. In the distance, towards the end of the straight, she could see a large milk tanker. If she got stuck behind that she knew there wouldn't be another chance to overtake for ages. Gunning the engine still harder, she tore down the road, hoping that she could pass the tanker before the slow left-hand bend that was at the end of the straight. She was beginning to think she was not going to get past when she saw the red brake lights at the back of the tanker light up. He's slowing down, she thought, I can just about make it. The Mini reached the back of the tanker just as it was entering the bend. The girl moved out to overtake only to realise that, due to the curve in the road, she could no longer see more than a few yards ahead. An instant later she saw two horse riders right in front of her and the girl panicked. There was no way that she could avoid them. She was going to hit them! The tanker driver, seeing the problem unfold, applied all the braking power that his vehicle could muster. Thanks to his efforts the tanker slowed astonishingly quickly, giving the girl a moment's hope as a gap appeared in front of the tanker. Desperately she swerved into the space but it opened too slowly to take the full length of the Mini. Her back wing clipped the front corner of the tanker, sending the small car into an uncontrollable spin. Now utterly helpless, the girl watched as the car narrowly missed the riders, giving her a second's relief before she realised that her car was spinning towards a bus stop. Her last memory was of the look of terror on the face of a woman as the car ploughed into her and her children.

At the top of the hill the sounds of the braking tyres made Vicky, Nathan, Carl and Julian look up. A second later the shrill sounds of a child screaming had them all on their feet rushing down towards the road. Halfway down the steep slope they were overtaken by the Old Man. He had emerged from the wood and was now bounding past the others with a confidence that seemed to ignore the heavily ploughed ground beneath their feet. After vaulting the field gate with an athleticism that belied his years, he paused on the road to take in the full horror of the scene that confronted him.

The Mini had struck the bus shelter full on, stopping only when the earth bank behind had absorbed its terrible momentum. Underneath the car the Old Man could see the legs of a woman, clearly pinned down. They were worryingly still. Alongside her a small boy lay on the roadway. He was barely conscious but sobbed quietly, rubbing his right leg which the Old Man could see was severely broken. The Mini must have struck him a glancing blow that threw him outside the main crash area but resulted in a fracture that folded his leg out to the side, horribly bent about the point of impact, a hand's width above the knee. The screams were coming from a second child, a girl slightly older than the boy. She appeared uninjured but was suffering from the shock of the unfolding nightmare. She ran wildly around the crash scene, desperately seeking help from any source. Seeing the Old Man she rushed towards him.

'Mummy's under the car! Get her out! Quickly, get her out!' she shouted. The Old Man placed his hand on the girl's shoulder, a movement which she saw as an unnecessary delay. 'Please, get her out! Please do it now!'

'Fear not, little one. Your mother will be fine. But you need to rest now.'

'No! No! Get my Mummy out! You must do it now!' As she spoke she turned towards the crash scene and so did not see the Old Man squeeze a seam of the old pouch hanging from his belt. Reaching across he smeared something on the skin beneath her nose. Instantly the little girl crumpled and fell into the Old Man's arms. Looking beyond the crash scene he saw two women holding horses. Approaching them, he laid the girl at the feet of the older one.

'She sleeps! See to her comfort!'

The woman, at first surprised by the authoritative tone, quickly realised the importance of the request. Taking off her coat she wrapped it around the sleeping child, nodding to the Old Man as she did so.

By this time the others had reached the scene of the crash. Nathan and Carl had vaulted the gate in the manner of the Old Man and so arrived slightly ahead of the other two, who had climbed over in a slower but safer fashion.

'Has anyone called the ambulance?' Nathan called to the two riders.

'I'm just doing it now.' A man's voice came from within the cab of the large wagon that had jack-knifed across the road in a desperate attempt to stop and now blocked the approach of any other traffic.

Having seen to the young girl, the Old Man approached his companions and issued them with instructions in a manner that demanded no query or debate.

'Nathan. I have need of eddswort. Return to the gate. Take a stride beyond the far gatepost and you will see a small yellow flower on a long stem. Dig beneath down to its roots, which are bright orange. Collect as much as you can and bring it to me.'

'What if there is none there?' replied Nathan, anxious to help but not wanting to waste time.

'Tis there. I can smell it. Delay me no more. Go!' As Nathan ran off the Old Man turned to Carl. 'Cyric, we need to move the Rover cart. Will your strength suffice?'

Confused by the strange name but quickly realising his task, Carl nodded and ran over to the crash scene.

The Old Man then turned to Vicky. 'This day we shall test your skills, Physic. Come.'

As they moved towards the Mini Julian realised that he had not been given a task. 'What should I do?'

The Old Man paused for a second. 'Get me some honey,' he replied.

'Honey?'

'It is from bees!'

'I know what it is but where am I going to get any around here?'

No answer came as Vicky and the Old Man rushed towards the bus shelter.

Initially Vicky moved towards the Mini, glancing through the shattered windscreen towards the driver. She saw a young girl, probably not yet 20, lying very still in the front seat, her head tilted to the side at an unnatural angle.

'She is lost,' said the Old Man, seeing the direction that Vicky was looking. 'We must treat those that might yet see tomorrow.'

'How can you possibly know that?' replied Vicky, shocked by his callous words. More in defiance than anything else, Vicky leaned into the car to feel for a pulse in the girl's neck. There was none. The Old Man was right.

Carl had managed to insert himself between the car and the grass bank behind the shelter. After a moment to steady himself he gripped the front of the car and pushed, giving out a great roar as he did so. Slowly at first but with gradually increasing speed, the car began to move. A second later it had been rolled back across the road, well outside the crash area, to reveal the children's mother.

The Old Man knelt down beside her. His initial examination of her unconscious form told him that most of her injuries were serious but not life threatening. Mostly bruises with the possibility of some small-scale fractures. However, as he brushed her hair from her forehead he saw something far more worrying. She must have been thrown backwards by the force of the impact, causing her head to whip backwards. Her temple had struck the metal frame of the bus shelter, resulting in a massive indentation to her forehead.

Vicky saw the injury a moment later. The dent was so large that it could contain a golf ball without touching the sides. The damage to the brain must be massive. Vicky knew that, although alive now, the woman could not survive for long. Her training kicked in and she turned to help the boy, some yards to her right.

The Old Man remained at the woman's side. Looking up, he spoke to Vicky. 'You wish to leave her? Can you give her no aid at all?' Without waiting for an answer he looked down the road towards the gate. 'Nathan, I have urgent need of that root. Bring whatever you have found at once.'

Nathan had managed to dig up a handful of the root, located exactly where the Old Man had told him to look. Holding the fibrous tubers in his palms he rushed over to the Old Man, who examined the roots and selected two of the thickest which he handed to Vicky.

'Chew these.'

'What!' said the young doctor, unsure of what she had heard.

'You wish to learn my ways? Your apprenticeship starts here. Chew these!'

Vicky accepted the roots offered by the Old Man. She brushed off the worst of the soil clinging to them before reluctantly placing them in her mouth and began to chew.

'Make haste,' shouted the Old Man, 'This woman's life is ebbing away.'

Vicky chewed for a couple of seconds. The roots tasted sour but not unpleasant as they quickly pulped down into a paste in her mouth. The Old Man held out a hand and gestured that he wanted Vicky to spit the paste into his palm.

'Move to her head,' said the Old Man. As she did so the Old Man moved to the woman's side. With his free hand he pulled up the woman's jumper and tore open the blouse underneath. Finally he lifted up her bra, exposing her left breast.

'What are you doing to her?' The angry voice came from the elder of the two riders, who had been watching from several yards away, alongside the sleeping form of the daughter. She quickly got to her feet and rushed across to the Old Man. 'Get away from her, you pervert. She needs a doctor, not some sicko!'

Vicky had also been shocked by the Old Man's actions but tried to calm the elderly rider. 'It's OK. I'm a doctor. `

As Vicky spoke the rider glanced away from the Old Man for a split second, long enough for him to touch the edge of his pouch once again and pinch his assailant under the nose. As with the young girl a few moments previously, the woman dropped like a stone.

'Carl, get this harridan away from me that I might work.' A moment later the elderly rider was lying alongside the young girl. The younger rider, having seen what had happened to her companion, chose to stay with the sleeping pair and make no further comment on the unfolding events.

The Old Man returned to the injured mother. Cupping the breast in his hand he smeared the pulp across the nipple, carefully rubbing it into the dark flesh. Once complete, he spoke to the increasingly stunned Vicky.

'Hold your hand over the head wound. You will feel the skin rise. You must allow this movement until the hollow is full. Then you must oppose it. Her life will depend on you ensuring the head does not burst.'

Though confused, Vicky did as she was told, placing her palm across the awful depression in the woman's skull. Once ready, she nodded at the Old Man.

At her signal he placed the forefinger of one hand alongside the woman's windpipe and pressed down firmly. With his other hand he reached up and pinched the woman's earlobe hard. Vicky felt the woman's body flinch with pain before relaxing into her previous position.

At first Vicky could feel no change but then slowly she felt the wound grow hot under her palm. A second later she felt the skin within the depression begin to move, slowly expanding to fill up the terrible wound. It was as if the pressure of the woman's brain had increased and was now pushing the damaged skull back into place. The speed of the expansion increased. Vicky could feel the damaged bones of the skull grating against each other as they returned to their former shape. It took only a few moments for the depression to be filled but Vicky could feel the pressure keep building. Suddenly she realised what the Old Man wanted. If she didn't hold the rising skin back the weakened skull would burst. She placed her other hand over the first to try and maintain the shape of the woman's forehead.

The Old Man noticed her movement. 'Is the skull now as it should be?'

Vicky nodded.

'Then you must hold on for an instant more. The bones must set before you can stop.'

Just as Vicky became convinced that she could not hold the bones back any longer she felt the pressure begin to fall. Looking across at the Old Man she saw that he was gradually easing the pressure that his finger was applying to the woman's throat. This pressure seemed to be controlling the whole treatment. After another few seconds he removed his finger and sat up.

'Cease. She will live. Now for the boy.'

Tentatively Vicky lifted her hand and glanced down at the woman's forehead. An angry red colouration was the only sign that there had been any injury. The young doctor reached down and replaced the mother's clothes. The Old Man gestured to Carl to move their patient to the roadside, alongside the other two sleeping forms.

Julian had spent the last few moments trying to understand the request made of him. Where was he supposed to get any honey out here? Tentatively he approached the lorry driver and younger rider, now tending to the three patients lying on the road.

'Excuse me, sorry to bother you at a time like this, but ...' he hesitated as he knew how this was going to sound, ' but I don't suppose that you have any honey, do you?'

The two looked at each other in confusion and then back towards Julian.

As the driver spoke, Julian could feel the irritation in his voice. 'What? Honey? No, we don't. Even if we did I'm not sure that honey is quite the top of our agenda just at the moment.'

'Of course. I quite understand. Sorry to have bothered you.' Julian could feel his embarrassment as he spoke the words. He wandered back towards the crashed car. What could the Old Man possibly want with honey? He must have known that there was none to be found around here. Then another thought occurred. Perhaps this was just a way of keeping him occupied, out of the way whilst the others did their thing. Annoyed, he approached the Old Man, who was now crouching over the boy.

'I'm afraid that there is no honey. No one seems to have any.'

The Old Man threw up his head and shouted at the heavens in frustration.

'Ahhhh! Why are you so useless? How can you possibly have forgotten so much? I told you. You get honey from bees. There are two bees` nests within your sight. One is over there ...' the Old Man gestured towards the hedgerow alongside the field gate, 'and the other is in that tree.' Again he gestured but his time to a large conifer behind the lorry. 'Any plain fool can smell them but you are clearly a special type of fool. Now, get me that honey and do so in haste!'

Suitably chastised, Julian ran over to the field gate, while the Old Man turned his attention to the boy. This time both Vicky and Nathan crouched alongside him, making full use of the space alongside but only for a second. Nathan had thought that he would be able to cope with this situation. In his short time with the police he had attended many road accidents and had seen some terrible injuries. However, when he saw the break in the boy's leg, the way that it lay, unnaturally, out to the side, Nathan could feel the contents of his stomach start to rise. Jumping to his feet he rushed to the other side of the road, arriving just in time for a fountain of vomit to erupt, spraying across the hedgerow. He knew that he could play no further useful role and so stayed back.

Meanwhile the Old Man had sized up his new patient and called out to Carl.

'I have need of that knife.'

Since buying the expensive blade, Carl had spent much of the time sharpening the cutting edge using a steel that was located inside the handle. He was proud of how sharp he had made it in such a short time. He jogged across from the car and handed it to the Old Man.

On receiving the blade the Old Man carefully examined the edge before he shook his head and handed it back to Carl. Getting to his feet he wandered past the ex-para and began to search around the crash scene. The impact of the car had damaged the grass bank immediately behind the bus shelter, tearing away the top few inches of turf to reveal the soil beneath. The Old Man carefully examined the surface of the bank before selecting two small stones. The first was a dark grey colour, smooth but with several irregular edges across the surface. The second was jet black and totally rounded, almost like a pebble. As he got to his feet he also picked two plants, a tiny blue flower and a type of grass. Returning to the boy, he handed the plants to Vicky. 'Hold these between your cupped palms. Be ready to crush them when I say.'

This time Vicky did exactly what she was told. She had learned enough that morning not to question his instructions.

The Old Man placed both hands on the boy's chest and pressed down hard, forcing the breath from his body and preventing any further breathing. He held that position for a few seconds until the boy started to show signs of discomfort.

'Crush the plants now but hold them sound within your palms. Let not the vapour escape.'

Vicky ground her hands together. She was becoming increasingly worried about the boy, who was now showing clear signs of distress under the crushing weight of the Old Man's hands.

'Now place your hands above his mouth. Do not release the vapour until I say.'

Again Vicky did as she was told. Once she was in position the Old Man suddenly lifted his hands. The boy heaved a single, deep breath.

'Now,' shouted the Old Man, 'open your hands.'

As she did so Vicky noticed a faint, grey mist emerge from her cupped palms. She could only see it for a second before it was drawn into the boy's lungs by his deep, heavy panting. Vicky started to move her hands to her face, keen to smell the vapour that she had created, but the Old Man stopped her.

'Best not, at least for a few moments,' he said, before turning his attention to the stones. Holding the edged one in the flat of one hand he picked up the pebble. After a moment of careful study he struck the pebble against one of the edges on the other stone. A thin flake broke off and fell into the Old Man's lap. He repeated the process several times, resulting in a small mound of the flakes, each no larger than a thumbnail. Discarding both stones, he carefully scooped up the flakes and dropped them into the palm of Vicky's hand.

Vicky looked at the flakes carefully. Watching the Old Man create them she had realised at once what he was doing. She had seen similar flint pieces, as she now knew them to be, in museums, but never as thin and delicate as these. Holding one up to the light she could see that it was translucent, the light showing through the grainy structure of the stone. She dropped it back into her palm only to see that it became embedded in the skin of her palm. Carefully she pulled it out. The cut was not deep enough to cause any bleeding but it had left a visible mark.

'Have a care, Physic!' The Old Man was clearly angered by Vicky's actions. He gently retrieved the flint flakes, selected the one that had become embedded and threw it away. Reaching into his pouch with his free hand he withdrew a handful of seeds, all of differing colours, shapes and sizes. 'Take out the almert and the knoisa and grind them into a dust.' Vicky's face reminded the Old Man of her limitations. 'The large grey ones and the narrow black ones. Swiftly now!'

Vicky picked out the seeds that the Old Man had described. Once she had a handful of both, the Old Man withdrew his hand and placed the remaining seeds back into the pouch. He then gestured to her to put her palms together and crush the dried seeds. Once she had begun this process he turned his attention to the boy.

Carefully placing the flint flakes on the grass he reached across to the boy's dreadfully deformed leg. Firmly gripping the point of the break with one hand he grasped the ankle with the other. With a single, strong, fluid movement he pulled the leg back into a straight position. The boy, semi-conscious until this point, screamed with the dreadful pain that the movement must have caused. As with his sister, the Old Man wiped a finger across the boy's top lip and he fell into a deep sleep.

'Why didn't you do that before you straightened his leg? You must have known that it was going to hurt?' Vicky asked.

'Not now, Vicky. Lessons must be for later. Just make sure that you have that dust when I have need of it.'

The Old Man now examined the boy's leg. As the boy was wearing shorts there was no need to cut away any clothing so he could clearly see the boy's skin. He carefully studied the surface, seeking the muscle structure that he knew lay beneath. After a moment's reflection he picked up one of the flint flakes and ran it gently down the front of the boy's thigh. The movement seemed to involve no cutting pressure but Vicky was astonished to see how the flesh just seemed to fall away under the flint edge, parting to reveal the damaged bone underneath. She noticed that the Old Man's cut had avoided all the significant blood vessels but she knew that such a major incision would still cause heavy bleeding. As she watched the blood start to flow into the open wound she was considering how the boy would survive without any transfusion facilities, when the Old Man shouted to her.

'Now, Vicky! Quickly! Blow the dust across his leg!'

Once again, she did as she was told without question. Cupping her hands, she gently blew the dust from the crushed seeds across the open wound. At his direction she ensured that all areas of the incision became coated with the fine, grey and black powder.

Once her palms were empty she sat back and watched. As the powder alighted on the spurting blood she heard a sizzling noise. A moment later the awful smell of burning flesh engulfed her, making her stomach heave. Fortunately she was able to hold back the wave of vomit that surged into her throat. When she was able she looked back into the wound to see that all bleeding had stopped, revealing the terrible damage that the thigh bone had suffered.

The boy's age had been an advantage to him. His young bones were still quite flexible so the damage was not a clean break but rather a severe 'greenstick' fracture. It was like someone had tried to snap a tree branch only to cause all the fibres to severely bend but not break. The straightening of the leg had realigned these fibres but the damage was still severe. Vicky could see that they might be able to save his leg from amputation but it would never again be a fully functioning limb.

As Vicky had carried out her examination, the Old Man had stood up and walked across to the crashed car and peered into it. A moment later he called to Carl and Nathan.

'I have need of the corpse. Take it out and lay it over by the boy.'

Both men hesitated for a second, worried as much about what he was asking as about what he was going to do with the girl's body. The Old Man saw their hesitation. 'Spare me your opinions and do as I say. Now!'

Both men and ran across to the Mini. After a few moments they managed to pull the corpse through the car windscreen and place it where the Old Man had indicated. He rolled the body over onto her front. Picking up another flint he moved towards the calf area of her left leg and cut through the nylon covering. Discarding the flint, he selected another with which he made two incisions across the leg, one above the ankle, the other some nine inches higher. A third, this time along the length of the leg, linked the first two cuts. Peeling back the skin he exposed a length of tendon. A further series of cuts detached tough, white flesh from the underlying muscle and bone. The Old Man lifted the object of this macabre surgery from the corpse and returned to the boy.

'What are you doing?' This time it was the turn of the lorry driver to shout out. 'You can't chop her up like some piece of offal. That's a human being you're dealing with!' He rushed across towards where Vicky and the Old Man were working. Nathan and Carl both stepped across his path, effectively blocking him from reaching his target.

'He knows what he's doing,' said Nathan, although he was just as horrified as the lorry driver. 'Please just let him finish and we'll talk about it afterwards.'

'I'm not standing by and watching this butchery.' The lorry driver was not going to be placated. Seeing that he was not going to succeed by persuasion, Nathan nodded to Carl.

The huge soldier grabbed the driver by the lapels and lifted him off the ground. Like Nathan, he had major doubts about what was unfolding but he also had a profound feeling that what was happening was best for the boy. Trusting his instinct, he pulled the lorry driver towards him.

'Look, mate. As I see it there are two ways forward here. The first is that you calm down, and go back over there. Then tomorrow, if you ain't happy, you can write to your MP. Second way is that I give you a little slap, then you calm down and go back over there. As with the first choice you can still write to your MP, only this time you'll do it with a bent nose. Which is it to be?'

The driver, shocked by the fearsome threat, returned to the younger rider. The two continued to mutter between themselves but kept away from the unfolding operation.

Throughout this confrontation the Old Man had continued to work. Vicky was horrified and fascinated in equal measure at the surgery that was being undertaken.

'What are you doing?' she whispered to him, not wishing to exacerbate the situation with the lorry driver. 'We don't do this sort of thing without the permission of the donor.'

'What is a donor?' the Old Man replied, looking up briefly.

'Well, in this case, her.' Vicky nodded towards the corpse lying in the road alongside her.

'She is beyond any debate. Besides, was she not the cause of all this?' The Old Man took Vicky's silence as confirmation of his point and so continued with his angry response. 'Surely you can smell the problem. She reeks of it. What is it called in these times? Mead, Ale, Wine? It goes by so many names but always brings the same sadness and grief. The only difference here is that she was riding in her Rover cart, which has made the whole problem many times worse. So tell me, Physic, which of your modern ways gave permission for this child to be crippled? Or his mother to be killed? Spare me your sermons until your words have more balance.'

He returned to the piece of tendon that he had taken from the corpse. Another few cuts with a fresh flint produced a series of thin strips. Reaching into the wound he fed each strip around the back of the fracture before bringing the ends together. Pulling each of them tightly around the bone, he tied them into small knots, cutting off any surplus length of tendon as he went.

'Honey! I have need of the honey now.'

Julian could be seen alongside the field gate, trying to reach into the hedgerow. Each attempt was repelled by the surge of angry bees that forced him back. His efforts became more and more desperate, especially when he heard the Old Man call out.

'I'm trying, but these bees keep stinging me!'

The answer clearly exasperated the Old Man who jumped to his feet and ran over to the gate.

'Why am I travelling with such an ignorant moron? Why are you so useless at carrying out even the simplest of tasks?'

As he ran he reached down and grabbed a handful of broadleaf plants that he rubbed over both of his hands. He plunged his arm into the hedgerow and withdrew a large handful of the bees' nest. As he ran back he removed as much of the outer covering as he could, favouring the honeycomb and the honey within. Once back with the boy he smeared the mixture, still including bits of nest, leaves and twigs, across the open surfaces of the wound. He then placed his hands on either side of the boy's thigh and forced the open edges of the wound together, holding them in this position for a few moments.

'Vicky, cut me some strips from that fabric,' nodding towards the boy's towel roll lying beside him. Again Vicky did as she was instructed, using the last of the flint tools. The Old Man took the strips and wound them around the boy's leg, tying them to provide a final support for the now closed wound. As he worked Vicky was surprised at how quickly the skin had knitted together. It was as if the combination of the honey and the dust that she had blown on earlier provided some form of glue that bonded the cut surfaces. The towelling strips almost seemed an unnecessary addition but, again, she chose to remain silent.

Once he had finished, the Old Man stood up and stretched.

'Our work is done here. Let us move on.' He looked around for a space in the hedgerow on the opposite side of the road to the gate and, having found one, plunged through.

In the distance Nathan could hear the ringing sound of an ambulance. He reckoned that it would be here in just a few minutes. 'Sounds like we'll have company soon. I suspect that none of us want to have to explain any of this morning's work?' He looked around and saw only agreement.

Pausing only to pick up their packs, they all followed the Old Man through the hedgerow and into the fields beyond.

CHAPTER 23

Edward Rylands' Flat,
Bristol
Sunday 26th August
10.30 a.m.

Rylands woke abruptly after an unsettled night. It was always the same when he was stalled on an investigation. Somehow the frustration seemed to worm into his head, making relaxation impossible. His mind had been buzzing for hours until the dawn light had granted him some fitful sleep. He knew that any more time in bed would be pointless so he got up and wandered into his kitchen to make some coffee.

It was just so galling. All his leads had come either to an end or to a point where he was waiting on others. Once again, he considered his lines of enquiry, reviewing each to see if he had missed anything.

Firstly, his police contact. It had been expensive but Rylands considered it to be money well spent, looking across at the photograph of the Old Man pinned above his desk in the open-plan living space. He was sure that the holiday fund given to the young PC would be spent quickly, leaving open the possibility of getting another call but only if he had any useful information. So, no call could only mean no news.

Then there was the hospital. The consultant was a definite no-go area. His reaction suggested that he knew more than he was saying but, Rylands knew, any further probing along that line would risk him being dragged into the public arena, probably with a formal complaint. Rylands had no worries about such a step – indeed many of his most successful programmes had used complaints as part of the publicity – but it was too soon in this case. He needed more to go on before he trod on the toes of the senior medical fraternity. The Ward Sister might prove a more fruitful avenue. Coffee in hand he walked across to his desk and made a note to remind himself.

He was sure that the technician had no more to give him. Rather limited in imagination, Rylands thought, he hadn't even considered the possibility of the equipment being suspect in some way. Another significant investment, but it had led him to Paternoster.

And finally, his friend in the financial sector. Tom was a strange character, living within an even stranger world. Of all the areas Rylands had tried to infiltrate, the world of finance was the most opaque. He was not sure if it was the vast quantities of money involved or the immense power that went with it. They were all tightly knit, happy to feed off each other's information but a closed book to outsiders like Rylands. Fortunately Tom was an insider, a former banker with the sort of contacts that other journalists would die for. A quiet word here, a traded titbit there, and suddenly doors opened to reveal a key piece of the jigsaw, before slammed shut once again. Rylands had worked with Tom many times since that first story about the senior politician with too many shares in too many companies that were getting too many government contracts. Enough time for Rylands to trust him, at least as far as the term stretched within the world of investigative journalism.

In a vain attempt to distract his mind into other areas, Rylands collapsed into a large armchair and pressed the button on the remote that brought the TV to life. He flipped through the many channels until he found one devoted to news. Distractedly, he watched the screen which showed a woman reporter doing a piece to camera. Behind her,

Rylands recognised the shape of one of the larger Bristol hospitals. Along the bottom of the screen ran a moving red banner bearing the message 'Breaking News – Bird Flu, Child Death'.

'.... *Doctors confirmed that the girl, who has not been named, died of respiratory failure at 03.00 hours this morning. She was one of the group taken in yesterday for observation following the death of two council workers from a local park. The hospital spokesman also stated that the results of tests are still awaited and so it is too soon to link her death with those of the two park keepers. It is still quite likely that her death was as a result of a pre-existing condition. The status of the other children ...'*

Rylands considered the news for a moment. He wondered if it was too late to buy some shares in the pharmaceutical sector. Walking back to his desk, he was making a second note on his pad when his mobile phone rang. The small screen gave him the news that he had been waiting for.

'Tom. Great to hear from you, and on a Sunday too. I am doubly honoured.'

'Spare me the flannel, Eddie. I know you from old, remember.'

'OK, niceties spurned. Talk to me about Paternoster. What have you got?'

'Well, on the one hand, very little but, on the other, a great deal.'

It was Rylands' turn to cut things short. 'Oh, for God's sake, Tom. Don't go all mysterious on me.'

'Sorry, Ed, but this one has been a real puzzler. How did you come across them?'

'They cropped up in the course of one of my investigations.' Rylands rattled off the old line. 'Come on, Tom, you know the drill. No names, no lawsuits.'

'You misunderstand me, Eddie. I'm not trying to muscle in on your story. Quite the opposite. What little I've been able to find out about them suggests that you should leave well alone.'

'Go on,' said Rylands, surprised by the caution in his friend's words. If this outfit has managed to put the wind up such a hard-bitten journo, then there must be quite a tale to tell.

'OK then, first the official stuff. Paternoster are a Private Unlimited Company, totally owned by the Eriksson family. This limits the amount of information that they have to put into the public domain. So very little by way of accounts, profit statements and suchlike is available to the likes of you and me. I checked with Companies House and found out that the current head is a John Eriksson but he is only the latest in a long line of Erikssons, stretching way back.'

'How far?'

'Well, the records go back as far as the middle 1800s when the law on company registrations was passed by Parliament. Paternoster seems to have been one of the first on the list, and the guy that signed the paper was one Ranulf Eriksson.'

'So he started it?'

'Hard to say. It seems to have been a very big operation, even then. I suspect that they had been going for some considerable time prior to then.'

'How big were they? In fact, how big are they now?' Rylands was anxious not to turn the call into a history lesson.

'That's the problem. The figures just aren't available. They have no legal requirement to publish them. It's just impossible for an ordinary member of the public to obtain that kind of information.'

'Fortunate, then, that you are not ordinary.'

'Well, that's where the unofficial stuff starts.'

'I knew I could rely on you, Tom. So which school chum did you call?'

'As you said earlier, Eddie, no names, no lawsuits. Sufficient to say that I do have a good contact within our friends in Her Majesty's Revenue and Customs. Being private doesn't get them out of paying taxes so that gives us another line to follow.'

'And your little playmate said ....'

'Eddie, they are huge. I expected any such private company to be little more than a family club, trying to dodge death duties or some such scam, but not this outfit. My contact followed lead after lead after lead. Every time he turned over a stone, expecting to reach the end, he just found another stone. They seem to have started in land acquisitions, which is still the largest part of their portfolio. They own land all over the country. Towns, cities, countryside – everything. You would be amazed at the list of property that they have, all of which is rented out at favourable rates on long-term leases and always through several layers of bureaucracy to keep things quiet. They seem to own most of the Peak District, for example. The rental income from this part of the business alone would put them in the FTSE 100 if they were a public limited company – which, of course, they're not.'

'You said that they started in land holdings. What else do they cover?'

'Well, when you have that much money you don't stick it in a piggy bank and put it under the bed. You diversify, and that is what they did. Boy, did they diversify. The range of organisations is staggering. Manufacturing, transport (road, rail and air), IT – the list just goes on and on. At one stage they toyed with some form of private detective agency, which turned into the largest non-governmental type of outfit in the UK. One spin-off of this agency is an outfit which is the world leader in DNA testing equipment, which is how your paths crossed. Another spin-off is what they call 'Security Support' but what seems to me to be a private army full of former paratroopers and suchlike. I shudder to think what they get up to.'

'So what's the bottom line? How big are they?'

'Well, that's why I am calling you now. Last time I spoke with him, my contact hadn't found the bottom line. He was still digging but he had already turned up enough to make them larger than a South American dictatorship.'

'OK, thanks for the info so far. Tell him to keep digging and call me again when you have the full picture.'

'No can do, Eddie. I've lost touch with him. He's not returning calls. He didn't show at a meeting we had set up yesterday. None of my other contacts have spoken to him. He seems to have vanished.'

'So now you're spooked and you're warning me to back off?'

'Look, Eddie, I know this sort of thing might happen all the time to you but it's not common in the world that I inhabit. All I know is that I started to ask questions about a massive organisation that is trying very hard to stay secret. How about this? I heard from another source that the Head of Paternoster Public Relations used to work for MI6. I thought that was a joke until my contact in HMRC disappears. I recall you saying that you didn't believe in coincidences. Well, neither do I. Anyway, I think I have found all that I'm going to about this outfit. So I think it best all round if I wish you good fortune and exit stage left on this one.'

'I quite understand, Tom. Thanks for the information and the warning.'

'Any chance that you'll take my advice and stop?'

'Not a hope in hell. Regards to the wife and kids.'

Rylands watched as the mobile phone screen went blank. Clearly Paternoster was far bigger than he thought and was quite determined to keep that size a secret. What other secrets, he wondered, were hiding behind that first one? It was a strange thing about him and secrets. Almost like a moth to a flame, he just couldn't help himself when it came to chasing them. So far he hadn't been scorched too badly but he also knew the fate that awaited most moths. Perhaps this was the flame which would burn him up. He was grateful when the arrival of a text broke this rather gloomy train of thought. It was from Alan Bradley, his contact from the police station. He smiled as he read the message:

Urite uncle Ed?
Fanks for the crackin holz, it was fab.
Iv got sum pics ready dat Ino yud luv 2 c.
Mayb Sundy lunch at our fave restaurant? C u @ 2?
Luv
Al

Rylands smiled at the inept subterfuge. One dodgy meeting with a journalist and everyone thinks they're James Bond. Still, a door that was closed had now opened again. He was whistling by the time he reached the shower.

—⚭—

Vicky glanced at her watch. The group had been walking for two hours since leaving the scene of the car accident. Desperate to quiz the Old Man about what she had seen, and participated in, she had tried and failed to draw him into conversation. All her efforts had been ignored with, at best, a wave of his hand or, at worst, snubbed completely. Finally, her patience ran out. She stepped in front of the Old Man, placed her hands on his shoulders and shouted.

'Enough of these games! I must know what happened back there. You will tell me now, this instant, or I will drop out of this pantomime.'

Her words seemed to draw the Old Man out of his reverie. Reluctantly he looked into her eyes, drew in a long breath, and spoke. 'What do you wish to know?'

Vicky was surprised. She had expected an argument rather than acquiescence, but took her chance anyway. 'Let's start with the mother.'

'Go on.'

'Well, what did you do? What did I do? What will happen to her?'

The Old Man grimaced. Always questions. He knew that there would be no end to them. Nothing he could say would ever stop them, only lead on to more. Yet he could see that Vicky had reached the end of her patience and she had proved to be useful at the scene of the accident. He knew that he would miss her if she chose to leave so he started to answer.

'The root was eddswort. It makes the heart pound more strongly, too strongly if given frequently. I needed you to chew it to a pulp as it only works on a woman if another woman has prepared it. In the same fashion, if the victim is a man, only a man can provide the pulp.'

'Why is that?' Vicky sensed that the Old Man had finally decided to open up, and she was keen to get as much information as possible.

In answer the Old Man closed his eyes, trying to control his temper. He answered as a teacher would speak to a small child.

'The 'why' is not important. Nature has made it so and I am simply applying her gifts.'

Vicky sensed her opportunity was passing and so chose to change tack. 'Why did you apply it through her nipple?'

The Old Man seemed happier with this question.

'It is close to her heart. Any other entry place would have taken too long to raise the pace of her beat.'

Vicky could see the logic of the answer. She pressed on. 'Why did you pinch her ear? I remember you did the same to Carl in the police cell.'

'Pain shocks the body. I needed that shock to boost the treatment's potency.'

Again, Vicky could see the sense of the answer. 'So the heart drug boosted her blood pressure, causing the brain to swell and push out the damage to the skull,' she said, more to herself than to the Old Man, 'and you pressed down on her throat to control that pressure until the surge abated.' She looked up at the Old Man for agreement.

'What is 'pressure'?' he replied.

Vicky chose to play him at his own game and ignored the question. She moved on to the second patient. 'Talk me through your treatment of the boy.'

The Old Man shrugged, 'Twas simple enough. The vapour that he breathed in lowered his heart's pounding. I made him draw it deeply by pressing on his chest. The crushed almert and knoisa burns the flowing blood, stopping the bleed for a short time. The honey binds the cut flesh and stops the wound from rotting.'

'You chose to tie up the thigh bone with the tendons from the driver.'

The Old Man looked puzzled. 'What would you have done in my stead?'

'I wouldn't have cut into the leg. I would have straightened it as you did, but then splinted it from the outside, binding it with sticks.'

The Old Man nodded. 'That was the Roman way. It works after a fashion but it takes weeks and the bone never fully heals. There is always a weakness at the point of the break. The boy would have walked with a limp for the rest of his days.'

'So where did you learn your way?'

'It was the way of the Celts. The binding of the bone is complete after a few days as the lashings – the tendons I think you called them - draw the broken surfaces tighter as they dry out, until finally they snap and are broken down by the mixture of honey and blood that flushes them away.'

'If it was so much better why didn't the Romans do things that way?'

'They shared your concerns with the use of the bodies of the dead. I never understood it. They were happy to maim and slaughter while the person was alive but not to use the corpse to cure others. A mystery to me.'

By this time Julian had walked up beside the pair. He had heard most of what they said but had seen little of the treatment process due to his fruitless search for honey. As sceptical as ever, he waded into the conversation. 'So you blew some seeds across them and everything will be happy ever after. Is that it?'

Vicky scowled at him, urging silence.

The Old Man smiled. 'So you have need of more evidence of my wisdom in these matters?'

'You can say what you like to the others, you antique fraud, but I know a con artist when I see one.'

The Old Man stooped down and picked up two plant stalks, seemingly at random. Two paces behind, Nathan noticed that the stalks were similar but from different plants. The Old Man handed them to Julian, carefully placing a stalk in each of his hands.

'Crush them in your palms.'

Julian obliged, feeling the moisture of the stems squeeze out from between his fingers.

'Now clap your hands together,' said the Old Man. The wistful smile upon his face should have given Julian some warning but the young man was blind to it.

As his hands came together a massive blue flash suddenly emerged from his palms. The sound of his hands coming together was drowned out by the loud crack of the blue flame. It lasted only for a fraction of a second but it was enough to knock Julian off his feet and onto his back. From that prone position he looked down at his hands. Apart from a slight stinging feeling they were undamaged.

All of them looked towards the Old Man.

'A foolish trick for the entertainment of knaves and children. 'Tis of no import.' Still grinning, he turned and continued along the trail.

Carl and Vicky helped the groggy Julian back to his feet.

'None of my business, Goldenballs, but it might be a good idea to stop winding the old gentleman up. Better for the health, y'know.' Carl grinned as he passed on the advice, knowing full well that Julian would take no notice.

Nathan had been shocked by this, so-called, foolish trick. As the others moved off to follow the Old Man, Nathan backtracked. Carefully he identified the two plants and pulled a stalk of each. Even more carefully he placed the stalks in different pockets. Once done, he turned and jogged after the others.

—∞—

The traffic delayed Rylands' arrival at the Mexican restaurant. It was almost ten minutes past the hour when he walked in and looked across the tables towards the corner booth where he expected to find his contact. Sure enough he saw someone sitting at the table, his face hidden behind the large, laminated menu that provided glowing descriptions of the fare on offer. The journalist moved across to the table and slid onto the plastic-covered bench.

'This better be good,' he said to the back of the menu. 'I normally charge overtime for Sundays.'

'Oh, I'm sure this will be truly wonderful,' replied a voice that was both familiar but unexpected, as his lunch partner lowered the plastic menu.

Rylands found himself staring into the smiling face of Police Sergeant Tony Johnson.

Looking back, Rylands was surprised at how calmly he reacted. Inside he felt complete panic. He was caught with his pants down, following up on a bribe of one of Her Majesty's finest. Ten years' incarceration was the most optimistic outcome. Then he started to notice things. He noticed that Johnson was wearing civilian clothes, a fact that gave him a foolish degree of comfort. He noticed that the expected avalanche of other police seemed a long time coming. After his previous arrest in the park, Rylands knew that numbers were usually the order of the day. So far all he could see was Johnson, smiling at him. He tried to sound calm, recalling his oft-repeated promise that, when his time came, he would go down quipping.

'Not sure that you'll like this place. All the furniture is screwed down.'

'The only thing screwed down here, my lad, is you. Coffee?' replied the police sergeant. Rylands nodded and the order was given to a passing waitress. Johnson continued, 'You know, I always had you journalists down as quite a bright bunch. All total bastards, of course ...' Rylands gestured a feigned agreement '... but mostly near the top of the intellectual tree. Yet someone like you, allegedly from one of the uppermost branches of said tree, uses someone like Alan Bradley.'

'Who?' Rylands knew that it sounded weak but denial seemed the best option.

'Let me tell you about PC Bradley. Over the years I have often wondered how some of my colleagues have got through the supposedly stringent selection regime. Perhaps they might be not too clever, perhaps they are too nervous, perhaps they are too ready to slap people around. However, I have always taken the view that the senior officers who take these decisions know their trade and perhaps it's me that's out of step. Perhaps such recruits have some deep-rooted talent that I just cannot see. I am, after all, only a sergeant, a small cog in the magnificent mechanism that is the Avon and Somerset Constabulary.'

Rylands listened in silence. He knew where this was going.

After a moment's pause, the sergeant continued, 'And then I meet recruits like Alan Bradley and all my doubts are blown away. One minute in Bradley's company and I am totally convinced that all the money spent on selection is totally wasted, that the officers involved are a bunch of arrogant tossers and the recruitment process is truly the shambles that I always thought it to be.'

'It's always good to have your stereotypes confirmed,' Rylands tried, and failed, to sound supportive.

'Let me be quite clear. In all my years in the force, Bradley is the most stupid, lazy and inept police officer that it has ever been my misfortune to command. And those are his good points. Amongst his many other failings, and the one that is most pertinent to this conversation, is his total and complete inability to keep a secret.'

Rylands winced at this news.

Johnson continued. 'So when I see him paying off the debts owed to colleagues and start to bring in magazines about Caribbean holidays, I think to myself something strange is going on here. So I call him into my office for a little chat that I know one of us is not going to enjoy very much. I'm quite good at those, you know.'

'I can imagine.'

'Anyway, about a millisecond later I learn all sorts of interesting stuff. About meetings in Spanish restaurants, about your interest in strange old men and, most interestingly of all, about your telephone details.'

As the policeman spoke, the part of Ryland's brain not involved in listening to this sorry tale started to query things. Something was not quite right here. Where were the cavalry? Why was he being told these things in a public place? Surely all this would have to be done as part of a formal interview if any charges of corruption were to stick. He decided to probe.

'Sorry to hear your views on Alan. He speaks very highly of you.'

Johnson smiled once again. For a brief moment, Rylands wondered if snakes could smile. Having taken the initiative, Rylands continued. 'Problem in my game is that you often have to play your hand with the cards you are dealt. Bradley was the only officer that I knew was on duty when the old man was processed. Apart from you, of course, but you didn't strike me as the chatty type. Well, at least not then. Now, well, I'm not so sure.'

The smile vanished from Johnson's face.

'Don't try to bribe me, you little shit. I'm not going to risk my career any further by letting you get your teeth in.'

'So we are now going to take a drive to the nearest police station, where you are going to interview me under caution, complete with sound and video? Is that the plan? OK then. It's a fair cop, guv'nor.' Rylands theatrically offered his wrists. 'Slap on the derbies and let's go.'

Johnson glanced around to see if Ryland's performance had attracted any notice. That was the moment when the journalist knew he was safe. There would be no arrest today.

'OK then, Sergeant. So what's going on here? If it's to be neither a bribe nor a ride in a squad car then what's the real reason for this meeting?'

The tension of the moment was broken by the arrival of the coffee. The waitress placed the cups in front of each of her customers before departing with her professional smile. Once she was out of earshot Johnson leaned forward. 'Before we begin, let me make one thing clear. I have taken a full statement from Bradley about your activities, made several sealed copies and distributed them amongst my colleagues. One call from me and they are to hand them to my boss, and every media outlet that you can possibly think of. If I don't call in regularly then they will distribute them anyway. If you don't agree with everything I'm about to suggest, or if anything nasty happens to me, or even if I'm just feeling pissed off about the weather then you will be roasted on the fires of both our professions. Is that clear?'

The feeling of control that had washed over Rylands a moment before evaporated. This time it was he that was being manipulated, not a feeling that he enjoyed. For want of alternatives, he nodded.

'Right then. I'm not sure what Bradley told you about my role in this little saga.'

'I seem to remember that he was surprised at your enthusiasm for the group to leave the police station.'

'That old bastard did something to me. I don't know how, but I was completely brainwashed. All I wanted to do was to help him. Instead of keeping him locked up I ushered the whole group out of the building. I even held open the front door while they walked out.'

'Was this condition temporary?'

'Too right. Ten minutes later I'm sitting in my office thinking what the fuck have I done.'

'I see your problem. I suspect the views of your inspector were not so transient?'

'He wanted to know why I had done it but I couldn't explain because I had no idea what had been done to me. I was given 12 hours to find them or I was to be suspended, pending possible prosecution for abetting their escape.'

'And then?'

'The bastard vanished. I had all my troops hunting him down. We put in road blocks, foot patrols – the lot, but they just disappeared off the face of the earth.'

'So, just to be clear as to your current status?'

The sergeant just glared back, unable to say the words, so Rylands continued.

'Now, I'm guessing here, but I would have thought that you've been suspended and you need to find this old guy and persuade him to get you off the hook?'

Johnson nodded.

'So, mindful of their own careers, all of your former pals have deserted you and so you need a new playmate to help you track him down. Then you discover my little transgression with Bradley and suddenly another way forward beckoned.'

Again Johnson nodded.

Rylands leaned back against the chair. He quickly considered the implications of the new situation. Clearly, saying no was not an option. Johnson had prepared his position too well. On the other hand, agreeing to the proposal had several positives - his continued freedom being the most appealing. Having someone with Johnson's contacts could prove quite an advantage. After a moment's thought he looked across at the police sergeant.

'It's a deal.'

CHAPTER 24

Chisbury Chapel,
Just outside Chisbury, a small village on the Wansdyke.
Monday 27th August
5.00 a.m.

Since 04.00 it had been Nathan's turn to stand watch. The Old Man had wandered off when the early dawn light had streamed through the stained-glass window of the ruined chapel. He had nodded to Nathan as he left but gave no word of his plans. They were all used to this early morning routine by now. Always the first awake, the Old Man spent the early hours walking around wherever they happened to be, continuing his everlasting trials of any new plants that he came across. He would return when he was ready.

Nathan reckoned that they had covered around 15 miles the previous day. Soon after they left the site of the road accident the Wansdyke had led them from open fields into the Savernake Forest. Although there were several defined tracks through the woodland, the Old Man kept stubbornly to his easterly course which brought them back into open fields leading into the village of Chisbury. Pausing only to replenish their supplies at the village shop, the group pressed on to another Iron Age fort on the outskirts of the settlement. Nathan expected the Old Man to call a halt to the day's journey but he pressed on still further to this chapel, on the south edge of the fort's ramparts. The Old Man seemed to know its exact location but was initially confused by the more modern farm buildings that surrounded it. However, once he had located it he pushed through the unlocked wrought iron gate that blocked the entrance and gestured that this was where they were going to spend the night. As was his usual custom, he lay down on the earthen floor and, without further comment, fell asleep.

Despite the physical difficulties of the journey, Nathan was starting to enjoy himself. The Old Man had been right about the benefits of a long walk with strangers. His mind had never been so clear, making his doubts and worries much easier to consider and, as he moved towards conclusions, address. He now realised that his chosen career might not be for him. His decision to join the police force had been prompted by a latent streak of helpfulness which, he now saw, was far stronger than he had originally imagined. He truly wanted to make a difference and had seen the police as a means of achieving that. Then another aspect of his character - stubbornness - kicked in, as all his friends and family tried to talk him out of taking such an important step. To be fair, the main issue that they had predicted - racism - had not become the problem he anticipated. A bit of banter at the beginning soon led to his new colleagues realising that he could give as good as he got, and after that it was 'all lads together'. The real issue was the role that he was asked to play, always having to react to problems that were so entrenched that it was impossible for him, or anyone else in the police service, to solve. These solutions lay elsewhere, beyond the bounds of his chosen profession. He now saw that police work, at least at his level, would always be reactive, never proactive. For him, that was the core of the problem. He saw himself as a solver of problems, not someone who only ever cleared up their aftermath. He now recognised the frustrations building up and knew that, in the end, they would overwhelm him. He was beginning to see that, once this little adventure was over, he would have to leave the police force.

He glanced around the little chapel. About twenty strides by ten, it had a beaten earth floor surrounded by old, roughly made flint walls that supported a thatched roof. Completely cleared of any furniture, it had obviously not been used for its original purpose for many years.

Nathan reckoned the stonework around the windows was from around the 13th century, making it the oldest building he had ever slept in.

Vicky rolled over on her travel mattress, making a sound that distracted Nathan from his thoughts. She was quite a girl, he thought. As far as he could tell she was the only one who was making this journey for others rather than for themselves, driven to learn the Old Man's knowledge in order to deal with the pandemic that she was sure was coming. Perhaps it was her example that had influenced Nathan. She was certainly influencing the Old Man. Since the road accident he seemed to have become more tolerant of her questions, more prepared to discuss the plants that he found along the way. On her side she had given up all pretence of making the questions conversational, choosing a more direct, almost blunt approach. She had even started to make a note of his answers in a small book that she kept in her coat pocket for easy access at a moment's notice.

Nathan glanced at Julian, lying alongside her, and asked himself once again what she saw in him. To others he was a brash arrogant bully but she must see things that were invisible to folk outside their partnership. Occasionally Nathan thought that he saw some strain between them but had always put it down to the rigours of the journey. But he could have been wrong. Or perhaps he was just hoping that it was time for her to move on, perhaps into a new relationship. Perhaps … but no, he thought, what could a rising doctor possibly see in an unemployed policeman. But then, maybe …

'Bugger me, but that's a sight for sore eyes first thing in the morning.' Carl had woken to the full sun streaming through the huge stained-glass window at the far end of the chapel.

'It is quite something,' replied Nathan. He had noticed it earlier, as the sun rose behind the ancient glass but now, in the full glare of the morning light, it could be viewed in the way its makers had created it for. The window was recessed into the thick walls. Its outside edge was defined by a carved stone frame, the main section of which comprised a series of glass panels, each held in place by strips of lead. These panels depicted some form of crowd scene, with groups of background figures cheering a monk or priest in the centre. This main character was dressed in a simple brown habit but with the cowl folded back to show his face. The medieval glass makers had taken great care to ensure that the area around the head was much lighter than elsewhere in the window, giving the obvious impression of a halo.

The figures surrounding this central character had been clustered into distinct social groups. On one side, a number of peasants were shown waving, their status demonstrated by their drab clothing. Another area had more prosperous figures, perhaps merchants or landowners. Yet another area had a group that looked like some form of soldiery, dressed in chain mail and carrying weapons. All the groups were finely illustrated into the glass panels, their faces carefully drawn to be smiling and cheering the triumphant entrance of the priest or monk.

'I wonder who he was?' Vicky had now woken up. Julian also stirred beside her. 'They all seem to be celebrating his arrival. Perhaps he was some form of saint.'

'Not in the beginning.' The Old Man had entered the chapel. 'He was a priest called Martyn and he was a complete ...' the Old Man paused. He seemed to struggle for the right word '... bastard!'

'Oh no. Sounds like it is going to be story time again. Do we have to listen before we have even had breakfast?' Julian made the comment in his standard stage whisper.

'For once, the servant speaks wisely. Make haste to break your fast. We have far to travel this day.' At the Old Man's words, emphasised with encouraging gestures, Carl began to break out the rations.

'So who was this Martyn? What did he do that upset you so much?' True or not, Nathan was always fascinated by the Old Man's tales.

The Old Man squatted down alongside the four members of his group and spoke as they ate.

'Martyn was the priest for the vill of Chisbury during the time of the third Edward. At his best he was a lazy, useless fool. At his worst he was a thief and a bully. On my first day here I found him threatening a penniless widow with damnation if she didn't give up her last loaf to him. Claimed that it was his by right of the priesthood. When I intervened he tried to strike me but I defended myself, smearing his cheek with arrocha.' The Old Man chuckled to himself. 'He spent the next three days on the privy, but was too stupid to see my hand in his plight. I had planned to move on, through to the next vill, but then the plague came. Many died in Chisbury, as in many other places in the kingdom. At the first death Martyn fled. Instead of comforting his flock, as was required by his office, he deserted them. Left them all to die.'

At this Vicky raised her head from the disgusting porridge that Carl had made. 'So this was the village? The one where you found the cure for the black death?'

'Twas so,' the Old Man replied hesitantly, fearing what was to come.

Vicky sensed his discomfort. 'Why?'

The others looked across at Vicky. That was not the sort of question that they had come to expect from her.

Without waiting for an answer she pressed on, 'Surely the plague is nature's way of culling the flock? In your philosophy, aren't such plagues a necessary evil?'

The Old Man just stared at the earthen floor.

'Once again. Why did you find a cure for this plague?'

'Because these villagers were kind to me,' the Old Man snapped back. 'Because, like very few other places I have journeyed, they took me in. They gave me warmth and companionship. For a short time they made me feel like one of their tribe, something that I have not met often, before or since.'

'So when the plague came you could not sit back and watch them suffer?'

'Yes. As I told you in the alehouse, I found a cure and so no one else had to die.'

'So you will help people when it suits you!' Vicky's accusative tone drew a scowl from the Old Man.

'How does this relate to Martyn?' said Nathan, anxious to move the conversation away from the developing row.

'Once the word had spread about the cure, Martyn returned. He claimed that the cure was a result of his prayers. When the villagers told him about my work he told them I was a witch. He wanted to burn me on a fire. They stood up for me but he threatened everyone with excommunication, something unknown to me but dreaded by them. Eventually he forced them to drive me away.'

'So why didn't you fight back? I'm sure that your herbal tricks could have changed things,' asked Julian.

'To what point? The warmth was gone. Nothing I did could replace it.' The Old Man looked up at the window. 'They made him a saint and built this place as a temple in his honour.' For a second he seemed lost in thought but then he roused himself. 'Enough of this chatter. Let us go.' He turned and walked out of the chapel, closely followed by Nathan, Vicky and Carl.

Julian finished collecting his sleeping things together. Closing his pack, he swung it onto his shoulder. He paused for a final moment to look again at the medieval scene. Suddenly he saw something that stunned him. Walking towards the window to check more closely, he saw a small figure in the top corner, missed by his companions. This figure was walking away from the main group but was drawn with his face looking back towards the priest. There could be no doubt about it. The villagers had not forgotten him. Julian was looking at the face of the Old Man.

In an instant he realised that the Old Man had been telling the truth all along. There could be no more room for doubt. Here in the ancient window glass was indisputable proof of his amazing story. For a second he considered calling out to the others but then he paused. This changed everything. It might be best if he kept it to himself, at least until after his plan had been implemented. Smiling at this new knowledge, and the power that went with it, he turned and walked out of the chapel.

—∞—

Eriksson glanced at his watch. It was nearly 8.30 a.m. Throughout his working life he had always been an early starter but this crisis had made him even more so. He had been at his desk for over an hour, unsuccessfully trying to deal with the huge pile of paperwork that went with running such a major enterprise. As he sipped his second coffee of the day, his phone rang.

'Yes, Mike?'

'There's a call on the line for you,' said his second-in-command.

'Can't you deal with it?'

'The guy insists on talking to you. It's that Professor of Archaeology that we sent to take a look at Maes Knoll. I'm not sure that they found much but I think he wants to thank you for the donation.'

'Very well, but before you put him on I see that you have taken on another IT specialist on what seems to me to be a rather generous salary. What's the story there?'

'We found him digging around in the company files for his previous employer. He was very good. Got far more information than I would have thought possible. I decided that I would rather have him inside the tent pissing out than outside pissing in.'

Eriksson winced at the vulgarity. 'The President Johnson strategy. Fair enough. Who was his previous employer?'

'Her Majesty's Revenue and Customs.'

'Sounds like a good career move. Have we applied the usual induction process for such newcomers?'

'We have sent him and his family on a Caribbean cruise with orders not to call home for a month. He seemed content with the arrangements.'

'I should think so. OK then, put me through to this eager academic.' Eriksson paused as various clicks came through the phone.

'Mr Eriksson?' said a nervous voice.

'This is he. Thank you for reporting in so promptly, Professor ...' Eriksson suddenly realised that he had forgotten to ask Aspinall for the man's name.

'Ferguson. Anthony Ferguson. I am Professor of Archaeology at the University of Taunton.'

'Of course. Please forgive me. The memory fades as the years go by. So, tell me, how did you and your team get on?'

'Firstly, may I thank you formally for the kind, and very generous, donation that you made to the department. In these hard times it is proving very difficult to advance the subject of archaeology and so without benefactors such as yourself ...'

'You really are most welcome,' interrupted Eriksson. He had heard such speeches many times before. 'We at Paternoster are always happy to support the realms of academia. However, I am rather pressed for time this morning so, at the risk of being rude, might I ask you to push on to the results?'

'Well, as you may know, the site is scheduled which means that we cannot put in any test pits without formal consent.'

Eriksson could feel his interest waning with every passing word. The idea of sending in the archaeologists had been Aspinall's. So far as Eriksson was concerned, their target had moved on so he didn't see what was to be gained.

The Professor continued. 'We were able to do some field walking and some limited survey work which confirmed all the published results of the site being an Iron Age enclosure, possibly a fort.'

'What was your view of the palm mark?'

'An excellent example of its type. Truly remarkable workmanship but not an unfamiliar sight at such locations. We think that it was used to confer some sort of authority to the site. Footprints are more common but palm prints are not unknown.'

Eriksson could see this was going nowhere. He reached for his coffee as he tried to think of a polite means of escape.

The Professor continued, 'So I'm not sure that we can add much more detail at present. I could request a permit to dig but that may take several months to acquire.'

Eriksson took a sip of coffee. 'Well, that may be something for the future but at present ...'

'It would be unusual for Maes Knoll to be surveyed only for its enclosure. Obviously, it is better known for other reasons.'

More out of politeness than any genuine interest, Eriksson posed the obvious question. 'Other reasons?'

The Professor sounded puzzled. 'I'm sorry, I thought you knew.'

Another sip of coffee. 'Knew what?'

'Traditionally, Maes Knoll is regarded as the start of the Wansdyke.'

Eriksson shot to his feet, sending coffee cascading down his expensive suit. `What!' he shouted.

'The Wansdyke. It's an ancient defensive earthwork that ...'

'I know what it is, I just didn't know where it was.' Eriksson's mind was now in turmoil.

'Some think that the start was further west, perhaps on the banks of the Severn but most credible historians think that ...'

'Professor, thank you so much for your input. I really have to go. Something monumentally important has just come up.' He dropped the phone and ran into the operations room.

Mike Aspinall had never seen his boss run anywhere so he knew that something important must have happened.

'Put the route of the Wansdyke up on the big screen, now!' Eriksson panted breathlessly.

'The what?' said Aspinall.

'The Wansdyke,' shouted Eriksson. 'It's an ancient earthwork that runs across the south-west of England.'

Aspinall still looked puzzled.

'It starts at Maes Knoll and goes eastwards. Sound familiar?'

By this time one of the operations room staff had been able to set up the display. All present stared at the screen on the wall.

'Now superimpose the route that we know our quarry have been following so far.'

A moment later and the connection was clear. The two lines coincided perfectly as far as the pub at Monkton Combe where the chase team were currently stuck.

Aspinall saw what Eriksson was getting at. 'So they have been following this Wansdyke, at least as far as that pub. Useful information for sure, but how does that help us? They could have left it at any time.'

'Or they could still be using it. I realise that it is a long shot but given our current dearth of options I think it is worth pursuing.' Eriksson turned to the screen operator. 'Can you tell me where the Wansdyke finishes?'

The operator bent over his keyboard for a second before replying. 'Sorry, sir, but that is not easy to say.'

'Force yourself!'

The operator scanned the screen, quickly taking in the information presented.

'The literature seems to suggest several locations. One is in the middle of Savernake Forest, others are more to the east.'

Eriksson thought for a moment. 'Which is the one furthest to the east?'

Again, the operator studied the screen. 'Furthest east? That would be a few miles to the south of a village called Little Bedwyn in Wiltshire.'

Eriksson turned to Aspinall, 'We'll tell Major Warren to divide the chase team into groups of four. I want them picked up by helicopter and dropped along the route of the Wansdyke, say, every five miles and one right at the end, near to this Little Bedstead place.'

'Little Bedwyn, sir.' The operator tried to sound helpful.

'Thank you. Your geography does you credit.' Eriksson returned to Aspinall. 'For each drop I want one pair to move out eastwards and the other to go westwards. That way we should cover the whole route before nightfall.'

Aspinall examined the screen closely. 'That's quite a distance to try to cover. Plus, as I said, they could have turned off at any time.'

'Perhaps I can help here?' Again the operator spoke up.

'All contributions greatly appreciated,' replied Eriksson.

'I have been monitoring the emergency services over the last few days, trying to weed out anything unusual. Problem is that there are so many things that might fall into that category. I have just pulled out a report from the Ambulance Service timed at yesterday lunchtime. It was a road accident just south of Marlborough. Seems that someone fixed up the victims before the crew arrived but did so using some rather weird first aid. It seems to have been very effective but made one of the ambulance crew puke.'

'Go on,' said Eriksson, his interest suddenly focussed. 'Why do you think that relevant?'

'Because the location given is exactly where the road crosses the Wansdyke.'

'That has got to be the Old Man. So they must have got that far at least,' said Aspinall, examining the screen. 'That cuts down the length of search considerably.'

'OK then. You sort out the helicopters. I'll go and update the good Major.'

—∞—

The Mission Impossible ring tone brought Colin Warren out of his musings. He was sitting at the bedside of his friend. Although the medics assured him that Choggy was physically fine, but merely sleeping, Warren was still worried. If that was all that was wrong, why had he not woken up for 48 hours?

He stood and walked out of the hotel bedroom, carefully avoiding all the medical paraphernalia surrounding the bed. Once on the landing, he answered the call.

'Yes, Boss.' He listened as Eriksson outlined the new developments together with his plans for the team.

'So the choppers will be here in half an hour? OK. We'll be ready.'

Closing the phone, he took a final glance at his friend before going down the stairs. A few minutes of organised chaos followed as the troopers quickly pulled together their kit for a rapid deployment. Less than 30 minutes later the helicopters arrived, landing in a field behind the pub. The troopers piled in and within a minute the chase was back on.

Inside the hotel, just as the noise of the helicopters faded away, Chogan opened his eyes.

After leaving the chapel, the Old Man led the group down a hillside towards a small village. The Wansdyke was completely invisible here but the Old Man continued to stride out confidently as if he were on a clearly marked roadway. As ever, his progress was interspersed with his ongoing examination of plants, most of which he tasted before spitting out. The others, now used to this relentless performance, ignored him and pressed on down the hill.

The ancient route did not follow any of the more recent roads that led into the village but rather through some private gardens, much to the discomfort of Nathan, who was pleased when they emerged without being challenged by any irate owners.

Had the group taken a more modern route into the village they would have passed a sign. Hand crafted by a local woodcarver, now retired, the sign welcomed all visitors to the community known as Little Bedwyn.

Chapter 25

Little Bedwyn,
Wiltshire
Monday 27th August
10.00 a.m.

Their path took the group down a narrow driveway between two tall houses. Looking up, Carl caught a brief glimpse of a helicopter flashing overhead, moving to the south. For a split second he was back in Afghanistan being transported across hostile terrain. Initially the thought warmed him as he recalled the job and the camaraderie that went with it. Then he remembered his capture and the warm feeling drained away. With an effort, he drove such memories from his mind.

The group emerged from the long passageway onto the main road that ran through the village. The Old Man led them across this road, towards a concrete footbridge that spanned a railway line and, beyond it, a canal.

At the base of the steps he paused. 'What manner of things are these?' he said, gesturing to the tracks and the waterway beyond.

'Well, in front of you is a railway line, probably from London to Bristol, and beyond it is a canal,' replied Nathan. 'I can see some signs on the other side but can't quite read them from here.'

The Old Man hesitated at the foot of the grey concrete steps.

'Think of them as alternative means of journeying,' said Vicky, noticing that the Old Man was becoming worried.

'So rather like his Rover cart?' said the Old Man, pointing towards Julian.

'Something like that, but much bigger,' said Julian, trying to be helpful.

'Bigger!' shouted the Old Man, getting more concerned with each further explanation.

'There is nothing to worry about,' said Vicky, 'it's really only a raised footpath. We'll cross it in no time at all.' As she spoke a canal boat emerged from some locks to their left. The slow pace and a cheery wave from the boat's owner seemed to calm the Old Man.

'So this Ka-nal is some form of man-made river?'

'That's a good way of putting it,' replied Nathan, sensing that the Old Man was beginning to calm down. 'Carl, you go first. We'll follow on behind you.'

With Nathan's encouragement, the Old Man began to follow Carl up the steps. Vicky and Nathan followed close behind with Julian bringing up the rear. Once they had reached the highest point the Old Man stopped and peered over the side of the bridge towards the canal boat that had now glided serenely beneath them. Comforted, he turned to look in the opposite direction, towards the locks with the railway line running alongside.

Suddenly Nathan saw the Old Man's face turn to a look of abject horror.

A second later the metallic scream enveloped the tranquil scene. A long passenger train pounded along the railway line and under their feet, causing a rhythmic thudding that started on the tracks but quickly moved up into the fabric of the bridge.

The sudden noise and vibration was too much for the Old Man. In a blind panic, he roughly pushed Vicky and Julian to one side and rushed down the steps that he had so reluctantly climbed a moment before. Once at the base of the steps he ran across the road and took refuge in the narrow alleyway beyond, squatting against the brickwork and pulling his arms over his head.

A few seconds later the train had gone and the tranquillity of the country village returned.

Vicky was the first to reach the Old Man. As she placed her hand on his back to comfort him she could feel his body trembling. He was clearly terrified by the sudden noise and vibration. It was going to be some time before he would be calm enough to try crossing the footbridge again. Sensing his need for comfort she sat down beside him, put her arms around his shoulders and hugged him. Slowly she felt his racing heartbeat abate, as his terror began to subside.

—◁∞▷—

Colin Warren was the last out of the helicopter. The two troopers with him had jogged away from the landing site, and were now kneeling about 30 metres away, scanning the surrounding countryside. Joining them he turned to wave away the pilot, who quickly ascended before flying off in the direction of his base.

Once the noise had died down Warren realised that his phone was ringing. A glance at the screen told him it was his Canadian friend. Relieved, he took the call.

'Choggy, how are you feeling?'

'Fantastic. Never better. The best sleep I have ever had.'

'Well, it was certainly the longest. What do you think happened?'

'I think it was some sort of drug, almost certainly applied to those berries that I chewed. It must have been a trap set up by our target. He really does know his stuff, doesn't he? I suppose I should be grateful that he set the dosage to send me off to sleep rather than kill me.'

'Are you fit for the fray again?'

'Damn right. I may still have to convince the medicos here but once they let me out I'll be with you ASAP. What has been happening? No one here seems to know anything.'

Warren took a moment to bring his friend up to speed. As he would have expected, Chogan spotted the flaw in the plan within seconds.

'So you are charging over 10 miles of this Wansdyke path hoping that they are still on it somewhere. How do you know they haven't turned off?'

'Well, we don't, but it was the only option on offer until you decided to end your little nap. Now that you are back on stream, what do you suggest?'

'I'm sure I can do better than getting the whole troop to run around like headless chickens.'

Warren winced at the sneer but chose to ignore it, mostly because of the ring of truth it contained. 'Thank you for your input. Now, once again, what do you suggest?'

'Do you still have access to the choppers?'

'Only a call away.'

'Good. Send one back for me. I'll get them to put me down at the mid-point of the route. I'll scout around and see if I can find any trace of them. If I can find their tracks then the chopper pilot can move me to the mid-point of the second half. If not, then he can take me back to the mid-point of the first half. If I can keep halving the sections of the route then I should be able to either find the quarry or, at least, where they have left the Wansdyke.'

'Sounds like a plan. I'll tell the pilot to get over to you. OK with you if the rest of us carry on with our arrangements?'

'Sure. It'll keep you out of my way and stop you from getting bored. Besides, you might get lucky and trip over the old guy by accident.'

Once again Warren winced. 'As I said, thank you for your input. Call me as soon as you find anything.' Warren ended the call before calling the changes through to Paternoster, requesting them to arrange for the helicopter pick-up.

Joining the other two troopers he saw that they were examining the screen of a hand-held computer which displayed a map of the area. A thick blue line indicated the predicted route of the Wansdyke, for which Warren was grateful as he could see no sign of anything in the field around them. A cross indicated their current position, at the most southern tip of the ancient earthwork. Looking to the north, in the direction of the blue line, he saw that the ground fell away slowly, running downhill towards what appeared to be a small river and a railway line. Increasing the screen magnification he realised that he had made a mistake. It was not a river but a canal, across which there was a narrow footbridge leading to a small village. The footbridge was about a mile away.

'That's our first milestone,' Warren told his companions, indicating the direction they were to travel.

As they fell into the brisk marching step of soldiers everywhere, one of the troopers spoke up.

'What's this place called then, Boss?'

Warren paused for a second to look at his screen. 'It's called Little Bedwyn.'

—❊—

'I care nought for your views. Such a creation has no place in Nature.' The Old Man had calmed down a little since his panic with the train but he was still extremely reluctant to cross the footbridge.

'I can see that it was a shock for you but, honestly, you have nothing to fear.' Vicky still had her arm around the shoulders of the Old Man who was still crouching in the narrow passageway between the houses. She could see that his pupils were starting to return to their normal size and his breathing was more subdued.

'Problem is that we are going to have to cross the railway at some stage.' Nathan had joined them. 'Unless, of course, you want to change to a different route?'

'At the cost of many extra days?' replied the Old Man. 'No, we must reach our destination with all possible haste. Somehow I must cross the path of that monstrous Rover cart.'

After a moment's pondering he seemed to reach a decision. Taking out the old pouch, he untied the drawstring and emptied the contents in his palm. Selecting two, quite different, seeds he replaced the others.

The larger seed, a black oval shape about the size of a fingernail, he gave to Vicky.

'When it is time you must crush this seed in your palm and blow it into my face. As you do, pinch my ear, hard. Harken to my words. Hard I say, lest I should slumber for many days.'

Vicky was confused. Was he asking her to treat him for something?

The Old Man turned to Carl. 'Carl. I would have you carry me across to the other side.'

The ex-para nodded his huge head. Somehow he seemed to know what was going to happen next.

The Old Man returned his attention to Vicky. 'Once we are over the bridge, on the far side of the Ka-nal, Carl will lay me down on the bank. That is where you must practise your new wisdom.'

Although still a little confused, Vicky nodded.

Once he had her agreement, the Old Man tossed the second seed into his mouth and began to chew. For a moment Vicky thought that the seed was having no effect but suddenly the Old Man started to cough violently. A moment later, still hacking, he sank to his knees and then rolled onto his back. Carl and Vicky both reached out in a failed attempt to catch him. As the coughing abated the young doctor quickly checked the Old Man's prostrate form and found that he was still breathing and his pupils were normal. Looking up, she nodded to Carl who lifted up the Old Man's body and threw him over his shoulder.

'Quickly, now,' he shouted as he sprinted across the road and over the footbridge. At the far end a series of steps, supported by a low brick wall, led down to the canal bank. Carl laid the Old Man down against the wall, not in a sitting position but with his back on the grass and his legs leaning up against the dark grey brickwork.

Seconds later Vicky caught up with them, closely followed by the confused Nathan and Julian. Kneeling down she crushed the dried seed into the palm of her hand which she then blew into the Old Man's face. With her other hand she reached up and pinched his ear lobe as hard as she could.

The Old Man's body suddenly convulsed with pain. 'Agh!' he shouted, gulping in a lungful of air and the crushed seed powder.

At first the Old Man seemed to return to his sleep. Vicky became concerned that she had not carried out his directions correctly. Slowly, he seemed to come round. Carefully he got to his feet, using the wall for support. Groggy at first but then with increasing confidence he straightened up and began to look around him.

Touching his ear, his first words were to Vicky. 'Not hard enough!' he said sternly. 'You must be brutal for that physic to work.' Seeing her disappointment, he quickly modified his words. 'Yet, not a bad beginning. You make a promising apprentice.'

Vicky found herself smiling at this praise but before she could answer the Old Man seemed to totter on his feet. She rushed forward and caught his arm, preventing him from falling.

'The pain has not cleared the sleep from my head. It will take a moment more for me to recover.'

As he spoke his eyes lighted on some signs fixed to the brick wall.

'What marks are these?' he said.

Nathan was the first to speak. 'One just has the number 93, probably an identification of the bridge. The other says Kennet and Avon Canal.'

The Old Man, now steadier, seemed to pause for a moment, as if trying to remember something.

'You say this Ka-nal was made by men?'

'That's right,' said Nathan.

'Perhaps by Irish men?'

'Possibly,' said Nathan, now puzzled at where this was going. 'They used large amounts of Irish labour when they built the canal system.'

'Perhaps by one Irish man called Callaghan?'

'It's a common Irish name.'

The Old Man nodded. ''Twas so. The man Callaghan worked this part of the Ka-nal, as far as a place called Wargrave, several leagues to the east of here.'

'How can you possibly know that?'

'Do you recall the young lord that tried to take both our lives? It was the evening of my Return?'

'I'm not going to forget him in a hurry.'

'Then you will remember that his name was Shaun Callaghan and that I assimilated with him. Since then his inner wisdom flows through me.'

Nathan glanced at the others. All three were listening but were as confused as Nathan.

The Old Man continued. 'Yet not just his inner wisdom but also of those that went before him, stretching through the generations, back to the beginning.' The Old Man paused, continuing to think hard.

'Go on,' said Julian, suddenly interested.

'One of his forefathers left the land of his birth to do the bidding of others. He spent many summers making this Ka-nal and he knew well the route it took. And his knowledge then is my knowledge now.'

'So how does that change anything?' said Nathan.

'It means that we no longer have to follow the Wansdyke. A more direct path lies along the banks of the Ka-nal.'

With that he stepped down onto the tow-path, crossed under the footbridge that had given them such problems a moment before, and walked off along the grassy track. The rest of them, confused but knowing better than to argue, followed along behind him.

The canal, and the tow-path alongside it, followed a long, slow curve so that within a few minutes the group were out of sight of both the footbridge and the village.

After a few minutes Vicky caught up with Carl.

'Something is bothering me,' she said to him. 'I need to ask you something.'

'No problem. Ask away.'

'Do you remember when you carried him ...' she nodded towards the Old Man '... across the footbridge?'

'Of course. `

'Well, when you got across the bridge you laid him down.'

'That was what he asked me to do.'

'Yes, but you laid him down in a very particular way, with his feet up and his back on the ground.'

'So?'

'Why did you lie him down like that rather than the more usual way, with his back against the wall? I watched you. You did it very deliberately. Is that something you were taught in the army?'

Carl stopped for a moment to look at Vicky. Up until then he hadn't even thought about it. 'Can't say why. Never done it that way before. Just seemed right. Something inside seemed to tell me so.' Again, Carl had a feeling that he had experienced several times since they had left Bristol. A sense of unexplained familiarity. Shaking his head he looked again at Vicky. 'Sorry, Doc. Can't explain it.'

Vicky shrugged. 'I'm sure it was nothing important.' She smiled and walked on, falling into step behind Julian.

—∞—

Five minutes later a group of three military-looking individuals emerged from fields to the south. Heading north, they approached a footbridge that crossed a canal and a railway line. At a steady jog they made their way across the footbridge and entered the village beyond. The one in the lead paused for a moment to examine the screen of a hand-held computer, checking that they were on the correct route. This modern device gave them such a high degree of confidence that they did not need to refer to any of the signs on the bridge to confirm their position. Had they taken this, quite unnecessary, step they would have seen that the bridge was individually identified.

It bore the number 93.

CHAPTER 26

Intensive Care Unit, Great Western Hospital,
Swindon, Wiltshire.
Monday 27th August
11.00 a.m.

'I'm sorry, Sergeant, but as I explained to your colleagues earlier, neither of these patients will be available for interview for several days yet.'

Johnson looked over the nurse's shoulder at the two people he sought, lying unconscious in the beds that made up the corner bay. The tubes and wires running from them, connecting them both to a wall of electronics, only served to confirm what the nurse was telling him. One of his unofficial police contacts had tipped him off about a mother and son who had been brought here the previous day after a serious car accident. Tragic, but hardly unique, had been his initial response, until he heard about the medical treatment that had been administered at the roadside. Decades of police work had given him an excellent nose for a lead which had twitched when he heard about this event. Rylands had not been keen but Johnson persisted, resulting in him now standing before the nurse and Rylands sitting in the car park.

'Don't be fobbed off by the official crap. Push her harder.' Johnson could hear Rylands` voice in the hidden ear-piece that the journalist had fitted. The microphone disguised as a pen in his top pocket was keeping Rylands informed of the conversation.

'I can understand your concern for your patients, Nurse, but you must also realise that the unusual nature of this accident means that we have to follow up all leads before they go cold.' Johnson trotted out the standard line that he had used with medical staff a hundred times before. It usually proved successful, but not today.

'You can get as heavy as you like with me but it won't change anything. These two need to rest and so we are keeping them sedated. All I can promise is that I will call you the moment they are available for interview, which is exactly the same promise that I have already made to your colleagues. So if you could give me a contact number, Sergeant ... sorry, but what was your name?'

Johnson frantically thought of some new direction to take the conversation. Unlike the nurse, he was acutely aware that he had no authority to be there. Not only was he currently under suspension but this hospital was in the domain of a totally different constabulary. He had hoped that his uniform alone, suitably stripped of any identification marks, would carry him through but that plan seemed about to go wrong. Fortunately a voice behind him provided an escape.

'There would be no point in speaking to them anyway. Pam was unconscious from the moment that the car hit her and I'm told that Adam went to sleep almost as soon as that old man touched him.' The voice came from an elderly woman who had entered the unit behind Johnson. Her confident manner, her steel grey hair and her green, waxed coat told Johnson that he was dealing with a member of the country set. Behind her was a younger version, also female, probably a daughter.

'And you are?'

'My name is Emma Whitehead and this is my daughter, Amanda. We rode past Pam and the children just before the accident happened. We came to see how they are doing.'

Nodding his gratitude to the nurse, Johnson turned back towards the two newcomers.

'I wonder, ladies, if I might buy you both a cup of coffee?'

An hour later Johnson was back in the car with Rylands.

'So the old bloke is on some form of hike across southern England. He has teamed up with the group that left the police station with him and now he is providing a gruesome first-aid service to strangers that he meets along the way.' Rylands' summary brought a nod from Johnson.

'I don't know what game Nathan Aluko is playing. If he gets caught with them he will be in even more trouble than me.'

'Is he the impressionable type?'

'Not really, although I don't know him that well. He has not been at the station long, but he seemed to be settling in, maybe a little slowly.'

'So perhaps the old man is playing the sort of mind games on him that you think he played on you?'

'It's possible. He certainly must be using something strong to keep that mad paratrooper quiet.'

'And where does this young doctor and her beloved fit in?' Rylands asked, more to himself than to Johnson.

'I really have no idea.'

'Well, all this is good background stuff but knowing where they have been is of limited use. I'm more convinced than ever that this old guy is something special so I'm still up for the chase. Are you?'

Johnson turned a fixed stare at his unlikely colleague. 'More than you can possibly imagine.'

Rylands started the car and began to drive away from the hospital, turning on the radio to diffuse the silence.

'... *resulting in Downing Street issuing a statement in which the Prime Minister has asked the public not to panic at the recent developments in Bristol. He also said that potential new outbreaks of the H1N1 bird flu strain reported in Birmingham and Middlesbrough had yet to be confirmed and are not considered to be related at the present time. The National Health Service spokesman said that adequate quantities of general flu vaccine are widely available for members of the public in the 'at risk' categories but admitted that a vaccine for this particular strain may be some weeks off.'*

Following the canal tow-path proved much easier than walking across open country and so the group covered several miles before Julian demanded a halt.

'I never expected to hear myself saying this but, in the absence of anything actually edible, I feel about ready for one of your rabbit-food bars.'

Carl looked at the Old Man for a decision. On getting the merest hint of a nod, the paratrooper slung the large pack from his shoulders and began to distribute the army rations. As was now his custom, the Old Man wandered further along the path to continue his ongoing experimentation with the greenery that he found along the way.

'Where are we now?' asked Nathan to no one in particular. The lush, green countryside along the canal had entranced him but they were now moving into a more urban area, with cheap-looking council housing starting to appear on the other bank.

'I reckon we must have got as far as Hungerford,' replied Carl. Unfolding his map to check, he pointed to the location that they had reached. 'We've done well. That's quite a jaunt that we've made since breakfast. We'll make a hiker out of you yet, Julie.'

Vicky winced at the airing of Carl's latest name for her boyfriend and awaited the riposte. To her surprise none came. Julian said nothing, but remained in deep, silent thought. This was new to Vicky. She had never seen this side to his personality. He was certainly a different person to the one that started the trip. Perhaps, she thought, he might be showing some benefit from this pleasant walk in such beautiful surroundings, especially since he was starting to overcome the physical demands. Then, she recognised a look that she had seen before, an expression that indicated a detachment, a focus on the mental task in hand. No, she decided, he was plotting something.

The Old Man wandered some distance from the group, around a long, left-hand bend in the canal that broke the line of sight between them. Like some large, scruffy butterfly, he moved from plant to plant, picking, tasting and spitting as he went. The moisture of the canal had brought about a change in the flora, resulting in many plants that he had never seen before. At one point he passed a stone bridge carrying a rough track over the canal and up to the housing estate on the opposite bank. He spied yet another unfamiliar plant, sprouting from the lowest row of stones at the base of the bridge. Picking a leaf, he chewed on it for a second before spitting it out onto the dusty track. The taste reminded him of something so he decided to extend his examination to the roots. Falling to his knees he began to dig into the earth with his fingers.

Perhaps it was his intense concentration, perhaps he was just getting careless. Whatever the reason, he did not hear a group of four youths cross over the bridge and gather around him and so was surprised when he heard one of them speak.

'What you doin', Grandad?' said one in an aggressive voice.

The Old Man looked back at the figures before him. They were all in their mid-teens but of varying sizes. Two were very large for their age, another somewhat smaller, and the last one smaller still. All were dressed in dark blue trousers of a fabric unfamiliar to the Old Man, together with hooded tops in a variety of colours.

'I said, what are you doin?' It was the smallest of the four who had spoken. At a glance the Old Man sized up the boy. He had seen such a youth a thousand times before. His stance, his aggressive manner, even his very odour told of someone struggling to establish his manhood, seeking to earn his place among his peers.

'You fuckin' deaf or something?' Again the feigned hostility.

The Old Man chose not to rise to the challenge. 'I seek knowledge in these plants, young sir,' he replied, calmly.

'He's stealing our weeds, Robbie,' shouted one of the larger boys.

The smallest youth, clearly the leader of the group, smiled malevolently. 'We don't like it when folk steal our weeds, you old bastard. I don't remember you asking permission.'

This made the other three laugh loudly, joined soon after by their leader. Slowly the Old Man got to his feet. Had they been watching, the youths might have noticed him grab a particular stem with his left hand as he stood up. His right hand reached into his coat pocket for a moment before returning to his side. As he spoke he rubbed the thumb of each hand along the side of each index finger.

'I seek leave from no man to explore the gifts of Nature, my young lord.'

'Forgot your manners, then? Maybe a dip in the canal will help you remember them.' The youth nodded towards his two large colleagues who lurched towards the Old Man. As they tried to grab him he swiftly raised both hands and struck each assailant on their top lips, just under the bridge of the nose. The blows were not hard enough to cause any great damage but were sufficient to halt the attack, forcing both assailants to step back.

The Old Man's defensive manoeuvre surprised all four youths for a moment. The leader was the first to regain his composure. 'Stop pissing about,' he shouted at the two assailants, 'Get him in that canal!'

Before he could add any more orders, his words were drowned out by a loud rumbling sound, coming from one of the larger youths. Looking down, they all saw a damp patch beginning to grow in the boy's groin. As the sound grew louder, so the patch spread until it covered the front and back of his trousers. Horrified, the youth looked down in time to see a thin brown liquid run out of both trouser legs, staining the grass beneath as an appalling smell of sewage filled the air. As his bowels continued to evacuate, he looked towards his leader for some sort of guidance. Getting none, he turned and waddled - the only possible description - back across the bridge, as quickly as his sticky clothes would permit.

The sight of one of his gang retreating only served to anger the leader even more. He was about to demand action from his remaining gang members when he noticed that the other assailant was now staring intently at the middle-sized youth.

Stepping forward, the larger one grabbed his friend in a bear hug. 'God,' he shouted ,'you're gorgeous,' and planted a wide kiss upon the lips of the startled youth, forcing his tongue deep down his throat.

The horror of his predicament gave the recipient a strength that he had never known before. Pushing away his unwanted admirer, he managed to break free of the embrace and fled over the bridge and back towards the houses on the other side. A second later his new admirer was in hot pursuit, calling desperately for him to return for more affection.

The gang leader realised that he was now alone, with the Old Man standing before him. In a blurred instant, he saw the Old Man's arm twitch and, suddenly, he found himself suspended by his throat over the dark waters of the canal. In the days that followed, whenever he looked back, it was the speed of the Old Man's reactions that had really shocked him. He recalled seeing a nature programme where a cobra struck out at a rat, catching it in the blink of an eye. Yet that was nothing to the instantaneous strike of the Old Man. One moment his hand was at his side, the next the youth was grabbed by the throat and hoisted off the ground, powerful fingers compressing his windpipe. The Old Man stopped squeezing just before the youth became unconscious.

'Harken to my words, my young lord. I see in you a worthy gift, a rare talent with which you might do great things. Men will do your bidding, even unto war and death. Yet you must learn to use this gift, for without wisdom only evil and wickedness awaits you. If you would listen I would give you your first lessons. Will you listen?'

Somehow the youth managed to nod.

'Firstly, never send your warriors into battle, but rather lead them.'

Again, a nod.

'Secondly, know your enemy before you draw your sword – for it is too late afterwards.'

Another nod.

'Now go and build on this lesson, so your tribe may prosper from your talents.'

With that the Old Man released the youth who disappeared into the dirty waters of the canal. He surfaced, gasping for air, but still managed to swim to the opposite bank, where he crawled out, and jumped to his feet. From this position of perceived safety he paused, as if to shout something at the Old Man, but thought better of it. Turning, he ran back into the pathway between the houses.

'Having trouble?' The Old Man turned to see Nathan leading the others towards him. They had seen the end of the encounter with the youth but had heard nothing of what was said.

'That boy. All the arrogance of his youth but with no experience to temper it. Yet in him I see great things, if only he is guided aright.' The Old Man paused for a moment, considering something. 'Perhaps we should tarry here. I would speak with his tribal elders, tell them the talents that I can see in him. Ensure that he is apprenticed to the right warrior.'

'Things don't work like that anymore,' replied Nathan.

'How so?'

'There is no tribe, no elders and no warriors.'

'So how will such a youth mature?'

Nathan shrugged.

'But without such guidance he is lost. Only evil awaits him. Surely your ways won't waste such talents?' The Old Man was appalled by Nathan's answer.

It was Carl's turn to speak. 'Maybe in some places. But from an estate like that ...' he nodded towards the houses, 'I don't give him much chance.'

The Old Man shook his head sadly. 'So many of your ways make no sense to me.'

With a final glance towards the houses into which the youth had disappeared, the Old Man turned and continued along the tow-path.

A couple of hours later found four of the group sitting around a window table at a café in the small village of Kintbury, a few hundred yards south of the canal. Reluctantly the Old Man had agreed to leave the tow-path for a short time, nominally to replenish their stocks of food and drink. This reluctance was, in part, due to the unwelcome delay to their journey, but mostly because he was watching a large flock of starlings flying around in complex patterns in the late afternoon sunshine. He had never seen such numbers before, possibly tens of thousands, and had been fascinated by the twists and turns of their impressive aerial display. The group almost had to drag him away to get him to take the short journey to the café where they now awaited the return of Julian.

'Where in God's name has he got to?' said Nathan, peering out of the window across the T-junction at the centre of the village. Nathan had also needed persuading to make this diversion but his concern was more to do with the risk of them being recognised.

Julian, the subject of the question, had tried to allay his fears by offering to go and buy the supplies based upon the suggestion that he was the least noticeable of the group. Even the Old Man had been surprised by the offer but, since none could argue with the logic, Julian had been dispatched with a list of requirements.

Carl responded to Nathan's question with an indifferent shrug. In his view, the chance of a hot drink more than offset the risks. Vicky put on her most relaxed smile, trying to hide her increasing concern about her boyfriend's strange behaviour.

The Old Man made no answer. His attention was drawn to the next table where two women, one elderly, the other of middle age, were having an argument. Or, more accurately, the middle-aged one was having a rant while the elder seemed to be sheepishly taking the brunt of the comments.

'Just because I married your son shouldn't mean that I'm lumbered with you.'

The older woman said nothing, only staring back.

The speaker continued. 'It's all right for him. He's off to work every day. It's me that has to put up with you. So I'm either stuck in the house all day making sure that you don't wander out into the road, or I take you out and I have to watch you like a hawk to make sure you don't get lost. Well, I'm sick of it.'

Again, the older woman made no reply, but tears welled up in her tired eyes.

Further along the main road through the village, out of sight of the café, Julian was shopping for something far more complex than groceries.

'So this thing will guide me to any location that I require, even at night?'

The owner of this outdoor pursuits shop tried to reply in as pleasant a manner as possible, despite the rather blunt tone directed towards him. 'Yes indeed, sir. This unit will take you over the roughest terrain, in the worst of weathers and in a blackout.'

'Let's leave the advertising drivel out for now, shall we? What about use in towns and cities?'

'Just as good, sir. It has a full UK street map already loaded. All you need to do is tap in the postcode and press go.'

A frown passed across Julian's face, giving the shopkeeper a momentary concern that this expensive sale might yet evade him. 'What if you don't have the postcode, only the address?'

'Again, no problem. You can enter that information into the unit instead, but it takes a bit more knowledge of using the set-up menu.'

Another thoughtful frown from Julian.

The shopkeeper pressed on regardless. 'But it is simple to get the postcode for any address. There are web-sites that can do that. Here, let me get it for you.' He turned to the open laptop on the counter beside him and waited for Julian to respond. After a second it was apparent that the information was not coming too readily. 'The address, please?'

Julian was struggling with a dilemma. On the one hand he really had no desire to give away any details of his plans to anyone, let alone a stranger. Yet he was also conscious that his talents with anything in the least technical were non-existent. A memory of his experience with a set-top box flashed through his mind, causing a brief shudder. If this device was to be of any use to him it must be all set up, ready for instant use, even by someone as technically inept as himself. With time running out, if his plan was to succeed his choices were getting limited. Reluctantly he reached into his pocket and took out a piece of paper and placed it flat upon the counter. Carefully covering the name with his hand, he slid the document across so that the shopkeeper could read only the address.

'Thanks,' said the shopkeeper, 'OK, then.' A moment later the information was entered into the laptop and the postcode noted under the address. In his experienced hands the data was transferred to the hand-held GPS device and the die was cast.

'So all I need to do now is to switch it on and it will guide me to this location?' Julian nodded towards the paper, still held on the desk by his hand.

The shopkeeper nodded. 'I can also programme in the start point of the trip if you wish?'

'That won't be necessary. I'm not quite sure where that will be yet.'

'Fair enough. In that case just switch it on and it will determine your location for you. Then just follow the directions on the screen.'

'Excellent. So how much do I owe you?'

This was the part the shopkeeper always dreaded. In truth the GPS unit was ridiculously expensive, which is why he was so keen to get rid of it. Kintbury had few residents rich enough or foolish enough to spend so much on such big-boys toys.

'That will be £675, please.'

As the shopkeeper feared, another frown appeared on his customer's face. This was not due to the magnitude of the figure - Julian was both rich and foolish enough to make the purchase - but because it would take up most of the cash that he was carrying. This would leave him with insufficient funds for the groceries that he was supposed to be buying. He quickly considered the alternatives. He could find a cash machine but that would take yet more time, and he was sure that his fellow travellers would be wondering where he was. Besides, it was far from certain that such a small village would even have one.

His only other option was his credit card. Despite the regular dire warnings given by Nathan, Julian was sure that the young policeman worried too much. He had used the card to buy the kit in Bristol and that hadn't caused any problem. Anyway, very soon it would not be his concern.

Smiling, he presented the card and tapped his PIN into the machine.

—∞—

Chogan, Warren and two troopers jogged down the hill towards Little Bedwyn, entering the hamlet, not through any formal road or pathway, but down a long thin passageway between two houses. All four looked tired and dejected.

The day had not gone well. As expected, the tracker had picked up the trail at the mid-point of the suggested route. By continually halving the residual distance he had made good progress until the point where his target had entered the Savernake Forest. Once inside the huge wooded area he had lost all trace of the Old Man and his group. The problem was not the natural areas of the forest, where he could easily track them through the grass and pine needles that covered the forest floor, but in the large number of tarmac paths and roadways that drove deep into the woods. There were no signs on the roadways that he had time to check, but there were so many that checking all of them was simply not feasible.

Warren's trio rendezvoused with the Canadian in the early afternoon. After a quick recap, they had to accept that the Old Man's group could have left the Wansdyke somewhere within the forest, and headed off in a completely different direction. If so, it was probable that their quarry had eluded them and it would be back to awaiting further mistakes.

In desperation Warren chose to stick with the Wansdyke path theory and so called in the helicopter to drop the foursome outside the forest, just beyond the small town of Chisbury. Here their luck changed. Chogan quickly picked up the trail which led them to an old chapel, alongside a farm. It was clear that this was where the group had spent the previous night.

As Warren reported their progress back to Paternoster, Chogan paused for a moment to admire the magnificent stained glass windows in the end wall of the chapel. He was in deep reflection about the possible story behind the figures in the coloured glass when Warren, his report completed, called the group back onto the trail. As they left, Chogan realised that none of his companions had even noticed the window. Had it existed at home in Canada, something so magnificent would have been treasured. Here it was completely ignored, as was the run-down chapel that housed it. Probably seen as only one of so many examples that could be found all over this country. History, he decided, was completely wasted upon Europeans.

The path from the chapel had led them into Little Bedwyn, where the Canadian was now carefully examining the area in front of a footbridge that carried travellers over a railway line and, beyond, a canal.

'Something strange has happened here.'

Squatting alongside his friend, Warren stared hard at the dust, sand and earth scattered around the base of the concrete steps. As so many times before, he could see completely nothing. 'So, go on then, astonish us.'

'Well, obviously, the main problem is that in the last few hours three large clowns came down these steps and performed some form of elephant mating dance here before moving on up that hill.' He grinned as he looked up at Warren. 'If you can find out who they were then someone should kick their collective ass.'

'Leave it to me, Choggy,' replied Warren, looking up at the two troopers standing behind Chogan. Both turned away to hide their smiles.

'Fortunately I can see the story beneath their antics. Less than an hour earlier all of our targets walked up these steps but then came down again soon after. One of them, the Old Man I think, was running very fast.' Chogan stood up and retraced his steps back towards the houses. 'They all regrouped here. But then ...' Chogan looked carefully at the marks in the ground, invisible to the others, 'only three of them walked back.'

'So one of them vanished?' Warren was in no mood for any more mysteries.

'No. The tracks from the big guy are deeper. He was carrying something. My guess is that he carried the Old Man over the footbridge.'

'Why would he do that?'

'Let's get over to the other side and see.' Chogan stood up and began to return to the footbridge. He stopped when he heard the Mission Impossible theme coming from Warren's phone.

'Yes, Boss,' said Warren into the handset. A broad smile spread across his face. He nodded to his three companions as he listened. 'That's brilliant. We'll get there as fast as we can.' Closing the phone he looked at the three faces watching him. 'We can stop this now. St Clere has just used his credit card at a shop five miles east of here.'

CHAPTER 27

The Four Seasons Café
Station Road
Kintbury, West Berkshire
Monday 27th August
4.00 p.m.

'Well, if he doesn't get back soon I'll have to go and find him!' Vicky was becoming ever more exasperated with her boyfriend. She could feel Nathan's tension.

'Well, what I always say is 'if in doubt – have a bacon sandwich',' said Carl, cheerily. Whether he was trying to diffuse the situation or this was part of his constant desire for food, Vicky wasn't sure but she was grateful for the help.

Nathan shrugged his shoulders, trying to show his reluctance, and looked towards the Old Man for support, only to see that he was still preoccupied with the two women on the next table.

'So that will be a black coffee for me and a tea for my mother-in-law.'

The young waitress noted the drinks order and started towards the kitchen before she was called back by Carl. 'Over here, my lover.' His loud voice only added to Nathan's fears of being noticed. As the girl approached the table his voice boomed out a second time. 'So I reckon that's bacon butties all round, and we should stand another mug of tea each.'

'So that's four bacon sandwiches and four teas?'

'No. Could you make that five? Best get one for Julie, especially as he's the one doing the paying.' Carl laughed at the irony but only got a brief smile from Vicky in return.

The girl noted the order and walked off around the counter and through a beaded curtain into, presumably, the kitchen beyond.

The strained silence returned to the group, who resumed their earlier pastime of staring out of the café window into the street beyond.

Warren had suffered mixed fortunes in his attempt to get his team to Kintbury. When word of St Clere's card payment had reached him, his first thought was to call back the helicopter, only to find that it was flying back for refuelling. All the others were back at base and so too far away to be of any use.

Fortunately the rest of his troop, after their failures on the Wansdyke, had all been picked up by the Transits and were now waiting for orders at Froxfield, a nearby town on the main London road. In no time they covered the short distance to Little Bedwyn and collected Warren, Chogan and their two companions. Now, less than twenty minutes after getting the call from Paternoster, the two vans were driving slowly into the heart of Kintbury.

'Park over there,' Warren instructed the driver, indicating a large space near to a T-junction in the centre of the town. Once stationary, he carefully considered the scene in front of him. From his position in the front seat of the van he could see a variety of shops on either side of the road, including a butcher's shop, a newsagent, a florist and a café.

'Too busy for my liking,' said Preston, looking over his colleague's shoulder.

Warren nodded. While it was not exactly heaving, there were several dozen shoppers using the pavements, crossing the street and standing in a bus queue a few yards along from where the Transits had parked.

'Right,' he said, both to the troopers in the back of his Transit and, via a microphone fitted to an earpiece, to those in the other van. 'We need to spread out and find the targets. They can't have got far. Everyone get miked up and start to mingle. Call in as soon as you see anything.'

'Not sure that we have got the right dress code.' This time it was Chogan who spoke.

Warren looked at his team, all dressed in black fatigues, and nodded. 'Choggy's right. We all look at bit conspicuous. Everyone change into civilian coats and jackets.'

For a minute, chaos reigned in the confined spaces of both vans as several large men all reached into back-packs and changed into the suggested attire. Once completed Warren spoke again.

'OK. I'll get out first. This van, wait for my signal. The rear van, get out when the front van unloads.'

He reached for the handle, opened the door and stepped onto the pavement.

'Where did you get to? You've been ages,' said Vicky as Julian walked into the café.

He placed several plastic bags on the table and allowed his frustration to vent. 'Look, do you want this job done properly or not? I'm sick of eating his rabbit food ...' a nod towards Carl, 'so I've tried to get something a little more appetising. That took time. Plus it seems that now is the time that the local peasants all buy their fodder so I was stuck with them in an appalling shop the size of a telephone box.'

Vicky had often been surprised at Julian's ability to offend those around him but, as she glanced around the café at the other customers now staring at him, she realised that this talent was truly Olympian.

'Well, now that you are back at least we can get back on the road,' said Nathan, getting to his feet.

'So don't you want the bacon sandwiches then? I'm just about to bring them out.' The question came from the waitress. She was walking past the table carrying a tray bearing two cups, one containing tea, the other black coffee.

'Sorry, but we have to get on,' replied Nathan.

'Steady, mate,' said Carl. 'Seems a shame to waste good food. Besides, we are going to have to eat sometime. Having this will mean that we can walk for longer before we bed down for the night.'

'The gorilla's quite right,' said Julian. 'Besides, I'm famished.'

Carl, momentarily unsure whether to thank or smack his new supporter, chose neither. 'Right then, who's with me and Julie?'

Nathan looked around the group. Their faces told him that he was going to lose this one so he sat down again.

'I'll bring them once I've taken this order,' said the waitress, walking off towards the next table.

Vicky had taken no part in the conversation. This was partly because she was unconcerned about eating, but mostly because she had been watching the Old Man. To an innocent observer he had been sitting quietly, his hands clasped together in front of him. However, Vicky had travelled with him long enough to know that what appeared as 'sitting quietly' was, in reality, a façade that he used to mask his actions.

She had seen him place his hand in his coat pocket and withdraw something, hidden in his closed fist. She knew that he kept various seeds in that pocket. As he brought his hands together she could see that the thumb of one hand was in the palm of the other, and the merest hint of movement of the knuckles told her that he was grinding something. Once that task was completed he separated his hands and sat back in the seat. As part of this motion, his hand swept across the tray that the waitress was carrying. Vicky saw a fine dust fall into the cup containing the tea.

His work complete, he returned his attention to the group's conversation. As his eyes swept across the group he must have thought that no one had noticed his actions, until he saw Vicky watching him. In an instant he realised that she had seen everything. A slow smile spread across his face, which she returned. Although no words were spoken Vicky could feel the bond between them strengthen and, for a split second, she had an insight into this man's complex character. As the moment passed, the conspirators returned their attention to their colleague's concerns about bacon sandwiches.

The waitress, unaware of the Old Man's actions, moved to the next table and served the drinks to the two women seated there.

A few minutes later, food duly delivered, the group had fallen silent as each enjoyed their meal. The Old Man had removed the slice of meat from the surrounding bread and was now nibbling at one edge. Having decided that he liked it he took a larger bite and chewed it slowly, evidently enjoying the flavour. Glancing around the table he saw that the others were all doing the same. For a moment a calmness spread across the table but it vanished just as quickly as he saw Carl suddenly tense up at something he had seen through the window.

'What have you seen, Cyric?' asked the Old Man.

'I've just recognised someone.'

Nathan looked in the direction of Carl's gaze to see a tall, fit man in his thirties who was climbing out of a dark blue Transit van. 'Who is he?'

'His name is Colin Warren. Major Colin Warren to give him his full title.'

'How do you know him?'

'He was in the Paras in Afghanistan. We were in different units but I remember him very well.'

As Carl spoke, Warren stepped onto the pavement directly across the street from the café. After a careful glance up and down the busy road, he slapped his hand onto the door panel. Immediately all the other doors opened and several men climbed out. It was then that Nathan noticed a second Transit, parked just behind the first. Yet more men climbed out of this second vehicle. Although all dressed in differing coats and jackets, all wore similar types of trousers and boots.

'Funny thing about Major Warren,' said Carl, also watching the steadily growing band. 'He disappeared from Camp Bastion at very short notice.'

The Old Man had been listening to this conversation with increasing concern. Carl's manner told him that something important was about to happen.

'So what happened to him?' said Nathan.

'Well, it was only a rumour but ...' Carl hesitated as he tried to recall the full story.

'Go on.'

'We all heard that he had bought a house in Hereford.' Carl paused to see if the full implications of his comment would dawn on his fellow traveller. He saw Nathan's eyes widen and so knew that he had understood.

'You mean he joined the Special Forces? The SAS?'

Carl nodded.

'So you think they have set the SAS on us?' Nathan was struggling not to shout as the impact of the information hit him.

'What is this SAS?' snapped the Old Man. 'Kingsmen?'

'Far more than Kingsmen,' replied Nathan 'Elite troops, probably the best in the world.'

'And you think they have been sent out to arrest this little group of misfits?' said Julian, condescendingly. 'Sure that your ego isn't tripping over your paranoia?'

'I remember that before we left the police station, the Inspector was talking about getting the army involved but I'm sure that was just to control the rioting. I just can't believe that we would merit such an over-reaction.'

'I'm sure it is just a coincidence. Perhaps they are just on some form of exercise,' said Vicky.

They watched as the group of men clustered around the Major, who was clearly giving them some form of instructions.

'Well, we will find out soon enough. Strikes me that we can't get onto the street without walking straight into them.' Carl was already looking for a back way out but he knew that it was futile. Within minutes, the troopers would be combing all the surrounding streets.

'There is no such thing as coincidence,' said the Old Man. 'We must act with all speed.'

As he spoke he looked around the café. Everywhere he looked all he could see were man-made objects and materials. Even the flowers on the tables were made of plastic. He thought of his pouch but realised that it contained nothing of any use in this situation.

Yet he could smell something. He had caught the odour as they had arrived and now he realised that it came from behind the counter. As he looked more closely at the bead curtain the waitress emerged with another order. He saw that the curtained doorway did not just lead to the kitchen in the rear but also through the wall into the shop next door. Clearly, the shop owner had two businesses, run in adjoining premises. Once again, he caught the smell on a draught of air coming through the curtain and this time he knew what was being sold next door.

The other business was a florist's.

Without explanation he stood and rushed past the counter, through the bead curtain and out of sight of the others. He returned a few moments later carrying several different types of flower heads.

'Carl, stand by the door. Ensure no one enters. Vicky, I have need of some type of parchment pouch. Find me one. Nathan and Julian, help me tap out the inner dust from these flowers.' The instructions were barked out in quick succession in a tone that did not encourage questions. All four set about their given tasks without a word.

After a short search Vicky found an envelope beneath the counter. She gestured to the increasingly confused waitress.

'May I have this?'

The waitress, turning her head for a second from Carl, now stopping her customers entering or leaving, nodded agreement. 'Take what you like but get him away from that door!'

Carl smiled at the girl. 'Now don't you be worrying, my darlin'. We'll be out of here in two shakes with no harm done.'

The girl smiled back but didn't seem convinced.

The rest of the customers watched in growing concern as the Old Man demonstrated the skill of tapping pollen from the various flower heads to Julian and Nathan. A moment later all three were busily engaged in the delicate task. A moment more and they had created a multi-coloured pile of dust on the plastic tablecloth. This was swept by the Old Man into the proffered envelope which he was about to seal when he paused for a second, as if considering some further action.

Reaching deep into another pocket he withdrew one of the many plastic bags that he had been filling with various types of plant along the way. Nathan recognised this bag as the one containing leaves from the rhododendrons that they had found several nights earlier. Carefully tearing them into small pieces, the Old Man swept them into the open envelope. Finally, he closed the flap and, having checked the seal, he gave the envelope a gentle shake, mixing all the ingredients together.

'We're closed! Bugger off!' Carl gestured to two teenage boys who tried to enter the café.

'No, Carl,' said the Old Man. 'Bid them enter.'

A different gesture and an open door brought the two youths in front of the Old Man.

'How are you called?'

The elder of the two answered, 'My name is Darren. This is my brother, Robert.'

'Well met, Darren and Robert. I have a task that I would have you perform for me. You should know that there might be some slight danger but you will both be handsomely rewarded.' The Old Man saw that at the mention of danger and reward the demeanour of the two changed from suspicion to interest. For a second he reflected on how some things had not changed over the centuries.

'What do we have to do?' This time it was Robert who spoke.

'And how much will you pay us?' said his brother, only a second later.

'Do you see that man, standing beside the Rover cart?' The two boys, although puzzled at the strange description of a Transit van, nodded. 'All I ask is that you take this to him. You must put it into his hand. For that simple task I will pay you both a sovereign.'

'What's a sovereign?' said Robert.

'We can see who is the businessman of the partnership,' said Julian. 'Let's say a tenner.'

'Each? Just to hand this envelope to that bloke across the road? Sounds easy. Where's the danger?'

'You will have to escape afterwards without being caught but even if you fail in that part they will only question you about me, and by then I will be long gone so you can tell then whatever you like.'

'But the real danger is if you take the money and run off without delivering the envelope,' added Nathan.

'Why's that?'

Carl leaned forward, placing his head at the same level as the boys. 'Because that's when I get involved, and I'm far more dangerous than anyone over there.'

'OK, Carl. No need to get heavy.' This time it was Vicky. 'They seem like clever lads, more than resourceful enough to do this small thing.' She smiled at them.

The Old Man could see that they were now hooked. Danger, money and the admiration of women - a combination irresistible to young males everywhere.

Darren glanced at his brother who nodded eagerly. A moment later they were outside the café with the envelope in Darren's hand and Julian's money in their pockets.

'Right, half of you walk up the street, the other half walk down it. Split off in pairs each time you pass a side road.' Warren was directing his forces, not an easy job as the troopers and passing shoppers made for quite a crowd on the limited width of the pavement.

'Major Warren?' said a young voice.

Warren turned to see two youths emerge from the shoppers, one of them offering him an envelope.

'Thank you,' he said. He accepted the offering before turning to Chogan, standing alongside him. 'Paternoster seems to be using younger messengers these days.' He turned back towards the youths, only to find that they had merged back into the stream of shoppers.

Without further thought he ripped open the sealed envelope.

A quarter of a mile away, unseen by anyone in the village, tens of thousands of starlings perched in trees alongside the canal suddenly took to the air.

Expecting some form of written message, Warren's fingers probed into the envelope. Finding nothing, he looked more closely, only to see that it contained some sort of multi-coloured powder, some of which had already adhered to his fingers. He poured the contents into his cupped hand before turning to Chogan.

The Canadian frowned. 'This is not from Paternoster. This is from our quarry. They must know that we're here.'

'What does it mean?'

'Based upon his past history, I suspect that we'll find out very soon.'

As they spoke Warren heard a dull, almost silent, plopping sound. Looking to one side he noticed a moist, white stain on his shoulder, evidence of the attentions of a passing bird.

Chogan smiled at his friend's misfortune. 'That counts as good luck in my tribe.' But his smile vanished when a second and then a third stain appeared on Warren's coat. A moment later several of the other troopers became peppered in white spots, raising several amused comments. However, a moment more and this amusement vanished as it became apparent that these were not isolated droppings. The sound of dull thuds steadily increased until it became obvious that the troop was under a sustained attack from the air. The shower of droppings continued, getting heavier with each passing second.

The sounds of a large flock of birds circling overhead made the crowd, troopers and shoppers, look up. The more unfortunate ones caught the corrosive white liquid in their eyes, a situation made even worse by the consequent rubbing action.

Warren heard the cries of pain and quickly realised that many of his troopers were, at least temporarily, out of action. The light shower progressed into a heavy white rain and then into a monsoon-like downpour. Everything within a 10-metre radius became coated with the terrible, glutinous, white liquid. People tried to move away, only to slip on the increasingly slippery pavement. Attempts to grab onto those alongside only caused further chaos as they, too, were dragged to the floor.

Just as the downpour reached its maximum intensity, the local bus drove into the maelstrom. In a second the windscreen turned an opaque white, causing the driver to switch on his windscreen wipers. The resulting smearing improved his vision for a second before further droppings re-coated the screen.

However, in that brief moment he saw that he was about to run down some shoppers who had fled onto the road to get out of the disgusting downpour. Instinctively he braked hard and swerved to avoid a collision. He missed them but his actions caused the bus to skid on the road, now also coated in the white-green slime. For a second he thought he had regained control, but his hopes were dashed when he felt the bus shudder as it piled into the side of the rear Transit. Driven on by its considerable momentum the bus continued on its destructive path, sliding along until it came to rest embedded in the rear of the front Transit.

The deluge abated as abruptly as it had begun. Warren and Chogan were two of the few left standing in the sea of white slush. The Major looked down at the sticky remnants of his troop, now reduced to thrashing around on the pavement trying to regain their feet. Chogan was looking around, trying to work out their next move.

Glancing across the street he saw the large window of a café, on the far side of the road, through which a group were peering at the unfolding scene. This group comprised an old man, a black man, and three others - one male, one female and one huge.

'It's them,' he shouted, to no one in particular, pointing in the direction of the café.

Warren looked in the direction his friend was pointing and saw the group. For a second his eyes locked onto those of the Old Man. 'Quickly, everyone get to that café.' As he stepped forward his feet shot from under him and he reached out to Chogan for support, only succeeding in dragging him down as well.

Looking back towards the café, he saw that the group had vanished.

Inside the café the group watched the scene unfold. In the space of a few seconds they had seen the street become a winter wonderland scene, but with snow replaced by vast quantities of bird excrement.

'How did you do that?' said an amazed Nathan.

Even the Old Man looked shocked at the outcome of his efforts.

'I was expecting something of this sort. The flowers were once used by farmers in the old times to make birds fertilise their fields. Yet I have never seen it happen on such a scale.' He plunged his hand into his pocket and withdrew a bag. He looked at it thoughtfully for a second. 'Perhaps I have misjudged this rho-de-den-dron. It might have some use after all.'

'One of them has seen us,' said Carl. The urgency in his voice made them all look back to the street where they saw one of the few troopers still standing point towards the café window. 'Time to leave, I reckon.' Then, to the waitress standing alongside him watching events on the street unfold, 'Right then, my lover. This is where you show us the back way out.' All five of them followed the girl through the bead curtain and into the kitchen beyond.

Once the group had left, the two women sitting at the table alongside also looked away from the street scene.

'Right then,' said the younger of the two. 'Time to get you home. That's quite enough excitement for one day.' As she spoke she started to rummage around the bottom of her large handbag. 'Now where did I put those car keys?'

'You put them in your coat pocket, dear. Left-hand side.'

To make the point she reached across to the coat, folded over the back of the chair, removed the keys and presented them to her astonished daughter-in-law. 'Now, I think I'd like to go to the library on the way home. There's a cookery book that I've been meaning to get for ages. Would you mind if I cooked the meal this evening? Sometimes it's nice to have someone else cook, isn't it? Something a bit different, perhaps with a bit more flavour?' She put on her coat with a flourish and breezed out of the café, pausing only to smile at the waitress. Through the open door she called to her companion, still standing at the table, her mouth open in amazement. 'Come along, dear. Don't dawdle.'

—∞—

The last rays of the setting sun saw the group settled down for the night. They had walked for a few more hours along the canal before setting up camp in some woods a few hundred yards off the tow path. They had eaten and were sitting around the dying embers of the small fire that they had lit to stave off the chill of the summer's evening.

The conversation had been sporadic. They had been shocked by the events at Kintbury and seemed reluctant to discuss them. Eventually it was Nathan who broke this temporary, unspoken agreement. 'If they have set the SAS on us then we can't hope to elude them for long.'

'They are one persistent bunch of bastards, and no mistake.' Carl clearly spoke from experience.

'Yet, such is their talent that we have been able to walk across most of Wessex before they crossed our path. I feel that you praise them too highly. Besides, now that we know that they seek us I can take steps to frustrate their purpose.' With these words the Old Man began to settle himself down for the night.

'I have a question for you.' It was Carl who spoke. The others all turned to listen. Nathan and Vicky were the usual source of questions. Neither could recall a single one from the big paratrooper.

'Go on,' said the Old Man, now lying down with his eyes closed.

'Every time the pressure is on, you call me by another name.'

'I call you Cyric.'

'That's the one. Why do you do that? What does it mean?'

The Old Man sat up and stared at Carl.

'Truly, you know not?'

Carl shook his great head.

The Old Man got to his feet, walked around the fire and sat down next to Carl. Reaching out he grasped Carl's right arm at the wrist and drew back the sleeve, exposing his intricate tattoos. These were an interlacing pattern of Celtic designs, strips that curved and twisted in complex shapes from his wrist to his shoulder.

'How did you come by these?'

'I had them done in a tattoo place in Aldershot years ago. Chose them from a book. Got to be honest, I was a bit plastered at the time.'

The word 'plastered' seemed to confuse the Old Man but he soon got the gist of what he was being told.

'Yes, but why these patterns? What attraction did they hold for you?'

'Can't really say. Just seemed to like them.'

'Do they mean something?' This time it was Nathan who spoke.

'For those with the skills to read, they have a message. The tightness of each curve, the width and length of each line. All combine to say something of the person wearing them.'

'So what do these say?' Carl again, now increasingly fascinated.

The Old Man lifted the arm again and ran his finger along the intricate lines of the patterns, as if reading from some great book.

'It says "I am Cyric, spearman of the war band of Tadc, and I have killed many Saxons".'

'What does it mean?'

'In a former life you were also a great warrior. You have walked these hills before in the times when Saxons spread like a plague across the land. You were a spearman in the company of a great warlord, Tadc. For many years your war band held the Saxons at bay, although after your death they finally prevailed. Your inner wisdom remembers this and so recognised the patterns from the book in Al-der-shot.' As he spoke, he reached out and ran a finger across Carl's top lip.

Carl paused for a moment, deep in thought at the revelations the Old Man was giving him. The Old Man fell silent but continued to stare at the ex-paratrooper, as if waiting for something.

Suddenly Carl looked up. 'I can remember now. It's as if a fog is clearing in my head. I can recall the fighting and my comrades. I can see Tadc. He was even bigger than me, a magnificent fighter. It's all coming back to me. I can remember so much. I remember …' Carl paused, as if to confirm his thoughts. Confident in his recollection, he continued '… you!'

The Old Man smiled and put his arm around Carl's shoulders. It was the first sign of real affection that any of them had seen from him and so was all the more surprising.

'Indeed. That was one of my Returns. We walked these paths together in those far-off days. Tadc made you my bodyguard, although I had no need of such assistance. Many years we spent together and, throughout all the centuries, I never found a better friend.'

A tear began to run down Carl's cheek, causing him to turn away in embarrassment.

The Old Man continued. 'I was delighted when the fates conspired to throw us together again in that Kingsman's Palace. Yet I could not tell you of our past until your damaged mind was ready. It is a great relief that you have reached such a condition.'

'I knew that something was happening. Ever since we started the journey I had this feeling of having done this job before.'

'So that was how you knew how to lay him down when I had to revive him by the canal bridge. You had a sort of deja vu?' said Vicky.

Turning towards her the Old Man replied. 'This word is unknown to me, but if it means reaching into our inner wisdom, the wisdom that is passed to us from our forefathers, then you are right. This 'deja vu' lies within all, only awaiting the right moment to emerge.'

'So that is what you tap into when you assimilate? Like you did with the guy in Bristol,' said Nathan.

'This is so.'

Carl sat in silence, the full implication of this revelation gradually dawning upon him. After a second he pulled back the sleeve on his other arm, revealing another set of complex Celtic patterns.

'So what do these say?'

'Ah,' said the Old Man reluctantly. 'There, I fear, your inner wisdom abandoned you. The patterns speak of things that I know to be false.'

'What do you mean?' said Carl, now looking concerned.

The Old Man lifted the huge arm and examined it carefully in the firelight.

'It says … ' he hesitated and examined the arm a second time. 'Sometimes the inner wisdom cannot be relied upon. The drink may have been your guide here.'

'So what does it say?' repeated Carl, now really worried.

'It says … ' again a pause. 'It says … that you are a great lover of sheep.'

Unable to contain themselves, Vicky, Nathan and Julian all began to laugh at the horrified look that spread across Carl's face.

CHAPTER 28

Embourne Copse,
Just south of the Kennet and Avon Canal,
Berkshire
Tuesday 28th August
1.00 a.m.

Julian waited until he was sure that Vicky had fallen asleep. He knew from experience that once she had drifted off it would take a great deal to wake her. Carefully he slipped out of the sleeping bag and moved out of the tent. He had left the flap unzipped, blaming the warmth of the evening, and had managed to hide the fact that he had not changed out of his clothes.

He hesitated for a second to glance back at his girlfriend. He had enjoyed their time together but knew that it was coming to an end. It was always the same for him. Women seemed to like his company at first but then his attraction seemed to diminish. Still, if this evening's plans were even half successful then he wouldn't be short of female admirers. She would soon change her tune then.

He crept over to where the Old Man was sleeping. As expected, he saw that the slumbering shape was not wearing his coat - the warm evenings had meant that it had been laid on the ground alongside his sleeping form. As carefully as possible Julian reached into one of the pockets and removed the otter-skin pouch. At first the slimy feel and rank smell almost made him gag but, mindful of his greater purpose, he placed it into his own pocket and, as silently as he could, he walked further into the copse.

Had he turned around he would have seen that the Old Man was not asleep, as the theft of the pouch had roused him. His ancient eyes followed Julian until he disappeared into the woodland gloom. Unconcerned, he rolled over and returned to his slumbers.

Julian walked for a couple of minutes before removing from his pocket the GPS that he had paid so much for in Kintbury. Pressing the 'On' button, as demonstrated so carefully by the shopkeeper, he waited for some response. At first none came. The unit seemed to be dead, leading to an angry reaction building up within him. But, just as he was about to throw it away in petulant disgust, the screen lit up and displayed a map of the area. His location was marked by a green dot and the route to his pre-programmed destination was highlighted in red. The screen told him that it was two miles away in a direct line, two and a half if the suggested route was followed. Grinning at his new technical competence, he strode out in the proposed direction.

At first his pace was slowed by the rough, wooded ground chosen by the GPS. Initially, he chose not to use his torch, relying on the light of the fortuitous full moon and clear sky. Just as he decided that he was far enough from the camp to risk the light, the GPS brought him out of the woodland and onto a country lane, enabling him to speed up considerably.

Three-quarters of an hour later he found himself in front of a pair of high metal gates through which he could see extensive gardens and, at the end of a long gravel drive, a large country house. Reaching into his pocket he took out his mobile phone and switched it on. He felt a small thrill of rebellion as the screen lit up. For Julian, Nathan's paranoia held sway no more. He quickly selected the number, added to the phone's memory in Vicky's flat days before, and waited for a reply.

Nothing happened.

After a few frustrating seconds he looked again at the phone screen to see the lack of any signal bars on the display. Cursing silently to himself he tried to think of a Plan B. He recalled that he had passed a telephone box a few minutes before reaching the house. It was probably vandalised but he was short on alternatives. He jogged back along his route until he found the iconic red structure. On opening the door his nose was assailed by the smell of stale urine. In any other circumstances he would have turned and walked away but this plan was too important to abandon now so he pressed on, lifting the telephone. To his immense relief he heard a dialling tone.

A few moments later, in a large bedroom on an upper floor of the nearby house, a telephone rang. An elderly man, roused from a deep sleep, rolled over to answer it.

The man was Sir Patrick Donelly. Widely regarded as the foremost businessman of his generation, he had started with nothing on a council estate in Leeds. He had earned his first million before his 25th birthday, following an approach that was to become a pattern for the rest of his life. This involved buying under-performing companies, ramping up their profitability using a combination of business acumen and low cunning, before selling them on at substantial profits. Now, allegedly retired, he was still on the boards of several multinationals and had been appointed as a special advisor on business issues to the Prime Minister.

'Leave it, dear. William will answer it.' The voice came from Joan, his wife of 38 years.

'No. We gave him the night off. Don't you remember, he has gone up to London?' With an effort he looked at the alarm clock and switched on the bedside light, much to his wife's annoyance.

'Well, let it go to the answerphone then.'

'It might be important. People don't normally call at this time unless there is a problem.' He lifted the phone. 'Hello, Pat Donelly.'

'Sir Patrick? I'm really sorry to call you at such a ridiculous hour. My name is Julian St Clere. We have met once or twice but you know my father, Alain, better.'

'Yes, Mr St Clere. I know your father very well. How can I help you?'

'As I say, I'm really sorry to call, but my car has broken down just down the road from you and I can't get a mechanic out until the morning.' Julian had always been surprised at his ability to lie smoothly. 'I know this is really impertinent, but could I beg a sofa for the night?'

Donelly covered the mouthpiece with his hand. 'It's the son of a friend of mine,' he whispered to his wife. 'He's broken down near here and needs a bed for the night. OK with you?'

His wife gave him a withering look that told him of her opposition to the idea. However, her reply was more equivocal. 'Whatever you think, darling. It's up to you.' For a second Donelly weighed his wife's obvious opposition against his own desire to help someone, even a distant acquaintance, in evident need.

On the other end of the phone line Julian held his breath as his plan teetered on the brink of failure.

After what seemed to be an age he heard Donelly's voice again. 'I'm sure that we could do better than a sofa. Where are you? Do you need me to come and get you?'

'No thanks. I think I'm only a few hundred yards from your house. I could be there in just a couple of minutes.'

'OK. That's settled. I'll open the gates. See you then.'

Ten minutes later Julian was sitting in the lounge of the country house, drinking coffee with his hosts. Both Sir Patrick and his wife, still wearing their dressing gowns, had come down to sort out their unexpected guest.

'How is your father? I've not seen him for a few weeks.'

'He's fine and sends his regards. It was his idea that I should call you.' Another lie but Julian was in too deep to care.

'Not a problem. Always happy to help out. Now, let's get you settled into the guest suite.'

'Before we do that, may I just use the bathroom? I'm afraid that I'm quite desperate. Might not even make it to the guest room.' A weak smile emphasised his predicament.

'Well, if things are that bad you had better use the downstairs loo. It's the first on the left, by the front door.'

'Thank you so much,' said Julian. 'I'll be back in just a moment. Sorry again.'

He left the lounge, closing the doors behind him, and moved into the large hallway. Ignoring the directions, he ran up the staircase and quickly located the master bedroom. Once inside he dashed into the en-suite toilet where he found two ornate wash basins, together with an impressive bath and shower area. Around one of the basins he saw a range of toiletries and cosmetics, around the other there was a can of shaving cream, a razor and a toothbrush. Grabbing the toothbrush with one hand he withdrew the Old Man's pouch with the other. He carefully rubbed the bristles of the brush around a section of the pouch. Once done, he paused for a moment, finally considering the magnitude of the step that he was about to take. A second later, the decision made, he placed the toothbrush in his mouth. Instantly he blacked out and collapsed onto the tiled floor.

—⚭—

A muffled cry from just outside the tent woke Vicky with a start. Finding that Julian was not lying next to her she initially thought that he had stepped outside on a call of nature. She looked through the open tent flap into the darkness only to make out the shape of the Old Man crouched over Carl's sleeping frame. 'What's happening?' she called out.

'Will there be no peace this night!' It was the Old Man's irritated whisper that came back to her. 'I must treat Carl while he sleeps or his demons will return.'

As her eyes became accustomed to the dark she could see that he was pinching at Carl's ear. It was his cry that had woken her. 'Have you done this every night?' she asked.

'Only at the start of our journey. Since then he has needed the hendle oil less and less.'

Vicky had never heard of hendle oil so chose to pursue a different avenue. 'Why must he be asleep?'

'It is vital that his mind knows nothing. He must think that the terrors are passing from him without any outside help. Only then will he emerge cleansed. He is almost back to his earlier state. That is why he could recall his former life.'

Vicky wondered how many other ways this strange man had helped people without their knowledge, or thanks. In so many ways he was certainly odd. Her thoughts returned to her missing boyfriend. 'Do you know where Julian is?'

'He is gone. I think that we will not see him again on this Return.'

'What do you mean 'gone'?' said Vicky, puzzled by the answer.

'He is putting his scheme into effect,' replied the Old Man. 'Now, let me take my rest.'

'What scheme? What are you talking about?' Vicky had now left her tent and was standing over the Old Man. Before he could answer she was joined by Nathan and Carl, now both awake, the latter blissfully unaware of the Old Man's ministrations.

'Is it not obvious? The scheme that he has been plotting since the beginning of our journey.' He looked for some comprehension but was only met by three blank faces. 'Surely you have read the signs. His words, his expressions, his actions?'

'I think you have the better of us in those areas,' said Nathan. 'Tell us what you think he is up to.'

'I had not realised that you had lost these skills so totally. How can you understand each other if you cannot read such signs? Without them all you can go by is a person's words and that is never …'

'This is no time for another lecture on the faults of the world. What has happened to Julian?' Vicky was getting worried.

'He has taken my pouch and has gone to find someone to assimilate with. Someone with a greater wisdom in a field he considers important. I suspect that gold will be at the heart of it. It usually is.'

'Why do you think that?' said Nathan.

'Surely you could see his purpose in his actions.' Again, he was met with three blank faces. 'Why do you think that he changed his mind so abruptly when he chose to join this expedition? Why do you think he has endured all the physical torment of the journey?'

Vicky had known there must have been a reason for Julian's actions but had no idea what it had been.

The Old Man continued. 'Assimilation was his goal. He has tried to steal my pouch before but became scared when he saw that I was awake. I suspect that being almost captured by the Kingsmen today forced his hand. Had he but asked I would have given it to him. It is nothing to make another. So now he is gone and you know about his scheme. I feel that we are better off without him. And so do you!' This last remark was directed at Vicky. 'You have already decided that you must part from him but have lacked the courage to tell him so. Well, now he has taken the decision for you. So then, let us sleep.' With that he lay down on the ground and rolled over, turning his back upon his companions.

'I'm not sure that you have thought this through,' said Nathan. 'If he does assimilate he will be in a deep coma for several hours. Correct?'

'That is so,' came the muffled reply.

'When that happened to you we all thought you were dead. Will it be the same for Julian?'

'Of course. If he assimilates this night it will be tomorrow's noon before he wakes. Longer if he uses too much, which likely he will.'

'What's your point, Professor?' said Carl, anxious to get back to sleep.

'Julian's assimilation will be seen as a suspicious death. Standard practice would be for him to be given a post-mortem.'

'So he could wake up in the middle of all that, with his important bits in glass bottles?'

Carl's gallows humour shocked Vicky into action. 'No. That can't be allowed to happen. No matter what my feelings are towards him we can't risk that.' She knelt down and shook the Old Man by the shoulder. 'When did he leave? Can we catch up with him?'

'He took the pouch very recently. It would be simple to catch him. But why should I want to? It is his choice. Besides, this world already has too much stupidity. One less fool should gladden the hearts of all that remain.'

'Oh no! I'm getting wise to you now. You trot out the standard line about not getting in the way of Nature's awful progress yet then anonymously help out a stranger with dementia. You pick and choose those who you wish to help. Well, as things stand Julian is due to die a horrible death and I cannot believe that you would want that. So get up and help us prevent it.'

For a second the Old Man did not move. Then, slowly, he rolled over and got to his feet. 'Very well. If that is your wish, let us go. Strike camp and follow me.' Without waiting he turned and jogged into the woods. The other three grabbed the tents and cooking materials and stuffed them into backpacks before heading after the Old Man.

The next thirty minutes were a revelation. All three struggled to keep up with the Old Man as they followed Julian's trail through the woods. The moonlight gave just enough illumination for them to progress without stumbling yet the Old Man ran as if they were in full daylight. He even had time to continue his ongoing testing of the grasses and leaves he found along the way, spitting out the results as he went.

The trail took them out of the woods and onto a series of country lanes until they found themselves outside a large country house. At the metal gates, left open for some reason, the group paused to catch their breath.

'So you think he went in there?' said Vicky.

'I have no doubt of it,' replied the Old Man. 'Let us proceed.'

Before they could move any further down the gravel driveway the stillness of the night was riven by an appalling scream. Starting impossibly high, the sound got lower and lower in pitch until it passed beyond the range of human hearing. Nathan recognised it instantly as the sound he had heard on the Bristol estate on the night of the riot. It could only be the sound of someone going through assimilation.

'That must be Julian,' he shouted, and sprinted towards the house, followed by the others. All at once they began to pound on the front door, which was opened by an elderly lady wearing a dressing gown.

'Is Julian here?' shouted Vicky.

The woman, stunned by both the scream and the pounding on the door, could only point the way up a staircase. Gently pushing past her all four ran up the stairs.

'Julian?' shouted Vicky.

'Through here,' called a male voice which the group followed, through a bedroom and into an en-suite bathroom in which an elderly man was supporting Julian's lifeless body.

'He's dead!' said the man, obviously very shocked. 'I don't know what happened. He said that he needed the toilet but we sent him to the one downstairs. Why he came up here I have no idea.'

'We need to get him outside,' said Nathan.

'No problem,' said Carl as he hoisted Julian over his massive shoulder and carried him out, followed by a distressed Vicky.

The Old Man noticed that his pouch and a toothbrush were lying on the floor of the bathroom. Picking them up he placed both into a pocket of his coat before turning to Nathan who was trying to comfort the elderly man.

'Bring him downstairs.'

Back in the elegant hallway the elderly couple were starting to overcome their shock at finding Julian's body.

'Who are you all?' said the elderly woman. 'What have you done with Julian?'

'Don't worry about anything,' said Nathan, in his best police officer voice. 'We will see to everything.' He glanced at the Old Man, nodding ever so slightly towards the elderly couple.

Taking his hand out of his pocket the Old Man reached out to both of them in turn. First he shook the man's hand. 'You have had a terrible shock.' Then he shook the woman's hand. 'Thank you so much for looking after our friend. We are most grateful.' In each case the handshake seemed slightly longer than was required for a normal farewell. 'I suggest that you go back to bed now. Things will seem so much better in the morning's light.' Still nodding, the Old Man walked back onto the driveway.

'Well, if that's what you think,' said the man.

'Seems a good idea to me,' said the woman.

Both were walking towards the stairs when Nathan gently closed the front door behind him.

Once outside, the Old Man, anxious to ensure they were not followed, directed Carl to carry Julian a few hundred yards from the house. They finally stopped alongside an old telephone box against which Julian was laid. Vicky tried to examine him but struggled in the half-light.

'Does anyone have a torch or something?' Her urgency was evident.

Carl reached into his rucksack and pulled out a head torch which he threw to Vicky. Switching it on, she adjusted the elastic strap around her forehead and set about the examination.

She quickly checked his pulse and pupils. Julian's condition was just the same as the Old Man's when she had checked him in the police cell. Apart from a slightly higher temperature, Julian had all the signs of being nothing more than a corpse.

'So what do we do now? Can you revive him or do we have to wait?' she called out to the Old Man.

From a ditch at the side of the roadway the Old Man replied. 'I have no desire to wait here all night. Returning him to his normal state of stupidity now, whilst undesirable, would at least be timely.'

'I thought he should now have all the cleverness of the old bloke, back there?' asked Carl, nodding in the direction of the house.

'Well, let us see what he has learned, shall we?' As the Old Man climbed out of the ditch he started to chew on some leaf stalks that he had found. He licked his fingertips, applying some of the chewed mixture to them. The remainder he spat out onto the ground where it landed just to the left of Julian's prostrate form. Reaching down, he grasped both of Julian's earlobes.

'Hold him steady,' he said to Carl and Nathan.

Once they were in position the Old Man squeezed both lobes very hard. For a second Julian's body contorted with the pain before relapsing back to his former position.

Vicky, worried that the treatment had not worked, leaned over and stared into Julian's face, looking for some small sign of life. As she did so he opened his eyes.

'What the bloody hell are you doing here?'

'As rude as ever. Glad to have you back.' As she spoke she could see his eyes begin to widen.

'Wait a minute. I'm beginning to remember, to understand. I can see it all now. How can I have been so stupid?'

For a second Vicky thought that Julian was expressing some sort of regret. As ever, she was to be disappointed.

'Now I know everything that Patrick Donelly knows. I can see everything so clearly.' Then, more to himself than anyone else, 'There was no way that I was ever going to make that project work with so little capital. The market would have been so much bigger if I offered a wider range of ... Perhaps I could segment it for different customer bases. Perhaps if ...' He looked back at Vicky, still staring into his eyes. 'I can see it all now,' he repeated. 'I'm going to be so rich. Sorry, dear Vicky, but from here on out I'll be way above your league. You're dumped!'

'As I feared. The pursuit of gold. I never understood how the Others always yearned for it,' said the Old Man as he returned to the ditch.

'Well, you old derelict, that's because you're the stupid one. What do you know?' As he spoke he could still taste the mixture from the pouch in his mouth. He remembered the toothbrush and the effect that it had had on him.

In an attempt to sit more upright against the telephone box Julian placed his hands on either side. His fingers touched the spittle, left behind by the Old Man a few moments earlier. At first he felt distaste at having come into contact with something so disgusting but then he looked at the Old Man in the ditch. As he watched Julian saw the Old Man spit out another chewed up combination of leaves and grasses, and an idea came to him.

'OK then, let's see what you really know!'

Almost at the same moment the Old Man realised what Julian was about to do.

'No!' he screamed, and dived towards the seated form.

Julian ignored the warning and smiled as he put his moistened fingers to his lips.

For the second time that evening the scream of assimilation ripped across the night sky. As before, Julian's open mouth started with a combination of high pitch and loudness that made the others clamp their hands over their ears. Then the pitch began to drop, although the loudness remained, resonating into the skulls of all present. After what seemed like an age the scream ended and Julian rolled over onto the road surface.

Vicky was the first to recover. She knelt alongside Julian, resting his head in her lap. Once again, she carried out the basic examination and got the same results, although this time his temperature was perhaps a little higher. She looked across at the Old Man, expecting him to repeat the revival treatment, but the look on his face frightened her.

'You can bring him round again, right?'

The Old Man shook his large head. 'Assimilation brings with it an agony that only the strong can survive, and then only once for each Return. Only the sleep of centuries can prepare the mind for another. He has chosen two assimilations within an hour. He is beyond my help.'

As he spoke Vicky became aware of the heat coming from Julian's head. She placed her hand on his forehead only to swiftly remove it again. His head was too hot to touch. She carefully lifted his eyelids to re-check his pupils but found that his eyes had become very bloodshot. Heat from his head now forced her to move position, taking it out of her lap and laying it back on the ground. With Carl and Nathan's help, she sat Julian up against the telephone box. By now his head was very hot although the rest of his body seemed normal. Then she noticed a small drop of blood run down his upper lip from one of his nostrils. As she checked the nostril she saw another one fall from his left ear onto his collar. Carefully turning his head she saw still more flowing from his right ear. Lifting an eyelid again she saw that his eyes were now completely blood-red. Looking more closely she realised that the liquid was not just blood but a viscous combination of fluids. She began to panic. Something beyond her experience was happening to Julian. Feeling helpless, she sat back to try and think what to do next, only to see that the red liquid from his ears and nostrils had now increased to a steady flow.

At that moment his jaw dropped, opening his mouth to allow a cascade of the horrendous liquid to erupt, driven by some massive build-up of pressure within the skull. Instinctively, Vicky swayed to one side to avoid the stream of the blood-red mucus, but not enough to avoid flecks peppering her arm and shoulder. Horrified, she looked up at the others for support, only to see Nathan and Carl looking on in appalled bewilderment. The Old Man just stared down impassively at the nightmare that was unfolding before them.

The release of fluid from the mouth seemed to lessen the pressure inside Julian's head, reducing the flow from his nose and ears. Again Vicky lifted Julian's eyelid but her stomach heaved at what she saw. The socket no longer contained an eyeball, or indeed anything else. She found herself staring into an empty skull, its contents now reduced to a viscous pool that stained the ground beneath them.

The Old Man wasn't sure if Vicky wanted an explanation but provided it anyway. 'The great heat causes the brain to melt like iron in a furnace. It bursts out through any route that it can find, leaving only emptiness behind. I have seen it many times but have never been able to halt it.'

Vicky stood and looked down at the corpse that had so recently been her partner. 'You were right,' she said to the Old Man. 'He was a fool. But, for a short time at least, he was my fool. And no matter what he said to me at the end, I'm going to miss him dreadfully.' She began to sob uncontrollably and, accepting Nathan's consoling arm, buried her head in his chest.

Within a surprisingly short time everything was arranged. Clearly someone had to stay with Julian's body and report his death to the authorities. Vicky quickly volunteered but declined offers from both Carl and Nathan to remain with her.

'Both of you,' she explained, 'have come too far not to see this journey through.'

The Old Man, once he realised that his suggestion of burying the body in the woods broke some form of social taboo, lost interest in the problem and announced that he must continue his journey, with or without them.

'Besides,' he said, 'once the Kingsmen are here to collect Julian's corpse it will be difficult for me to escape their clutches. It would be better if I was long gone by then.' So all three said their goodbyes to the young doctor before turning and walking back towards the woods.

Only the Old Man hesitated, as if wanting a private word with Vicky before he left. 'It is a great sadness to me that you will no longer be my apprentice. I was beginning to enjoy our learnings together.'

Despite her grief Vicky was also sad at their parting, realising that she would never share his knowledge of plants and medicine, her plans for curing bird flu now abandoned by this awful bereavement. 'I shall miss our little chats,' she replied. 'I had learned just enough to realise how much there is still to know.'

The Old Man nodded and turned to leave once more but hesitated again. 'Perchance there is still hope. I cannot delay my journey for too long, as the bad times are coming and I must find my Rest ahead of them. But if you can escape from the Kingsmen then I will wait for you at some place further along our path.'

'That would be brilliant,' said Vicky, keen to grasp at any opportunity, however slim. 'Where do you suggest?'

The Old Man thought for a moment. 'Calleva,' he said. 'We shall wait for you tomorrow in the late afternoon at Calleva.' Without waiting for an answer he turned and followed the other two into the darkness.

Once they were out of sight Vicky opened the door of the telephone box. She had agreed with Nathan's suggestion that she should not use her mobile phone, so she called the emergency services from the land line. That done, she sat down on a fallen tree trunk to await their arrival.

Only then did she start to think about the likelihood of catching up with the group. As she thought through all the reasons that might get in her way, and how she could overcome them, she realised that there was still one significant problem.

Where, on earth, was Calleva?

CHAPTER 29

The Mortuary
Royal Berkshire Hospital
Reading
Tuesday 28th August
7.00 a.m.

The clatter of a hospital trolley woke Vicky from her uncomfortable sleep. Chairs were for sitting, not sleeping, she thought. In fact she had learned over the years that the chairs placed in NHS corridors were not that suitable even for sitting.

She moved upright and stretched to ease the stiffness in her limbs. Although the last few hours had been a blur she had to admit that things had gone surprisingly smoothly. The arrival of the ambulance, the transfer to the hospital, the inevitable police questions – all had run their course without any major hitch. Even the telephone call to Julian's parents, although the most difficult thing she had ever had to do, went far better than she could possibly have hoped. They had been utterly distraught to hear of their son's death yet Vicky could sense that they were not overly surprised. It was almost as if they expected him to get into more trouble than he could cope with sooner or later. They were now driving to the hospital from their London house and promised to be with her inside an hour. A glance at her watch told Vicky that she had not slept for long and so their arrival was imminent.

Her thoughts moved on to her own mother, still lying in the Bristol hospital, or so she thought. Vicky had not been in contact for several days so perhaps she might have been sent home by now. Out of habit she stepped into the small office alongside the mortuary corridor, picked up the telephone and rang a familiar number.

'Ward B3. Sister Sampson speaking.'

Vicky was relieved that her friend was on duty. 'It's Vicky, June. Sorry I've not been in touch but things have been rather hectic.' She quickly summarised the events of the last few days.

'Vicky, I'm so sorry. As you know I was never a fan of Julian but it must have been awful for you to go through all that.'

'Thanks, June. How's Mum? Is she still with you in the hospital?'

'She is really fine. All the tests are indicating that the cancer has simply vanished.'

'That's great news. When do you expect her to be going home?'

Vicky noticed that her friend seemed to lower her voice before replying. 'That's where the problems start. Mr Courtney is determined to keep her in for ever more tests. He has not been able to find any explanation for her recovery and is not allowing her home until he does.'

'Well, I should be back in Bristol in a few hours, so I'll sort things out then.'

'So you've given up any hope of catching up with old man. That seems a pity.'

'Not totally, but it does seem unlikely that I will be able to get clear of all this and be in Calleva by late this afternoon.'

'Where?'

'Calleva. I've never even heard of the place so it's even more unlikely that I'll get there in time.'

'Well, don't worry about things this end. I'll do my best to look after your mum until you get back, whenever that is.'

'Thanks, June. I'll try to keep in better contact. Bye.'

As June Sampson replaced the telephone she looked out of the ward office to see James Courtney walking towards her. He was smiling as he entered, closing the door behind him. June had learned to adopt a cautious approach whenever he tried to be pleasant.

'Have you heard anything from Vicky Snow yet?'

'Nothing, Mr Courtney. I'm sure that she would speak with you first.' June knew that she wasn't a good liar.

'Well, I know that you are good friends so I just wondered. No matter.' Courtney turned to leave.

'I was wondering when you were planning to discharge Mrs Snow. I see that all her tests have come back fine and I know that she is very keen to get back to her own bed.'

'Ah yes, Mrs Snow.' Courtney's face grew serious. 'I still think that we should conduct further tests. None of us want a relapse, do we?'

'What other tests do you have in mind? Surely she has had all the usual ones and, as I said, they're all fine.'

'Sometimes it's hard to tell from the basic ones. I'm thinking of something a little more, how shall we say, intrusive.'

His hesitant reply only served to put June even more on her guard. 'What do you mean, intrusive?'

'I have planned for her to have biopsies taken from her lymph glands, her lungs and, if they show nothing, her brain.'

June was appalled. 'But that would mean surgery under full anaesthetic, with all the attendant risks. How can you possibly justify that, especially on a patient who is fit and well? How can that be in her best interests?'

'Sometimes we have to take a wider view. For the greater good, you understand.'

'I understand very well, Mr Courtney. I understand that something amazing has happened to this patient and that you are desperate to discover what that is.' June was surprised by her courage in standing up to the consultant and decided to press on before it ran out. 'I understand that you seem to be prepared to do anything to achieve that end, regardless of what is best for the patient. But haven't you forgotten something?' You cannot operate without her permission and there is no way that she will ever give it, especially after I've spoken with her.'

'I'm sorry that you don't share my natural inclination to find out how this patient returned to full health. My only desire is to find a way to share this medical landmark with all cancer sufferers.'

'We both know that this is more to do with a Nobel prize than this 'greater good', but this is all academic. I'll make sure that she won't be signing anything.'

James Courtney had needed to acquire many skills to become a top consultant. His medical knowledge had provided him with a good starting point but his work now required skills in management, control and, where required, intimidation. Calling upon this last skill, he leaned across the table until his face was almost touching the seated nurse.

'You have been a valuable member of this hospital for longer than either of us would care to admit. It would be most unfortunate if your years of excellent service were to come to an abrupt end, as it most certainly would if you oppose me on this. Besides, your sacrifice would be wasted. The matter has been taken out of Mrs Snow's hands.'

'What do you mean?'

'For several days now I have been concerned about this patient's mental health. To be brought back from the point of death must have been an awful trauma for her. Last night I was able to get a colleague of mine, a consultant psychiatrist, to consider the case and he is in full agreement with me.' A sly smile spread across his face.

June listened in horror. She knew where this was going.

Courtney took a piece of paper from his pocket and waved it under June's nose.

'I have just come from his office. We have both decided that, in the best interests of the patient, she should be sectioned under the Mental Health Act. From now on, faced with the regrettable absence of any next of kin, all decisions relating to her medical well-being have been placed in the hands of a designated consultant - in short, me. I will be carrying out the first of these operations as soon as there is a space in the theatre programme, which I understand to be around early evening today. Don't cross me on this one, June. You will lose.' He turned and stormed out of the ward office.

In an abject panic, June picked up the telephone and tried to call back the number used by Vicky a few moments before. The unavailable tone only served to heighten her fears. She tried Vicky's mobile number, only to get the answerphone message that she had heard so often over the last few days.

She realised that she had no way of contacting her friend in time. Without Vicky's direct involvement as next of kin there was no way that Courtney could be stopped.

Her eyes alighted on a business card sticking out from a pile of papers on her desk. The card read 'Eddie Rylands, Journalist' and gave a contact telephone number. As she dialled the number she realised that this was the last, the most desperate, of her final straws.

—∞—

After spending an unsettled night in yet another wooded copse, Nathan, Carl and the Old Man had risen early and had been walking all day. Having left the canal, they were now following another of the Old Man's invisible pathways leading, he assured them, to the Roman town of Calleva. The mid-afternoon heat and the events of the previous night had minimised the conversation so it was something of a surprise when the Old Man spoke.

'After the great stain that you call Bristol I'm worried what I am going to find at Calleva. It was a large city when I last walked this road, one that the Romans called a civitas.'

'Regional capital,' said Nathan to Carl.

'I did wonder,' replied Carl, sarcastically.

'I'm surprised that we have not seen any sign by now. I would have thought that the city would have spread out at least as far as this.' The Old Man looked around at the open fields that surrounded them.

'What was it like then?' asked Nathan.

'As I said, it was a large city, built around a central forum and surrounded by a strong defending wall, over a league's distance around its edge.'

'About a mile and a half,' said Nathan, again to Carl.

'Within the walls were all manner of trades. Brewers, fullers, workers in metal and stone, together with all the activities involved in government.'

Again, Nathan turned to Carl. 'Brewers, you already know. Fullers were …'

'Do you want a smack?' The big soldier smiled. 'If you don't know by now that I'm allergic to education then I've a well-tried way of convincing you.'

Nathan took the hint and returned his attention to the Old Man who had now stopped and was looking at something in the distance. Nathan followed his gaze and saw, across the large field in front of them, the unmistakeable flint and mortar walls of a Roman city.

'Calleva Atrebatum,' said the Old Man. 'It seems to be the same size as my last visit, which surprises me.'

The sight of the walls seemed to spur them on and within a few minutes they were standing before what Nathan realised was the western gateway. The straight path that they had been following all day had led them right to it. Clearly, they had been following yet another Roman road.

The walls either side of the gateway were built in layers of flint and slabs of stone, up to a height that reached four metres in some places. Even though the top part of the gateway had long disappeared and no barrier blocked entry to the city, the walls alone, stretching for hundreds of metres on either side, gave testament to how great a stronghold Calleva must once have been.

The Old Man barely gave the walls a glance as he pressed on into the area within. Once inside he stopped in his tracks and let out a gasp, heard by the other two as they caught up with him. Inside the massive walls of this Roman city there was - nothing. All that they could see were open fields covered in grass, stretching in all directions to the encircling walls beyond.

'So it is all gone,' said the Old Man, mostly to himself. 'All the houses, temples, workshops have just been allowed to rot away. I am surprised that such a large city should be allowed to vanish so completely, yet I should not be.' He turned to Nathan. 'Note this well, my friend. No matter how great the works of the Others, Nature will always be victorious in the end.'

Carl noticed movement over to his left. 'Something's happening over there,' he said, pointing towards a collection of portable cabins in one of the smaller fields. 'Let's take a view.'

The Old Man nodded.

As the three men approached they could see that the field was being excavated as part of some sort of archaeological project. Once closer, they could see a large sign that read: '*University of Dunstable, Department of Archaeology, Summer School.*'

'Can I help you?' The question came from a girl in her late teens, dressed in shorts, army boots and a tee shirt bearing the motto 'Archaeologists dig it deeper!'

'What is happening here?' said the Old Man.

'We're doing our summer dig. The Uni has been coming here for the last few years, trying to find out more about the Roman city. My name is Sophie and I've been given the job of Tour Guide for today. Would you like me to show you around, explain what we're doing?'

'Thank you. That would be great,' said Nathan.

Sophie led the trio onto the site that seemed to consist of a series of trenches of varying depths, running in seemingly random directions that criss-crossed the area. Many, but not all, of the trenches were occupied by people dressed in a similar fashion to their guide, all carefully removing earth and gravel. This was shovelled into wheelbarrows for transport onto a series of spoil heaps around the edges of the site. One of these, some five metres high, had been surrounded by scaffolding poles and covered in planks of wood, turning it into a viewing platform, giving an elevated view across the whole area. It was to this structure that Sophie led her guests, as she chose to call them.

'We are digging in this area,' she told them, pointing to a plan of the whole city as it would have been in Roman times. 'We think that it was an area occupied by artisans, mostly metal workers.'

'Yes,' said the Old Man. 'They chose this corner so that the wind would blow the smoke from the furnaces away from the forum at the city centre over there.' He gestured towards the centre of the ring created by the walls.

'Well, that's certainly a possibility,' replied Sophie, rather distracted by the confidence with which he spoke.

'My friend has a keen interest in this site,' explained Nathan, trying to allay her evident confusion, but the Old Man's next remark only made the situation worse.

'That was Merula's workshop over there.' The Old Man pointed to one particular pit to their left. He was a coppersmith, but not a very good one.'

Sophie gave him a kindly smile, not wishing to give any offence, but then remembered that the materials from that trench had contained a metallic slag, bearing trace levels of copper. Before she could say anything, the Old Man pointed to another trench.

'And that was where Bestia worked. He worked in bronze and had a real talent for it, as long as he was sober, which was rare.'

'I'm sure Sophie doesn't want to hear all this foolishness.' Nathan was anxious not to draw attention to the trio. He could see that Sophie was perplexed, probably regarding her elderly guest as rather demented, and she was unlikely, at present, to call in any of the more senior site staff.

Ignoring Nathan's remarks, the Old Man pressed on. 'The real talent was with Ralla the goldsmith. His work was renowned across all Britannia. Yet he kept all his best work for himself. I remember that he once told me about a secret chamber that he had made deep under his workshop. That would be a real find for you, So-Fee.'

'So where was his workshop, then?' The question came from Carl, suddenly interested at the mention of gold.

'It would have been ...' The Old Man paused, trying to get his bearings in relation to the city walls, '... right here. Just where we are standing.'

'You mean under this massive spoil heap,' said Carl with a chuckle. 'So all these clever buggers have buried the best bits under a couple of tons of muck and stones. Ha!'

Nathan decided to abandon his futile attempts at keeping a low profile and decided to seek out the toilets in the Portakabins on the edge of the site. As he walked away he glanced at Sophie and saw that she was caught between disbelief at an old man's ramblings and taking action on a chance that was just too good to ignore.

He knew exactly how she felt.

A few minutes later, call of nature resolved, Nathan stepped down the metal staircase from the toilets. To the side he saw several green plastic trays full of broken pottery, obviously found during the digging. They had been carefully washed and left out to dry in the afternoon sunshine. He paused to look at them for a moment, his interest in history momentarily revived. He was reflecting that these pots had last seen daylight almost two thousand years before when a familiar voice called out behind him.

'PC Aluko! We're a long way from the Woodburn estate.'

Nathan turned to find himself staring into the angry eyes of Sergeant Johnson.

Stunned, he looked about for others, either police or military, but only saw a smaller, more rotund figure standing slightly behind his former boss.

'I didn't bring the heavy mob with me this time, Nathan. There's just me and this tame journalist. I think that the formal introductions can wait for a better time. However, just in case you are thinking of doing a runner I've brought this along.' Johnson lifted the edge of a newspaper covering his forearm to reveal a small hand gun.

Rylands was horrified at the sight of the weapon. 'What on earth is that for? Guns were never part of our deal.' This was said in a whisper, but forcefully put.

'It's OK for you, Rylands. All you want is a good story but if I don't get this mess sorted out then, at best, my career is down the pan and, at worst, I'll be in prison for the next five years. Do you know what happens to ex-policemen in prison?'

Rylands made no reply.

'So, don't go all 'Guardian reader' on me now. Just keep quiet and don't get in my way.'

He returned his attention to Nathan. 'As you may have guessed this little episode does not bear the full stamp of formal police authority. The trick pulled by your new friend back in Bristol has led to the temporary withdrawal of my warrant card. So please see this ...' he lifted the paper a second time, ' ... as a little encouragement to get you back there. Now, let's go over and introduce Mr Rylands to your new chums.'

Nathan saw that he had no choice and so walked back to the viewing platform. As they approached the Old Man recognised Johnson and tried to approach him.

'Well met, Sergeant. Tis a wondrous day to renew our acquaintance.' He extended his hand for Johnson to shake, brushing against the coat pocket as he did so.

'No thanks. It's shaking your hand that has got me into this mess.'

Carl took a menacing step towards Johnson only for him to lift, once again, the edge of the newspaper. He was careful to ensure that the guide did not see the weapon underneath.

'Back off, Squaddie! Everyone just keep calm and we'll all be merry and bright!' Then, to Sophie, 'Sorry, love, but I'm stealing your audience. Time to get back to your scratching. We all need to go somewhere a bit more private.'

The group walked down the earthen ramp and back to the field entrance, where Sophie left them. Confused on several different levels, she felt the need to go somewhere quiet to think.

'So where to now?' asked Nathan.

'We did a bit of background reading when we got here,' replied Johnson. 'You'd have been quite proud of us, Nathan. It appears that there is an amphitheatre just outside the city walls. It's not open to the public at the moment but the archaeologists aren't in there either. Just the place for our little heart-to-heart. So let's go. It's that way.'

Unknown to the group, as they walked along a trackway that bisected the long-vanished city, another pair of eyes watched their progress from the top of the walls.

A few minutes later, the group entered the ruins of the city's amphitheatre. Nathan looked around the wide oval space marked out by a low wall, built from the same flint and stone as the far more massive counterpart that surrounded the city. Beyond this inner wall, no higher than a man's waist, rose the stone terracing that would once have been filled with blood-thirsty crowds but was now covered in a thick mat of weeds, grass and small trees. The only other entrance framed the far end of the gravel-covered arena.

Johnson and Rylands directed the trio to a small gap in the walls, about halfway around the oval shape. Clearly this had once been some form of antechamber, perhaps where ancient gladiators had paused before entering combat. Nathan looked around the narrow space and realised that it must have been, for many, the last place of refuge before a violent death. Not a good omen for their current predicament.

Carl had been watching Johnson closely during the walk to the amphitheatre, waiting for an opportunity to disarm him. Reluctantly he had to admit that the policeman had been very careful, always just out of range of a desperate lunge. Carl had hoped that the end of the journey would give him a better chance. Now that they had arrived, his hopes were dashed. The small gap in the wall was out of sight of anyone passing either entrance. Once again, Johnson had positioned himself carefully, too far for Carl to reach him without being able to get off at least two shots. The odds being against him, Carl decided to bide his time.

'Right, then,' said Johnson, once the trio had been backed into this walled, roofless chamber. 'This is the way things are going to pan out.

I'm going to put in a call to my friends in Her Majesty's Constabulary, telling them that a group of wanted fugitives are in my custody, and calling for assistance. Even the yokels out here must be able to respond moderately quickly. Once they are here I am going to stay with you until we get back to Bristol, where a very interested Inspector wants to hear all about how you got me to help you escape.'

Once again Carl mentally measured the distance to Johnson. Perhaps two shots wouldn't be enough to stop him from reaching the policeman.

Johnson continued. 'While we are waiting for the local plod, my friend and colleague wants to ask you a few questions. Full and frank answers are required. Anything less might result in this gun going off by accident.'

'I'm really sorry about this,' said Rylands. 'The gun was really not part of any plan that I had.'

'Never mind about that,' said Johnson, reaching into his pocket for his mobile phone.

'Pardon me.' Suddenly a woman's voice came from behind Johnson and Rylands.

Both spun around to see Vicky standing behind them. As they turned she held up her outstretched palms and blew hard. A flurry of blue dust covered Johnson and Rylands, causing them both to start to cough violently.

The coiled spring that was Carl exploded into action. He took a single stride and launched himself towards the two figures, now coated in the blue powder. The impact knocked all three to the floor, the gun falling from Johnson's hand as he fell.

Nathan was the next to react, rushing forward to pick up the gun.

The Old Man jumped out of the walled enclosure and climbed onto the grassed terracing above, where he began to search urgently for a particular plant.

'Am I glad to see you,' said Nathan to Vicky.

'Pleased to be back,' she replied.

The Old Man, having found the plant that he required, ran over to Carl, still lying on the ground. He was coughing from some of the blue dust that had spilled onto him as a result of his efforts.

'Quickly, water!' he called to Nathan and Vicky.

Nathan retrieved a water bottle from his rucksack and passed it to the Old Man who opened it and squeezed some juice from the plant stem into it. Lifting Carl's head the Old Man carefully poured a few drops into his mouth. The coughing stopped instantly and the big soldier struggled to his feet.

'You should drink some of this too,' said the Old Man to Vicky. She shook her head and took a plant out of her pocket. The Old Man saw that it was the same as the one that he had just found on the terrace.

'So you had both the weapon and the cure? You are indeed an excellent apprentice.'

Vicky beamed at this rare praise.

'How did you get here?' said Nathan.

'It was Julian's parents. I decided to explain everything to them when they came to see his body. Both saw the importance of the situation and agreed that I must catch up with you all and learn as much as I can from him.' She nodded towards the Old Man, now standing over Johnson and Rylands who were still lying on the ground. 'It turns out that Julian's father studied history at Oxford and knew exactly where Calleva was. He drove me straight here from the hospital. I saw you from the city walls and followed you down here.'

Slowly Johnson's and Ryland's coughing receded and eventually stopped. However, as each of them tried to get to their feet they discovered that a weariness had taken over their legs. Despite several attempts neither could get up. As they lay on the ground they felt this feeling spread to their arms, making any attempt at movement impossible. The Old Man stood over both of them and watched, making no attempt to give either the curative water.

'Aren't you going to revive them?' asked Vicky, who was becoming increasingly concerned at their condition. She did not want the first time that she had used her new skills to result in someone's death.

The Old Man just shrugged.

All four watched as the tiredness spread to Johnson's and Rylands' chest muscles, making breathing increasingly difficult. Vicky could see terror in their eyes as they realised that they were both about to suffocate.

'Restore them or I will!' shouted Vicky.

Her shout seemed to rouse the Old Man into action. He stepped forward and, lifting Rylands' head, he allowed a single drop of the water to fall into his mouth. The effect was instantaneous. Rylands began to take great gulps of air into his heaving chest, a massive relief evident on his face.

The Old Man moved to Johnson. He did not administer the cure straight away but stared into the policeman's face instead.

'You threatened to take life from me and from my companions. You are now my enemy. So know you this, Kingsman. In all the world, I am the worst enemy that there has ever been, can ever be and will ever be. This time I spare you. Make it your lifelong purpose that we do not meet again. I have never spared anyone twice!'

With these words he poured a single drop into Johnson's mouth. Again, the group watched the heaving chest and the overwhelming relief as the man dragged himself back from the brink of death.

However, unlike Carl a few moments earlier, neither man was able to get to his feet.

'Why can't we get up? What have you done?' shouted Rylands.

'I've given you enough for a slow recovery. You will regain your vigour over the next few hours. Until then, even if you are still foolish enough to want to follow us, you will not have the strength.'

Rylands, still breathing heavily, called out from the ground. 'Dr Snow! Thank you for getting him to save us.' He nodded towards the Old Man. 'Life is full of irony. In saving us, you have probably also saved your mother.'

'What do you mean?' said Vicky, puzzled at how he could know anything of her mother's situation.

'June Sampson called me. That's how we knew that you would all be in Calleva this afternoon.'

'Why should June tell you that? She is a close friend. She wouldn't endanger me for anything.'

'She had no choice. It was the only way of getting an important message to you.'

'Go on then, tell me,' said Vicky, now increasingly concerned.

'James Courtney has had your mother sectioned under the Mental Health Act. It appears that he is going to operate on her brain to get samples to try to explain her recovery.'

Instantly Vicky reached into her pocket and took out her mobile phone. Nathan was about to remonstrate with her about using it but the glare she gave him told him to remain silent. She made two calls. The first involved a great deal of shouting, the second a more passive tone, but with a steely resolve in her voice. Once done, she turned back to Rylands, still lying on the ground at her feet.

'Thank you,' she said. 'She is now in good hands. Perhaps when all this is over I may yet be able to give you your interview.'

Leaving the two men lying on the ground, the four travellers picked up their packs and walked out of the amphitheatre. Nathan caught up with the Old Man. 'You weren't really going to let them die, were you? You just left it late to give them a bigger fright. That is right, isn't it?'

The Old Man just shrugged and went off in search of more plants.

—⚭—

In a large country house several miles away an elderly couple were watching the evening news.

'Casualties have now been reported from all the major cities across the United Kingdom. Unconfirmed reports suggest that the death rate amongst those that contract the influenza is around 80%. The government has announced that all

motorways will be closed for the foreseeable future to minimise contagion. Flights to all European and North American destinations have been cancelled as countries are refusing to allow planes from the UK to land.'

Sir Patrick Donelly glanced across at his wife to see that she was looking worried.

'It's getting serious, isn't it Pat?'

Her husband nodded. 'I've heard that the PM is about to call a state of emergency. Seems to be the only way that stands a chance of stopping riots breaking out.'

Both returned their attention to the TV screen, which showed a picture of Julian.

'Local News now. The body found early this morning in woodland outside Newbury has now been formally identified as Julian St Clere, a businessman from Bristol. Police have said that they are treating his death as suspicious.'

'That is so sad. Such a young life,' said Sir Patrick.

'You knew him, didn't you?'

'I met him once or twice, years ago. I knew his father better. We worked together on some government committees.'

'We should send some flowers.'

'Yes, that would be kind,' he replied, his mind now moving on to other things. 'I'm not sure why, but that reminds me. Have you seen my toothbrush?'

CHAPTER 30

Paternoster Headquarters,
Cambridge.
Tuesday 28th August,
3.15 p.m.

John Eriksson looked across at the accountant sitting opposite him and realised that she was waiting for an answer.

'I'm so sorry. Could you repeat that? I'm afraid that I'm a little distracted today.'

'I said would it be better if we used the revenues from the ….'

She was interrupted by an urgent knock on the office door. Both of them looked up as Mike Aspinall burst in, without waiting for an invitation. Seeing the accountant he paused for a moment to collect his thoughts, adjusting the words to hide the facts but still convey the urgency.

'There has been a development on the Core Purpose that I think you would like to be involved in.'

Instantly Eriksson was on his feet.

'I'm sorry, Miss Charmers … '

'Chambers,' interrupted the accountant.

'Absolutely!' replied Eriksson, his mind now focused elsewhere. 'I'm afraid that something important has come up and we are going to have to postpone our discussions until another time.'

'Well, if you insist, Mr Eriksson, but these accounts must be ready for the board meeting next month.' She looked down at her diary, laid open on the table. 'How about Friday at 2.30?' She looked up for confirmation only to find that she was alone.

'What's happened?'

'Victoria Snow has used her mobile phone.' Aspinall was struggling to keep pace with his boss as they walked down the corridor towards the control room. 'She made two calls. One to the hospital where she works, the other to a firm of solicitors specialising in medical issues.'

'Do we know what was said?'

'In the first call she spoke with the hospital's Director of Medicine. It seems that there are plans to do some operations on her mother that Snow is dead against. A consultant called Courtney, Snow's boss, has had her mother sectioned and so got the right to proceed without the patient's written authority.'

'What was the outcome?' Eriksson was not keen on hearing all the details.

'The Director agreed to halt all operations until her return.'

'What was the second call?'

'She has arranged for solicitors to sit alongside her mother's bed, twenty-four hours a day until she calls them off.'

'So she didn't believe the doctors. Smart girl.'

By now the two had entered the control room. The large screen on the wall displayed a map of the countryside around Silchester.

'So where was the call made from?'

'She called from the middle of an amphitheatre, just outside the Roman city of Calleva.'

'And when?'

'Within the last five minutes.'

'Excellent. Where are the chase team?'

'We've got them on standby at a company safe house near Newbury. I reckon they could get to Calleva in around three-quarters of an hour.'

'Get them moving. Problem is we can't assume that our target will remain there.' Eriksson pondered for a moment. 'Show me all the ancient roads that are centred on Calleva.'

The screen operator pressed a few keys and the large display changed.

'So, we have three roads entering, broadly, from the west. I think we can say that they came in on one of those and so it is unlikely that they will leave on any of them.'

'Seems logical,' said Aspinall.

'That leaves three - one going north, one south and one east.' Again Eriksson pondered the lines on the screen. 'If we look at the route they have taken so far it has always been eastwards. It's possible that they could now strike north or south but I think it more likely that they will continue east and I'm going to gamble that it will be along that old Roman road.'

'The Devil's Highway,' said the screen operator, who had a clearer picture of the road name.

'Pardon?' said Eriksson.

'It's called the Devil's Highway,' the operator said again. 'I was born around there so I know it from my childhood. It leads all the way to London. It's quite a pleasant country walk for most of the route, but it does get built up once you near the suburbs.'

That seemed to settle something in Eriksson's mind. He turned to Aspinall.

'How many helicopters can we put up?'

'Probably four immediately. More within a couple of hours.'

'Right, send two along that Devil's Highway, trying to spot the group from the air. Hopefully we can get a sight of them before they hit London.'

'And the other two?'

'We should hedge our bets. Get one to cover the northern road and the other to cover the southern. Same plan. Call in if they see any group of five walking along those routes.'

'Four, sir.' This time another screen operator called from another corner of the room.

'Sorry?' replied Eriksson.

'Just found a report from Reading police. It appears that the body of Julian St Clere was found in woodland near Newbury last night. Major head trauma. They are treating it as a suspicious death. We took a while to spot it because they had spelt his name wrongly.'

Eriksson glanced at Aspinall.

'This could pose a problem. The last thing we want is to have any more police involvement. Do we have any more details?'

'Just coming in now, sir,' continued the operator. 'It was reported by Dr Snow, who accompanied the body to the mortuary. She stayed long enough to hand over to the parents before disappearing.'

'To turn up at Calleva a few hours later making urgent calls to Bristol,' said Aspinall. 'I wonder how she got there?'

'And how she found out about her mother's situation once she arrived? It must have been both sudden and urgent for her to have used her mobile phone,' replied Eriksson. 'Too many questions for now. Let's focus on catching up with them.'

Aspinall nodded and began to make some calls.

—⁕—

They had been walking for several hours. Carl was surprised at how much more quickly they could travel without Julian to slow them down but had decided against commenting on it, especially to Vicky. She had been rather silent during their journey, seemingly deep in thought. He looked at his watch. It was 8.30 p.m., probably time to be thinking about finding somewhere to camp for the evening.

As with most of the other days, their journey had taken them in a straight line heading unrelentingly eastwards. Carl didn't need Nathan to tell him that it was another Roman road, as he was getting used to the signs.

The route had been a mixture of woodland and open fields, with very little sign of civilisation apart from the occasional distant farmhouse and the even more occasional roadway. For the last few minutes they had been walking along a tree-lined path between a series of large fields to their left and, on their right, what seemed to be gardens bounded by high wooden fences. Curiosity compelled Carl to clamber up one such fence, beyond which he saw an extensive garden leading down to a large house, one of several that he could see to the right and left. As he allowed himself to drop back onto the trackway, Nathan pointed to a heavy wooden gate in the fence bearing a sign warning off intruders with threats of legal action.

'Natives don't seem too friendly, then,' said Carl, smiling.

'They never were.' This came from the Old Man, standing ahead of them, on a set of stone steps that led up into a churchyard.

'We seem to be coming to some sort of village,' said Vicky as she looked beyond the gravestones to a church, a village green and some more houses. Of particular interest to Carl was a pub, called the Queen's Oak, almost certainly named after the single, old tree in the centre of the green.

'I think we should see if they have any rooms for the night,' said Vicky. 'I didn't get any sleep last night, and I'm sure you three didn't get much either.'

'A good meal and a pint of the local brew would go down well,' agreed Carl.

'But how could we pay for it?' said Nathan. He was conscious that he always seemed to fall into the role of Chief Parade Rainer. 'After our narrow escape at Kintbury I'm not sure that credit cards are a great idea.'

'Julian's father gave me some cash,' replied Vicky. 'It won't last forever but it should be enough for tonight.'

They all looked at the Old Man who gave his customary shrug by way of agreement.

As they walked across the green and into the pub Carl, bringing up the rear, looked up to see a helicopter in the sky above his head.

He couldn't be sure but for a moment it seemed to be hovering. A second later it climbed steeply and flew out of sight, much to the relief of the ex-para. Well, we are getting close to London, he thought. Choppers will be far more common around here than along the route so far. His worries alleviated, he turned and followed the others into the pub.

Inside there were two rooms, one slightly larger than the other, both served from a common bar that ran between them. The group entered the larger one and, having got some drinks and placed an order for food, all sat down at the only available table, in the opposite corner from the entrance. Over the next thirty minutes the strain of the last few hours seemed to lift from the group. Conversation began to flow and they all began to settle down for a restful evening.

The Old Man was watching some of the other patrons, mostly couples enjoying some time together on this late summer evening. As he watched, the door opened and a young man entered. Casually dressed in jeans and tee shirt, he glanced at the group on his way to the bar, where he ordered a pint. Once served, he leaned against the counter and took a long pull on the cool beer before taking out a mobile phone to make a short call. Once the call was completed, he returned his attention to the beer, pausing only briefly to glance again at the foursome in the corner.

The Old Man had watched this newcomer from the moment he entered. As the brief phone call was made, Vicky noticed her mentor begin to tense up. At the newcomer's second glance the Old Man began to stand but before he could finish the movement, chaos engulfed the quiet pub.

The entrance door flew open under the force of a short, sharp kick. In the space of a second a dozen men ran in. Dressed from head to foot in black fatigues, they wore helmets fitted with visors that covered their faces. Many of them were carrying plastic riot shields that reached from their knees to above their heads, together with short batons held in their other, gloved hands. Worryingly, those without shields carried machine pistols.

As they burst into the pub they all shouted, creating an eruption of noise that terrified and, more importantly, froze all present. A professional manoeuvre that Carl immediately recognised as one designed to disorientate.

Once inside, all the shield-bearers rushed past the other diners and towards the Old Man and his companions in the corner of the room. As soon as all were in place they locked the shields together, forming an impenetrable barrier. In a single, well-rehearsed manoeuvre they all moved forward, sealing the group within the shield wall. Once they were six feet from their quarry a shouted command halted their progress. A further six men, all similarly dressed but unarmed, ran into the room.

'EVERYONE OUTA HERE! NOW!' The command came from one of the group carrying machine pistols. Below average height with thick black hair and a tanned complexion, he was evidently the leader of the evacuation team. The newcomers manhandled all the other diners out of the bar and into the car park beyond.

Carl and the Old Man had jumped to their feet at the second the door had been kicked in, and Nathan only a moment later. All three now faced the wall of shields, the Old Man in the centre with Carl and Nathan on either side. Vicky stood behind them, frantically wondering what she could do to help her friends in the battle she was sure was about to take place.

A few seconds later, the room now clear of diners, the leader spoke.

'Sir, my name is Major Colin Warren. Let me assure you that none of us mean you any harm. I have orders to hold you until my superiors can get here. Please do not try to oppose us. I repeat that I do not wish to cause harm to any of you.'

The Old Man glared at Warren through the clear plastic of the riot shields.

'Well met, Major. My congratulations on a well-executed plan. You are clearly a master of your trade. Yet know this. I will never be taken by any agent of any King. I will draw my breath freely or not at all. And if this day is to be my last then many others will not see tomorrow's sunrise.'

As he spoke he seemed to draw his eyes deeper into his furrowed brows, while the hair on his head and his beard flared outwards giving it the appearance of a lion's mane. With the final word he flung his head back and gave out an awesome roar. Carl, Nathan and Vicky recognised it immediately as the terrible sound that they had heard in the Bristol garden, days before. But none of the troopers had ever heard anything like it. The depth and power of the dreadful sound assaulted their senses at a primeval level, tapping into long forgotten terrors of immense pain and violent death.

To their credit none of the troopers flinched as this terrifying wave of noise flooded over them, although several were suddenly aware of a warm liquid running down the inside of their trousers.

As the feral roar came to an end Carl picked up a wine bottle and smashed it on the edge of the table. As he waved his new weapon towards the shield wall he shouted, 'Same goes for Cyric! Come and get some, you Saxon bastards!'

A silence fell over the room as both sides hesitated, waiting for the other to make the first move.

The silence was broken by the muted music of 'Mission Impossible'. Warren quickly rummaged deep into his pocket, withdrew his phone and tossed it across the bar to the young man who had entered just prior to the assault. In a single movement he caught it, opened it and answered it.

'No, Boss. It's Mark Preston. Major Warren is a bit busy at present.' On the other end Eriksson said something to which Preston replied, 'We've got them cornered but they don't seem to want to come quietly.' Within the shield wall Carl again waved the broken bottle. 'I think we may have to call you back in a few minutes.'

The troopers moved the shields closer together, preparing for the charge that Warren was about to order.

'Sorry, Boss? Didn't catch that. Please say again.'

Warren flicked off the safety catch on his machine pistol. He knew that he was under orders not to harm the Old Man but neither was he going to watch while his men died. He held up his hand, ready to give the order.

'OK, Boss. Got that. So what do you want me to do?' Preston was still talking to Eriksson. 'What, just that? Nothing else?'

'Troopers. Let's get this job done.' Warren dropped his hand and the shield wall moved forward.

'MAZAK!' screamed Preston at the top of his voice.

'CEASE!' shouted the Old Man, placing his hand on Carl's arm.

Warren saw the expression on the Old Man's face change. 'Fall back!' he shouted, causing his soldiers to stop just before any contact had been made and return to their original positions.

'Who calls me this?' shouted the Old Man.

In answer, Preston proffered the still-open mobile phone through a gap that had opened in the shield wall. The Old Man took the phone gingerly before immediately passing it to Vicky.

'What does Mazak mean?' she said, as confused as anyone else in the room by what had just happened.

'It is a name by which I was once known, many Returns ago,' replied the Old Man, still clearly puzzled by the unexpected turn of events.

Glancing at the mobile phone Vicky realised that the Old Man would struggle with normal use and so switched it to speaker mode. 'You can just talk normally now,' she said as she laid it on the table.

'Who speaks?' said the Old Man.

'My name is John Eriksson,' came the voice from the table. 'I have something of great importance to share with you. I can be with you within the hour. I beg you to remain there until my arrival.'

'What do you know of Mazak?'

'I shall answer all your questions when we meet. I promise that, once we have spoken, you and your companions will be free to go.'

'So what do you want from me? The Others always want something. It is in your nature.'

'I want nothing from you. The truth is quite the opposite. So, Mazak, will you wait for my arrival?'

The Old Man thought for a moment and then nodded.

'He has agreed, Mr Eriksson,' said Vicky, realising that nothing had been said.

'Thank you, Dr Snow. I will be there as soon as possible.'

As she passed the phone back she wondered how he knew her name.

'Well, now that you've all stopped shouting, will someone tell me what the bloody hell is going on?' The landlord, relatively safe behind the bar, had sensibly held back up until this point but felt he could do so no longer.

In answer Warren passed him the mobile, still connected to Eriksson.

The landlord listened for a moment before speaking. 'Well, that's all very well but I have a pub to run here.' Another pause. 'Oh. I see. Well, that's very generous. I'd be a fool to say no. Thank you very much, sir.' He closed the mobile phone and passed it back to Warren, before turning to the astonished patrons in the smaller room trying to follow events by peering across the common bar. Reaching up he took hold of a thick piece of rope attached to a bell hanging above him, which he rang twice. 'Time, gentlemen, please,' he shouted. 'We are now closed due to a private function.'

The hour seemed to pass very slowly. Even by his own standards the Old Man was unusually withdrawn. Any attempt by Vicky or Nathan to make conversation drew only a blank response. In the end, at Carl's suggestion, they moved to the other side of the room to give him the space he clearly needed.

Apart from Warren and Preston all the troopers had left the pub. Looking out of the window, Nathan could see that they had set up a secure cordon around the perimeter, politely discouraging any potential diners from entering.

The noise of a helicopter landing on the green attracted Nathan's attention, causing him to look out of the window a second time. He saw several figures jump out and start to move towards the pub.

'Looks like things are about to start,' he said to Carl and Vicky. They moved back to stand alongside the Old Man, ready to provide whatever support they could.

Warren opened the door to allow his boss to come in. The Old Man rose as he entered the room.

Eriksson was the first to speak.

'Sir, firstly, may I say that it is a privilege to meet you. I cannot tell you how many times I have dreamed of this moment. It is my duty to tell you that, many years ago, my family took on a sacred task, one that was to be handed down through my lineage until the vow that was made had been fulfilled. Throughout the intervening years my ancestors have tried to fulfil that promise but always without success.'

The Old Man said nothing. All his senses told him to be suspicious of the man before him.

Eriksson continued. 'Now, after almost forty generations, it falls to me to be the one who has the honour to discharge this promise.'

He nodded to Warren who opened the door to allow two small children to enter. The older one was a boy. He was short for his age, which was about eight, but had a stocky build which gave him the appearance of rude health. The second child, a girl, was about six. She shared the stocky build of the boy but seemed shy by comparison, almost hiding behind him as he led her across the tiled floor. In her hand she held a small doll, made of grasses tied together. Although clearly very old, indeed almost falling apart, it was evidently very important to her as she held it tightly in her other hand.

Vicky glanced at the Old Man to see that he was thunderstruck by the arrival of the two children. His eyes were wide open, his mouth gaping.

The boy, leading the girl by the hand, walked across the room and stood in front of the Old Man. He looked up, smiled into the ancient face, and spoke with a voice that tried to sound confident, but crackled with emotion.

'Hello Father.'

CHAPTER 31

The Queen's Oak Public House,
Finchampstead,
Berkshire
Tuesday 28th August,
9.15 p.m.

At Eriksson's suggestion the Old Man had taken the two children into the smaller bar, now cleared of the earlier customers. He was seated on a corner bench by the side of the fireplace with the boy on one side and the girl on the other. Both children had wrapped their arms tightly around the Old Man and showed no signs of letting go.

For several minutes the trio sat in silence, still reeling under the implications of their reconciliation. It was the Old Man who spoke first.

'I tried so hard to find you. Your mother was to send you to your grandfather's farmstead outside the city so I went there after I left the shop only to find that you had not arrived. By the time I could get back all of York was ablaze. I sought you everywhere but could find no trace.'

The boy loosened his grip and sat up. The girl took the chance to move even closer to her father, hugging him even more tightly. 'Mother said that it was too dangerous to make the journey. She hid us in the cellar under the shop.'

At this the Old Man closed his eyes in anguish. A tear seeped out and ran down his cheek.

'So you were in the shop all the time. You heard all that happened?'

'The soldiers hurt Mother and then you killed them.' It was the little girl's turn to speak.

'So where did you go?' The Old Man was keen to keep the conversation away from his wife's dreadful death.

'When we got out of the shop the street was full of soldiers hurting people and setting fire to houses. Erik the Coppersmith and his family were running out of the shop next door. He told us to come with them.' The boy spoke with such confidence that his father could see that he had practised this explanation many times.

In his mind's eye, the Old Man recalled his neighbour. Erik had always been a good man. Such a kindness, even as his own world was falling apart, was typical of him.

The boy continued. 'He took us to grandfather's farmstead, but the soldiers had already been there. All the animals were killed and the buildings were on fire. We couldn't find any bodies so we think that they had escaped but we couldn't find them.'

The Old Man nodded. 'It was the time of the Harrying.' He remembered the reports that he had heard in later Returns. 'William the Bastard bid his troops kill all creatures that drew breath for three days` march in all directions around the city. They were commanded to destroy all that might give comfort to those that escaped. Farmhouses, barns, even crops in the fields. The famine that followed blighted the people for three generations. I have never trusted a King or a Kingsman since, nor ever will I again.' He looked down at the two small faces and realised how inappropriate such a grim story was for such a happy reunion. 'So where did you go? How did you survive?'

'Erik took us and his family to Denmark. He had relations there and we stayed with them for many years,' said the little girl. 'We came back to England with Erik's great-grandson.' The boy paused in his story. The obvious question was about to come up, and he had waited many centuries for the answer. 'But we didn't get old. We have always been children, never growing up, not even by a single day. Yet I did just as you told me, but I must have done something wrong. What did I do wrong, Father?' There was sadness mixed with desperation in the boy's voice.

'Did you follow my instructions? The ones that I gave you in case of such peril?'

'I did exactly as you showed me,' replied the boy. 'I took the staria seeds from the bowl in the shop and prepared them just as you said. Once we got to Denmark we both took the powder and fell asleep but we woke up the next morning as if nothing had changed, except that we never aged. Please, Father, tell me. What did I do wrong?'

The Old Man thought for a moment. The preparation of the seeds was quite a simple process. He had taken his son through it many times, always resulting in the correct outcome. The Old Man closed his eyes and called upon his incredible memory. He thought back almost a thousand years, to the events of that terrible morning. He had always tried to drive that sight from his mind but he could never forget the look on his wife's face as he entered the shop. Then there was the fight with the Norman soldiers. He had never enjoyed killing, having seen life taken too cheaply in so many Returns. Yet that day he had taken satisfaction in the death of her murderers. He recalled their response when they saw him. Their initial bullying, the violence that followed, the damage to the tables and the pots set out upon them. Suddenly he recalled something. He looked down at his son.

'The staria seeds. Were they dry?'

The boy had to think for a moment. Fortunately, he had his father's gift for memory. 'No. They were all sticky. But I washed and dried them before I prepared the powder.'

The Old Man sighed. So, this simple error, carried out in haste so long ago, had brought them back together.

'The seeds had been lying in amthol oil from a bowl that had been overturned during the fighting. Washing removes the outer liquid but some always seeps into the centre of the seeds.'

The boy put his face into his hands. 'I knew that I had done something wrong. It's all my fault.'

The Old Man put his arms around his son's broad shoulders. 'You are right. The oil strips away all the sleeping powers of the staria. Instead it causes growth to cease so that any who take it will never age. Yet, do not be hard on yourself, my son. You cannot have known. But also, think of this. Through your actions, we are now together again.'

'Can the effects of the powder be reversed?' said the boy.

'Once I can find some elmthrop, 'tis but the work of a moment.' He smiled at the relieved expression on the two faces. 'But first we must get some staria and commence your first great slumber. The more I discover about the times of this Return the greater my worry about the pestilence that is to come. Will you join me on my journey?'

Both children smiled. The little girl gave the Old Man another huge hug. The boy saw in his sister's face a look of secure contentment that he had not seen for so long. He could see that she was safe at last, and so his work was finally done. He turned his back on the happy pair, not wishing them to see his face.

For the first time in almost a thousand years, a small boy cried for the loss of his long-dead mother.

Back in the other bar Eriksson was having a drink with Nathan, Carl and Vicky, busily explaining the background to the evening's events.

'So your family have been looking after these children since the days of the Normans?' Nathan had been getting used to accepting outrageous tales but this moved the boundaries still further.

'It was the only thing to do. My ancestor already had quite a large family. Adding two more was not such a burden. They fled the Norman rule and returned to Denmark. You must remember that Northern England had built up strong links with Scandinavia over the previous 300 years. York must have been more Viking than Anglo-Saxon then, which made William the Conqueror all the more determined to crush any rebellion.'

Nathan nodded before looking towards Carl to see that he was also nodding.

'I was just about to say that,' said the big ex-para, with a grin.

'So what about the hundreds of years between then and now?' asked Nathan.

Eriksson shrugged. 'As you can imagine, it came as something of a shock when they realised that the children never seemed to age. At first their explanations were treated as childish delusions, perhaps a result of their mother's death and their father's disappearance. However, the family archives speak of their amazing knowledge of plants and how they could be used to cure even the most crippling illness. It appears that they had learned much in the short time they had spent with their father. After that, their tales of his slumbers and returns didn't seem so incredible.'

'So what happened then?' said Vicky.

'The family stayed in Denmark for a couple of generations, returning to England when they felt that some stability had returned. With the children's knowledge of plants the Erikssons began to prosper - a process that has continued over the centuries resulting in some limited success in one or two areas.' The words were spoken in a modest, understated tone that, Nathan could see, belied the actual position.

'So all this ...' Nathan waved a hand towards the window, with the troops and helicopter beyond, '... is your idea of a limited success?'

Eriksson shrugged. 'The family business has grown somewhat over the centuries but it has always been in pursuit of the Core Purpose.'

'The Core Purpose?' said Vicky.

'Reuniting the children with their father. From the very beginning my ancestor, Erik the Coppersmith, vowed to bring them back together and Paternoster has been devoted to achieving that ever since.'

'Paternoster?' asked Vicky

'The name of our organisation. Chosen by one of my distant ancestors who had an eye for the ecclesiastical. I see that Nathan has made the connection.'

Carl and Vicky turned to see that their friend was smiling.

'Paternoster,' he explained, 'Latin for 'Our Father'.'

The explanations were interrupted by the arrival of Mike Aspinall, accompanied by Warren, Preston and Chogan. After the customary introductions Aspinall gave a summary of the current situation.

'We are going to have to send the helicopter back to base. It can't stay here overnight as it is attracting too much attention. I have arranged with the landlord for rooms for us all tonight but I was wondering about the plan for tomorrow?'

'I was just coming to that,' said Eriksson. 'It rather depends on our new friends, here.' Then, to Nathan, Carl and Vicky, 'We've been chasing you ever since you left Bristol but we have been unable to work out where you are heading. Now that we have caught up with you, I can offer you the not inconsiderable resources of Paternoster to assist you in your task. So where are you going and how can we help?'

'We are looking for some staria.' It fell to Vicky to explain. 'The Old Man, Mazac I suppose I should call him now, discovered that his supplies had fallen through a hole in his pouch.' As she spoke she reached into her rucksack and took out her notebook computer. 'When I tried to find something about the plant I discovered that it was extinct.'

'So he cannot go back into long-term hibernation?' said Aspinall. 'So he is stuck here until he dies?'

'Well, not quite,' replied Vicky. 'I was able to find a possible source for the seeds that he requires in preparing the powder.' She turned around the computer screen so that all could see the website that was displayed upon it. 'It appears that they might have some here.'

'A good plan.' Eriksson nodded as he studied the details on the small screen. 'May I ask how you were going to persuade them to part with such a rare commodity?'

'He - that is, Mazac - wasn't big on sharing his plans but, having seen him in action, I'm sure that he can be very persuasive if he wants to be,' replied Nathan.

At a nod from Eriksson, Mike Aspinall broke away from the group and started to make telephone calls from a table on the other side of the room. Eriksson continued with his questions. 'And after that?'

'I'm afraid that the plans get even thinner,' said Nathan. 'All that I can say for sure is that he wants to get back to what he calls his 'Rest' as quickly as possible. He is not impressed with the mess mankind has made and is convinced that we are heading for some form of major disaster.'

'He is especially concerned about the arrival of bird flu,' added Vicky. 'He sees that as Nature's way of thinning out the herd, taking it back to sustainable numbers.' She watched as the implications dawned upon the members of the Paternoster team. 'Yet I'm sure he could stop it if he wanted to. He says he has done it before.'

'You mean the plague in the 1300s?' said Eriksson.

'You know about that?' said Nathan, surprised at the remark.

The Paternoster CEO nodded. 'You must remember that my forebears have been following Mazac very closely. They almost caught up with him many times. Once they heard about a high survival rate in a small hamlet, whilst all surrounding villages were wiped out. They took a keen interest but sadly by the time they reached the hamlet he was long gone. They didn't have our tracking skills then ...' he nodded towards Chogan, 'so the trail was lost.'

Vicky continued. 'I've been trying to get him to share some of his secrets with me. I've learned a little but only enough to realise how much more there is to know. There is also the problem that, while he seems happy to help individuals and small groups when he chooses to, overall he seems to think that wiping out a major chunk of the world population is actually quite a good idea. He keeps describing it as Nature's way.'

'So you are hoping to persuade him to delay his slumber, at least until you are able to learn some form of cure?' said Eriksson.

Vicky nodded, but further discussion was interrupted by the return of Aspinall. He looked rather serious as he sat down at the table. 'I've been in touch with the Director of the Establishment that interests you.' He nodded towards the computer screen, still showing a picture of their objective. 'He was not pleased to be contacted at home, which may have been a factor in his outright refusal to even contemplate giving us any of the seeds.'

'Surely there must be some formal procedure that we could follow?' said Eriksson.

'It appears that they do release seeds to accredited laboratories but none of our labs meet their criteria ...' Eriksson was about to interrupt but Aspinall continued before he could speak '... and the accreditation process takes several months to complete.'

'Perhaps some financial contribution?' asked Eriksson. 'These places are permanently short of money.'

'I tried that too. That was when he put the phone down. It seems that we are dealing with someone with principles.'

'How very tiresome,' replied Eriksson. He thought for a moment. 'I think that we may need to adopt a strategy that is a little less - how should I say - passive?' He looked across at Warren. 'Major, I think that we may have need of your talents once again.'

—∞—

The tanker driver looked at his watch. It was 9.10 a.m., bang on time. The instructions that he had received in the early hours had specified exactly when he must take up his position. The site staff, the instructions said, would all have arrived but the general public would not be admitted until 10.00 a.m. As the double-length milk tanker rounded the bend of a country road leading to Haywards Heath, West Sussex, he saw the large sign directing visitors to Wakehurst Place, the country estate of the Royal Botanical Gardens, Kew. The sign spoke of several acres of formal gardens and woodland surrounding an Elizabethan manor house.

He pulled the huge vehicle into the lay-by across the site entrance, turned off the engine and switched on the hazard warning lights. He picked up a small notebook computer from the passenger seat and typed in a series of numbers and letters. This caused a digital message to be sent down a cable that ran under the dashboard to the engine's central processing unit. An instant later, in response to this instruction, the fuel pump was immobilised, the air-brakes were locked on and the automatic gearbox was fixed into the 'park' position. This tanker, the driver thought, was going nowhere until he got the order to move. Taking out his mobile phone he selected a pre-programmed number.

'Aspinall speaking,' came the voice from the phone.

'Objective one achieved. Entrance gate blocked.'

'Excellent. Please hold that position until you hear from me. Aspinall out.'

The driver closed the phone, reached out for his newspaper and switched on the cab radio.

'*... what this government doesn't seem to realise is that this country survives on commerce and business. Forced closures, however temporary, will have a massive impact on our profitability so who is going to pick up the tab? That's what I want to know.*'

'*Thank you, caller. You raise an interesting question. You are listening to the Morning Starts Here programme on BBC Radio 2. Today we are discussing the government's handling of the bird flu epidemic. If you have a view please call on 0800 ...*'

The driver tuned to a different station, seeking something with a bit more music. Had he looked at the Wakehurst Place sign more closely he would have noticed that another, very different, activity was also based there. The sign told interested parties a little of the activities that were undertaken, inviting them to visit the facility on any day from 10.00 a.m. onwards. The driver, who could never have been described as an interested party for anything involving biology, remained in his cab.

Sometimes Alan Forster just could not believe his luck. If someone had told him that one day he would be in charge of a major biological project he would have laughed at them. Yet here he was, in his perfect job. He could not have planned it better. It had everything. It involved plants and seeds which had been his passion since childhood. It meant working with some of the top minds in the field, which included him, but he was far too modest to say so. It was doing something that really mattered, something that he really believed in, and not in some back-room laboratory – although that would have been fine for him – but in possibly the most prestigious project currently being undertaken in modern biology. In truth, he would have agreed to do the job for nothing but, even more fortunately, the Trustees offered him a very good salary. It was just perfect. As he entered his office that morning he felt that his life was complete. He took off his jacket, hung it on the coat stand and put on his lab coat. As he did so he glanced at the name badge. It was a task that he did every morning, just to be sure that it was not a dream. As with every other day the badge proclaimed his ideal reality.

It read 'Dr Alan Forster, Director, Millennium Seed Bank.'

Having been involved in the seed bank project since the late 1990s, he and his team had now established a store of over one and a half billion seeds, together with laboratories investigating better methods for collection, storage and revival. With an average of one species becoming extinct every day, the project was put in place to try to arrest this appalling statistic. Now, with almost one hundred per cent of UK species protected and nearly ten per cent of species worldwide either stored in the bank or with overseas partners, he felt that they were starting to make a difference. The thought that, in some future time, humanity might suffer for the lack of some long-dead plant horrified him and gave him new impetus at the beginning of each working day. With that thought in mind he sat at his desk and began to read his correspondence. For a second he was distracted by the sound of distant helicopters but his concentration soon returned to an e-mail on the topic of the Rosy Periwinkle that had increased survival rates in childhood leukaemia almost tenfold.

Three helicopters, two smaller, the other slightly larger, emerged from the low cloud base and flew in formation across the futuristic buildings of the Seed Bank. The smaller ones moved to a point above a field to the left of the half-round structures, hesitating for a second before coming into land. As soon as they touched the ground the doors flew open and two teams of troopers hit the ground running. With a well-practised air they fanned out, one team forming a protective ring around the centre of the field, the other running to secure a farm gate that led, through a series of pathways, to the Seed Bank entrance. At a signal from Mark Preston, leader of the gate team, both helicopters took off and disappeared from view across the wooded horizon, to be replaced by the larger helicopter that now came into land in the centre of the newly-established protective ring. At another signal from the leader of the protective-ring team, Pierre Chogan, the doors of the larger helicopter opened. The first person out was Colin Warren, followed by another two troopers. They were quickly followed by Carl, carrying the unconscious body of the Old Man. Clearly at home in such an operation, Carl ran across to the protected field gate and carefully laid the prostrate form on his back, with his legs vertically upwards against one of the gateposts. The first group were followed by Vicky and Nathan, with Eriksson and the two children close behind. At yet another signal, this time from Warren, the larger helicopter followed the other two back into the air and over the horizon. Warren knew that the arrival of helicopters was always going to attract attention, most notably from the laboratory windows some 150 yards away, but it was the best plan that he could hatch for getting the team in, the objective achieved, and affecting a withdrawal as quickly as possible, certainly quick enough to escape the attentions of the local police. Once called, Warren reckoned on them responding within about 15 minutes, hopefully longer if the trick with the milk tanker worked. By then, he hoped, this whole circus would be back in the air.

Vicky ran over to the Old Man. She took out the black oval seeds that he had given her before they took off. His horror of cars had meant that getting him, conscious, into the helicopter was out of the question so he had chosen this, unconscious, method of making the journey. Crushing the seed into a powder, she blew it into his face and prepared to pinch his ear, as she had done on the canal bank.

'Not like that!' The voice came from the small girl, now crouching beside her father. Roughly pushing Vicky aside, she reached down and pinched her father's ear with a vigour that Vicky could never have mustered. As the Old Man quickly returned to consciousness Vicky realised that he now had a new nurse who was not going to be supplanted by anyone.

With his main charge now conscious, Warren ordered his forces to cross the open ground that led up to the main entrance to the Seed Bank. The crack troops ran towards the large glass door, passing several large raised beds full of flowering plants. The others followed as quickly as they could apart from Eriksson, who seemed to prefer an elegant stroll to a sprint, and the Old Man who stopped to examine some plants in the raised beds.

As they approached, the large glass door failed to open. Warren glanced at his watch and realised that, at 9.25, the mechanism had not been set to receive visitors. At a nod from him another trooper placed a metal box on the frame of the doorway and began to press buttons. Seconds later, the large plates of glass glided smoothly apart.

To Warren's annoyance, the first to enter the large, marbled reception area was Eriksson, whose ambling had brought him to the doorway just as it slid back. Clearly, Warren mused, Eriksson had his own ideas on the 'Presidential Levels of Personal Protection' that had been the over-riding instructions given that morning.

The reception area comprised several exhibits on the activities of the Seed Bank around the world, together with a large flat-screen TV, running a continuous loop describing work undertaken and giving examples of the results achieved. Windows to the right and left gave glimpses of the laboratories beyond, now full of white-coated staff peering at the arrival of the intruders.

Eriksson made an unhurried progress through the reception area, ignoring the displays. He stopped at the desk located at the far end and occupied by two uniformed, middle-aged ladies who had been staring at the group in open-mouthed amazement. The fact that all of the weapons carried by the troopers were set to safe-mode did nothing to reduce their intimidation value.

'Good Morning, ladies,' he said in a confident voice. 'My name is Eriksson. This is a bank, yes?'

The taller of the two reception staff managed a nod.

'Excellent. We have come to make a withdrawal.'

'Perhaps I might be able to help you?' The voice came from a white-coated individual who had entered the reception area from one of the laboratories, prompted by the arrival of the helicopters.

'Your name, sir?' said Eriksson.

'I am Alan Forster, Director of the Seed Bank.'

'Just the person that I need to see. As I was explaining to your charming, yet strangely silent, colleagues, I am John Eriksson, CEO of Paternoster Industries.'

Again, Warren inwardly winced. He wasn't sure of the finer points of carrying out a bank raid but was fairly sure that introducing yourself was not normally part of the proceedings. He glanced at his watch: 9.31a.m. They could only count on nine minutes before the police arrived.

The Director recognised the name of Paternoster from the previous evening's telephone call. Glancing beyond Eriksson he saw the assault team, now spreading out across the large reception area. His concern began to grow into fear as he saw their intimidating weaponry. He had always wondered, if his principles towards the seed bank were ever to be tested, whether he would have the courage to stand by them. Today, it would seem, he would find out. Bravely, he took in a deep breath and replied. 'I remember your company from last night's rather unwelcome conversation. I assume that this intrusion is related to that request. As I explained to your colleague, we only allow seeds to be used in approved research programmes, following extensive investigation into the propriety of the laboratories involved. We do not just pass them over the counter like some form of scientific garden centre. In our view the work of this Institute is of the utmost importance to the future of life on this planet. I am not prepared to compromise our values unless there is a significant benefit to the work of the project, and I am not talking of some tawdry attempt at bribery such as your colleague tried to pass off last night, nor of some common bullies however well equipped.'

The courage of the man was evident for all to see. Eriksson saw that he would have to change tack if he was to get a result. 'I think that you might be interested in meeting our patron. He knows a little about plants.' As he spoke he looked around for the Old Man. After a second Eriksson saw him looking at the large TV display at the rear of the reception area. He had clearly taken no interest in the confrontation so far. 'Mazac!' he called out. 'I wonder if I could introduce you to the keeper of this great venture?'

Reluctantly the Old Man drew himself away from the screen and joined the others. 'Does Erik's son speak the truth?' he said to the Director. 'You are responsible for the saving of the seeds? You do this purely for those that are yet to come?'

'Well, it's not quite as simple as that but, in essence, yes.'

Clearly the Old Man was impressed. He gestured towards the windows and the laboratories beyond, filled with faces watching the events unfold. 'And you lead this tribe that does naught but keep the seeds safe?'

The Director nodded. 'That is the case. It is important work and we take it very seriously, which is why I cannot give you the seeds that you require.'

Warren looked at his watch. 9.32 a.m. Their time was running out. He decided to try a more direct approach. Placing his hand on his pistol he took a pace towards the Director. 'Now listen to me. We need to get these seeds off you and fast. We can do it the easy way or ...'

'NO!'

No one present had ever seen anything like it. In an instant, or even a fraction of an instant, the Old Man stepped forward and, faster than any striking snake, grabbed Warren by the throat and lifted him off the ground. The other troopers moved forward to protect their leader but Carl stepped between them and glared defiantly.

'From the very beginning of this Return all I have seen of this world is rank and foul. This is the only man who is trying to make the world sound again. He will suffer no harm while I breathe.' The Old Man's actions and words silenced all those around them.

Eriksson was the first to react. Leaning over, he whispered softly into the Old Man's ear. 'I'm sure that the Major meant no real harm. Perhaps it might be best if you were to put him down? `

Seemingly unconcerned by the effort of holding a grown man off the ground with a single hand, the Old Man considered Eriksson's request. With a shrug that Vicky, Carl and Nathan recognised, the Old Man released his grip on Warren, who collapsed in a heap on the floor. Eriksson reached down and helped him back to his feet. As he did so he whispered ,'I seem to recall suggesting that you shouldn't underestimate this man. Do you recall? Tanks and florists?'

It was Nathan's turn to step forward. 'I think I may have a solution to this impasse.' Reaching into both coat pockets he took out two small sealed plastic bags, each containing a leaf from a different plant.

Once the Old Man saw the plants he let out a sigh. 'This is no time for children's tricks.'

'Please give me a chance with this,' whispered Nathan. 'I really think it will make a difference.'

The Old Man gave another shrug. 'If you think so. Yet have a care. I have only ever used leaves fresh picked from the plant. I cannot say how the trick might play with leaves some days old.'

Nathan smiled in reply. 'We'll just have to risk it.' Then, to the rest of the group who were looking increasingly bemused by his actions he said, 'As with all the best tricks I am going to need someone to help me.'

'I'm sure that Major Warren would be only too happy to play the role of the beautiful assistant, if only to show his regret at his earlier misunderstanding.' Eriksson smiled at Warren who nodded, if a little reluctantly.

'Excellent. Now please could you hold out each hand, palms upwards.' Warren did as he was told. Nathan placed one of the leaves on each palm, taking care that they should not touch. 'Now please crush the leaf in each hand by clenching your fists.'

Again, Warren carried out the request.

'Good. Now, please clap your hands.'

The Old Man had been right to be concerned. The older leaves caused an effect far greater than had been experienced by Julian several days before. Even before Warren got his hands together a huge electric-blue, spark flashed between his palms with a loud crack, illuminating the whole area for a split second and launching him several feet into the air. He landed against one of the exhibition stands, knocking it over and causing the contents to fall to the floor with a crash.

Nathan spun round to face the astonished Director. 'Electrical energy from plant matter! And not just any plants but ones that are regarded as weeds. I'm no botanist but I'm sure that I've seen these growing all around the world. Think of the benefits such a discovery would have, improving the lives of people in even the poorest of countries. Surely this would count as 'a significant benefit to the work of this project?' Surely this would be worthy of a trade for a few staria seeds?'

The Director looked across at Warren, now groggily getting to his feet. He recalled the power of the blue flash and considered the potential of such a discovery. He smiled at Nathan. 'Yes,' he said. 'I think it would.'

CHAPTER 32

A Wooded Glade,
Somewhere in Derbyshire
Thursday 30th August,
11.00 a.m.

'OK. You can remove your blindfolds now.' At Eriksson's instruction Vicky, Carl and Nathan reached behind their heads and took off the velvet bands that they had been told to wear some 30 minutes earlier. Initially they all struggled with the bright sunlight of the summer morning but soon their eyes became accustomed to it. Climbing out of the minibus they stepped into a beautiful grassed area, surrounded by mature trees and bushes. Broadly flat, the glade floor rose slightly at one end, giving the impression of a large crescent, as high as a man in the centre but falling away on both sides to some small rocky outcrops, randomly spread around. Looking through the trees Nathan could see that they were on the top of a small hill, the land falling away gently in all directions to give extended views of the surrounding countryside. As he looked around he could see no sign of civilisation, no roads, no farm houses, nothing. It was, he thought, a truly tranquil location.

As he waited for his turn to get out of the minibus, Nathan reflected on the previous 24 hours. Events had moved quickly since they had left the Seed Bank. Agreement had been reached surprisingly quickly on the terms of the deal to develop the new power source. Eriksson took charge of the negotiations and, within minutes, a partnership, funded by Paternoster, had been proposed and accepted. The only concern expressed by the Seed Bank Director related to the distribution of any profits but this was blown away by Eriksson committing all profits to the Seed Bank in perpetuity. With a wave of his elegant hand he casually stated that Paternoster already had more than enough money.

Within an hour of their arrival the group were back in the air. Aspinall had been left behind to progress arrangements. Warren and his team departed in the two smaller helicopters, leaving Eriksson, Vicky, Nathan, Carl and the children to take the larger machine. The Old Man had reluctantly agreed at the Queen's Oak that walking was not an option if they were to cover the distances involved in the time-scale required. However, despite the urging of his children, he would not even consider entering anything mechanical whilst conscious so, once again, Carl had to carry his prostrate form into the helicopter.

Secure in the Old Man's pocket was a small packet of seeds. The object of their journey had been achieved.

They flew north for about two hours. The noise of the engine had made any attempts at conversation difficult so Nathan had been unable to discover where they were being taken. Eventually they landed on an immaculate lawn in front of a large stately home, deep in its own surrounding countryside.

Once on the ground, Eriksson had welcomed them to Coppersmith Grange, the ancestral family home. Each person had been allocated a sumptuous bedroom where they had rested for the remainder of the day.

Only Nathan, Vicky and Carl had come down for dinner, Eriksson having sent down apologies for himself, the children and the Old Man. They were, he explained, deciding on the next stage of their journey.

The following morning all were provided with breakfast in their rooms, together with a note asking them to meet in the main entrance hall at 10.00 a.m. At the appointed time Vicky, Nathan and Carl, bearing the now familiar burden of the unconscious Old Man, joined Eriksson and the two children in a Paternoster minibus. A few minutes into the journey Eriksson had asked the three friends to put on the blindfolds.

'Undoubtedly an unnecessary precaution, but I'm sure that you will understand once we arrive at our destination,' he explained, speaking over his shoulder as he drove the minibus deeper into the beautiful countryside.

The Old Man's noisy return to consciousness brought Nathan back to the present. Once he saw that the Old Man had fully recovered, Eriksson called the group together in front of the grassy crescent. 'As you all are aware, the children have been seeking their father for almost a millennium. When the task of supporting them was passed to me, I also began to plan for the day when they would be reunited. I anticipated that Mazac would want to take his children into his next Rest, something that they have all now decided to do.'

Nathan realised that this was the start of a farewell speech and looked across at the Old Man who met his gaze but remained silent.

Eriksson continued. 'The children had told me of the rather uncomfortable places that their father tended to pick for his slumbers, usually more from enforced circumstance than comfort and security. I therefore decided that my contribution to this history would go beyond the ongoing search, and create somewhere for them all, once reunited, to sleep away the centuries until the time of their next Return.'

Reaching into his pocket he withdrew a small key-pad and entered a pass code. From deep underground came the noise of equipment becoming energized. Nathan could feel vibrations under his feet as a large section of the grassy surface moved slightly forward and then slid to the side, revealing an underground chamber, instantly illuminated by electric light. Inside Nathan could see a large, flat floor space upon which were placed three platforms, each the size of a single bed, upon which lay a mattress made from some sort of dense foam material. The remainder of the cavern was empty, save for a series of cupboards built into the surrounding walls.

'I really hope that you like it, Father,' said the little girl, the excitement barely contained in her voice. 'We both designed it for you.'

The Old Man peered into the chamber and looked around the brightly lit space. 'It will serve us well,' he said to the two children, who beamed with the satisfaction of his approval.

'Now I see the need for the blindfolds,' said Vicky, 'but how did you keep it secret? Surely you must have had all sorts of people here to build it? They must all know of its location.'

'All the construction work was done by a team of Latvian builders, helicoptered in directly from Riga,' replied Eriksson. 'Like you, they were blindfolded for the majority of the journey. We told them they were in northern France and gave them no reason to doubt it. None of them spoke any English or French, and we restricted them to this site for the whole of the build phase. Even the materials were helicoptered in, using Paternoster pilots who were all paid handsomely for their silence. As part of the deal they agreed to emigrate to Australia or New Zealand as soon as the project was complete. They all know that if any word of this venture ever leaked out then all of them would lose everything that we have given them. It seems to have been incentive enough.'

'But what if all this kit goes wrong? What if the door mechanism fails or the power supply gets interrupted? Surely then it turns into just a high-tech tomb?' asked Nathan.

'All the components have been tested to destruction and have a design life of over five hundred years. The electricity comes from a small power plant built deep into the hillside which, my boffins assure me, will last for over a thousand years. Finally, even if all that fails, the door can be opened manually from the inside.'

'Enough chatter,' said the Old Man. 'It is time for us to take our rest.'

The two children started to walk down into the chamber. After a few steps they stopped, turned around and ran towards Eriksson. Throwing their arms around his neck they both hugged him.

'Thank you so much,' said the girl.

'We owe you and your ancestors more than we can ever repay,' said the boy.

Crouching down, Eriksson returned their embrace. 'I shall miss you both enormously,' he said, 'but this is the moment that we have all worked so hard for. Now is the time for you to rejoin your father.' He kissed them both gently on the forehead. They turned back and ran into the chamber, from which came the sound of gentle sobbing.

The Old Man approached Eriksson and shook his hand. 'I must add my thanks to those of my children. Erik the Coppersmith was my good friend but what your family has done for them goes far beyond the bounds of simple friendship.'

'No thanks are needed. Your children are a delight and it will be strange not having them around. Besides, they are the power behind Paternoster, which has brought my family many other blessings.'

'I understand. Yet still do I offer you my greatest thanks.'

'And what of the future? The main reason for Paternoster's existence is now over,' continued Eriksson. 'The Core Purpose is now complete. Do you have any final instructions for me?'

The Old Man thought for a moment, carefully pondering the question. 'Firstly, I was much impressed with the work of the Seed Bank. I would that their enterprise prospers.'

Eriksson nodded. 'Consider it done. Anything else?'

The Old Man looked towards the trio standing beside the chamber entrance. 'Nathan and Vicky,' he said. 'They have been good companions to me on this Return. I would that their remaining days were spent in peace and useful labour.'

'I'm sure that we can find a place for them. But what about the big fellow?'

In answer, the Old Man turned towards Carl. 'When we met in the Kingsman's palace at Bristol I proposed that we should walk together until the end of days. I repeat my offer now. We have walked together in the past and in this present. Will you be my companion on future Returns?'

Although the offer came as a shock to him, Carl did not hesitate for a second. 'There is nothing to hold me here. My family are all dead and my old life ended when I became addicted. You offer me a brighter future than anything I can expect here. Count me in.'

Eriksson leaned forward and whispered into the Old Man's ear. 'I hate to be the practical one, but the chamber has only three beds. I can get another one fitted but it will take me some little time.'

'Fear not,' replied the Old Man, again in a whisper. 'Don't tell the children but I have never found a bed that is better than the good earth. Cyric can sleep on the one allotted to me.'

Carl turned to Vicky and Nathan. 'Looks like this is where we part company.' He wrapped his huge arms around each of them in turn.

'Good luck, Carl,' said a tearful Vicky. 'I hope you find some peace. You certainly deserve it.'

'And I was just getting used to having you around,' said Nathan, smiling. 'Another few days and folk could start to describe you as being educated.'

Carl laughed. 'Well, perhaps that's the best reason of all for me to go.' With a final wave of his hand he entered the chamber and disappeared from their sight.

The Old Man then spoke to Nathan. 'I told you that a walk with a stranger would help you resolve your anxieties. May your future pathways be clearer than the ones that you are about to abandon.'

'You're right,' replied Nathan. 'I'm not sure what I'm going to do next, but it will not be as part of the police force.'

The Old Man shook Nathan's hand before turning to Vicky. 'So, for a second time we say farewell. As I said then, I'm sorry that we had no more time together. You are an excellent apprentice.'

'Can you not stay with us for just a little longer? There is so much more that I want to learn from you.'

'Since Bristol all I have wanted to do is bring this Return to an end and leave this fetid world to those that have despoiled it. Nature will not be subdued for long and now I must ensure that my children do not suffer the catastrophe that is to come. It is time for me to go.'

The two embraced briefly before the Old Man turned and, nodding a final farewell to Eriksson, walked towards the underground chamber.

At the entrance he hesitated, as if struggling with some inner conflict. After a few seconds he seemed to achieve some form of resolution and he turned to face Vicky. 'I can offer you something,' he said. 'But I warn you that the price might be more than you wish to pay.'

'I will do whatever it takes,' replied Vicky.

The Old Man gave that familiar shrug of his shoulders and reached into his coat pocket. He took out the old pouch that Nathan had first seen in the police cell, the one that he had used throughout the journey, the one that Julian had stolen to assimilate with the businessman.

Nathan immediately realised what the Old Man was proposing. 'No!' he shouted. 'Nothing is worth that!'

The Old Man tossed the pouch to Vicky. As she caught it she looked back to see the Old Man spit into the palm of his hand, which he then extended towards her. 'I offer you the knowledge of a lifetime of lifetimes and hope that you have the wisdom to use it.'

'Absolutely not!' shouted Nathan. 'Remember what happened to Julian. The risk is too great.'

'Julian was a fool. Vicky is not,' replied the Old Man. 'Yet I must warn you that great pain and a risk of oblivion always attend those who take this path. You must choose, Vicky. It is all that I have left to offer you.'

Like Carl before her, Vicky did not hesitate for a moment. She squeezed the corner of the pouch between her fingers, stepped towards the Old Man's outstretched hand and dipped her fingertips into the sticky mucus. Nathan rushed to stop her but he was unable to prevent her putting the fingers to her lips.

A great scream issued from her mouth, shattering the tranquillity of the woodland glade. High pitched to start with, the awesome sound fell until it became lower than any female throat had ever made. It stopped as quickly as it started just as Vicky collapsed into Nathan's arms.

With a final nod to Eriksson the Old Man turned and walked into the chamber.

A second later the grassy door closed, returning the glade to its earlier, tranquil state.

Nathan and Eriksson carried the still form of the young doctor back to the minibus. Although they knew the effects of the assimilation process, both were inwardly concerned at her condition - pale, limp and with no sign of any discernible breathing – anyone who had not witnessed the previous few minutes would have confidently said that she was dead. Laying her carefully across the wide seats, Nathan contrived to fit the seat belts around her to prevent her from rolling off during the bumpy return journey. Eriksson handed a blindfold to Nathan, who fixed it around his head as the minibus pulled away.

Unable to see the surrounding countryside, Nathan used the journey to reflect on the events of the last few days. In what had seemed like an age, but had been little over a week, he had gone from confused junior member of the police to ... what? He had decided days ago that he did not want to be part of the police force. He saw his future in solving problems rather than containing them. What that meant in practice he had no idea.

His thoughts turned to Vicky, lying across the seats behind him. In many ways he envied her sense of purpose. She had a clear vision of what she wanted to achieve, although the methods for doing so were less well defined. If she survives this assimilation ... he quickly corrected himself... when she survives, she might need a helper to support her. Perhaps she might want someone who was more than that. Maybe ....

'You can take the blindfold off now. Once again, my apologies but I'm sure that you can understand my reasons for asking.' Eriksson spoke in a casually apologetic tone.

'No problem,' replied Nathan, removing the strip of material.

For a few minutes the two drove in silence before Nathan recalled something that had been bothering him.

'So, by the sound of things, your team have been following us right from the beginning.'

'That's right,' replied Eriksson. 'We picked up Mazac's trail at your police station.'

'How did you do that?'

'Your colleagues took a DNA sample, probably while he was still assimilating. I can't imagine him agreeing to it while he was conscious. Can you?'

Nathan smiled in agreement. 'But how could you access the results? Surely they were held within the police system.'

It was Eriksson's turn to smile. 'Your naivety does you credit. I hope that you retain it for as long as you can. We have arranged matters so that all DNA samples are tested on Paternoster equipment. By a little digital sleight of hand, all the results are copied to our head office in Cambridge where we have managed to build up quite a database. Once his results came in, they set our system whirring and so the chase was on.'

Nathan was about to mention the Data Protection Act but stopped when he recalled the naivety jibe. 'So you were able to compare it with samples that you had taken from the children?'

'We didn't need to.'

'Then you must have had his DNA from before? From an earlier Return?'

The minibus rocked slightly as Eriksson drove around a tree stump. Both men looked back at Vicky to check she was still secure on her seat.

Eriksson continued. 'Once again, we didn't need one. Obviously, there was no mistaking Mazac's DNA. He is quite unique, you know.' He caught a glimpse of Nathan's puzzled expression before going on. 'My God, you haven't realised.'

'Realised what?'

'Did friend Mazac never strike you as being a little, well, different?'

'How do you mean?'

'His appearance. His physical prowess. The way he thinks. Did none of this seem odd?'

Nathan reflected over their time together. From the very beginning there had been something different about the Old Man. His head appeared rather large, his brows rather deep. He recalled how the Old Man had lifted up Warren in the Seed Bank. His strength was prodigious and the speed of his movements had been astonishing. Then Nathan recalled the terrifying, feral roar that he had heard in the Bristol garden and again in the Queen's Oak.

'I see that you are starting to put things together. Did he ever refer to himself as being different?' said Eriksson.

'Several times he referred to a group called 'the Others' but he never made it clear who they were. I remember him saying that when we knew them we would know much about the problems of the world.'

'And whom do you think these 'Others' are?'

Nathan shook his head. 'I have no idea.'

'We are the 'Others'. You and me and everyone else that walks the face of the earth today. Homo sapiens. We are the group that Mazac holds responsible for all the world's ills.'

'But, surely he is part of that group? How can he see us as 'Others'?'

Eriksson halted the minibus and turned towards Nathan.

'Because he is not part of that group, that species. He is not Homo Sapiens. That's why his DNA signature was so striking.'

Nathan took a moment to let Eriksson's words sink in. 'Not Homo Sapiens?'

'No. Not Homo Sapiens. He is Homo Neanderthalensis.'

Nathan's jaw dropped.

'That's right,' continued Eriksson. 'For the last few days you have been walking with the world's last Neanderthal.'

Epilogue

Passenger Compartment of a Paternoster Helicopter,
5,000 feet above the Derbyshire Dales,
Friday 31st August,
6.00 p.m.

The recently appointed Director of the Paternoster Botanical Research Institute looked out of the helicopter window at the fields and woodlands passing beneath her. It was as if she was looking at the English countryside for the first time. As before, she saw the inspirational scenery but now she saw so much more. This time she also saw a storehouse of boundless raw materials together with the potential for an infinite number of possible combinations, some tried but most still tantalisingly unknown.

Vicky had 'slept' for about twenty-four hours, waking just a few hours earlier feeling massively refreshed. Physically she did not feel any different from before the assimilation, although she was conscious that her senses, especially taste and smell, seemed far more acute. However, her mental capacity was now massively different. In part it was the body of knowledge that her memory now contained. She could recall all the knowledge of the Old Man's life, especially the details of plants that he had discovered in his continuous experimentation.

Nathan had told her of the Old Man's Neanderthal past. She had sat and listened politely but, in fact, she already knew. She could see the face of his mother and the sight of his tribe being drowned in that terrible flood that separated Britain from the European mainland. She could even feel his pain at the death of his wife and the joy of his reunion with his children. She could recall all this in an instant, as if she had experienced it herself.

Yet the most surprising thing for her was the way that she now thought. She now knew that if she mixed the petals of alsmond with the roots of genation, then the resulting paste would cure toothache. However, yesterday she would have wanted to know why this combination worked so well, what were the component parts and how they interacted. Today she had no such interest. The fact that the combination worked was sufficient, although further experiments by adding other plants to the paste fascinated her. It was as if the analytical part of her brain had now been shut down to be replaced by a purely empirical approach; a change that worried and excited her in equal measures.

When she had woken, both Nathan and Eriksson had wanted her to rest for a few days. They had watched her body turn into a corpse which showed no sign of improvement until the moment she recovered. She understood that it must have been a worrying time for them but they could not know how revitalised she felt. She had insisted that her work must start at once, save only for a visit to Bristol to resolve her mother's predicament. When she had explained her ideas to find a cure for the unfolding bird flu epidemic, Eriksson had immediately put the full resources of Paternoster at her disposal. He suggested an initial budget that had made her eyes water and instantly sent out instructions to find and equip suitable premises.

She looked across the cabin to Nathan who was also looking out of the window. She knew he too wanted to return to Bristol, mostly to resolve his issues with the police force. To his credit, he wanted to explain what happened at the police station so that Sergeant Johnson would escape charges. He then wanted to resign with immediate effect but expressed a concern that he had broken some important rules by going AWOL, and also that he would have to serve some form of notice period. At this Eriksson had simply laughed, saying that his lawyers would rejoice at the chance to tie the constabulary up in legal knots until they agreed to his early departure.

Nathan saw her looking at him and smiled. The noise of the helicopter engine made conversation impossible so all she could do was smile back. Another of the Old Man's skills that she seemed to have acquired was his ability to read body language. Since she had woken she had noticed several instances when Nathan had clearly shown an interest in her that went beyond simple friendship. She wondered what his plans would be after he had left the police force. Would he, perhaps, be interested in assisting her in setting up this new venture? Would she, perhaps, want him to be more than just a colleague?

She reflected on all this as she stared out of the window at the unfolding scenery beneath her. They were flying over a village, as traditional as it could be, complete with church, pub and an oak tree in the centre of the village green. She noticed that the leaves on the tree were slightly darker than they should have been at this time of year. With some difficulty she fought back a desire to chew on one.

—∞—

In the pub beer garden, several thousand feet below, two men watched the progress of the helicopter as it moved across the bright summer sky.

'Seems that your contact was right,' said Rylands, shading his eyes from the sun.

Johnson nodded. 'When you owe me the sort of favour that he does, it can be quite dangerous to get it wrong.'

The previous day Johnson had taken a call from a 'colleague' in Air Traffic Control, telling him that a helicopter with a Paternoster ID code had left the south-eastern air space and flown to Derbyshire. This lead, coupled with Rylands' knowledge of Paternoster's extensive land holdings in the county, had been enough to justify their journey north.

'Don't see many of those anymore.' This came from the landlord as he brought out two pints and placed them on the table in front of his two new customers.

'I'm surprised that you see any at all in a quiet place like this,' said Rylands, using a style of conversational inquisitiveness that had always seemed to come naturally to him.

'These days you are right, but a couple of years ago we used to see loads of them. Big buggers too, much larger than that one.' He nodded towards the helicopter, now disappearing from view. 'No one around here had any idea what was happening. All very secret, like.'

'Pity,' replied Rylands. 'Mysteries can be frustrating when you never find the answer.'

'We managed to get some idea.'

'How did you do that?'

'One night this group of foreigners suddenly burst in. Russians, I reckon. Whatever they were, none of them spoke a word of English. Wasn't a problem though. Thirsty men find their own language and, my God, but they were thirsty. Drank us out of vodka within a few minutes so they turned to any spirits that we had, all washed down with copious amounts of lager.'

'What did they have to do with the helicopters?' said Johnson.

'Possibly nothing, but we managed to work out that they were builders and they were making some form of cellar. Hard to be more specific, what with the language barrier and the drink. I tried to find out where they got all the materials from. My brother-in-law runs a builder's merchants in Buxton, you see, and I thought he might pick up some business. That's when the subject of the helicopters came up. It seems that both them and all their kit were flown in by helicopter, really secret like.'

'Sounds like an interesting night,' said Rylands. He tried to make his question seem nonchalant. Too much interest tended to put people off.

'Could have been even better but just when it was getting lively this bloke bursts in. I could see straight off that he wasn't a happy bunny. Turns out that he was their foreman or such like. He starts to shout the odds and the builders all rush out to this minibus waiting outside. I got the strong impression that they shouldn't have left the building site. They must have sneaked out for a quick drink or ten, without the foreman's knowing. Anyway, once they are all back in the bus the foreman comes back in. He spoke no English either and I reckon he had no idea where he was. He paid the bill in euros and he kept calling me 'Monsieur'. Foreigners, eh? You've got to laugh.' With this he collected some empty glasses and walked back into his pub.

'Sounds like we're on to something at last. May not be anything to do with the Old Man but it's all we have at the moment,' said Rylands.

Johnson took a pull at his pint and nodded. 'Worth a look.'

'Are you really sure you want to do this? I got the distinct impression that you may not be a welcome guest at the next reunion.'

'I've no choice. I either bring him in or spend the next few years in prison. A no-brainer, as they say. But what about you? I'm here because I've got to be. You have a choice.'

Rylands looked towards the countryside that surrounded the village. 'You're wrong,' he replied. 'I have no choice. It's a story, and the more that I find out the more I'm convinced that it's a big one. Chasing big stories is what I do. I never let up. I'm like a moth to a flame.'

Both men finished their drinks and walked out of the beer garden and onto the pavement beyond. In silence, they followed the rough country road towards the distant hills and the secret that they might contain.

Printed in Great Britain
by Amazon